THE LOST SYMPHONY

Jack Rogan Mysteries Book 6

GABRIEL FARAGO

This book is brought to you by Bear & King Publishing.

Publishing & Marketing Consultant: Lama Jabr
Website: https://xanapublishingandmarketing.com
Sydney, Australia

Cover Design by Giovanni Banfi

First published 2020 © Gabriel Farago

ISBN: 978-0-9876283-3-6

Signup for the author's New Releases mailing list to get a free copy of *The Forgotten Painting** novella and find out where it all began ...

https://gabrielfarago.com.au/free-download-forgotten-painting/

* I'm delighted to tell you that *The Forgotten Painting* has received two major literary awards in the US. It was awarded the Gold Medal by Readers' Favorite in the Short Stories and Novellas category and was named 'Outstanding Novella' of 2018 by the IAN Book of the Year Awards.

THE LOST SYMPHONY

GABRIEL FARAGO

CONTENTS

AUTHOR'S NOTE

Very few cities in the world today have as tortured a soul as St Petersburg. The wheel of history has been particularly cruel to this remarkable place. Bloody revolutions, uprisings and assassinations resulting in untold misery, and devastating wars causing the deaths of millions have shaped this city, and the echoes of a painful past can still be felt today by visitors who are prepared to observe and listen.

Inspired by Venice and Amsterdam, this spectacular 'Versailles on the Neva' – Peter the Great's 'window into Europe' – became the capital of Russia in 1712. I visited this fascinating city in September 2019 to prepare the way for the release of *The Curious Case of the Missing Head*, Book 5 in *The Jack Rogan Mysteries Series*, and to continue my research for a novella, *The Lost Symphony*, which I'd had in the back of my mind for some time.

But things don't always turn out as planned.

Actually visiting this jewel on the Baltic and being surrounded by its extraordinary history had a profound effect on me. It is important to mention this at the very beginning, as it has a bearing on how the storylines unfolded, and how the many fascinating characters who shape this book came to life.

Initially, *The Lost Symphony* was planned as a short novella about a tormented genius and one of my favourite composers – Pyotr Ilyich Tchaikovsky – who visited St Petersburg often, and died there in 1893. I referred to this in chapter 62 of *The Curious Case of the Missing Head*, part of which has been incorporated into the opening scene of the Prologue and explains how the storylines of this book fit into *The Jack Rogan Mysteries Series*, which doesn't always follow Jack's life chronologically.

At the time of my visit, I thought St Petersburg and its turbulent history would provide a most suitable backdrop and setting for the novella. Then, several things happened that changed all that:

The first was a wonderful concert. One of my readers, an eminent Russian musicologist I had corresponded with for years, knew I was planning to delve into Tchaikovsky's life and times, and kindly arranged tickets to a concert showcasing Tchaikovsky's sublime music.

During the stirring fourth movement of Symphony No.6, the *Pathétique*, with its sense of gloom and foreboding, my mind began to wander and the first shoots of a new, much wider storyline began to emerge. I have no doubt this was all due to the spell of this remarkable city, which was soon to captivate me and hold me in its grip. I also recalled the words of my friend at the beginning of the concert: 'If you want to get to know the soul of Russia, listen to its music.'

The next event that had a bearing on all this was a visit to the Cathedral of St Peter and St Paul where the Romanovs are buried. In addition to the Tchaikovsky research, I also wanted to explore the tragic history of Tsar Nicholas II and Rasputin, that enigmatic, evil genius who contributed so much to the tsar's downfall. The tsar and his entire family were brutally slaughtered by the Bolsheviks in Yekaterinburg in July 1918, two and a half years after Rasputin himself had been murdered in the Yusupov Palace in St Petersburg. I have been fascinated by these cataclysmic events and what followed for years, and had planned to make them the centrepiece of the next book in the series. But first, I was going to write the novella about Tchaikovsky.

However, all of these plans evaporated as I stood in front of the Chapel of St Catherine the Martyr, where Tsar Nicholas II and his family were finally laid to rest on 17 July 1998, eighty years to the day after their murder. It was a deeply moving moment. For some reason I still can't explain, I kept hearing the sombre notes of Tchaikovsky's sixth symphony, my eyes firmly fixed on the last tsar's modest sarcophagus in front of me, and wondered ...

A flash of inspiration often lasts only a millisecond, but it can have a profound influence on the creative process that shapes an entire book and ignites the passion needed to write it. And that is exactly what happened during a moment of reflection in that solemn place that day. The idea was simple enough: why not combine the storylines of the novella with the next book, and create a Russian epic worthy not only of a great composer, but of a tragic chapter in Russian history that changed the modern world?

The next day, my Russian friend took me to the Peterhof Palace, and it was while strolling through the stunning palace gardens with their spectacular fountains, golden statues and waterfalls that the ideas and story-threads all came together, forming the inspiration for this book. It was like opening a window to let in the sunshine.

Once that window was opened, there was no turning back. I pulled the little notebook I always carry with me out of my pocket, sat down on a bench overlooking the fountains, and began to jot down an outline for this book.

That was how it all began. What is contained in the pages that follow is the product of an inspired idea that floated into my mind's eye on that grey autumn afternoon as a whisper, and then turned into a literary symphony I hope you will enjoy.

Gabriel Farago
Leura, Blue Mountains, Australia
November 2020

PROLOGUE

Kuragin chateau, just outside Paris: 26 July 2018

'You're up early,' said Jack and walked over to Rahima, his mother, sitting in the conservatory overlooking the garden. With the morning sun streaming through the open windows and making the palm fronds glisten, the conservatory was an idyllic place where Jack had done a lot of writing during the summer.

'Come, sit next to me,' said Rahima. 'I had the best night's sleep in months. This is so beautiful here. So peaceful and serene. So safe.'

Rahima pointed to an exquisite mahogany music box on the mantelpiece. 'I believe that's yours,' she said.

'Katerina told you about it?'

'She did. But she didn't tell me the whole story. She said that would be a matter for you. Apparently, it used to belong to my aunt and she left it to you. A couple of years ago, I believe. Is that right?'

'That's correct. There's an amazing story attached to this little gem. It's all about a letter, a desperate tsarina and a long-lost masterpiece created by a musical genius just before he died.'

'How intriguing. Katerina did say you are quite a storyteller,' interrupted Rahima, a glint in her eyes. 'As we are about to visit my aunt's memory trees later today, would this be a good time for you to tell me the story?'

'I suppose it would. But I have to warn you, this story isn't altogether a happy one. There's treachery, betrayal and murder, and a family tragedy so cruel it's almost impossible to put it into words. History written in blood.'

'My goodness!'

'Do you still want to hear it?'

'Absolutely!'

Jack settled back into his comfortable wicker chair and looked pensively at his mother. 'I've just finished writing a book about this,' he began. 'The manuscript is with my editor in New York right now.

In fact, I wrote most of it sitting over there next to the mantelpiece. The music box was my inspiration. It spoke to me ... It was like taking dictation from the past.'

'I can't wait.'

Jack stood up, walked over to the mantelpiece and pointed to the music box. 'I had it restored by a horologist in Paris, specialising in antique mechanisms just like this one made by Symphonion Musikwerke in Leipzig, Germany in 1888. It works perfectly now; listen.' Jack pulled out a small lever on the top of the box to activate the mechanism that turned the disc. Moments later, a delightful Russian folk melody drifted across from the mantelpiece, reminding Rahima of her childhood spent with her aunt, Madame Petrova, and her family a long time ago.

'It all began when Madame Petrova died suddenly eighteen months ago. As you know, it turned out she was my great aunt, a connection I had only discovered by chance because of this,' said Jack. He reached inside his shirt and pulled out the exquisite little Fabergé cross he wore around his neck. 'How this eventuated is just as fascinating as the story of the music box I'm about to tell you.'

During the next hour, Jack told his mother how the chance discovery of a letter hidden a long time ago set a chain of events in motion, which brought to light a masterpiece created by a musical giant that would, but for that letter, have been lost forever. Rahima listened in silence as Jack — a natural storyteller — described not only the extraordinary events, but the incredible cast of characters as well. He did it in a way that transported mother and son into a past filled with drama and tragedy so real and moving, that Rahima had tears in her eyes by the time Jack finished.

'These are some of my breadcrumbs of destiny, as I'm fond of calling them,' said Jack, 'which inspire my writing.'

'This is without doubt one of the most remarkable stories I've ever heard,' said Rahima quietly, and looked adoringly at her son. 'And you almost died—'

'Thankfully, that's all in the past now,' interrupted Jack, still reeling from the horrors he had experienced in Russia the year before. 'Some things are best forgotten, don't you think?' Jack reached for his mother's hand. 'I can live with the scars, but not the memories,' he added quietly, becoming emotional. 'I still can't believe I've found you after all these years, and that you are actually sitting here, right now, with me. And all thanks to Madame Petrova and—'

'Destiny?'

'Oh yes, let's not forget destiny,' said Jack, and gently kissed his mother's hand.

PART I
MADAME PETROVA'S MUSIC BOX

Modest Tchaikovsky's apartment, St Petersburg:
5 November 1893, 10:00 pm

The mood in the top floor apartment at 13 Malaya Morskaya belonging to Modest, Tchaikovsky's brother, on that gloomy, freezing winter's evening was sombre and subdued. The relentless, icy grip of approaching death could be felt everywhere. Pyotr Ilyich Tchaikovsky, arguably Russia's greatest composer, was dying.

The doctors had left after diagnosing a classic case of cholera, as there was nothing further they could do to help their famous patient. Originating in Bombay, the deadly disease had entered Russia via Arabia, causing a pandemic that had been raging since 1881.

Propped up by pillows, covered in sweat and with his kidneys and eyesight failing, Tchaikovsky lay in his bed. Realising the end was near, he was working on a complex score like a man possessed. Fuelled by creativity set on fire by the raging disease consuming his frail body, his exceptional mind was bursting with inspiration and musical ideas that he desperately wanted to record before it was too late.

Tchaikovsky had been secretly working for years on a grand Russian symphony that was going to capture the soul of the country he loved with a passion. Due to his enormous workload, this had only been possible during furious bursts of creativity between concerts and other demanding commitments. As one of the most celebrated composers of his time, Tchaikovsky had wowed adoring audiences throughout Europe, lifted his baton in all the major concert halls, and had even travelled as far afield as America to showcase his work and present it to the world.

Sadly, all this fame and adulation could do little to calm the inner torment that was consuming his soul. Homosexuality in ultra-conservative and deeply religious Russia at the time was not only a serious crime, but carried with it a social stigma so heavy and destructive that it would not only have disgraced the celebrated composer, it would have destroyed him, his reputation and his family, and placed an ugly stain on his musical genius for generations to come. For these reasons, Tchaikovsky had gone to great lengths to keep his homosexuality a closely guarded secret. In his thirties he even got married, to keep up appearances. Unfortunately, the marriage only lasted a few days and his distraught, humiliated and disappointed wife left him after a hysterical scene that had ignited gossip and speculation and set society tongues wagging.

Then, quite unexpectedly, matters came to a head in 1893. The celebrated composer suddenly found himself standing at the edge of catastrophe. Tchaikovsky became infatuated with his young nephew Vladimir 'Bob' Davydov, also a homosexual. Unable to control his feelings, this almost desperate infatuation was noticed even outside his innermost circle of loyal friends protecting him, and sent ripples of curiosity across a social establishment that was always on the lookout for scandal.

Exhausted, Tchaikovsky put down his pen, satisfied that the melancholy chorus of bassoons towards the end of the work would do the symphony justice as a celebration of the Russian soul. Standing in the shadows, Modest was anxiously watching his failing brother. 'Is there anything I can do for you?' he asked, choking with emotion, his voice barely audible.

'Yes. Please send Bob in. I want to talk to him. There isn't much time.'

Looking tired and dishevelled, which wasn't like him, and with deep rings under his teary eyes, Bob – a handsome young man in his early twenties with a striking face that had an uncanny resemblance to his famous uncle – quietly entered the room.

'Come; sit,' said Tchaikovsky, and pointed to the side of the bed.

'You know I have loved you from the moment I saw you as a baby in my sister's arms,' began Tchaikovsky softly, his voice quivering with emotion. 'I knew then, as I do now, that it was destiny.'

Shocked by his uncle's appearance and aware of the gravity of that fateful moment, Bob sat in silence on the edge of his uncle's bed. Tchaikovsky reached for his hand.

'During the past two years, you have become my best friend, my soulmate and confidant and have shared my innermost thoughts, fears, dreams and desires,' continued Tchaikovsky. 'But all this is about to come to an abrupt end. Before that happens, there are some important matters you need to know about me and what is happening here tonight, and why ...'

'Oh? What kind of matters?' asked Bob.

'Before I tell you, you must promise me on our love not to divulge a single word of what I'm about to tell you to anyone, and that includes Modest. Understood?'

Bob nodded, momentarily overcome by emotion welling up from somewhere deep within and making him feel dizzy. 'I promise,' he whispered.

'A few days ago,' continued Tchaikovsky, 'I was summoned to attend what turned out to be some kind of "court of honour" convened by my former classmates at the College of Law right here in St Petersburg.'

'How curious. What was that all about?'

'A very delicate matter, but one with potentially devastating consequences. I was accused—'

'Accused of what?' interrupted Bob, frowning.

'Of being a despicable deviate because of what I am. Because of what we are, you and I—'

'You speak in riddles,' interjected Bob again, becoming agitated.

'I don't think so. I'm sure you know exactly what I mean. There was a letter of accusation written by a duke close to the tsar about this, which if delivered and made public would cause a scandal so devastating it would destroy not only me and my work, but all those close to me, and that includes you.'

'I ... I don't understand,' stammered Bob.

His vision blurred, Tchaikovsky let go of Bob's hand and looked intently at his nephew. 'No matter,' he said. 'You will in good time. What is important for now is that the court of honour gave me a way out. The letter of accusation would not be delivered to the tsar, my reputation would remain intact and most important of all, my work would pass into history untarnished in return for ...' Tchaikovsky paused, and took a deep breath.

'In return for what?'

'My death.'

'What are you saying?' shrieked Bob.

'Quite simple really. I was told to commit suicide.'

'This is absurd! You can't be serious, surely!'

'Oh, but I am; deadly serious. You do remember I drank some unboiled water at Leiner's a few days ago?'

'Yes. You surprised us all, especially your brother. You made a public spectacle out of it for all to see. A reckless one. And in a crowded, popular restaurant frequented by gossiping socialites of all places. Drinking unboiled water during a cholera epidemic is madness. We all told you so!'

'You did, but this was quite deliberate, you see. It was part of a plan.'

'What plan?'

'To cover up my suicide.'

'What are you talking about?'

'Arsenic poisoning has very similar symptoms to cholera: dehydration, acute diarrhoea, kidney failure, then death. Even the timeframe is similar, certainly close enough to confuse even the doctors.'

For a while there was complete silence in the room as the implication of what Tchaikovsky had just suggested began to sink in. 'Are you saying that you poisoned yourself with arsenic to make it look like cholera?' asked Bob, stunned.

'Precisely. And drinking unboiled water, while obviously reckless and unwise, would provide a plausible explanation for how the disease was contracted, and when. The doctors certainly thought so, and so did Modest. As you can imagine, I wanted to avoid the obvious stigma of suicide and all the wild speculation and innuendo that would inevitably go with it, at all cost. Dying of cholera would definitely be preferable, don't you think? A tragic but befitting end for someone like me, especially here in melancholic Russia. Cut down by cholera, a classic exit to remember and easy to accept, especially in the current climate of fear of disease. Almost theatrical, wouldn't you say?'

Bob went down on his knees and looked intently at his uncle. 'Oh my God,' he stammered and reached for his uncle's hand. 'You *are* serious!'

'There is more,' said Tchaikovsky, his voice weak. He pointed to the papers on his lap.

'What's this?' asked Bob.

'My parting gift to Mother Russia and the world. My legacy.'

Bob stared at the pages – obviously a new score – covered in notes and comments in the margins, all in Tchaikovsky's distinctive, spidery handwriting.

'I just finished it. It's a symphony I've been working on for years. I believe it's the pinnacle of my work and I am entrusting it to you here, right now, just before I die.'

'Why me?' stammered Bob. 'What do you want me to do with it?'

'Deliver it to the tsar. I have dedicated it to him. He will know what to do with it, of that I'm sure. He will present it to the world, and the world will listen.'

Exhausted and barely able to speak, Tchaikovsky sank back into the pillows. To an artist like him a quick, albeit painful death in exchange for posthumous glory, admiration and love by his country, and a place in history, was a fair bargain and a small price to pay for immortality.

Tchaikovsky gathered up the pages with a limp, shaking hand and handed them to Bob. 'Now, please take this and leave me, and remember the good times we had together, not this misery here. Remember me as the proud man – baton in hand – conducting a symphony orchestra in a packed concert hall full of admirers, and not the pitiful shell of a man at death's door that I have become. Now, please go before my heart bursts!'

Bob stood up – tears streaming down his pale cheeks – kissed his uncle tenderly on the forehead and without saying another word, walked slowly out of the room.

Pyotr Ilyich Tchaikovsky, one of the greatest composers Russia had ever known, died at three am the next morning, aged fifty-three.

Three days later, on 9 November 1893, Tchaikovsky was granted the great honour of a spectacular funeral service in the Kazan Cathedral in St Petersburg. This was the first time such a privilege had been bestowed on a commoner. Tsar Alexander III offered to pay for the funeral himself – an almost unheard of gesture – and instructed the Directorate of the Imperial Theatres to make the necessary arrangements for what promised to be a grand occasion.

And a grand occasion it was, with thousands of silent mourners lining the streets to pay their final respects and watch the funeral procession move slowly towards the cathedral, and later to the Tikhvin Cemetery at the Alexander Nevsky Monastery.

Kazan Cathedral could hold six thousand mourners and admission was by ticket only. More than sixty thousand people applied and eight thousand were finally admitted. As Bob followed the coffin slowly into the cathedral, he understood why his uncle had decided to follow the suicide path suggested by the honour court. Instead of ending his days in disgrace, shunned by the public, his reputation in tatters and his music cast aside, Tchaikovsky was being carried into the cathedral like a hero, admired, mourned and celebrated by the country he loved. Like his sublime music, Tchaikovsky would come as close to immortality as a human could possibly aspire to.

Bob had brought the precious score of the symphony his uncle had entrusted to him to the funeral. He thought it was appropriate for this to be done, and it was safely tucked into the inside pocket of his overcoat.

Later, at the Tikhvin Cemetery where Tchaikovsky was laid to rest next to such great composers as Mussorgsky, Glinka and

16

Borodin, Bob sensed that the symphony in his pocket had just begun an astonishing journey to an uncertain future, in which he would play an important part. Little did he know just how surprising that journey would turn out to be, or how long it would take for the symphony to reach its final destination.

1

Sydney Harbour: Boxing Day 2016

Sydney Harbour on Boxing Day was certainly the place to be. On this day each year, the yachting elite of the world of sailing descend upon Sydney to compete in one of the most gruelling ocean races, for glory and a place in the nautical history books.

The picturesque harbour was crowded with all kinds of pleasure craft jostling for the best vantage points, and thousands of excited spectators lined the harbour foreshores to watch the start of the famous Sydney to Hobart Yacht Race.

Sponsored by Rolex and hosted by the Cruising Yacht Club of Australia, where Jack was a member, the iconic race was about to begin. Leaving the confines of the harbour was always a challenge, especially for the huge super maxis that needed space to manoeuvre properly. But being among the first to get out of the harbour before turning south to begin the 630-nautical-mile journey through the treacherous Tasman Sea and Bass Strait, and then up the River Derwent to the finish line in Hobart, was every skipper's dream. The start was therefore always chaotic and a matter of survival as eighty-eight yachts of all shapes and sizes, with eleven hundred sailors pumped with adrenaline and excitement, waited for the signal to begin their long journey to Tasmania.

Jack, who knew the harbour well, had strategically positioned his small sailing boat early in the morning to make sure they had a clear view of the starting line. The perfect weather and the sparkling harbour were a cameraman's dream, as TV crews from around the world began beaming the exciting event to millions of viewers.

'Not long now,' said Jack and prepared to come about once more before the race began. He had arrived two days earlier from Paris to watch the start of the race and spend New Year's Eve in Sydney with

18

Professor Alexandra Delacroix, a close friend. Now an internationally celebrated Nobel laureate who worked at the Gordon Institute in Sydney and still lived in Jack's apartment, Delacroix had recently come up with a revolutionary treatment that had saved the pope's life. She and her team were currently developing a drug based on the late Professor K's work that could be a gamechanger in the fight against cancer, and save the lives of millions.

Watching the start of the iconic race was a treat that Jack had been looking forward to for a long time.

'This is amazing,' said Alexandra, salt spray in her hair and cheeks glowing with excitement as she watched two of the giant super maxis heading for the starting line just ahead of them, the activity on board frantic as the crew trimmed the huge sails for the start in the hope of catching a favourable breeze.

Moments after the starting cannon fired, Jack felt his phone vibrate in his shirt pocket. Holding the tiller with one hand, he managed to pull the phone out of his pocket and glance at it. It was a call from Countess Kuragin in France. *Must be important,* he thought, frowning. The countess rarely called him and would certainly not have phoned on Boxing Day during the start of the race, which he knew she would be watching on TV, unless it was urgent.

'Who was that?' shouted Alexandra.

'Katerina,' replied Jack, looking worried. 'I'll call her back as soon as things here calm down a little.'

After the spectacular start, Jack headed back to the sailing club. He had reserved a table on the terrace weeks before with the club secretary, whom he knew well, and was looking forward to a seafood lunch to celebrate the start of another Sydney to Hobart race. As soon as he had tied up the boat, Jack called the countess.

'Sorry to bother you on this special day, Jack, but I have some sad news, I'm afraid,' said the countess, her voice sounding distant.

'Oh?' said Jack, bracing himself.

'Madame Petrova passed away during the night. The nurse found her this morning ...'

'Oh no!' said Jack, feeling a lump in his throat. 'What happened?'

'She was in good spirits the night before, even played bridge they told me, and had a glass of champagne, but at ninety-six ...'

'Quite. Sad, nevertheless. She was my only living relative that I know of.'

'That's why I called you straight away. I suppose you will come back?'

'Of course. I'll come as soon as I can.'

'I am so sorry, Jack, I know what she meant to you. I will make the funeral arrangements. You know what she has asked for ... and we promised.'

'I do, thank you. And we'll carry out her wishes to the letter.'

'Of course. Let me know when you are coming and François will meet you at the airport.'

'Thank you, Katerina. This is a sad day ...'

'It is, for both of us. One of my mother's closest friends. She was the last one.'

Seeing the expression on Jack's face as he slipped the phone back into his pocket, Alexandra knew something was wrong. 'What is it?' she asked.

'My great aunt passed away during the night.'

'Madame Petrova? Oh Jack, I am so sorry!'

'A little sad, yes, but passing away in your sleep at ninety-six after a game of bridge and a glass of champagne with friends isn't all that bad, is it now?' said Jack, smiling. 'It's the way I know she would have wanted to go. Come, let me buy you lunch and we'll lift a glass, or two, to celebrate her remarkable life. And what a life it's been!'

'You're on,' said Alexandra, pleased to see the change in Jack's mood. The sudden, almost upbeat reaction to the sad news was typically Jack, she thought. Always looking at things on the bright side through a glass always half full.

'I can recommend the Sydney rock oysters and the snapper fillets; superb,' said Jack without looking at the menu he knew by heart.

20

When in Sydney, he was a regular diner at the sailing club, which wasn't far from his apartment on the harbour.

Jack ordered a bottle of his favourite New Zealand sauvignon blanc and waited until the waiter had left their table before lifting his glass.

'To Anna Petrova, prima ballerina extraordinaire. May she entertain the angels with her sublime dancing for all eternity,' said Jack, tears glistening in the corners of his eyes. 'Anna Petrova somehow doesn't sound right,' added Jack. 'She was known in Paris as Madame Petrova, the celebrated dancer, and she preferred to be called by that name.'

'To Madame Petrova, then,' said Alexandra, touching glasses with Jack. 'I haven't told you this before,' continued Alexandra, 'but the last time I saw Madame Petrova, she was in your arms.'

'Oh? When was that?'

'On Christmas Eve at the Kuragin chateau four years ago, almost to the day. She stayed at the chateau overnight, remember? You were carrying the old lady upstairs to her room after dinner.'

'Ah yes, I do remember. You saw that? She was too frail by then to climb stairs and she hated her walking stick with a passion. As there was no lift in the chateau, carrying her upstairs seemed the right thing to do. She was as light as a feather.'

'I'm sure she was,' said Alexandra, a sparkle in her eyes. 'And I'm sure the old lady enjoyed it.'

'Do you know what she said to me at the time?'

'Tell me.'

'It's been a long time since a young man swept me off my feet. That's the kind of lady she was,' said Jack, becoming a little emotional. 'Coquettish like a teenager, with an irrepressible sense of humour, a wit as sharp as a razor blade and a memory to match.'

'Quite a lady. How did you two first meet?'

'I was introduced to her by Katerina. Madame Petrova was her late mother's closest friend. I was doing some research on the Ritz in Paris during the war, and Madame Petrova had actually lived there for several years during the occupation and knew all the high-ranking Germans, even the bombastic, half-crazy Reichsmarschall himself.'

'Goering? How amazing.'

'And she had a collection of remarkable photographs on her grand piano to prove it. There were photos of her as a stunning young woman with the entire Nazi hierarchy fawning over her. Von Stulpnagel, the military commander of Paris, was one of them, and Canaris, the head of the Abwehr – the German intelligence offices in Paris – had his arm around her insanely slim waist. He was a double agent, you know. And then there were photos of Coco Chanel and Marlene Dietrich. She knew them all.'

'Incredible!'

'But that wasn't all. There were also the writers and the wild parties. Jean-Paul Sartre and Simone de Beauvoir – Hemingway's drinking buddies – were two of the worst when it came to grog and drugs.'

'A wild girl.'

'And a very popular one, with a smart head on her shoulders and an exceptional memory that hadn't faded over the years. She gave me some valuable leads at the time, remember?'

'To do with the scandal of the crystal skull. It was the talk of Paris in 1941. You dealt with that in your book *The Hidden Genes of Professor K*.'

'Exactly. It was the crucial lead that opened the door to Senora Gonzales's past and a lot more.'

'Isis's grandmother?'

'Yes.'

'Your breadcrumbs of destiny as you are so fond of calling them.'

'Quite.'

'How did you find out Madame Petrova was in fact your great aunt?' asked Alexandra, changing direction. 'You never told me.'

Jack refilled their glasses and looked pensively at Alexandra. 'Destiny and fate,' he said.

'I expected something like that,' replied Alexandra, smiling. She let herself sink into her comfortable wicker chair and looked expectantly at Jack.

'It all happened because of this,' began Jack, 'quite by chance.' From the neck of his shirt he pulled out the gold chain with the beautiful little jewel-encrusted cross he always wore, and held it up.

'Ah, the famous Fabergé cross. I know all about that and its remarkable history.'

'The pawnbroker in Brisbane; Soul, the jazz singer; and the incident in Central Park in New York?'

'Yes. All that and more.'

'Then you will remember that only two of these were ever made, and by none other than the famous Alexander Fabergé himself as a special order for a friend, Madame Petrova's father, who actually designed the little cross. He gave one to Madame Petrova and one to her sister as Easter presents in 1930.'

'Breaking with tradition? A Fabergé cross instead of the famous Easter egg?' observed Alexandra.

'Quite. When Katerina took me to that astonishing retirement home for ageing aristocrats, and introduced me to Madame Petrova – one of the most famous residents – Madame Petrova noticed the little cross I was wearing around my neck, and it all went from there. That was in 2012.'

'Tell me.'

'All the missing pieces of my past suddenly came together when we visited Madame Petrova's memory trees—'

'*Memory trees?*' interrupted Alexandra. 'What on earth are memory trees?'

'A beautiful idea, and it all began as a pact between six friends, all elderly ladies who lived in the retirement home during the twilight of their lives.'

'How curious.'

'There were six of them and they all entered the retirement home at the same time. One of them, Marguerite, a countess, actually set it all up. It was her family chateau. They had known one another for many years and had shared much: the war, careers, lovers, tragedy.'

'And the pact?'

'They agreed that whenever one of them, or one of their close friends or relatives, passed away, they would plant an oak tree in the grounds in that loved one's memory. There would be no graves or gravestones, only trees.'

'What a wonderful concept. Quite beautiful, don't you think?'

'It is. And it was there, sitting under the trees with Katerina and Madame Petrova, that I found some surprising answers to some questions about my past which had troubled me for a long time. That sure was a moment of destiny, as Tristan would call it.'

'Care to tell me about it?'

'Perhaps another time. It's complicated.'

Alexandra sensed this was not the time to probe further into Jack's past and decided to change the subject. She held up her empty glass. 'A little more wine?'

'Certainly,' said Jack, appreciating Alexandra's tact, and reached for the bottle.

'When are you leaving?'

'As soon as I can arrange a flight, which won't be easy with all the tourists in town at the moment, but Katerina and I have a promise to keep ...'

'To plant a memory tree?' ventured Alexandra quietly.

Jack looked thoughtfully across the harbour glistening in the afternoon sunlight and nodded – a distant look on his face – as a strange, yet familiar feeling washed over him. Some of the most exciting stories and adventures always seemed to find him in the most unexpected ways. For reasons he couldn't quite explain, Jack sensed this could well be such a moment.

2

Madame Petrova's Memory Trees: New Year's Eve 2016

Due to the popular Sydney to Hobart Yacht Race, obtaining an airline ticket to Europe turned out to be almost impossible. It had taken all of Jack's ingenuity and contacts and several hours on the phone to finally secure a business class seat on Qantas. The breakthrough came when one of the booking clerks took pity on him after he had explained his situation over and over, pleading compassionate hardship.

Jack's plane was late, but François – Countess Kuragin's butler-cum-gardener and chauffeur – met him at the airport in Paris, greeted him like a long-lost friend and took him straight to the Kuragin chateau. Despite a ferocious snowstorm, when the car finally reached the familiar bridge and crossed the moat, Jack began to relax.

To a restless rolling stone like Jack, who had lived in many places without calling any of them home, the Kuragin chateau came as close to a notion of home as Jack had ever experienced since leaving the family farm in Queensland as a teenager during a dreadful drought that almost destroyed his father. This was in no small way due to the fact that after Jack found her lost daughter, Anna, in the unforgiving Australian outback six years earlier, Countess Kuragin had opened her heart and her home to Jack, and made him part of her family.

This had a wonderful, stabilising effect on Jack, who spent several months a year at the chateau, writing and sharing precious time with Tristan, who had grown into a formidable young man after the countess had taken him under her wing. Jack had brought Tristan to the chateau after the tragic death of his Maori mother, Cassandra. Tristan and Anna had forged a close bond and were able to communicate in strange, unexpected ways that didn't require words or even gestures. They just seemed to be able to read each other's thoughts and moods. Jack was used to this, and often joined them while Anna was painting in her studio with her little boy by her side, and Tristan was doing his school homework.

On those occasions, they sat for hours in total silence, but they were never alone. Because writing is such a solitary endeavour, Jack found this unusual arrangement calming and relaxing, allowing him to focus on his writing without having to withdraw from the affairs of the world and lock himself away.

After a hearty dinner down in the basement kitchen next to the old samovar, and a good night's sleep in his familiar room overlooking the now-frozen pond, Jack rose early. Feeling energised and refreshed after the long, tiring flight, he was sitting in his favourite chair in the warm conservatory, surrounded by ferns and palms and enjoying his first strong coffee of the day, when he heard footsteps approaching from behind.

'I thought I would find you here,' said the countess and sat down next to Jack. 'Isn't this beautiful? Look at you. Sitting in the tropics surrounded by exotic plants, watching the snow falling outside? I love the tracery of the tree branches over there, don't you? And look at the pine trees: bearded old men in white fur coats; straight out of *Lord of the Rings*. It's going to be a harsh winter, I think. Heavy snow like this around Christmas is always a sign.'

'When I left Sydney, it was thirty-two degrees. Hard to believe looking at this winter wonderland,' said Jack. 'I find international travel on this scale almost too fast. The body is already here, but the mind still needs a little more time to catch up and do the same.'

'I know what you mean,' said the countess and poured herself a cup of coffee. 'You were late.'

'The plane was delayed in Singapore. Put us back three hours.'

'So much for spending New Year's Eve on Sydney Harbour watching the fireworks. You'll be watching them here on TV instead, I'm afraid.'

Jack reached for the countess's hand and squeezed it. 'No matter, I wouldn't miss this for the world. And besides, a promise is a promise.'

'I know. Are you ready to do this today?'

'I am. On the last day of the old year. Quite appropriate, wouldn't you say?'

'I suppose it is. How about noon? It may be a little warmer by then.'

'I doubt it, but noon sounds fine.'

'I will ask François to make the necessary arrangements.'

'There isn't much to do, surely?'

'No, not much. Just a few things. Leave it to me,' said the countess.

'Just you and me?'

'Yes, I think that would be best.'

'I agree.'

For a long moment, Jack and the countess sat in silence, lost in thought, and looked out into the garden and watched the large snow-flakes drift slowly past the windowpanes. They both remembered Madame Petrova and the promise they had made to a remarkable old lady who had finally joined the many friends who had gone before her into the great unknown.

At twelve pm sharp, François pulled up outside in the old Bentley. He had gone to the retirement home earlier that morning to make the necessary arrangements for what was to come.

'Wow!' said Jack, as he held the back door open for the countess. Wearing a stunning, full-length fur coat that had belonged to her mother, and a matching Russian fur hat, the countess looked like a celebrity who was about to attend a reception at the tsar's Winter Palace in St Petersburg. The only things missing were the horse-drawn sleigh and uniformed guards.

'You make me feel decidedly underdressed.' Jack pointed to his well-worn leather bomber jacket and thick woollen scarf he had wound around his neck in a hurry before stepping outside. 'You look absolutely stunning!'

'I rarely get to wear this stuff. So I thought, why not send the old lady off in style? She would certainly have liked that, don't you think?'

'Absolutely! Let's go.'

Despite treacherous black ice and snow covering the road, the drive to the retirement home only took half an hour. Jack smiled as they drove through the ornate iron gates leading into the extensive, park-like grounds now covered in a blanket of heavy snow. The gates brought back memories of his first encounter with Madame Petrova four years earlier.

'Aren't you cold?' asked the countess, turning to Jack sitting next to her. 'An old sweater that has definitely seen better days, that infernal leather jacket, a scarf and a slouch hat? You look like the spy who came in from the cold.'

'Straight out of the John le Carré novel. I can live with that.'

'Is that the best you could come up with?' teased the countess, ignoring the remark.

Jack shrugged. 'You know me. Clothes are definitely not my forte. And I came out of a hot summer Down Under, not in from the cold, remember? As for being cold, I have you to keep me warm. This fur coat is big enough for both of us.'

'There is no doubt about it,' said the countess, raising an eyebrow. 'It's definitely true what they say about you.'

'And what's that?'

'That you are an incorrigible rascal.'

'Not that old chestnut again, *please!*'

'Look, we are almost there,' said the countess, changing the subject, and pointed out the window as François pulled up in front of the entrance.

'Don't we need some, you know, stuff to do this?'

'Don't worry, François has arranged everything; haven't you, François?'

'I certainly have,' replied François. 'Everything's ready.'

'And I have the important bit with me right in here,' said the countess and pointed to the muff on her lap.

'In that case, let's go,' said Jack and opened the door.

The short walk through pristine snow to Madame Petrova's memory trees at the back of the chateau only took a few minutes. François stayed behind and would be waiting for them in the car. The snow clouds had parted, revealing a blue sky so bright it made the eyes water.

'This reminds me of something you said the first time we met,' said Jack.

'Oh? What?'

'As I recall it, we were sitting down in the old kitchen in the chateau. It was late at night, and you had just explained to me what a samovar was and where it came from. I think you called it a tea urn that warmed generations.'

'I do remember,' said the countess, a smile creasing the corners of her mouth.

'And then you said something I have never forgotten. You told me that the kitchen was your grandmother's favourite place and that you sat there with her often as a girl, listening to stories of long Russian winters and sleigh rides through magic forests frozen in time.'

'That's right. You have a good memory.'

'Somehow, this place here, right now, reminds me of that wonderful image.'

'Ah, those memories, they are the precious echoes of the past,' said the countess, linking arms with Jack.

'There's certainly nothing sad about this,' said Jack as he remembered pushing Madame Petrova's wheelchair along the same path four years earlier towards that fateful moment of destiny which had revealed so much about the family he didn't know he had.

'Here we are,' said the countess as they approached a grove of oak trees covered in snow. 'Madame Petrova's memory trees.'

Jack looked at two trees set a little apart from the others and remembered what Madame Petrova had told him about them. Both had been planted by her: one for her sister and one for her niece, Jack's mother. 'What's that?' he said and pointed to a small wrought-iron table with a marble top, which had been placed under the two trees. 'An ice bucket with a bottle of champagne and two glasses, and a crystal vase with fresh flowers? Is that what François has been up to? We are having a party?'

'Kind of,' replied the countess, smiling. 'A little touch I added to what we are about to do. I'm sure she would have liked this.'

'Champagne?'

'Her favourite.'

'And what's this?' asked Jack, pointing to a small, twig-like tree without leaves in a wooden tub.

'What do you think? Madame Petrova's memory tree, of course.'

'An oak?'

'Yes, a very young one as you can see.'

'We are not going to plant it now, in the middle of winter, surely?'

'Of course not; we'll do that later when the weather is kinder, but for now, it will do. Could you please open the champagne?'

'Certainly.' Jack let the cork pop, filled up the two glasses and looked at the countess. 'What now?'

The countess pulled a small, ornate silver box out of her muff and placed it on the table next to the flowers.

'Is that what I think it is?'

The countess nodded, tears in her eyes. 'Yes, her ashes. We had her cremated straight away just as she had asked. She didn't want her cadaver lying on some slab in a morgue like a side of lamb on a butcher's block, she used to say.'

Jack smiled as he remembered his great aunt and her very special, if somewhat eccentric, sense of humour. 'In that case, this is definitely the time to toast a very special lady, don't you think?' he said.

The countess nodded, becoming a little emotional. Jack handed her a glass of champagne and held up his own. 'To Madame Petrova,' he said. 'Prima ballerina extraordinaire, who was already famous in her teens as one of the baby ballerinas of the Ballet Russe de Monte Carlo before becoming a celebrated movie star. May she entertain the angels with her sublime dancing for all eternity,' he added, repeating the earlier toast he had made with Alexandra on the terrace of the sailing club in Sydney a few days before.

'To Madame Petrova,' said the countess, her voice quivering with emotion. The countess pointed to the silver box on the table. 'Would you?'

'Now?'

'Yes. You do remember what she asked for?'

'Yes. She wanted to have her ashes scattered right here, next to the memory trees she had planted for her sister and her niece—'

'Your mother,' added the countess, her eyes misting over.

Jack put down his glass and reached for the box. As he turned around to face the trees, he noticed that dark clouds had rolled in again, blotting out the blue sky and the sun. He took off his hat and slowly walked over to the trees, their bare branches like outstretched arms of welcome, promising an embrace. As he opened the little box, it began to snow.

The heavens are weeping, thought the countess and began to cry, overcome by the sad beauty of the moment.

First, Jack scattered some of the ashes under the tree belonging to Sister Elizabeth, his grandmother who had died at the Coberg Mission in Queensland where he was born. When he turned towards the other tree dedicated to his mother, a strange feeling came over him. It was as if the tree were somehow whispering to him.

What if she isn't dead? the tree seemed to ask. *Have you considered that? What if I was planted before my time? What if ...?*

Jack heard the tree whisper over and over. Slowly, he scattered some of the ashes under that tree and then tipped the rest over the little tree in the wooden tub and closed the lid of the box.

Taking a step back, Jack just stood there in silence for a moment, staring at the tree. Then he began to pray. It was a little prayer Jana Gonski, a dear friend, had taught him after an unforgettable encounter in Ethiopia a few years ago. It was the only prayer he knew:

Love is always patient and kind.
It is never jealous.
Love is never boastful or conceited.
It is never rude or selfish.
It does not take offence and is not resentful ...

Before he turned around to face the countess, Jack sensed this was another moment of destiny and made a promise to himself. It was Madame Petrova who had led him to his mother under the very trees where he now stood and she had been laid to rest. It was now up to him to take the next step and find out what really happened. Now that he knew who she was, he would investigate further his mother's disappearance all those years ago, and answer the question posed by the tree once and for all.

3

The Prophet of Salvation, St Petersburg: December 1894

Vladimir Davydov, a vulnerable and sensitive young man, had taken his uncle's death very badly. The trauma of witnessing Tchaikovsky's final hours coupled with the shock revelation of his suicide had not only resulted in great anxiety and stress, it had caused considerable psychological damage as well, from which the impressionable young man would never recover.

This was exacerbated by the fact that Tchaikovsky had made his nephew his heir. He had left all the royalties from his extensive works to his beloved 'Bob' and had all the copyrights assigned to him as well, with instructions to divide the proceeds among certain relatives. This placed a huge responsibility on Davydov, ill-equipped to deal with such an unexpected and onerous burden.

It was therefore hardly surprising that he put the score of the Russian symphony dedicated to the tsar, which Tchaikovsky had entrusted to him just before he died, out of his mind, and neglected the task of delivering it to the tsar as instructed. This issue came to a dramatic climax with the sudden death of Tsar Alexander III on 1 November 1894. With the tsar dead, delivering the score with the dedication had now become impossible, which put further pressure on Davydov. In despair and finding it difficult to cope, he turned to morphine and alcohol, and soon developed a serious addiction to both, which would stay with him for the rest of his short life.

For the next year, the precious score languished among Tchaikovsky's many papers and letters Davydov kept in a wooden trunk in the attic of a house he owned just outside St Petersburg. Yet the guilt caused by failing his beloved uncle was never far away, and it tormented Davydov. Instead of fading over time, it became stronger as more time passed, and even haunted him in his sleep. Not even the ever-increasing doses of morphine and countless bottles of vodka could help ease the pervasive guilt and pain, and failed to provide even the briefest of escapes from the torment tearing his mind and soul apart. Frequent breakdowns, hallucinations and chronic pain became unbearable, causing a relentless downward spiral of addiction and despair. Davydov was rapidly hurtling towards self-destruction.

Then, quite unexpectedly, help came from an unlikely quarter. A young man whom Davydov had met during his time in the army and had a brief affair with, came to the rescue and threw Davydov a much-needed lifeline. He told him he knew of a medium who could contact the spirits of the dead. So, why not try to make contact with Tchaikovsky's spirit and ask him for guidance and forgiveness in the matter? he argued.

At first, Davydov dismissed the idea as absurd. But as time went by, and he became increasingly desperate and obsessed with the score in his possession and what to do with it, he decided to give it a try, and a séance was arranged.

Russia at that time was gripped by a fascination bordering on obsession with the occult, mysticism and everything supernatural, from telepathy and hypnotism to fortune-telling and chiromancy. All kinds of questionable practitioners, self-proclaimed preachers and prophets and 'mediums' – many of them opportunistic charlatans – appeared as part of a fervent spiritual searching that swept across Russia like a plague and engulfed the educated classes during what became known as Russia's Silver Age.

Igor Borodin was a cunning, drunken rogue who had spent time in jail for fraud, rape and seducing a minor. Tall, with a grey beard, penetrating eyes that seemed to look straight through you and a deep voice commanding authority, he was an imposing figure. After his release from jail, he reinvented himself and became a popular preacher who claimed to be able to summon the spirits of the dead and communicate with them. He called himself the 'Prophet of Salvation', and soon he had a dedicated circle of followers, many of them impressionable young society women who fell under his spell and were prepared to do almost anything for him. Rumours of unspeakable debauchery and drunken orgies held during his séances soon circulated throughout St Petersburg, yet despite all this, or perhaps because of it, many flocked to his sermons that promised salvation.

Borodin was a gifted, almost zealot-like speaker with a magnetic personality, who was able to whip up passion and excitement wherever he went. In Olga Gutnik, a stunning, ruthless Polish woman without morals, he had found a kindred spirit, and soon a successful partnership was forged to trick the gullible and exploit the desperate, looking for a spiritual experience. Olga, a former actress who had also spent time in jail for soliciting and fraud, became the medium, and Borodin was the preacher-prophet interpreting her 'messages'. The Borodin séances became fashionable and famous, and people were prepared to pay a small fortune for an invitation to participate.

The setting for these séances was a large, vaulted underground cellar in an old, dilapidated house on the outskirts of St Petersburg. The house provided an almost stage-like, theatrical backdrop to the spectacular séances, full of ingenious props and cleverly concealed special effects that were accepted without question as real by those who wanted to believe, and did.

Borodin preyed on the vulnerabilities, weaknesses and hopes of his subjects and tailored the séances accordingly. He interviewed potential subjects and their friends before each séance. This was done for the sole purpose of obtaining information to be used later during the séance in the medium's answers, as proof of her ability to access the spirit world, and summon spirits at will to answer questions, and provide guidance and advice.

So successful and sought-after were these séances that one had to book them several weeks, often months in advance. Many came to ask questions and seek comfort from their dear departed; others came out of curiosity or for entertainment and debauchery, for which the séances were well known. Borodin and Olga had something for everyone.

When a subject wanted to make contact with a spirit, Borodin preferred small groups of three or four participants. When the subjects came for entertainment, the groups were larger and the participants chosen accordingly.

Two days before the séance, Borodin had interviewed first Davydov then his friend, to find out why Davydov wanted to summon the spirit of Tchaikovsky and ask questions. Desperate and eager to believe this was truly possible, Davydov shared his innermost fears and hopes with Borodin. Borodin was an excellent listener and an expert in extracting information. He appeared genuinely interested, compassionate and prepared to help.

The séance was arranged for ten pm on a Saturday. Due to the sensitive nature of the questions to be asked, the only participants would be Davydov and his friend. To fortify himself and be able to cope, Davydov had injected himself with a large dose of morphine before attending. Borodin and Olga were consummate performers who knew how to put on a show to dazzle even the most hardened sceptics.

Davydov and his friend arrived half an hour before the séance was due to start and were shown to an eerie waiting room in the cellar that looked like an ossuary. One wall was entirely covered with rows of grinning skulls on rusty spikes, many of them with candles burning inside, sending crazy shadows floating across the stone floor like a dance macabre. A library of mortality reminding the visitor of the fragility of life and the certainty of death.

A young woman, her firm breasts exposed and wearing theatrical makeup that made her eyes appear feline and huge, showed them to a red velvet lounge facing the wall of skulls, and served vodka and champagne.

'What did I tell you?' whispered Davydov's friend and took a sip of champagne. 'Spectacular, isn't it?'

Davydov nodded, obviously impressed, the excitement and anticipation welling up from somewhere deep inside him, making him feel dizzy. Then the heavy, iron-studded wooden door at the far end of the large chamber creaked open and Borodin appeared. Looking like a wizard in a long black caftan embroidered with gold thread that shimmered in the candlelight, Borodin took a bow and pointed into the other room. 'This way please, gentlemen. Everything is ready.'

4

Madame Petrova's music box.
Kuragin chateau, La Saint-Sylvestre: 2016

After scattering Madame Petrova's ashes around her snow-covered memory trees, Countess Kuragin and Jack returned to the chateau to celebrate New Year's Eve. The countess had instructed the cook to prepare a special dinner, as tradition demanded.

'So, what have you got planned for New Year's Eve?' asked Jack as he helped the countess take off her heavy fur coat.

'A traditional meal, of course, but with a few surprises.'

'Can't wait. I'm starving.'

'You are always starving, Jack. Your eating habits are like your wardrobe: chaotic!'

'Not today, please,' pleaded Jack, rolling his eyes. 'Any guests?'

'No, I thought we'd keep tonight strictly a family affair, bearing in mind where we've just been and what we've done.'

'Good idea. I was hoping that was the case. I don't have to dress up, then,' added Jack, grinning mischeviously.

The countess shook her head, exasperated. 'No. Pre-dinner drinks in the music room at seven-thirty, dinner at eight.'

'I'll be there.'

'I hope so. What are you going to do now?'

'Reflect a little on what we did today, watch the Sydney fireworks and call Alexandra to wish her a Happy New Year.'

The countess put her hand on Jack's arm and looked at him. 'A day like this takes a lot out of you, doesn't it?'

'It sure does. Emotions can be draining. And thank you for arranging everything so ... well, you know, with love and care.'

'I did it for both of us.'

'Just the same. Facing the finality of death is never easy.'

'No, neither is the relentless march of time.'

'Quite so. Only the three of us, then, now that Tristan has decided to desert us and spend time in Venice instead. You and me, and Anna?'

Very much in love, Tristan had moved to Venice to spend time with Lorenza, the celebrated *Top Chef Europe* winner. He was staying at the Palazzo da Baggio, helping to set up her restaurant and reopen the boutique hotel after an ordeal that had almost cost her life.

'Who can blame him? Young love. Tristan and Lorenza have been through a lot together,' said the countess, remembering Lorenza's abduction and Tristan's heroic efforts to save her just a few months before.

'They make a great couple,' conceded Jack. 'I hope it works out.'

'Don't be such a cynic.'

'I miss him ...'

'I know you do.'

'François and cook will join us as well, of course,' said the countess. 'They are family.'

'Excellent! May I make a suggestion?'

'Go ahead.'

'If it's only the five of us, why don't we have our New Year's Eve dinner in the kitchen? That wonderful old table, full of memories. What did you call it? A table rubbed smooth by countless elbows propping up tired chins of generations past, looking forward to a meal? Far less formal ...'

The countess looked at Jack, surprised. 'I can't see why not. It's a great idea. In fact, it would make things a lot easier, especially for François and cook. And you certainly don't have to dress up,' she added, smiling. 'And as you know, Anna loves that kitchen and feels very comfortable there.'

'It's all settled then. Seven-thirty in the kitchen. I'll take care of the drinks.'

'You're on. I'll let cook know.'

The informal New Year's Eve dinner in the Kuragin kitchen, smelling of roast goose and spices, was a great success and the perfect conclusion to a solemn day, celebrating an extraordinary life. Jack the storyteller was in his element. He asked everyone at the table to tell a story about the most memorable New Year's Eve they could remember.

When his turn came, Jack reminisced about an outback New Year's Eve at the remote family homestead in Queensland. He described sitting under the stars as a young boy, at the end of a searing-hot day, with Aboriginal drovers drinking beer on the veranda, telling yarns of rainbow serpents living in the sky and Dinkarra, the mysterious Dreamtime hero, and Djumbud, the spirit country of revered ancestors long gone.

After a splendid meal of foie gras, oysters and roast goose, expertly prepared by cook for the occasion and washed down with vintage champagne from the Kuragin cellar, and a spectacular Bombe Alaska, specially prepared for Jack as a surprise, everyone retired just after midnight.

'Night cap?' said the countess, linking arms with Jack.

'Sure.'

'I have a surprise for you.'

'Oh? I like surprises.'

'Let's go to the music room, a most appropriate setting for the surprise as you will see.'

'I can't wait.'

'Warm up the brandy snifters. I won't be long.'

Fifteen minutes later, the countess joined Jack in the music room. François had built a cosy fire in the huge fireplace during the afternoon, giving the intimate room an inviting, festive glow. The first thing Jack noticed as the countess came walking slowly towards him was the familiar Fabergé gold cross she wore around her neck. The last time Jack had seen that cross was in Madame Petrova's retirement apartment four years earlier, when he had discovered that she was his great aunt. It had been that very cross that had been instrumental in exposing the remarkable connection between them.

Instinctively, Jack reached for his own identical cross he wore around his neck and held it tight. The countess placed a large parcel wrapped in gold paper she was carrying onto the coffee table in front of the fireplace, and turned to face Jack.

'In case you are wondering,' she said, following Jack's gaze and placing the tips of her fingers on the little jewel-encrusted cross around her neck, 'Madame Petrova left it to me. As you know, her father gave it to her as an Easter present when she was a teenager. He gave the other to her sister, your grandmother. You are wearing a replica of it around your neck.'

'Amazing,' said Jack, his eyes misting over as he remembered that tragic incident in Central Park four years earlier, when he had saved Soul's life. Once again, the little cross had played a significant part in that. He looked at the cross as a link of fate, opening doors to a past that would have otherwise remained hidden, preventing the discovery of precious family secrets and connections.

'How very appropriate,' said Jack. 'Another bond between us.'

'You know you are family, Jack, even without this.'

Jack nodded. 'Still ...'

'And she left you something, too.'

'Oh?'

The countess pointed to the parcel on the table. 'Open it.'

Jack put down his glass and began to peel away the gold paper. 'What's this?' he asked, opening the plain carton and peering inside.

'What does it look like?'

'Some kind of music box?' ventured Jack, lifting the curious item out of the carton. 'How beautiful,' he said, and placed the intricate little music box on the table.

'It is,' said the countess. 'But not just any music box. This is a rare antique. Apparently, it used to belong to Madame Petrova's mother, Countess Marya Bezukhova.'

'You don't say,' said Jack. 'Another unexpected link to the past.'

'She also left you all the photographs on her piano, which you so admired during your last meeting. She called them her little "memory windows" into her long life and wanted you to have them.'

'Thank you,' said Jack, and gave the countess a peck on the cheek. 'Do you think it works?'

'Why don't we try it and see?'

'Do you know what to do to make it go?'

'She did show me. Here, let me ...'

Slowly, the countess activated the mechanism, careful not to break anything as the box had not been in use for a long time. When she finally turned the lever at the back, the disc began to turn and a strange, muffled, mournful sound drifted out of the box.

'Ouch!' said Jack, covering his ears. 'Not what was once intended, surely.'

'I think not,' agreed the countess, laughing. 'The passage of time must have stolen a few notes, I'd say.'

'Sounds like it. Must be damaged inside.'

'Most probably. Hardly surprising when you consider its age. I know a wonderful clockmaker and restorer of musical instruments in Paris. He looks after all our clocks here. I'm sure he could investigate the problem, see what's wrong and hopefully repair it.'

'Excellent. Let's do that.'

Jack reached for the two brandy balloons on the mantelpiece and handed one to the countess.

'The day is full of surprises. To our inheritance,' he said. 'I wonder what tales this little music box could tell if only it could speak.'

'Who knows? Perhaps one day, it will,' said the countess and touched glasses with Jack. 'Happy New Year!'

5

The Séance, St Petersburg: December 1894

As Davydov followed Borodin into the séance chamber, he could hear the strange, mournful sound of a flute-like instrument in the background. A feeling of dread came over him and he began to tremble. If there was truth in what he had been told, he was about to come face to face with his uncle's spirit, the realisation filling his morphine-muddled brain with terror.

'In case you are wondering, what you can hear is a Turkish *Mey*, a double-reed aerophone,' said Borodin. 'It is an ancient musical instrument reaching all the way back to Hellenistic Egypt. It helps in making contact with the spirit world and relaxes our medium.'

The séance chamber had been carefully set up by Borodin and Olga for maximum effect. Exposed bricks, a vaulted, cobweb-covered ceiling and the stone floor gave the chamber a chapel-like feel, like a hidden place of worship in the catacombs of ancient Rome. The chamber smelled of sandalwood and was lit entirely by candles inserted into a rusty iron chandelier dangling from the centre of the ceiling. It appeared much larger than it was, with flickering shadows creeping along the walls like fingers pointing into the afterlife. Positioned directly under the chandelier was a round black marble table with a small silver bell on top, and four chairs, one of them with a back much higher than the others.

'Please take a seat,' said Borodin and pointed to the table, 'but leave this chair empty.' Borodin pulled the chair with the high back away from the table, sat down next to it and closed his eyes to let the tension grow. 'As I told you before, I will be your guide. If you carefully follow my instructions, no harm will come to you.'

Davydov and his friend sat down as instructed, and listened to the seductive melodies drifting through the chamber. Then the music stopped abruptly, plunging the chamber into silence. After a while,

Borodin opened his eyes again and reached for the ornate little bell in the middle of the table.

'This is an antique Buddhist singing bell from Tibet,' he said. 'It is used for sound healing and meditation in the Himalayas. Its chime will summon the medium; listen.'

Borodin rang the bell by gently tapping it with a small bamboo stick, the clear, almost ethereal sound banishing the silence.

'Now close your eyes and listen,' continued Borodin and rang the bell again.

'Now open your eyes.'

Davydov did as he was told and gasped. Sitting in the high-backed chair opposite was a striking woman in a green silk dress, her face covered by a translucent veil, making her large, hooded eyes glow in the semi-darkness as she stared at Davydov. For a while, Davydov's heavy breathing was the only sound in the chamber.

'Spirit world, open your gates,' began Borodin, his deep voice echoing through the chamber. 'We beseech you, allow the sprits within to reach out to the living, seeking comfort and advice.'

Olga closed her eyes and began to take deep breaths.

'Who is seeking comfort and advice?' asked Olga, her voice sounding strange, as if it didn't belong to her body but was emanating from somewhere else.

'Vladimir Davydov, beloved nephew of Pyotr Ilyich Tchaikovsky,' replied Borodin, 'who is in great need of comfort that only the spirit of his uncle can provide.'

Olga nodded, opened her eyes and looked up at the ceiling. 'Oh, spirit of Pyotr Ilyich Tchaikovsky, we summon you,' she whispered, her voice again sounding distant and strange. Suddenly, a cold puff of wind blew through the chamber, making the chandelier candles flicker and extinguishing several of them, almost plunging the chamber into darkness. 'Are you there?' asked Olga, opening her mouth.

Mesmerised, Davydov saw something that looked like green fog drift out of her mouth and then spiral upwards towards the ceiling like smoke. Moments later, Olga's body began to shake uncontrollably as more green fog came out of her nostrils, like steam from the flared nostrils of a brewery horse pulling a heavy cart on a cold winter's morning.

'I am,' said Olga, her voice now sounding deep like a man's. 'Oh, my beloved Bob, I have yearned for you so.'

Borodin looked at Davydov and nodded. This was the prearranged signal, telling Davydov that he could now speak and ask questions.

'Uncle?' croaked Davydov, tears in his eyes.

'Yes, it is me. You look so thin. Are you unwell?'

'I live in torment. I cannot sleep and cannot find peace.'

'Why?'

'Because I have failed you,' sobbed Davydov.

'How?'

'I have failed to deliver the score of your Russian symphony to our beloved tsar as you requested. And now he's dead and has been succeeded by his son.'

For a long moment there was complete silence in the chamber. Davydov interpreted this as a sign that his uncle was disappointed, perhaps even angry with him, and had withdrawn.

'No matter, my dear Bob, as long as you still have the score, all is well,' continued the voice. 'You do have it still?'

'Oh yes, I do,' replied Davydov, relieved. 'It is safe.'

'Then all is well and it is not too late to make amends.'

'It isn't?' said Davydov through his tears. 'Please tell me how that could be so.'

'I will. Now, please listen carefully. This is what I want you to do.'

6

Countess Bolkonskaya's promise,
St Petersburg: early December 1894

Instead of bringing some much-needed peace of mind and calmness into Davydov's troubled life, the Borodin séance had the opposite effect. Despite the forgiveness, encouragement and hope that Davydov had been so desperately yearning for, he found contact with Tchaikovsky's spirit not only disturbing, but he was filled with doubts and anxiety about what he had been requested to do.

Towards the end of the séance, after Davydov had confirmed that he still had the original score in his possession, the spirit had asked him to hand it to Countess Bolkonskaya, one of the tsarina's closest friends, with a request to deliver it to Tsar Nicholas II. This would fulfil the promise Davydov had made at Tchaikovsky's deathbed. The spirit reassured him that the new tsar would honour the dedication made to his father, Tsar Alexander III, who had passed away on 1 November, and deal with the symphony accordingly.

At first Davydov was elated, as this was a clear indication of the forgiveness that would absolve him from all guilt and further responsibility in the future. However, for some reason he couldn't quite explain, elation soon turned into alarm when Borodin told him at the conclusion of the séance that Countess Bolkonskaya was a frequent visitor and well known to Borodin and the medium as someone who made regular contact with the spirit world. He insinuated that this was most opportune in the circumstances and obviously something the spirit was well aware of, as a meeting with the countess could easily be arranged to facilitate the handover of the symphony. Borodin offered to be the go-between. He would explain the situation to the countess, introduce her to Davydov and prepare the way.

This was classic Borodin, who used every available avenue to exploit his subjects and their weaknesses to advance his own position and reputation, and make money along the way. Borodin, a rapacious master manipulator, knew that knowledge was power. The séances were about just that, as these carefully orchestrated sessions were the perfect vehicle to obtain confidential and often hidden information about individuals and situations that would otherwise never have seen the light of day.

In the fascinating Davydov–Tchaikovsky situation that he had just discovered concerning the symphony, he recognised a huge opportunity to gain entry into sought-after court circles and ingratiate himself with someone close to the tsarina. If what Davydov had revealed during the séance was true and he did in fact have access to an original score of an unpublished symphony by Tchaikovsky dedicated to the tsar's late father, then this was explosive intelligence that, if handled correctly, could be of enormous value. Borodin intended to take full advantage of this little gem and exploit the unexpected windfall to the fullest.

The necessary groundwork had already been laid in the way the séance had been conducted by Olga, and the direction it had taken. Knowing the countess was the key to this cunning plan, all Borodin had to do was bring the countess and Davydov together. Davydov would find peace of mind and the absolution he so desperately craved, and the countess, an ambitious woman who could be manipulated, would be handed something she could not have imagined in her wildest dreams: a Russian musical treasure that would make history, and she would be the one to present it to the tsar. As for Borodin and Olga, they would make sure the countess never forgot who had made it all possible, and how. She would remain forever in their debt and, if managed correctly, do their bidding in the future. With that, the door to the Imperial family would have been prised open at last.

All that remained to be done was to arrange a meeting as soon as possible while the impressions of the séance were still vivid, and make sure Davydov handed the symphony to the countess. The rest would take care of itself.

Two days later, Borodin contacted Davydov's friend with good news: a meeting with Countess Bolkonskaya had been arranged for that evening, and she had agreed to deliver the symphony to the tsar. As a close friend and confidante of the young tsarina, she had free and regular access to the tsar himself.

When Davydov heard the news about the meeting, he almost had a panic attack and immediately drank half a bottle of vodka to calm his nerves. Plagued by indecision and doubts, he stared at the score on his desk, unable to make a final decision. It was only after his friend had reassured him and pointed out all the logical reasons for going ahead, that Davydov finally agreed to the meeting. As soon as he was alone, however, Davydov turned to morphine for courage and injected himself with a huge dose to banish the demons haunting his feverish mind.

Countess Bolkonskaya had arrived earlier and was waiting for Davydov in the séance chamber. Borodin had carefully chosen this setting for the meeting, as it would remind Davydov of the recent encounter with the spirit world and provide an opportunity to call on the medium at short notice to quickly make contact with Tchaikovsky's spirit again, should that become necessary.

Countess Bolkonskaya, a striking woman in her thirties, had presence. Dressed all in black – she was still mourning her own recently departed husband – and wearing jewellery her friend the tsarina would have been proud to own, she radiated class and style. Since her husband's sudden death six months earlier, she had turned to mysticism and the occult for comfort, and to attempt to make contact with his spirit for advice and support. This was how she had come across Borodin and Olga.

It had only taken one séance to turn her into a believer, and she immediately became one of Borodin's most fervent followers, singing his praises at court. The Imperial family at the time was not immune from the spiritual searching and fascination with mysticism, the occult and all matters supernatural, sweeping across Russia. Alexandra, the newlywed tsarina – Nicholas and Alexandra had been married in the Winter Palace in St Petersburg on 26 November – in particular, was also very interested in spiritualism.

After introductions were made, a reluctant Davydov placed the precious score he had been guarding since Tchaikovsky's death and which had so tormented his guilt-riddled soul, on the marble table for all to see.

'May I?' said the countess and reached for the bundle of faded pages full of vertically aligned staves and clefs braced and barred together, and with numerous musical notations and instructions in the margin, representing the musical ideas of a genius. As she quickly leafed through the pages, her eyes fell on the dedication to the late Tsar Alexander III and signed by Tchaikovsky, which she read with interest.

Convinced of the authenticity of the document, the countess put the bundle of pages back on the table and looked at Davydov, who was looking uncomfortable and fidgeting in his seat.

'Are you sure about this?' asked the countess. Noticing Davydov's unease, Borodin decided to step in before Davydov had an opportunity to reply.

'May I make a suggestion?' he asked quietly.

'Please, go ahead,' said the countess.

'Why don't we ask the maestro himself?' suggested Borodin, carefully watching Davydov out of the corner of his eye. 'This would make everything clear and remove any uncertainty.'

Davydov looked at Borodin gratefully. The need for making a difficult decision had just been removed. Moments later, Olga the medium made a dramatic entrance and took a seat at the table between Davydov and the countess. Tchaikovsky's spirit was summoned and duly appeared during the carefully choreographed séance Borodin and Olga had worked out before the meeting.

After several questions about the score, Davydov asked his late uncle's spirit for guidance. He asked if he should hand over the symphony to the countess. After a long silence, the spirit replied:

'The answer to your question, my beloved Bob, rests in a simple promise. If Countess Bolkonskaya is prepared to promise on the memory of her late husband to deliver my symphony to the tsar, then yes, please hand it to her now ...'

Borodin looked at the countess, the question on his face obvious.

The countess turned to Davydov, tears in her eyes. 'I promise,' she whispered, momentarily overcome by the gravity of the moment.

Relieved, Olga closed her eyes, tilted her head back and began to tremble, a clear signal that the séance was over.

During the years that followed the handover of the symphony, Davydov sank deeper and deeper into despair. Despite the promise made by the countess, Davydov heard nothing further about the fate of the symphony, or if it had even been delivered to the tsar as promised. Numerous attempts to contact the countess failed. Even Borodin refused to help and indicated there was nothing he could do. He claimed not to have had any further contact with Bolkonskaya.

Riddled with doubts and regrets, and finally deserted by his friend who could no longer take the violent, alcohol and morphine-fuelled outbursts and irrational behaviour, Davydov reached a point of no return. He stood on a clifftop of desperation with nowhere to go.

On the morning of 27 December 1906, aged 34, he shot himself, his suicide causing not even a ripple in the fabric of St Petersburg society. Cast aside and forgotten, he was buried in the Dem'ianovo Cemetery in the town of Klin, where he had helped to set up a museum to commemorate his famous uncle's work and life.

7

The Letter, Paris: 7 January 2017

Jack was sitting in his favourite chair in the conservatory, writing, when Countess Kuragin walked in.

'I thought I'd find you here,' she said. 'I just had an interesting call from Claude.'

'Claude? Claude who? Enlighten me.'

'Claude Dupree, a wonderful man. He has repaired our clocks here for years. I sent your music box over to him to see if he can, you know, do something to make it go.'

'Of course. I remember.'

'Well, he just called. It was all very strange.'

'In what way?'

'He would like to see us.'

'Oh? Why?'

'Apparently, he discovered something inside the music box he wants to show us. In person.'

Jack pushed his laptop aside and looked at the countess.

'How interesting. Did he say what it was?'

'No, I couldn't get it out of him. But he did say the music box is now working perfectly.'

'At least that's something.'

The countess looked outside. 'The weather isn't too bad today—'

'What's on your mind?' interrupted Jack. 'I know you.'

'I thought, why don't we drive into Paris and pay Dupree a visit – his workshop is in Montmartre – and then we can have a nice lunch?'

'Great idea. You have somewhere in mind?'

'I do.'

'Care to tell me where?'

'No,' said the countess, smiling. 'It's a surprise.'

'How nice. Do I know the place?'

'Oh yes, you do.'

'Any hints?'

'You had an unforgettable experience there not that long ago.'

'Now you've made me really curious. I've been to a number of places in Paris the last year.'

'I know you have, but this one made quite an impression if I remember correctly,' said the countess, a sparkle in her eyes.

'Great, I'm always ready for surprises. I've had enough of writing today anyway.' Jack closed his laptop. 'Just can't seem to get my act together. Cabin fever.'

'You need another adventure,' teased the countess. 'I thought last year was more than enough excitement for a few years at least.'

'You know how it is; itchy feet.'

'Poor boy.'

'When do you want to leave?'

'Say, in an hour? And wear something decent,' said the countess.

'Oh, *that* kind of place?'

'I just don't want you to feel out of place.'

'Me? Never! I'm sure François will tell me where we're going.'

'I doubt it.'

'We'll see.'

'No, he won't.'

'You seem very sure.'

'I am. Do you want to know why?' said the countess, smiling.

'Tell me.'

'Because I haven't told him yet where we are lunching.'

'Any reason you're keeping this a secret?'

'Yes, because the place would give it away ...'

'Give what away?' asked Jack.

'The identity of the person we are having lunch with.'

'Very cagey of you. Someone I know?'

'Oh yes,' said the countess, enjoying herself.

'You've been planning this all along, haven't you? You're not setting me up; not some kind of date, I hope?' said Jack, looking alarmed.

'No, don't worry. It's all part of a promise.'

'A promise? How intriguing. I'll get ready.'

Because traffic was unusually light, it took them just over an hour to reach Paris, and François manoeuvred the old Bentley carefully through the narrow streets of Montmartre until he could go no further. 'You'll have to walk from here, I'm afraid,' he said and parked the large car in front of a set of stairs leading up a hill.

'No problem, it isn't far from here,' said the countess and got out of the car.

Located at the end of a narrow, cobblestoned alley, Dupree's workshop reminded Jack of Jakob Finkelstein, the famous Watchmaker of Warsaw. He had come across the eccentric Finkelstein ten years earlier, and was wondering if perhaps this marked the beginning of some danger and excitement, just as that unforgettable encounter had done all those years ago.

Same clutter, same smells, same dimly lit walls covered with all kinds of clocks, thought Jack. Even the sounds were similar, the regular tick-tock of a hundred intricate mechanisms trying in vain to move in unison.

However, that's where the similarities ended. Dupree was a man in remarkably good shape for someone well into his seventies. Tall, of athletic build with a full head of white hair and a neatly trimmed moustache, he looked more like a senior politician than a retired police officer who had once been a top detective in the Paris Police Prefecture and in charge of several sensational murder cases. After his retirement almost twenty years ago, he had decided to pursue his passion for antique clocks and, following in his father's footsteps, became a horologist.

'How good of you to come, Countess,' said Dupree and ushered his visitors to the back of the workshop. 'Lovely to see you.'

'You made us very curious, Monsieur Dupree,' said the countess.

'And with good reason.' Dupree pointed to the music box on his workbench. 'A splendid example, one of the best I've seen in a long time. An antique Regina 15 ½-inch disc music box with four discs; Cuban flame mahogany. It was manufactured in Gohis, Germany, in 1885. Quite rare. Excellent quality, and it works perfectly now. Here, listen.'

Dupree activated the mechanism at the back of the music box and within moments a cheerful Russian folk song chimed through the workshop with great clarity and a pleasing tone.

'How lovely. A little different from last time,' observed Jack.

'Not surprising,' said Dupree, 'when you consider why it didn't work.'

'Oh? Is that why you wanted to see us?' asked the countess.

Dupree nodded, took off his glasses and began to polish them with a crumpled handkerchief. Delighted to have such distinguished visitors in his workshop, Dupree took his time. He didn't have many visitors these days and besides, there was little demand for someone with his eclectic interests anymore. Times had changed.

Slowly, he put his glasses back on and looked at the countess. Then he reached for a dented tin with deep scratches sitting on the workbench, opened it and pushed it towards her. 'Here, please have a look, Countess. This is what we found inside. It was blocking the mechanism; that's why it didn't work.'

The countess pointed to the tin. 'This is yours, Jack. Better have a look and see what it is.'

Jack peered into the tin. 'What do you think this was doing in the music box in the first place?' he asked.

'I think it was hidden in there. That's the most logical explanation,' said Dupree. 'To open the back of the box wasn't difficult and could easily have been done without causing damage.'

Jack reached into the tin and took out a neatly folded piece of paper the size of a handkerchief. 'What's this?' he asked.

'A letter,' said Dupree, becoming excited. 'But not just any letter, as you will see in a moment.'

Jack unfolded the piece of paper and looked at the neat handwriting covering both sides. The ink had faded, but the words were clearly visible, and so was the date in the top right-hand corner – *Yekaterinburg, 16 July 1918*.

'How interesting,' said Jack.

'It's more than that,' said Dupree. 'I had a close look at it and showed it to my son. I hope you don't mind. He helped me with the repairs.'

Dupree turned around. 'Philippe, come over here please,' he called out. Moments later, the curtain at the back of the workshop parted and a man in his late thirties walked into the room. Shortish, with long, unkempt hair and restless eyes staring through thick glasses, and wearing a leather apron, he looked like he had just stepped out of a Dickens novel.

'Philippe studied history at the Sorbonne, specialising in palaeography,' said Dupree, sounding proud. After his wife had died, Dupree had used his modest retirement pension to put his only son through university.

'The study of handwriting,' said Jack. 'Fascinating.'

'Correct,' said Philippe, sounding surprised. Most people had no idea what palaeography was. 'It's a bit more than that, actually. We authenticate and date ancient texts mainly, but palaeography is also useful in the general study of history, especially letters and diaries.'

'Tell them what you've found out about the letter so far,' prompted Dupree.

'I've only had a brief look at it, but to begin with, we have this here,' began Philippe, and pointed to a printed crown at the top of the page and a kind of crest consisting of two intertwined letters, the letters A and N, below. 'This is very significant because it tells us something about the origin of the paper. Stationery like this was used by the Russian Imperial family, especially Empress Alexandra, the wife of Nicholas II. Several letters written on paper like this with a crown and crest at the top have survived.'

'Are you suggesting this could be such a letter?' asked Jack, looking serious.

'I am. And there are several reasons for this. When you look at the signature on the next page, you will see the letter is signed *Alix*, short for Alexandra. The empress only signed her name like this when she wrote to family members or close friends.'

For a moment no-one spoke as the possible implications of this began to sink in.

'There were, of course, several Alexandras at the Imperial court during the tumultuous reign of Nicholas II,' continued Philippe. 'And without further evidence, we cannot assume this was written by the tsarina. That said, we have this here.' Philippe pointed to the date at the top. 'A place, Yekaterinburg, and a date, sixteen July 1918. Both are significant.'

'The Russian Imperial family was imprisoned in Yekaterinburg in 1918,' said Jack. 'And they died there.'

'Correct,' said Philippe. 'And in that context the date, sixteen July, is extremely important because the entire family was murdered by the Bolsheviks in the cellar of the Ipatiev House during the night of seventeen July.'

'Extraordinary,' said the countess. 'Do we know to whom the letter was addressed?'

'We only have this here; a salutation,' replied Philippe: '"*To my dearest little Snow Queen*", but without an address or further clues. Perhaps there once was an envelope that would have had the full name and address written on it, which is likely, but it wasn't in the box.'

'How fascinating,' said Jack. 'But I see the letter is written in English.'

'That's not unusual,' said Philippe, warming to the subject. 'Nicholas and Alexandra spoke English and German in family circles, although Alexandra, a German, did speak Russian. Many of the tsarina's letters have survived and most of them are written in English.'

'What about the content?' asked the countess. 'Any clues in that?'

'I only looked at it briefly,' lied Philippe, 'but it is certainly fascinating and warrants further careful study.'

'Now you can see why I wanted to discuss this with you personally,' said Dupree, patting his son on the back. 'Good work, Philippe.'

'Yes, thank you both so much,' said Jack. 'This has been absolutely fascinating. I will certainly look into this further and try to find out what it all means.'

'I'm sure you will,' said the countess, smiling.

On their way out, the countess thanked Dupree and his son for being so helpful, and Jack carefully carried the music box. The letter was in his pocket.

'Happy?' asked the countess as they walked down slippery, snow-covered stairs and made their way back to the car. 'You are beaming like the proverbial cat.'

'Is it that obvious?'

'You should see yourself.'

'I did have that feeling when you gave me the music box on New Year's Eve, you know,' said Jack.

'What kind of feeling?'

'That another story had just found me.'

'A long-forgotten voice reaching out from the past, trying to be heard, you mean?' teased the countess. 'Destiny in action?'

'Something like that.'

'Looks like you were right.'

'I hope so.'

As soon as Jack and the countess had left the workshop, Philippe made a call on his mobile. 'They've just gone,' he said.

'I can see them,' said a voice on the other end of the line.

'The man's name is Jack Rogan, some kind of writer. A good friend of the countess. He's the owner of the music box, not the countess. The letter belongs to him.'

'Good work, Philippe. Madame Malenkova will be pleased. Payment as usual. Perhaps even a bonus.'

'There is more ...'

'What do you mean?'

'There was something else hidden in the box that would interest you.'

'Oh? What exactly?'

'We should meet and have a chat about this first ...'

'I see. Usual place?'

'Yes,' said Philippe.

'I'll let you know when.'

'Glad to be of service.'

'Here they come now. We'll take it from here.'

8

Lunch at La Closerie des Lilas, Paris: 7 January 2017

As soon as François, who had remained tight-lipped about their destination, turned into the busy Boulevard du Montparnasse, the penny dropped and Jack knew where they were heading.

'La Closerie des Lilas,' he said, pointing out the window. 'Our lunch spot?'

'Very good,' said the countess, smiling. 'That's where we are going.'

'*Oh no*!' Jack cried out. 'Then I also know who will be joining us for lunch.'

'You do?' asked the countess, enjoying herself.

'Mademoiselle Darrieux! Please tell me I'm wrong.'

'Right again. I'm sure she's already waiting for us at her usual table by the window.'

'That's why we are arriving in the family limo; appearances count. Nothing like pulling up in a vintage Bentley, right? I was wondering about that.'

'Now that you know who it is, please be nice to her. She's been asking about you for months, and I promised ...'

'You engineered this,' said Jack, shaking his finger at the countess.

'You wouldn't have come otherwise, admit it. And she did help you with your Professor K enquiries and Ritz questions, and gave you a vital clue, remember?'

'The scandal of the crystal skull. That's true, she did.'

'And she wrote that wonderful biography about Madame Petrova, your great aunt.'

'*The Darling of Swan Lake;* that's also true.'

'Then what are you complaining about? And besides, she could come in useful with that intriguing letter in your pocket. No-one knows more about Madame Petrova and her life and times than she does.'

'You're right. That hadn't occurred to me. Sheer coincidence.'

'Funny thing to say for a man who believes in destiny and fate.'

Jack looked at the countess sitting next to him and burst out laughing. 'You got me there. I promise to be nice to her irrespective of what outrageous attire might greet us when we arrive.'

'And please kiss her on both cheeks as I showed you last time? It's really important, especially in public.'

'Promise.'

'Did you hear that, François?' said the countess.

'I certainly did,' replied François, grinning, as he pulled up in front of the restaurant.

La Closerie des Lilas – one of Paris's most famous literary cafes with a long, colourful history – was one of Darrieux' favourite haunts, where she was well known and fawned over by the staff, and could therefore entertain friends in style.

Darrieux, an eye-catching Paris socialite and author, had perfected the art of being noticed. To ignore her was almost impossible. The fact that many laughed behind her back didn't seem to bother her. A flamboyant dresser in her late fifties – she only admitted to forty-something – she liked to show off her figure and considerable bosom by wearing daring designer outfits only worn by the reckless or the very brave, twenty or so years younger. She had never married – her relationships never lasted long – and she went through men faster than birthdays. Her lovers became younger as she got older.

Despite all this, she was very well liked and respected as a serious and talented writer, and her biographies of Coco Chanel and Marlene Dietrich, and more recently, her book about the famous Paris Ritz during the war years, were a huge success. Paris society embraced likeable eccentrics, and Darrieux passed with flying colours – literally.

'There she is,' said Jack as the maître d' showed them to the table. 'Wow!'

'Look cheerful,' said the countess. 'And try to ignore the dress – and don't let your eyes fall into her décolleté. They might get stuck!'

'I'll do my best,' hissed Jack, 'but it won't be easy.'

Aware that all eyes in the crowded dining room were upon them, the countess and Jack approached Darrieux' table.

'How wonderful to see you, Adrienne,' said Jack, and obediently kissed Darrieux on both cheeks as he had been instructed to do. More difficult by far, was to ignore the formidable bosom bursting out of a designer dress several sizes too small for a lady of her generous proportions, pressing against his chest.

'And you, Jack. I've heard so much about your escapades in Istanbul last year; it's a wonder you made it out in one piece. It was all over the papers.'

'I often wonder myself,' said Jack and ordered champagne. He realised that alcohol was the best medicine in situations like this.

'See? I kept my promise,' said the countess cheerfully and sat down next to Darrieux. 'Here he is.'

'Firstly, please accept my deepest condolences, Jack. Losing a wonderful relative like Madame Petrova is a huge loss,' said Darrieux sadly. 'And you, my dear, have lost a special friend. I know how much she meant to you,' she continued, turning to the countess.

Jack waited until the waiter had poured the champagne and left the table. 'This definitely calls for a toast,' he said and lifted his glass. 'To Madame Petrova.'

'To Madame Petrova,' echoed the countess and Darrieux. After that, everyone began to relax.

Darrieux' capacity to drink was only matched by her capacity to talk. Jack did his best to ignore the predictable chitchat and small talk, punctuated by shrill laughter that got louder with each glass of champagne, and tried to focus on the letter in his pocket. He had carefully read the entire letter in the car on their way to the restaurant and wondered what it all meant.

Could this really be an authentic letter written by Alexandra the day before she and her family were murdered? thought Jack. *And who is 'my little Snow Queen'? And why was the letter hidden in a music box belonging to my great aunt? What does it all mean?*

'Jack, did you hear that?' asked the countess, looking sternly at Jack.

'I'm sorry, what was that?'

'I just told Adrienne about that curious letter we found in the music box that your great aunt left you ...'

'Oh yes, very strange indeed.'

'Would you like to show it to her?'

'Sure.'

Jack reached into his pocket and put the letter on the table in front of him.

'May I?' said Darrieux.

'Of course, please go ahead.'

Darrieux picked up the letter and began to read it. As her eyes devoured the lines, the expression on her face changed. The flamboyant, outrageous socialite turned into the serious author who had written several meticulously researched books and could barely believe what the words were telling her. After having read the letter a second time, she put it on the table and for a long, tense moment just looked at it, lost in thought.

'Amazing,' she said at last, the expression on her face one of deep concentration. 'This letter is bristling with information,' she said. 'To me, it has an air of urgency and desperation about it. It seems to have been written by someone in a great hurry who is desperately trying to convey certain important information before it is too late, but in a way that only the person to whom the letter is addressed would fully understand and appreciate.'

'That's how I read it, too,' said Jack, impressed by Darrieux' interpretation and prescient insights. 'The fact it was found hidden in a music box that belonged to Madame Petrova,' continued Jack, 'has to be significant, surely. As you know her past better than anyone, does all this mean something to you? Can you throw some light on what is contained in the letter? Do you have any idea who "my dearest little Snow Queen" could be?'

Darrieux turned to Jack and put her hand on his arm. 'Before I answer that, I would like to listen to a couple of interview tapes I made – you know I recorded all of my sessions with your great aunt – and go over some of my notes. I have kept all the material I used for the biography.'

'I would really appreciate that,' said Jack, patting Mademoiselle Darrieux' hand. 'Who knows; this could be the beginning of something big, don't you think? Perhaps even a fascinating addendum to the biography?'

'Could be,' said Darrieux. 'It all depends on what I find in my notes ...'

'I suppose so, and where that might take us,' added Jack, looking dreamily into the distance, the writer in him sensing another fascinating story rising out of the past.

'Could you send me a copy of the letter?'

'You'll have it this evening.'

'Now, how about some more champagne?' said the countess, tactfully changing the subject that was threatening to take over the entire lunch.

'Excellent idea,' said Jack and signalled to the waiter.

9

Frieda Malenkova's villa, just outside Paris: 8 January 2017

Frieda Malenkova's art collection was legendary. Well known in art circles and auction houses throughout Europe as an astute collector with a seemingly bottomless purse, she had gone to great lengths to surround herself with an air of mystery and speculation. She never attended auctions in person, but preferred to bid over the phone or send one of her agents, usually a striking young woman, to do the bidding for her.

What began as a way to heal old wounds and forget, had turned into an all-consuming passion: an almost insatiable avarice for art and all things rare and beautiful. No-one knew what she looked like as she never appeared in public, nor gave interviews. She lived like a recluse in a converted church on the outskirts of Paris, surrounded by high hedges and security fences to keep out prying eyes and an inquisitive world she had withdrawn from many years ago.

But it hadn't always been that way. Recognised in her early teens as a figure skating prodigy in East Germany, she had been destined for great things from the very beginning. As the daughter of a high-ranking official working for the State Security Service – the notorious Stasi, one of the most effective and brutal intelligence and secret police agencies of the Cold War – she had enjoyed a privileged upbringing, and was hailed as a young hero of the GDR. As the reigning world champion, she had been due to represent her country at the winter Olympics in Lake Placid in 1980 and, it was expected, to bring home a gold medal and shower her country with glory.

The pressure on young Frieda was enormous. She was the apple of her doting father's eye, who left no stone unturned to provide her with the best available coaches sourced from his native Russia, to give Frieda every opportunity to reach her destiny. Known as the Beria of Berlin, Frieda's father had a fearsome reputation. Secretive and ruthless to the core, he was the architect of the highly successful dob-in your-neighbour-and-spy-on-your-family regime that supported the GDR for years, and created an era of suspicion and fear that only ended with the fall of the Berlin Wall in 1989.

A lofty position ruled by fear and terror created many enemies both within the Stasi, and on the outside. During a routine training session two weeks before the Olympics, disaster struck. Frieda was going through her breathtaking routine, practising an ambitious triple axel, one of her signature jumps. The triple axel was her secret weapon, which if completed flawlessly would put her ahead of the competition and into an excellent position for a gold medal. It required exceptional body strength, agility and control to gain sufficient height to attempt a jump of such complexity, but Frieda had mastered this challenge and was one of only a handful of skaters in the world capable of such an ambitious feat.

Everything went perfectly until the landing. This was the most difficult and dangerous part of the exercise as the skater had to land with a strong enough base after having completed the rotations, to absorb the enormous force generated by height and speed. As Frieda landed and touched the ice, just as she had done countless times before, her skate collapsed and she had a devastating fall, crushing her ankle. This ended her illustrious career and turned her into a cripple. It was rumoured that her skates had been tampered with, and that one of her father's enemies had been behind it as part of a revenge attack on a man feared and loathed by many.

When she acquired a new piece that she coveted, Malenkova would look at it for hours, and listen. She believed she could commune with objects – especially works of art – and draw energy and inspiration from the genius behind their creation. Over the years, Malenkova had turned into a bitter, ruthless woman who never got over the tragic fall that had destroyed her life. The once lithe and athletic girl capable of breathtaking feats, had become an obese, pudding-faced woman with a badly deformed foot, who needed a walking stick to get around.

Instead of moving on, she had turned to art to sustain her, and built a dark empire of shady art deals and questionable transactions where everything was possible, for a price.

Stolen paintings, antiquities and artefacts, books and manuscripts, even jewellery and rare musical instruments, would find their way to Malenkova from all over the world. Well known as someone who could find a buyer for almost anything – no questions asked – she was in great demand as a well-connected celebrity fence with access to the rich and powerful, prepared to pay handsomely for what she had to offer.

Secretive, manipulative and competitive by nature, Malenkova had channelled her energy and thwarted ambition into a different chase. Instead of chasing gold medals and fame, she now thrived on different challenges, often triggered by items she came across in unexpected ways. She was always on the lookout – usually for paintings, objets d'art and rare manuscripts – and had 'spotters' in many places.

Art galleries, libraries, universities, exhibitions, research institutes and the like around the world were all places of interest and part of her extensive network. Among the individuals she frequently did business with were archaeologists, university professors, art gallery curators, politicians, auctioneers, even palaeographers like Philippe. She always paid handsomely for leads and information she considered useful to her eclectic quests.

The physical challenge of her youth to attempt the impossible on ice, had been replaced by an intellectual challenge to unravel secrets and mysteries of the past that had eluded others, and profit from them along the way. Malenkova prided herself in being able to see what others couldn't, and muster the resources and ingenuity needed to turn that knowledge into results. She pursued her objectives with a stubborn, ruthless determination, and would stop at nothing to achieve her ambitions. With excellent connections to the Paris underworld, she was able to call on muscle if needed, and use more heavy-handed tactics should that be necessary. Over the years, she had accumulated a considerable fortune, which allowed her to indulge her extravagant tastes and pursue her expensive ventures.

After her devastating accident that brought her illustrious career to a sudden end, she went over to the dark side and became her father's assistant at Stasi. This gave her access to confidential material and intelligence concerning individuals and organisations only available to a privileged few. Over the years, she had carefully put aside some of that valuable intelligence and built up a small hoard of dossiers she intended to use in the future, when the time was right.

Then in 1989, the GDR collapsed, the Berlin wall came down and the hated Stasi disintegrated. Malenkova's father returned to Russia and joined the KGB. Malenkova left Berlin and went to live in Paris.

Now in her late fifties, Malenkova looked ten years older than she was. She sat in her wood-panelled study where once an altar had provided spiritual solace to the faithful. Hunched over her desk, she looked like a dangerous spider waiting for unsuspecting prey to become ensnared in her web of intrigue and greed.

Surrounded by books and manuscripts, she was carefully studying the letter Philippe had alerted her to. It was, of course, only a photocopy, but sufficient to have immediately aroused her interest. Apart from the few fascinating titbits Philippe had told her about the letter, she found its provenance and the way it was discovered of particular interest. And then there had been the lunch at La Closerie des Lilas with Mademoiselle Darrieux, Countess Kuragin and that interesting man, Jack Rogan, the author.

Malenkova had come across Mademoiselle Darrieux before and knew of her work, especially her biographies. She had heard of Countess Kuragin and her chateau, but had never met her. As for Jack Rogan, he was unknown to her, until now. She had carefully studied all the available material on the internet, which was extensive and very informative, and was beginning to piece together a picture of Jack, the intrepid adventurer with a literary streak. But that was only one of the links. Much more important as far as Malenkova was concerned, was the connection between Jack and Madame Petrova and the music box.

Malenkova read a certain passage in *The Darling of Swan Lake* – Madame Petrova's biography – a second time, and took off her glasses. *Fascinating,* she thought and underlined a short paragraph in the letter with a highlighter. She found that dividing a text, in this case a letter, into several distinct parts was a good way of analysing it and making sense of its content. An original letter from Empress Alexandra, the wife of Russia's last tsar, would be interesting enough, she thought, but what made Malenkova particularly excited was the content, or rather the questions raised by the curious way the letter was constructed, and what it was insinuating and hinting at without spelling it out.

Less than an hour after discovering the letter, the countess and Rogan have lunch with Petrova's biographer, thought Malenkova. *Coincidence? Hardly.* Malenkova didn't believe in coincidences, only analytical deduction and reason. She looked again at the letter and slowly ran her fingertips along the passage she had underlined earlier. *I wonder what it means?* she thought, a wave of excitement washing over her. Then she sat back and rang the bell on her desk.

Moments later, her PA, a young Polish woman, entered.

'Zuzanna, please tell me again exactly what happened yesterday from the moment you saw the two of them leave Dupree's workshop.'

'Certainly. They got into a waiting car and I followed them on my scooter to the restaurant.'

'La Closerie des Lilas?' said Malenkova.

'Yes. Mademoiselle Darrieux was waiting inside. The countess and Mr Rogan were shown to her table. It was clear from the way they greeted one another that they are friends, or at least know each other very well.'

'What happened next?'

'Champagne. Lots of it.'

'I want to know about the letter,' Malenkova said impatiently, 'not their drinking habits.'

'Rogan showed it to Darrieux. She took her time reading it. After that, they had what looked like an animated discussion about it. The letter was on the table and Rogan held it up several times, obviously to make a point.

'Then what?'

'Rogan put the letter into his pocket and they had lunch. After an hour or so, they stood up, said goodbye, and went their separate ways.'

Malenkova nodded, looking pleased. 'Now tell me about that phone call.'

'I just spoke to Philippe again a short while ago. He wants to meet.'

'Why?'

'Apparently, there is more to all this.'

'In what way?'

'The letter wasn't the only thing he found in the music box. There was something else.'

'Oh? Did he say what it was?'

'No. I got the impression he's after more money, before—'

'I see,' interrupted Malenkova, frowning. It was obvious she was annoyed. 'I think Philippe is playing a little game here. He could have told us this earlier.'

'I thought that, too,' said Zuzanna.

'Very well. Philippe shall have his meeting, but not exactly what he had in mind. I don't like games. We'll do this my way,' said Malenkova, steel in her voice, 'and teach him a lesson he won't forget. And at the same time, we send a message to others who might have similar ideas ...'

'Sure. What do you want me to do?'

'I'll tell you later, but first I want you to find out everything you can about Jack Rogan and Mademoiselle Darrieux. I've already found a lot of information about Rogan on the Net. Fascinating man. I want you to pay particular attention to Darrieux, understood? I want to know everything about her, particularly her past. Everybody has a weak spot, something to hide, a secret, especially someone like Darrieux. I want you to find it. Clear?'

'Absolutely,' said Zuzanna, used to Malenkova's devious ways and abrupt instructions. Investigating a person she had just come across was by no means unusual. To Malenkova, intelligence was power. She had learned that much from her father. 'I will get onto it straight away,' said Zuzanna.

'You do that.'

'Will that be all?'

'Yes, for now.'

10

Enter Rasputin, Peterhof Palace,
St Petersburg: 1 November 1905

Countess Bolkonskaya met Grigori Rasputin on the same day he was introduced to the tsar and his wife at Peterhof. This fateful meeting set in train a tragic chain of events with catastrophic consequences for the tsar, his family and Russia. The first of November 1905 was a cold and windy day. Part of the canal was frozen in patches and heavy fog hovered over the sea like a shroud. Rasputin had arrived in the afternoon, but his reputation preceded him. The simple peasant from the Siberian village of Pokrovskoye in Siberia had a meteoric rise during 1905 after his arrival in St Petersburg from Kazan. Doors seemed to open for him wherever he went and he rose from the bottom of the society ladder to the very top in less than a year, an unheard of accomplishment for a man like Rasputin in Imperial Russia at the time.

Hailed by some as a *starets*, or holy man and mystic with healing powers, he soon became the darling of the aristocratic elite – especially the women – who couldn't get enough of him and flocked to every salon he was invited to, just to hear him speak. His magnetic personality and strange ways were the talk of St Petersburg, yearning for something new, and fascinated by spiritualism and the occult.

As soon as he entered the palace, Rasputin took off his heavy peasant coat and stopped briefly in front of a mirror, adjusted his hair and smoothed over his unruly beard, and then followed the guard up the stairs leading to the apartments occupied by the tsar and his family. The fact he was about to meet one of the most powerful and revered men in all of Russia didn't seem to concern him.

As a seeker and man of God, all that mattered to him was his relationship with the Almighty, which dominated and defined his persona. Everything else came second. While many were put off by this arrogance and blind self-belief, and considered him nothing more than a charlatan, others were drawn to him because of these very character traits and revered him as a holy man and prophet. An eloquent, inspirational speaker with an exceptional knowledge of the scriptures and uncanny insights into human nature and behaviour, he mesmerised all who came in contact with him. This included senior clergy and the upper echelons of St Petersburg society, impressed by this simple, pious man of God, untarnished by the ways of a world ruled by jaded and cynical aristocrats, out of touch with the millions of ordinary people toiling in the fields, barely able to eke out a living.

Nicholas and Alexandra met with Rasputin in the small drawing room next to the tsar's study on the first floor of the palace. The meeting lasted for almost three hours, and the royal couple were impressed by Rasputin and the surprising way he expressed himself and dealt with complex and sensitive, mainly spiritual subjects of great interest to them. Alexandra in particular, was instantly drawn to him and fell under his spell.

Countess Bolkonskaya had known about the meeting for days, and was anxious to meet Rasputin and see for herself what all the rage was about. An unexpected window of opportunity presented itself as Rasputin was leaving. As he was putting on his coat downstairs after the meeting, Bolkonskaya walked up to him and introduced herself. Rasputin just looked at her with those famous piercing eyes, which seemed to look straight into her soul. Bolkonskaya looked away and began to shiver. After a while, Rasputin embraced her and kissed her on both cheeks.

Instead of being shocked by this unexpected intimacy, Bolkonskaya found his touch comforting and was instantly at ease as a sense of peace washed over her. There was nothing indecent or offensive about the sudden embrace, only surprise and a feeling of wellbeing. Rasputin was well known for kissing and embracing when meeting people even for the first time. This was almost unheard of in aristocratic circles and viewed as crass and offensive behaviour only practised by simple, ignorant peasants.

'Your soul is troubled and your heart is full of regrets,' said Rasputin, his voice gentle. 'But have no fear, God sends us mercy and is never far away. When our soul becomes despondent, our head is confused. If you turn to God and ask for guidance and forgiveness, all will become clear.'

Rasputin buttoned up his coat and looked at Bolkonskaya with his penetrating eyes. 'We'll meet again, of that I am sure. Should your soul still be troubled by then, I will show you the way ...'

Then, without saying another word, Rasputin turned and walked out into the cold, leaving Bolkonskaya sobbing.

How could he possibly know? she asked herself over and over. Since that fateful Borodin séance all those years ago, Bolkonskaya had been deeply troubled. It was as if the symphony entrusted to her by Tchaikovsky's spirit and the promise she had made, were bringing her nothing but misery and anguish.

At first, she'd had every intention to deliver the Tchaikovsky score to the tsar as promised, and couldn't wait to present it to him. As one of the first to extend the hand of friendship to a shunned and lonely Alexandra, a German, upon her arrival in Russia just before her marriage in 1894, Bolkonskaya's friendship with Alexandra had begun to blossom. But when she became the tsarina's confidante and was later appointed a lady in waiting, Bolkonskaya began to hesitate. How would she explain the way she had obtained the score in the first place? What would the tsarina's reaction be? How would she view Bolkonskaya's obsession with the supernatural and the occult? Could this endanger their friendship and threaten her position at court?

Deeply troubled by these questions, Bolkonskaya had made a fateful decision: instead of delivering the score to the tsar as promised, she took the coward's way out and decided to do nothing. She ignored Davydov's numerous attempts to get in touch with her, distanced herself from Borodin, and eventually put the entire matter out of her mind. However, the little accusing demons refused to be silenced, especially at night, and haunted her even in her sleep.

When Rasputin therefore appeared to allude to this very torment and gave her hope, Bolkonskaya instantly became one of his acolytes. If a stranger she had just met could look into the deepest recesses of her soul and discover her innermost secrets, she told herself, then surely he could become her saviour as he had promised: show her a way out, and bring peace. What Bolkonskaya couldn't possibly have known at the time, was that instead of being her saviour, the self-proclaimed holy man from Siberia would become her nemesis and destroy her world and everything she held dear.

11

The fire in Dupree's workshop, Montmartre: 9 January 2017

Just after ten pm there was a knock on the door. Claude Dupree, who was still working, went to the front of the shop, opened the door and looked at the young woman standing in a pale circle of light. 'We are here to see Philippe,' said the woman. A man stood behind her in the shadows, watching.

'Philippe? At this hour? Is he expecting you?' said Dupree, surprised.

'Please tell him *Le Fantôme* would like to see him,' said Zuzanna. She always used an alias when dealing with contacts like Philippe.

'Le Fantôme? How curious. Please come in, I'll get him.'

Dupree went to the back of the shop to get his son. Moments later, Philippe appeared, a concerned look on his face. 'Not here!' he hissed. 'The usual place. I told you, *tomorrow*! Please leave.'

'Why? We are here now,' said Zuzanna, giving Philippe her best smile. 'And you asked for a meeting. Madame couldn't wait. You made her curious, you see. So, what's this about?'

'Come to the back and I'll tell you,' said Philippe, his eyes darting anxiously around the room.

'Is everything all right?' said Dupree and walked up to his son.

'Yes, fine. Please leave this to me. A new job, that's all.'

'You must be Philippe's father,' said Zuzanna, extending her hand. 'I always wanted to meet you, Mr Dupree.'

Looking alarmed, Philippe bit his lip. He certainly didn't want his father to become involved and find out about his surreptitious business arrangements with Le Fantôme.

'We are here about the music box,' continued Zuzanna cheerfully. 'Or to put it more accurately, about what was found inside it.'

'I don't understand,' said Dupree, looking confused.

'I'll explain later,' said Philippe, stepping in. 'Why don't you go upstairs and leave this to me. *Please*?'

'No, please join us,' said Zuzanna. 'I think you should hear what Philippe has to tell us.'

'*No!*' blurted Phillip, looking alarmed.

'But I insist,' said Zuzanna, enjoying Philippe's discomfort. 'And so does my friend here.' Zuzanna pointed to the burly man with the boxer's face standing behind her, chewing gum.

Philippe realised this was not the time to argue. 'As you wish,' he said, shrugging his shoulders. 'This way.' He pointed to the back of the workshop.

'You may not be aware of this, Mr Dupree, but we have been doing business with your son for some time,' said Zuzanna in a conspiratorial tone.

'I don't understand. What kind of business?'

'He sells us information.'

'What kind of information?'

'You know, useful stuff about your customers, like that fascinating letter you found the other day in that music box.'

Dupree looked shocked. 'Is that true, Philippe?' he asked.

'I'll explain later,' mumbled Philippe, brushing the question aside.

Zuzanna turned towards Philippe. 'Now, what else did you find in the music box that was so important?' she asked softly. 'Do tell us.'

'Nothing; forget it. I made a mistake. I was going to tell you tomorrow,' lied Philippe, beginning to sweat, his eyes wide with fear.

Zuzanna turned to the man behind her. 'Do you believe that, Jean-Paul?'

The man shook his head.

'Neither do I. So, one more time, Philippe, what else did you find in the music box?'

'Nothing,' croaked Philippe.

'Not good enough! Jean-Paul,' said Zuzanna, turning her back to Dupree. 'I think we should help our friend here to remember, don't you?'

Jean-Paul moved very fast for a man of his size. Philippe only saw a shadow flash past in front of him before Jean-Paul's massive fist smashed into his face, causing crazy sparks to dance in front of his eyes. Just before he lost consciousness, Philippe lost his balance, staggered backwards and fell against the workbench behind him, blood gushing from his open mouth. Jean-Paul was about to follow up with another punch, when Dupree hit him over the head from behind with a piece of wood he had picked up from the work bench.

'Stop! That's enough,' he shouted, pointing the piece of wood at Jean-Paul. For a moment, Jean-Paul stood perfectly still. Then he turned slowly around to face his attacker and began to rub the back of his head, surprise and disbelief on his angry face. Dupree saw the rage in Jean-Paul's eyes and remembered similar situations during his time in the Paris Police Prefecture when he had faced attacks by dangerous men just like Jean-Paul. *He's going to kill me*, he thought as he realised that he was no match for someone like Jean-Paul. The big man began to flex his chest muscles, a clear sign he was about to attack.

Fear can turn into a powerful shield if harnessed correctly. It's all about presence of mind and instant decisions. In Dupree, it produced an adrenaline rush, which in turn created a moment of clarity lasting long enough to allow him to assess the situation and make a split-second decision. He dropped the piece of wood and reached for a small bottle on the workbench he had spotted earlier. Taking a step back, he quickly unscrewed the top and held up the open bottle, waving it from side to side like a weapon.

'Merde!' shouted Jean-Paul and charged. Just before his clenched fists made contact with Dupree, Dupree threw the contents of the bottle – acid used for cleaning metal parts – at the enraged face closing in on him. The acid penetrated Jean-Paul's left eye, momentarily blinding him and sending a shaft of excruciating pain to his brain. With both hands pressed against his face and howling, Jean-Paul staggered backwards. A candle burning on a small table fell over as he crashed against it, igniting the curtains behind it and instantly sending flames racing to the wooden ceiling and setting it alight.

'Good God!' shouted Zuzanna. 'We must get out of here!' By then, Jean-Paul's sweater had caught fire and he was screaming in agony, unable to see. Dupree was trying to lift his unconscious son off the floor and drag him towards the door as smoke filled the room, flames spreading quickly all around him.

Realising that she couldn't save Jean-Paul, Zuzanna decided to save herself. She covered her mouth with her hand and, coughing violently, staggered towards the front door. Gasping for air as she stepped outside, she looked up as the windows on the first floor exploded – showering her with broken glass – and the old building drowned in a sea of flames.

We were told to teach him a lesson he wouldn't forget. Looks like we've done a great job, thought Zuzanna and disappeared into the night.

12

Hôpital Cochin, Paris: 10 January 2017

Jack was chatting to cook in the kitchen and enjoying a slice of the orange tea cake she had just baked, when the countess burst in, breathless and excited. 'I just had a call from the Hôpital Cochin.'

'What about?' said Jack, munching happily.

'Dupree. He's in the burns unit, badly injured.'

'Good heavens, what happened?'

'Apparently, there was a big fire in his workshop last night ...'

'How bad is he?'

'They didn't say, but he's in intensive care and wants to see us both – *urgently!*'

'Did they say why? We aren't family.'

'There is more terrible news.'

'Oh?'

'His son, Philippe, died in the fire,' said the countess, close to tears.

Jack stood up and put a comforting arm around her. 'That's awful.'

'We'll take my BM. I'll drive,' said the countess, wiping away a few tears. 'We should leave straight away.'

'Of course. Let's go.'

The notorious Paris traffic was particularly heavy that morning, and it took them almost two hours to reach the hospital. A senior nurse met them at reception leading to the burns unit, and directed them to Dupree's room.

'Fifteen minutes. No more,' she said. 'He really shouldn't have any visitors, but we are making an exception because he was so insistent, and we couldn't calm him down.'

'Understood,' said Jack. He reached for the countess's hand and followed the nurse down the corridor.

'Ready?' asked the nurse and held open the door to Dupree's room. 'He's in a bad way.'

The countess gasped as she entered the room, and Jack squeezed her hand in silent reply.

Lying propped up in the bed with various tubes connecting him to a blinking machine, most of his face and head bandaged, and only his eyes, mouth and nose visible, Dupree looked like the mummy in a silent horror movie. Both bandaged hands were held up by a frame, like the hands of a preacher blessing the faithful.

'He's conscious and can talk,' said the nurse, pre-empting the obvious question. 'Fifteen minutes. No more,' and then she closed the door.

The countess locked eyes with Dupree, who was watching her come closer. 'What on earth happened?' she asked.

Step by step, Dupree took them through the turbulent events of the night before, holding nothing back.

'It seems that Philippe's inexplicable actions somehow brought this upon us. Everything is somehow connected to that music box. I am very embarrassed about all of this and can only apologise to you both for this breach of trust, but sadly, Philippe paid the ultimate price for his actions, however misguided,' said Dupree, his voice fading away. 'I couldn't save him. I had almost dragged him outside, when the ceiling collapsed, trapping us both. If the firemen hadn't arrived soon after, I wouldn't be here. Unfortunately, it was too late for Philippe.'

'Hush now,' said the countess. 'None of this matters. What matters is you and your recovery.'

'Thank you, you are very generous, Countess. Just before he died, Philippe regained consciousness. He was lying on my chest with a burning beam pressing down on him when he told me ...'

'Told you what?' said Jack.

'About something else he had discovered in your music box.'

'What was it?' asked Jack, bending down to hear better.

'It's over there on the little table. He had it in his pocket.'

Jack looked at the small table next to the bed. The only items on the table were a glass of water and a small brass key with a metal tag. He reached for the key and held it up. 'This here?'

'Yes,' said Dupree. 'It seems my son died because of it. Someone was very determined to get hold of it.'

'Do you know who?'

'I did ask Philippe.'

'And?' prompted Jack.

'The last thing he said before he passed away were two words.'

'What were they?'

'Black widow.'

'Do you have any idea what they mean?'

'No, but I intend to find out. As soon as I get better.'

'Do you know the meaning of the key?'

'No. That's a matter for you ...'

Jack nodded. 'Thank you. Thank you very much. I will do my best to find out what all of this means.'

Just then, the door opened and the nurse appeared, a stern expression on her face. It was apparent she didn't approve of the visit. 'That's enough. Please leave now.'

'Of course,' said the countess. 'Thank you, Monsieur Dupree, and thank you for being so conscientious, especially in the circumstances. You are an honourable man. I am so sorry about your son. Both Mr Rogan and I will keep a close eye on your recovery and do what we can to help.'

'Thank you,' said Dupree, sounding a little stronger now that something heavy had been lifted from his troubled chest.

'Poor man,' said the countess on their way back to the car, clearly shocked. 'Can you believe this? Someone else is interested in the contents of Madame Petrova's music box, and has gone to such painstaking lengths to get hold of what was hidden inside? And how did they find out about it all in the first place?'

'Philippe?' suggested Jack.

'Must be. Still crazy! Doesn't make sense!'

'It's certainly weird, that's for sure,' said Jack, smiling. 'But everything has a purpose. Something like this doesn't happen without a very good reason.'

'You are loving this, admit it,' said the countess. 'This is typical Jack Rogan stuff, isn't it?'

'I feel very sorry for Dupree, that's the first thing.' Jack held up the little key. 'As for this here, it's about as good a mystery as you can get, don't you think? Bigger and more challenging than the letter, I'd say.'

'Perhaps they are connected. Can I have a look?'

'Sure.' Jack handed the key to the countess.

'What do you think it is?'

'Don't know. It's too small for a room key, but the tag could be a clue. Looks old.'

The countess looked at the round metal tag attached to the key by way of a keyring, like the room number of a hotel room key, only smaller.

'Have you seen this?'

'Yes. Two letters engraved, H and E, and a number: thirty-three.'

'How interesting. Any ideas?'

'Not yet, but it's early days,' replied Jack, smiling.

'No more writing for a while then, I take it?' teased the countess.

'Not until I find out what all of this means.'

'I thought as much.' The countess handed the key back to Jack. As he slipped it into his pocket, a familiar feeling of excitement raced through him as he followed the countess to her car.

PART II
FABERGÉ'S SECRET EASTER EGG

13

St Petersburg: December 1906

Rasputin's astonishing rise and influence – especially over the royal family, and Alexandra in particular – continued during 1906. The tsar even appointed him as his *lampadnik*, his lamplighter. As the man in charge of keeping the lamps in front of religious icons burning, Rasputin now had an official position with regular access to the palace and the royal family. But the real breakthrough that elevated his power and influence came from a different direction altogether: haemophilia. Alexei, the tsar's only son and heir to the throne, suffered from the inherited bleeding disorder. This considerably restricted his life and created a serious, ever-present danger that caused constant anguish and fear in his mother, trying to protect him.

Rasputin had gained a reputation as a faith healer early on, and many stories about his almost miraculous powers circulated throughout St Petersburg at the time. During October 1906 after Alexei, then aged two, had a fall and began to haemorrhage internally, Rasputin prayed with the boy and the next morning the bleeding stopped. A grateful Alexandra was overjoyed and after this episode, Rasputin became indispensable to her and could do no wrong.

Rasputin's many critics were either silenced or ignored by Alexandra, and even the tsar refused to believe the many rumours and accusations about his debauchery, drunkenness, religious heresy and even rape, and dismissed them as vicious gossip trying to discredit a holy man.

Aware of his growing power, Rasputin became bolder and more confident, and freely accepted bribes and sexual favours from his many admirers, especially society women who flocked to his apartment for enlightenment and guidance. Ambitious and manipulative with no moral compass, Rasputin used his elevated status to expand his influence, which according to many close to the royal couple, included political influence over the tsar. It was even whispered in the society salons that he was having an affair with the tsarina. Aware of these rumours, Rasputin fought back and successfully silenced many of his critics by having them discredited or removed from office.

The way Rasputin justified and explained his immoral ways was ingenious: he used the word of God. He argued that repentance was essential for salvation, and repentance only came into play if there was sin. Sin, repentance and salvation were therefore inextricably intertwined and had to be viewed as necessary steps along the path leading to God.

Rasputin maintained it was possible to be both a holy man and a sinner, and to Rasputin that meant sex and drink. These arguments were part of his teachings and his many, mainly female followers embraced them with fervour in order to be 'saved'.

The day after little Alexei's bleeding stopped and he was beginning to regain his strength, Rasputin returned to the palace to pray with the tsarevitch and his mother. Rasputin was just leaving the nursery when he found himself momentarily alone with Countess Bolkonskaya in the corridor. They had seen each other on several occasions since his return from Siberia earlier that year, but had never spoken privately.

Rasputin stopped and looked at Bolkonskaya with those piercing eyes. 'I can see your soul is still troubled,' he said softly. 'The light is there for all to see who truly seek it. I can help you and show you the way.' Rasputin put his hand on Bolkonskaya's arm, his touch sending a shiver of excitement through her body. 'Would you like me to show you the way?' he whispered seductively.

'Oh, yes please,' whispered Bolkonskaya.

'Then come to my apartment tomorrow and we shall pray together. You know where I live.'

Bolkonskaya nodded. Rasputin withdrew his hand and quickly walked away. So powerful was Rasputin's hold over women in particular, that this was all it took to pull them into his orbit and bend them to his will.

Bolkonskaya's affair with Rasputin began the next day. At first they prayed together, but soon prayer turned to carnal desire, all in the name of repentance on the path to salvation as part of God's inscrutable plan.

As one of the tsarina's closest friends and confidantes, Bolkonskaya was privy to court gossip and information that Rasputin was eager to access. He cunningly used these liaisons not only for pleasure, but as useful sources of information to further his influence and keep his critics and enemies in check.

When Rasputin began to question Bolkonskaya about her troubles, he was surprised to find that contrary to what he had assumed, they had nothing to do with her position in the royal household, nor her relationship with the tsarina. At first, Bolkonskaya was reluctant to confide in Rasputin and tell him what had been tormenting her all these years, but as he drew her ever closer to him, using passion and desire, and his own calculating interpretation of the scriptures to manipulate her, Bolkonskaya's reluctance began to wane. However, the event that finally caused her to capitulate and open up, was Davydov's suicide on 27 December. Shocked and distraught, Bolkonskaya met Rasputin in his apartment the day after Davydov had shot himself.

'You look like someone who has just seen a ghost,' said Rasputin as he helped Bolkonskaya take off her coat.

'In a way, I have. A ghost from the past.'

'Would you like to tell me about it?'

'Yes.'

Rasputin lit a candle and sat down facing Bolkonskaya, his eyes boring into her like inquisitive beacons in search of hidden secrets. Taking his time, Rasputin reached for Bolkonskaya's hand, closed his eyes and began to pray. The comforting words seemed to relax Bolkonskaya, and the shock of Davydov's sudden suicide began to ease.

After a while, Rasputin stopped praying and opened his eyes. 'Now, tell me what is troubling you so,' he said, stroking Bolkonskaya's hand. 'God is listening ...'

'It's about this,' said Bolkonskaya. She reached into her bag, pulled out the Tchaikovsky score and put it on the table in front of her.

'What is it?' asked Rasputin.

'Something very precious that has been entrusted to me, but I failed ...' Bolkonskaya's voice trailed off and she looked at Rasputin, her sad eyes close to tears.

'Failure, like sin, is part of the path to salvation,' said Rasputin.

Encouraged by these words, Bolkonskaya told Rasputin the story of the Tchaikovsky symphony, holding nothing back. She told him how the precious score had been entrusted to her during the Borodin séance and the promise she had made, and then broken, and the shame and torment it had caused over the years, culminating in Davydov's tragic suicide the day before, for which she felt, in some strange way, responsible.

Rasputin listened in silence, stroking Bolkonskaya's hand. Then he picked up the score and examined it. When he read the dedication to Tsar Alexander III and saw Tchaikovsky's signature, he realised the importance of what he held in his hands, and decided to act.

'I can see you deeply regret what has happened. If you truly repent, all will be forgiven. I can show you the way ...'

'Oh, yes please!' said Bolkonskaya. She reached for Rasputin's hand and kissed it.

'Your soul will not find peace until the symphony has been delivered to the tsar and your promise fulfilled.'

'But it's too late!' said Bolkonskaya.

'No, *it isn't!*'

'What are you saying?'

'There is a way ...'

'There is?'

'I will deliver the symphony to the tsar. I can do that in a way that will explain the delay and the long journey involved. I can also keep your name out of it, so no blame will fall on your shoulders.'

'Is that really possible?'

'I believe it is,' said Rasputin, stroking Bolkonskaya's hair as he worked out how to distance her from the tsarina and remove her from court. This was necessary because he had no intention of handing the symphony to the tsar as promised. Instead, he decided to keep it and use it to maximum advantage later, when the time was right.

First, Rasputin stopped seeing Bolkonskaya. He told her this was necessary as part of her repentance. Next, he gradually turned the tsarina against her by hinting that Bolkonskaya's presence had a detrimental effect on the tsarevitch. Blinded by her unshakable faith in Rasputin, the tsarina believed him and shortly after Christmas, Bolkonskaya was dismissed without an explanation and banished to her remote estate just outside Moscow, where she gradually sank into obscurity. Lonely and forgotten, she died a few years later without having had any further contact with the tsarina, or the royal family she had loved so dearly.

Bolkonskaya's sudden removal from the tsarina's inner circle left a vacuum Rasputin was eager to fill. He already had a replacement in mind: Countess Marya Bezukhova, the wife of Count Vasily Bezukhov, one of the tsar's closest friends and supporters. What made her such an attractive candidate was her blind devotion to Rasputin and the aura of carefully cultivated mysticism surrounding him.

14

Kuragin chateau: 20 January 2017

'She's here,' said Countess Kuragin and pointed out the window as Darrieux pulled up in her red 1980 Citroën 2 CV. First introduced in 1948 as a low-cost, low fuel-consumption motor vehicle designed to help farmers – who still depended on horses and carts – to motorise, the 2 CV was without doubt the most original and innovative motor vehicle since the Ford Model T.

'Can you believe this? She's driving one of these? A museum piece,' said Jack, laughing.

'Fits, don't you think? Just what you would expect from a flamboyant eccentric like Adrienne who thinks she's twenty or so years younger than she is.'

'I suppose so. I hope it doesn't break down and she has to stay here indefinitely.'

'Let's go and say hello to your admirer,' teased the countess and headed for the front door.

After Darrieux had called two days earlier indicating that she had some exciting news about the music box, Countess Kuragin had invited her for the weekend.

'What a magnificent home, Katerina,' said Darrieux and handed a huge bunch of flowers to the countess. Wearing a full-length fur coat of dubious origin that had seen better days, and a hat that would have turned heads at the Ascot races, Darrieux looked like an ageing actress auditioning for a Humphrey Bogart movie.

'I must say, you made us curious,' said Jack as he helped Darrieux out of the fur coat that was a little too tight around the chest and a little moth-eaten around the collar.

'François will show you to your room,' said the countess. 'You may wish to freshen up—'

'That can wait,' interrupted Darrieux breezily. 'What I could do with right now is a drink. The traffic was diabolical. And all that snow!'

The countess looked at Jack and winked, careful not to burst out laughing. 'Excellent suggestion. Let's go into the music room and Jack will open some champagne for us.'

After her third glass of vintage champagne, Darrieux began to relax. Not one for subtleties, and realising that the countess and Jack were too polite to ask, Darrieux decided to cut to the chase and broach the subject on everyone's mind that had been the reason for her invitation.

'I reviewed all the relevant material I had kept after completing Madame Petrova's biography. I'm sorry it took so long, but there was quite a lot to go through.' Darrieux paused, and looked at Jack. 'One of the questions you asked me was if I had any idea who the "little Snow Queen" in the letter could be, remember?'

'That's right. It could be the key to solving this perplexing riddle about the letter and what it could mean.'

'Quite. I have good news,' said Darrieux and held up her empty glass. Smiling, Jack refilled it at once. 'One of the first things I did with Madame Petrova at the beginning of our little project, was to put together a family tree. This was going to be our reference point and help us place people and events in her life. She had an exceptional memory for dates, places and people. She could remember what someone wore on a special occasion, say, in the Ritz during the war, and who was present. In her own way she lived in the past, as many old people who had such an exciting life tend to do. And there was certainly no lack of excitement in Madame Petrova's life, that's for sure.'

Darrieux opened a crocodile leather handbag that would have made a conservationist cringe, pulled out a sheet of paper and placed it on the table in front of her. 'This is her family tree. There are a few gaps, but by and large it's complete and makes for fascinating reading. Of course, this concerns you personally, Jack, as we are talking about your relatives here.'

'Distant,' interjected Jack.

'Perhaps so, but relatives nevertheless. As for your question of who the little Snow Queen might be, I may have an answer. Of course, I couldn't find it in the family tree as such, as this is obviously a nickname, a term of endearment between two close friends. For that reason alone, it is very significant. I found a brief reference to it on one of the tapes. I discovered it quite by chance as I was looking for something else. I believe it's the only mention of a Snow Queen in the entire body of material I collected.'

Darrieux pointed to a name on the family tree and looked at Jack. 'I believe the little Snow Queen is none other than Countess Marya Bezukhova, Madame Petrova's mother.'

For a while there was silence and Jack stared at Darrieux, his mind racing.

'Before we go any further, could you please tell us how you came to that conclusion?' he asked.

'Certainly. When I questioned Madame Petrova about her ancestors, she went through various family members she could remember. She did this by telling me stories and anecdotes about them. That's how she recalled people and even events and places. Apparently, Countess Bezukhova was quite a character. Her husband, Count Vasily Bezukhov – Madame Petrova's father – left Russia in 1915 during the First World War, just after the tsar took personal control of the army. He came to live in France and settled here permanently.'

'What about his wife; did she go with him?' asked Jack.

'Curiously, no. She remained in St Petersburg. She was very close to Alexandra and her children. Countess Bezukhova left Russia shortly after Nicholas abdicated in March 1917, and joined her husband in France. They purchased a chateau not far from here, where Madame Petrova was born and grew up. She was born in 1920.'

'How interesting,' said the countess. 'I didn't know any of this.'

'The tsar's decision to take control of the army had disastrous consequences. Count Bezukhov – a close adviser to the tsar – had strongly counselled against this, but Nicholas wouldn't listen and went ahead regardless,' continued Darrieux, who had extensive knowledge of Russian history and was passionate about it.

'Count Bezukhov and the tsar had a falling out. Apparently, this rift was engineered by Rasputin, who had the ear of the tsar at the time even in matters of state, and was a very divisive and controversial figure in Russia during these turbulent times—'

'Ah, the mad monk Rasputin,' interjected the countess.

'Leaving Russia in early 1915 before the catastrophe that followed and coming to live in France was a far-sighted decision,' observed Jack. 'The count must have seen the storm clouds forming in St Petersburg. He clearly had an inkling of what was coming.'

'He must have, yet his wife stayed in St Petersburg for another two years. By then the catastrophe you mentioned was well underway, and the Imperial family was under house arrest in the Alexander Palace. Bezukhova was devoted to Alexandra and the two of them remained friends even after the countess left Russia in 1917 and joined her husband in France,' said Darrieux. 'And as we now know, they corresponded.'

'How fascinating,' said Jack. 'But what about the Snow Queen?'

'Ah. I was about to come to that. That's about Hans Christian Andersen,' said Darrieux, becoming animated.

'Fairytales? Please explain,' said Countess Kuragin, looking perplexed.

'Apparently, Marya Bezukhova was a wonderful storyteller and very popular with the Romanov children. Fairytales were her forte, and Hans Christian Andersen was her favourite.'

'Of course! *The Snow Queen*,' said Jack. 'One of Andersen's most famous stories.'

'Correct. But wait, there is more.' Darrieux took another sip of champagne, enjoying the anticipation in the room and being the centre of attention. 'According to Madame Petrova, who was very adamant about this by the way, the nickname "little Snow Queen" was given to her mother by no other than ...?' Darrieux paused and looked expectantly at Jack. 'Can you guess who?'

'Alexandra?' ventured Jack, frowning.

'Very good. Marya Bezukhova was not only a close friend of the tsarina, but also one of her ladies in waiting. She told young Alexei stories at bedtime to help him fall asleep, especially when he wasn't well. Andersen's *Snow Queen* was his favourite bedside story.'

'Incredible!' said Jack. 'And Madame Petrova told you all this?'

'She did. It's all on the tapes.'

Jack pulled the music box letter out of his pocket and put it on the table in front of Darrieux.

'Do you know what this means?' he asked.

'I sure do. The letter appears to be authentic, and was written by Alexandra herself and sent to her friend Countess Bezukhova, Madame Petrova's mother, in France.'

'Astonishing,' said Jack, shaking his head.

'According to Madame Petrova, the tsarina and Marya corresponded regularly,' continued Darrieux. 'Until the very end,' she added sadly. 'And this letter was obviously the last one. The date tells us that. The day after the tsarina signed the letter, she and her entire family were brutally murdered at Yekaterinburg.'

'Are you aware of any other letters like this?' asked Jack.

Darrieux shook her head. 'Unfortunately, no. This is where the good news ends.'

'Perhaps not,' said Jack, smiling. He reached into his pocket again, took out the little key Dupree had given him and placed it on the table next to the letter.

'How come?' asked Darrieux. 'What's this?'

'What does it look like?'

'I know what it looks like, but what does it *mean?*'

'This too, was found hidden in the music box,' said Jack, dropping the bombshell, and then explained what happened in Dupree's workshop.

'Good heavens! This story is becoming more incredible by the minute. I need another drink!'

As Jack filled up her glass, Darrieux' eyes fell on the metal tag attached to the key. 'Wait a minute. What's this?' she said and picked up the key to have a closer look. 'H E and a number,' she said. 'Amazing ...'

'Does this key mean something to you?' asked Jack, surprised.

Darrieux held the little key up to the light and carefully examined it from all angles. 'Could be. As you know, I have recently written a book about the Ritz here in Paris during the war. As you can imagine, there was a lot of research involved and I've come across a lot of trivia about the Ritz and the people who stayed there.'

'Yes, *Scandal in Place Vendôme*. Very popular, I believe.'

'Thank you. It's doing rather well. But back to the key. I have seen one just like it not that long ago. Compact, quite heavy for its size, distinctive design, old fashioned. But most interesting of all is the tag here.'

'In what way?'

'Here, have a look at this: H E. These are the initials of Hans Elmiger.'

'Who's Hans Elmiger?' asked the countess.

Darrieux turned to face the countess and smiled. 'Hans Elmiger was the manager of the Paris Ritz during the war. He was running the hotel during the German occupation. The Nazis used it as their headquarters. Goering lived there in the Imperial Suite, and many celebrities lived at the hotel during the war. The hotel was a hotbed of scandal and intrigue.'

'It's all in your book,' said Jack. 'I read it. But how is this relevant?'

'It is relevant because keys just like this one here were given by Elmiger to special guests staying at the Ritz during the war. The keys gave the guests access to their personal strong box allocated to them by Elmiger and kept in the hotel's walk-in safe in the basement. The guests kept their valuables in there during their stay. Cash, jewellery, stuff like that – and who knows what else.'

'And this could be such a key?' asked Jack.

'Yes, it looks just like the one I saw recently. I was doing some research at the hotel about Coco Chanel and her jewellery.'

'And are these strong boxes still kept at the hotel, do you think?' said the countess. 'It has just been extensively renovated. It was closed for years and was only reopened last year.'

'Correct. But let's not forget, the Paris Ritz is one of the most famous hotels in the world with a history like no other, and the guest always comes first. I would be surprised if the safe hasn't been retained intact. It was a very special safe, you see. I even saw the original ledger kept by the hotel during the war.'

'What kind of ledger?' said the countess.

'The ledger recording the names of the guests and the number of the strong boxes allocated to them. All in Elmiger's neat handwriting. He was a stickler for detail and procedure. All classic Ritz tradition.'

'So, do you think it could all still be there? The safe, the strong boxes, the ledger?' asked Jack, becoming excited.

'Why don't we ask the manager?' suggested Darrieux. 'I know him well, and since the publication of my book, I am rather popular at the Ritz,' she added. 'It's all about publicity. We could have a drink in the Bar Vendôme – perhaps a Rainbow, like last time – followed by lunch at L'Espadon. What do you say?'

'You're on,' said Jack, remembering an unforgettable dinner with Darrieux at the Ritz six years earlier, which had lasted well into the early hours of the morning and had given him a mighty hangover.

'I remember that occasion,' said the countess cheerfully. 'Jack came home early in the morning, and we didn't see him until lunchtime ... But he did rave about the evening, especially the fancy cocktails, didn't you Jack?'

'This is very exciting,' said Darrieux and put the little key back on the table. 'Who knows, perhaps this key can open more than just an old strong box left over from the war?'

'Let's find out,' said Jack.

'It's all settled then. I'll arrange lunch for the three of us. Would next Wednesday suit you?'

'Absolutely,' said the countess. 'Lunch at L'Espadon. We'll be there, won't we, Jack?'

'Absolutely. I can't wait! Now, who would like a little more champagne?'

15

The Ritz, Paris: 24 January 2017

'This is going to be interesting,' said Jack, playing with the little key in his pocket.

'We are late,' said the countess, as François pulled up in front of the imposing entrance of the hotel at number 15, Place Vendôme. They had left the chateau in a snowstorm that morning, which had brought the traffic on the autoroute to a virtual standstill.

Jack was about to reply when the back door of the Bentley opened.

'Good morning, Countess,' said the doorman, helping Countess Kuragin out of the car. 'Mademoiselle Darrieux and Monsieur Aubert are waiting for you in the Bar Vendôme. Please follow me.'

Jack smiled as he followed the countess and the liveried doorman into the lobby. *Just like last time*, he thought, admiring the superb floral arrangements as they crossed the newly refurbished foyer.

Darrieux was sitting at her usual table next to the grand piano. Strategically positioned in clear view of the entrance and everybody else in the crowded room, she was impossible to miss. She was talking animatedly to a distinguished-looking gentleman of about fifty, sitting next to her and listening patiently.

'Last time it was daffodil yellow; today must be pink Wednesday,' whispered Jack.

'Pull yourself together and be nice,' said the countess, waving at Darrieux as they walked across to her table, aware of curious eyes following them every step of the way.

'This is Monsieur Aubert, the manager of this wonderful establishment,' said Darrieux in a loud voice, making the introductions.

'It's a pleasure to meet you, Mr Rogan,' said Louis Aubert in perfect English as he shook hands with Jack. 'Mademoiselle Darrieux has told me a lot about you and the extraordinary discovery of the key.'

'I bet,' said Jack, rolling his eyes. Used to dealing with the arrogant rich and the unpredictable but always demanding famous, Aubert oozed charm and confidence, but something about his urbane, almost patronising manner made Jack feel uneasy and on guard.

'But you are, of course, no stranger to the Ritz here in Paris,' continued Aubert affably. 'It features quite prominently in your book *The Hidden Genes of Professor K.*'

'Ah, yes. The scandal of the crystal skull. That was quite a story and all thanks to Mademoiselle Darrieux, who first alerted me to it.'

'You have no idea, Mr Rogan, how many times I'm asked about that famous scandal since your book has been released,' continued Aubert. 'Our guests cannot get enough of it.'

'I suppose a little notoriety doesn't hurt?' said Jack, grinning.

'It certainly doesn't, and the Ritz has been – how do you say? – a magnet for notoriety. And much of it is due to Mademoiselle's wonderful book, which has certainly put the Ritz on the literary map, *non?* Centre stage.'

'You are too kind, Louis,' said Darrieux, patting Aubert on the back of the hand.

'Just last week, we sold over a hundred copies of *Scandal in Place Vendôme* in our gift shop alone,' continued Aubert. 'That reminds me, we have to order more copies.'

'You've made my day, Louis.'

Aubert, a busy man used to reading people and their moods, sensed in Jack a certain impatience and purpose that had nothing to do with a social occasion, which had brought most of the guests to the fashionable Bar Vendôme that morning, so he decided to come straight to the point.

Aubert turned to face Jack. 'You have already heard about our famous ledger, I believe?' he said.

Jack nodded. 'I sure have. Mademoiselle Darrieux seems to know every intimate detail about the Ritz; even its secrets.'

Darrieux looked at Jack and beamed.

'She's not only a Ritz expert, but our celebrated historian,' said Aubert loud enough for all sitting close to their table to hear. 'I have already examined the entries, Mr Rogan,' he continued, lowering his voice. 'And you will be pleased to hear that Countess Bezukhova was provided with a strong box – number thirty-three – in November 1942.'

Jack smiled at the countess as a familiar feeling of excitement made the hairs on the back of his neck tingle. He took a deep breath, reached into his pocket and took out the key. 'And could this be the key to open the box?' he asked, sounding hoarse.

Aubert picked up the little key and held it up. 'Certainly looks like it,' he said. 'But why don't we find out?'

'Let's do that,' said Darrieux, delighted to be once again the centre of attention.

Aubert stood up. 'We'll go first to my office and I'll show you the ledger. Then we can go down into the basement and inspect the safe ...'

'How exciting,' said the countess, 'I can't wait!'

'Why don't you put Countess Bezukhova's great-grandson out of his misery, Monsieur Aubert?' said Jack, falling in beside Aubert as they walked to the lifts. This was a shrewd remark, as it signalled Jack's standing and entitlement in the matter to Aubert.

'And how could I do that?' asked Aubert, well aware of both the question and the answer.

'By telling him if box thirty-three is still in the safe? That would be an excellent start.'

Aubert stopped at the lifts, pressed a button and then slowly turned around to face Jack. 'It is, and it doesn't appear to have been opened since the war,' he said, holding the lift door open for the ladies.

Aubert's office was a palatial room full of antiques and paintings, and overlooked the square. Furnished entirely in Empire style, it radiated Napoleonic charm and class.

'This is it here,' said Aubert and pointed to a large, leather-bound book the size of an atlas on his desk.

'Looks impressive,' said Jack, barely able to contain his excitement.

Aubert opened the ledger at a certain page that had been previously marked. 'There were one hundred active strong boxes in the safe during the war,' said Aubert. 'Coco Chanel had her own box, of course. It was number five as you would expect, after the famous 1921 fragrance in that iconic bottle. And then there was Marlene Dietrich's box, number eight, her lucky number signifying action, change and movement. Reichsmarschall Goering had two boxes, number twelve and number one – his birthday. He was born on the twelfth of January 1893. The Duke of Windsor and Wallace Simpson shared a box: number forty.'

'I understand that von Stulpnagel, the German military commander of occupied Paris also had his own box,' Darrieux cut in. 'I wonder what he kept in there? Cyanide, just in case it all went wrong? And then there was Canaris, the head of the Abwehr, the German intelligence offices in Paris. He too had his own box, I believe. Perhaps he kept his most important dossiers in there, about the guests staying at the Ritz? Who knows?'

Aubert smiled at Darrieux. 'But the one that interests us right now, is this one here,' he said. Then he pointed to an entry – a single line written in German in neat handwriting – and ran his finger along the line as he read the entry aloud: 'Graefin Marya Bezukhova; Schluessel thirty-three. Twenty-five November 1943. That's the date the key was handed over and the strong box became Countess Bezukhova's property, so to speak. There was also a password that was recorded elsewhere,' added Aubert, but he didn't elaborate.

'A password, you say?' said Jack. 'How intriguing.'

'Yes. The password was chosen by the guest and had to be provided every time access to the box was requested. For security purposes, I suppose. Guests often sent their maids to fetch something for them. As you can see, after the date here,' continued Aubert, 'there is space for another entry after the word *geschlossen* – meaning closed in German.'

'I see,' said the countess. 'But there is no entry. It's been left blank,' she observed.

'Precisely,' said Aubert. 'And that tells us that the box is still active. Shall we go and have a look?'

The countess reached for Jack's arm and squeezed it. 'Yes please,' she said and followed Aubert to the lift.

They caught the lift down to the basement. 'It's stairs from here, I'm afraid,' said Aubert. 'The safe is further down where the old air raid shelters used to be, in case the place was bombed ... Please follow me.'

Aubert led the way down a narrow set of stairs and then through a heavy fire door and along a dimly lit corridor smelling of rising damp, which came to an abrupt end. 'This is it here,' said Aubert, and pointed to a massive steel door set into a concrete wall. This has been here since the 1920s.'

'I've only heard about this place,' said Darrieux, 'but I have never been down here. How wonderful!'

'Please give me a moment,' said Aubert, fiddling with a set of large keys he had brought with him. 'The mechanism is quite old-fashioned and complicated, but it works.'

'How about this, Jack?' said the countess. 'Definitely up your alley, wouldn't you say? Following the breadcrumbs of destiny?'

Jack didn't reply. Instead, he watched Aubert intently as he went through the necessary steps to open the safe door. Finally satisfied, Aubert turned two keys simultaneously, the locks clicked into place and the heavy door opened. 'Always a good feeling when it works,' said Aubert. 'Let me turn on the lights.'

'Wow!' said Jack, stunned, as he stepped into the small room. 'This is amazing!'

Illuminated by a crystal chandelier dangling from the centre of the high ceiling, the elegant space looked more like an intimate dressing room fit for the Sun King than a walk-in safe in the bowels of a large hotel. Set deep into solid concrete along one of the walls were the one hundred strong boxes Aubert had mentioned, most of them disused long ago and empty. Arranged in neat rows and with only their square, polished steel opening doors visible, they looked like letterboxes in an exclusive Paris apartment block, their shiny black enamelled numbers reflecting the light from above.

However, the most striking feature of the room by far, was the amber panels surrounding a large mirror that almost covered the entire wall facing the strong boxes, making the room appear much larger than it was. Amber panels also covered the rest of the walls and the vaulted ceiling, giving the room a magical glow, like a pirate cave filled with stolen treasure.

'So, this is where it ended up,' said the countess. She was joking, of course, and pointed to one of the spectacular amber panels next to the mirror. 'The mysterious Amber Room reappears in the Ritz in Paris, presumably brought here by the Germans from the Catherine Palace in Tsarskoye Selo near St Petersburg during the war.'

'Looted, you mean,' interjected Jack. 'To make Goering feel at home, I suppose. He was obsessed with gemstones.'

'Yes, one could be forgiven for thinking that,' replied Aubert, smiling. 'It does look a bit like the legendary *Bernsteinzimmer*, the Amber Room, only much smaller, of course, and without many of the features of the Russian original.'

'This is incredible!' exclaimed Darrieux, taking in the stunning features of the room. 'The original Amber Room was given by the Prussian King Frederick William to Tsar Peter the Great in 1716.'

'And looted by the Germans during the war. All six tonnes of amber dismantled and removed,' said Jack. 'Sent back to Germany only to disappear along the way ... Present whereabouts unknown.'

'One of the great mysteries of the war,' said the countess.

Aubert turned to Jack. 'May I have the key, please?' he asked, changing the subject.

Jack handed him the key.

'Before we try to open the box, I have to tell you something,' said Aubert, looking serious. 'As you would have expected, I have, of course, discussed all this with senior management and the Board of Directors.'

'Naturally,' said Jack.

'It has been decided that as the original guest key appears to have surfaced in rather exceptional circumstances, supporting a claim by Mr Rogan, we should, if possible, open the box and examine its contents.' Aubert paused, searching for the right way to continue. 'It may be empty, of course, but then again it may not. In any event, I am not at liberty to hand over the contents right now. That would have to wait and be cleared by the directors and their lawyers. I'm sure you understand. Mr Rogan's entitlement will have to be examined and verified before that can happen, and that may well take some time.'

'Understood,' said Jack, who had been expecting something like that.

'Well then, let's see,' said Aubert, relieved, and turned to face the wall of strong boxes. 'This is it here, number thirty-three. To open the box works like this: There are two keys. One belongs to the hotel, this one here.' Aubert held up a key. 'The other one belongs to the guest.' Aubert held up Jack's key. 'Both keys are needed to open the box. One without the other cannot operate the lock. I will insert the hotel key here, and Mr Rogan can insert his key next to it here. All right? Let's do it.'

Aubert inserted the hotel key and turned it in the lock. Then he handed the other key to Jack and stepped back. Slowly, Jack inserted his key, turned it, and held his breath. Everyone in the room stared at the door of the box. Then a soft click broke the silence as the key engaged the lock, pushing the door open like an invitation to enter a long-forgotten world of secret memories and hidden treasure. A message from the long-departed to the living, prepared to listen.

'There's a metal tray inside the box you can pull out to make examining the contents easier,' said Aubert.

Jack opened the door fully and then pulled out the metal tray covered in red velvet. The countess and Darrieux stepped forward for a closer look.

There were only two items in the strong box. A bundle of what looked like letters with a white ribbon neatly tied in a bow around it, and a cube-shaped blue box, a little larger than Jack's hand. The countess's eyes went straight to the gold crest on top of the box, the corners of her mouth creasing into a knowing smile as she recognised the familiar logo.

'Why don't we see what's inside the box?' suggested the countess, her voice quivering with excitement.

Jack looked at Aubert standing next to him. 'May I?'

'Please, go ahead.'

Jack carried the tray over to the small marble table in front of the mirror, put it down and then lifted the little box carefully off the tray. It was quite heavy for its size, and he 'Before I open this, let's take a step back,' said Jack, a seasoned storyteller who knew how to make a point and let the excitement grow.

'This strong box was allocated by the Ritz to a guest, Countess Bezukhova, in 1942 and has apparently not been opened since the war. A key was provided to her, the one we've just used to open the box with, and has not been returned. According to the hotel's ledger, the arrangements between the hotel and the guest – Countess Bezukhova – regarding the strong box have therefore been active and on foot ever since, and have remained so to this very day.' Jack looked again at Aubert. 'Am I correct?'

'Yes, you are.'

Jack reached for the box and, taking a deep breath, slowly lifted the lid. Suddenly, all four sides of the box separated and opened up like the petals of a flower, exposing the unique treasure within.

The countess gasped.

'Good God!' Darrieux exclaimed, tears in her eyes. 'Do you think it could be?'

'Oh yes, I think so,' said the countess.

Aubert stared at the box for a while in surprise and disbelief. 'Congratulations, Mr Rogan,' he said. 'I believe we are witnessing another astonishing chapter in the hotel's exciting history. Don't you think so, Mademoiselle Darrieux?'

'Definitely,' said Darrieux, barely able to contain her excitement as her glowing cheeks competed for attention with the theatrical makeup covering her face like a mask.

16

Frieda Malenkova's study: 25 January 2017

Hands folded behind her back and squinting through her thick glasses, Malenkova stood in front of a large whiteboard next to the window overlooking the garden. It was getting dark and the open fireplace behind her was radiating a pleasant, welcome warmth on that freezing winter's evening. Her father had always used whiteboards when he worked on a difficult case that really excited him. As far as Malenkova was concerned, the 'Petrova Letter', as she called her latest project, was just such an endeavour.

As a seasoned veteran of many challenging projects, she had developed a sixth sense that rarely let her down when it came to following the trail of long-forgotten secrets and hidden treasure. And the key to following such trails and finding that treasure always came down to two simple things: information, and people.

Malenkova's father had been very resourceful when it came to obtaining information in imaginative ways and Frieda had been an attentive pupil. Many would say she had surpassed her father in tenacity and ruthlessness, which were often the key to success. She never hesitated to go where others feared to tread, and was prepared to take risks that would have made a fearless tightrope walker pale.

Just like her father, Malenkova was a master manipulator who knew how to use people and bend them to her will. How she did this was both subtle and clever. Based on instinct and an intuitive understanding of human nature, behaviour and emotions, she carefully tailored her tactics and approach in ways that would have impressed even the most practised psychiatrist. She also believed in destiny and followed her instincts with the certainty of a somnambulist.

Malenkova had read Darrieux' *The Darling of Swan Lake* – Madame Petrova's biography – cover to cover in one session. This had allowed her to create a picture in her mind of Madame Petrova's fascinating personality, her times and her remarkable life, which she then used to interpret the information about the Petrova Letter case as it unfolded.

As more information came to light, she added it to the whiteboard. Just like in criminal investigations, she concentrated on plausible, often hidden connections, motive, and opportunity based on facts and meticulous, rational deduction. At the same time, she carefully eliminated blind alleys, and rejected irrational conclusions hanging by the fragile thread of hope and speculation, rather than logic. While many would have considered such an approach old fashioned, too laborious and out of date, it had produced remarkable results for Malenkova over the years.

Perhaps the most remarkable feature of her methodology was the fact that she rarely, if ever, left her home. She used carefully chosen 'operatives', as her father used to call them, sourced from all walks of life and backgrounds to carry out her sometimes dirty and dangerous work. This had allowed her to distance herself from anything that could implicate her and bring her to the attention of the authorities. Her father had told her early on that staying in the shadows was the best way to stay alive.

Malenkova attached another extract from the Petrova biography to the whiteboard, limped over to her desk and rang the bell.

Zuzanna entered almost at once. As Malenkova's dedicated personal assistant and confidante, she was privy to most, but not all of her boss's plans, and also some of her secrets. She knew what was expected of her.

I am very lucky to have her, thought Malenkova, watching Zuzanna out of the corner of her eye, *yet I hardly know her at all.* She still couldn't quite understand why a sophisticated, cultured young woman like Zuzanna had accepted her invitation to join her and become her personal assistant two years earlier, and then, even more surprisingly, had decided to stay. For reasons she couldn't quite explain, Malenkova still felt somewhat uneasy about that. Instinct had told her to be cautious, but she dismissed those feelings as nonsense, as Zuzanna had not only demonstrated her dedication and loyalty time and again, but had become almost indispensable to her, especially after Celine's tragic death.

Malenkova had met Zuzanna Badowski, a young Polish woman, at an auction in Paris. At that time, Malenkova was still attending auctions and doing all the bidding herself. As one of the items going under the hammer was a rare painting by the Chan Buddhist painter Liang Kai, which she just had to have, Malenkova – an experienced tactician when it came to bidding at art auctions – only entered the bidding at the pointy end when most of the bidders had thrown in the towel. As part of her tactics, she dramatically raised the bids using amounts that were intended to intimidate and give the remaining bidders cold feet and make them stop.

Usually this approach worked, but not that time. One bidder was left who stubbornly stayed with her and continued the bidding until the amount had reached stratospheric heights well above the reserve. As the bidding continued, the crowded room fell silent and all eyes were on the two women bidding against each other.

Malenkova smiled as she remembered what had happened next. Suddenly, the young woman – Zuzanna – stopped bidding and turned towards her. Malenkova could still recall the exact words she said to her: 'Madame, I can see the passion in your eyes. This painting should belong to you. There will be no more bids from me.'

After the auction, Malenkova had invited the young woman to lunch, and it all went from there. *Strange,* thought Malenkova. *She has never told me much about herself or her background. Even after all this time, I don't really know who she is. Yet, she is watching me all the time. Weird.*

'Take a seat,' said Malenkova. She pointed to a chair facing her desk. 'Well? How did it go?'

It had taken Zuzanna longer than she would have liked to prepare her report on Darrieux. But following the leads she had uncovered had taken time and had even involved a brief trip to the US.

Malenkova, a tough and demanding taskmaster, would accept delays when justified, but never hurried shortcuts resulting in sloppy mistakes. In the risky, high-stakes games she liked to play, mistakes were not only costly, but could easily be deadly. She ran her small organisation based on tried and tested Stasi principles, and was proud of it.

'It's been a worthwhile trip with many surprises,' said Zuzanna. She had spent several days in the US following up certain leads about Darrieux, and had returned earlier that day from Louisiana.

'You asked me to find out everything I could about Darrieux' past.' Zuzanna paused and locked eyes with Malenkova. 'As you said, everyone has a weak spot, a secret, something to hide. Well, Mademoiselle Darrieux doesn't disappoint in that regard. She has plenty of all three. She certainly has a past, a surprising one. It wasn't easy to lift the lid on it, so to speak, because she has gone to great lengths to hide that past. And with good reason ...'

Malenkova held Zuzanna's gaze, trying in vain to suppress a strange feeling of dread building inside her. For an instant she thought that Zuzanna was talking about *her*, and not Darrieux.

Nonsense, thought Malenkova and reached for the cognac bottle on her desk. 'Would you like one?'

Zuzanna shook her head and waited until Malenkova had poured herself a large brandy.

'Darrieux was born in the Deep South near New Orleans and grew up in a shack on the banks of the Mississippi. Her father was a violent man who beat her mercilessly when he was drunk, which was most of the time,' began Zuzanna. 'Not surprisingly, she ran away from home as soon as she could. She lived on the streets as a teenager and began to work as a prostitute in New Orleans.'

Zuzanna paused again to let this sink in. It was difficult to imagine Darrieux, the flamboyant Paris socialite and celebrated author, working as a prostitute in New Orleans. But Zuzanna had saved up the best for last. 'Her real name is Maurice Moreau,' she said quietly. 'At least, that's what's on her birth certificate and the court records—'

'But that's a man's name?' interrupted Malenkova, shaking her head.

Zuzanna smiled. 'It is, and that's where the story becomes really interesting.'

Malenkova sat up, her curiosity aroused, took another sip of cognac and looked intently at Zuzanna. 'Go on.'

'Darrieux was born a male and worked for years as a male prostitute just off Bourbon Street.'

'*What*? Are you sure?' asked Malenkova, looking incredulous.

'Absolutely. Then came the event that changed all that ...'

'What kind of event?'

'A murder trial.'

'*What?*'

'And thanks to the court records, which Darrieux couldn't hide or suppress,' continued Zuzanna, 'we now know a lot about her, her past and what happened to her. In short, we know about her weak spot, her secrets and what she has tried to hide all these years.'

'Amazing.'

'Maurice Moreau was accused of having killed a coloured man from Santo Domingo in the Caribbean. His name was Armand Baudin. Apparently, a fight broke out when Baudin tried to force himself on Moreau. Moreau stabbed him to death, *twenty-eight* times ...'

'What happened?'

'A sensational trial followed. Moreau argued it was self-defence; the prosecution maintained it was a frenzied, drug-and-alcohol-fuelled murder. Despite overwhelming evidence, the jury found Moreau not guilty. This caused a racial riot among the black population. Moreau had to leave town.'

Malenkova shook her head. 'How did Maurice Moreau become Adrienne Darrieux?'

'That was the difficult part. After he left New Orleans, the trail went cold and Moreau disappeared for almost ten years, until another police matter, this time in Florida, threw him, or shall I say *her,* once again into the spotlight.'

'How?'

'Moreau was arrested for a petty break and enter in Miami. Only this time he called himself Estelle Montplaisir. She'd had a sex change, but fingerprint records linked her to the past. A journalist got wind of this and exposed the full story. Estelle spent two years in jail. After that, she changed her name again, left the US and came to live in France. Estelle Montplaisir became Adrienne Darrieux. How she managed this is unclear, but there you have it.'

Malenkova looked impressed. Her mind was already racing to find the best way to use this new, explosive information to advance her project. 'How did you manage this in such a short time?'

'I had a good teacher: *you*.'

'Are you sure it's her?'

'Yes. I engaged a private investigator in the States. One of the best. We've used him before and he came up with the important answers.'

'Ah. Good call. Always go to the top if you can. It's the most effective way to spend your money. You get results and you can sleep at night; another plus.'

'There is more good news,' said Zuzanna, basking in the rare compliment. Any form of praise from Malenkova was precious.

'There is? Tell me.'

'As you know, while I was in the States digging up Darrieux' past, I told Anielka to look after things here. A bit risky, I know, but how she handled the situation is remarkable.'

'It would appear so. I was able to use her when it really mattered. I sent her to the Ritz.'

'I think she's ready,' said Zuzanna. 'But that's only part of the good news.'

'She's a psychopath ...'

'I know that, and that is precisely what makes her so useful.'

'You think so?'

'Yes.'

'What makes you say that?'

'If handled correctly, psychopaths can be an awesome tool. She's exceptionally bright and totally without fear or any moral restraints. She can think on her feet and improvise in ways that leave you breathless. I've never come across anyone quite like her before, not even close. And apart from all that, she's a head-turner; stunning. Always an asset, don't you think? Men go crazy over her.'

'Exceptional then?'

'Yes, I believe she is.'

'Could she be a replacement for Celine?' said Malenkova with sadness in her voice.

'I know she was your favourite, but she's gone ... forever.'

'Please answer my question.'

'Yes. In good time, but we have to start somewhere. Give her a chance to prove herself. If handled correctly, she could be awesome.'

'And are you the one to handle her?'

'Yes, I believe so.'

'It could be risky.'

'Everything is risky. That's what we do. The secret is to assess the risk correctly, minimise it and act accordingly.'

Malenkova nodded as she recognised lessons in Zuzanna's remarks her father had taught her.

'And besides, she depends on us for everything,' continued Zuzanna. 'She has nowhere else to go, not after the prison ...'

'You are right. So, what's the good news about?'

'We had Darrieux under surveillance all this time, just as you asked. We know all her movements: where she goes, whom she meets, what she eats for lunch; everything.'

Malenkova nodded. 'And the good news?'

'It's about what Anielka found out at the Ritz yesterday while I was in the air coming home. I think we struck gold.'

'In what way?'

'As we know, Darrieux paid a visit to the Ritz.'

'That's not unusual. She wrote a whole book about the hotel and is well known there.'

'Quite. But *why* she went there this time, whom she met and what was discussed is remarkable.'

'Oh? In what way?'

'Because it has a direct bearing on our project. Anielka has done some investigating of her own. She actually sat near Darrieux' table in the Bar Vendôme and overheard a lot of things ... I told you she could improvise like no other. She has a memory as sharp as a razor and remembers everything. Very gifted.'

'Good. What exactly did she overhear?'

'I think it would be best if you could hear that from her.'

'I agree. When?'

'First thing tomorrow morning.'

Malenkova nodded. 'Impressive! We could do with some good news, especially after that Dupree fiasco.'

'That was an accident,' said Zuzanna, instantly on the defensive.

'We were lucky you were in disguise as usual. The muscle man is dead and the old man, Philippe's father, is in hospital with severe burns.'

'Barely alive, I'm told. He's no threat, even if he can somehow remember me later.'

'Perhaps not, but all the evidence has been destroyed in the fire. Pity about that. We may never know what else Philippe found in that music box.'

'Not necessarily,' said Zuzanna, smiling.

'*You know something?*' said Malenkova, her interest aroused.

'Let's wait until tomorrow and hear what Anielka has to tell us.'

'All right.'

'I will have that brandy now, if you don't mind,' said Zuzanna, and began to relax.

17

Yusupov Palace, St Petersburg: 16 December 1916

During the early years of World War I, Rasputin's power and influence over Nicholas and Alexandra became even more pronounced. Deeply opposed to war, Rasputin sensed that Russia was spiralling towards political and social catastrophe and the days of the Romanov dynasty, and therefore his own, were numbered. This had a devastating effect on his already shocking lifestyle and he sank deeper and deeper into a life of almost constant drunkenness and debauchery. Yet still, petitioners – mainly society women seeking political favours at court – flocked to his apartment offering bribes and sexual favours, which Rasputin accepted with abandon.

Emboldened by his power and ever-growing influence in high places, Rasputin made reckless political pronouncements that angered many. One of those bold statements involved an offer to go to the front to bless the troops. The Commander-in-Chief's reply was both swift and unambiguous: he would hang Rasputin from the nearest tree should he dare to show up.

Perhaps in response to this humiliating rebuff, Rasputin told the tsar that he'd had a revelation. Russia would not succeed in the war unless the tsar took personal command of the armies. So great was Rasputin's influence by then, that a weak and desperate Nicholas took this revelation as a sign from God and, encouraged by Alexandra, he took personal command of the Russian army. Ill-equipped for such a crushing responsibility, this had devastating consequences not only for Nicholas personally, but for the whole country, bringing the monarchy a step closer to collapse.

Instead of losing his grip, Rasputin's control over the tsarina increased further while Nicholas was at the front, losing the war. Rasputin became Alexandra's confidant and personal adviser, and encouraged her to remove his opponents from office and replace them with his own, handpicked protégées whose wives he had slept with earlier.

On 19 November 1916, Vladimir Purishkevich, a firebrand and outspoken critic of Rasputin and the tsarina, made a stirring speech in the Duma, accusing the tsar's ministers of having turned into marionettes whose threads had been firmly taken in hand by Rasputin and the Empress Alexandra. The speech made a huge impression on all who were present as it expressed what everyone felt, but was too afraid to say.

One of those present was Prince Felix Yusupov, who was married to the tsar's niece. He had been secretly plotting with Grand Duke Dmitri Pavlovich and others for some time to assassinate Rasputin, to save Russia and the tsar. After the rousing speech, Yusupov walked up to Purishkevich and invited him to join the conspirators. Purishkevich's enthusiastic acceptance set in train a chain of dramatic events that would make history, plunge Russia further into chaos, and instead of saving the royal family, seal their fate.

By December 1916, Rasputin was well aware he had made some powerful enemies who were plotting to kill him. He had become fearful, moody and reclusive, and rarely left his apartment. In a letter addressed to his family, he wrote these prophetic words:

A disaster is threatening us, a great misfortune is drawing near. The face of Our Lady has darkened and the spirit is disturbed in the calm of the night. This calm will not last. Terrible will be the wrath. And whither shall we flee? It is written: Watch, for ye know neither the day nor the hour. This day has come for our country. There will be cries and blood. In the great darkness of these griefs I can now distinguish nothing. My hour will soon strike. I am not afraid, but I know it will be bitter ...

During the afternoon of 16 December, a number of close friends visited Rasputin. Surprised to hear that he had accepted an invitation from Prince Yusupov to visit him at the Yusupov Palace later that evening, they tried to warn him about going out so late, but he wouldn't listen. The reason for this was predictable: Rasputin had been told by Yusupov that women would be there who were eager to meet him, but wanted to do so in private, well away from the prying eyes of curious society. To Rasputin that meant only one thing: a late-night orgy.

Just after midnight on the seventeenth, Yusupov rang the bell. 'Are you ready?' he asked. Dressed in a heavy coat and large fur hat that almost concealed his face, it was difficult to recognise him.

'I am,' said Rasputin and followed the prince down the stairs. They got into Purishkevich's motor car and drove to Yusupov's palace at 94 Moika. Dressed in a chauffeur's uniform for the sake of authenticity, Dr Lazovert was driving.

The conspirators had met at the palace earlier. Pavlovich; Sergei Sukhotin, a young officer in the Life Guard Infantry Regiment; and Dr Stanislaw Lazovert, a Polish physician who knew Purishkevich and had served under him in his military unit had spent several hours that evening carefully preparing the cellar where the murder was to take place. First, they put up curtains and laid carpets, and then brought in furniture. Tables and elegant chairs and even a samovar were arranged to create a cosy and inviting atmosphere. Aware that Rasputin liked music, they made sure there was a gramophone available and that it was working.

Next, they prepared the poisoned cakes that were to be offered to Rasputin by sprinkling enough cyanide powder on the petits fours to kill several grown men instantly, and also poured poison into two glasses in case Rasputin asked for some wine, which was most likely.

Just before one am, Yusupov and Rasputin arrived at the palace and went down into the cellar. They sat down, drank tea and Yusupov offered his guest the poisoned cakes. Rasputin ate several, but to Yusupov's surprise, nothing happened. Rasputin then asked for some wine and enquired where the women were. Yusupov obliged and offered him a glass of Madeira laced with poison and said they would arrive shortly. Again, nothing happened. The poison should have taken effect within minutes. By now, Rasputin had become irritable and suspicious and was drinking more and more wine.

Looking at the clock above the fireplace, Yusupov was becoming nervous; something was clearly wrong. He excused himself and hurried upstairs to where the others were anxiously waiting. When Yusupov told them that Rasputin was still alive because the poison had failed to have any effect, they began to panic. Yusupov saw Pavlovich's revolver on his desk and made a decision: he would go down and finish what he had begun.

Yusupov went downstairs into the cellar, loaded gun in hand, and entered the room. Having drunk more wine, Rasputin, by now quite drunk, was slumped in his seat, half-asleep. Yusupov walked up to him and shot him in the chest. Holding his chest and screaming, Rasputin tried to stand up, but collapsed onto the floor, blood gushing out of a huge wound.

Yusupov lifted the gun to finish the job, when Rasputin began to speak, his voice barely audible. 'Come closer, I have something important to tell you. It is a sin to refuse the last request of a dying man,' he said, cunning and devious to the last.

Holding the gun in front of him, Yusupov knelt down beside Rasputin. 'Say what you have to say and make peace with God.'

'If you spare me, I will give you something that will make history,' said Rasputin, blood trickling out of the corner of his foul mouth, 'and Mother Russia will be forever grateful and proud of you.'

'Give me what?'

'Come closer,' whispered Rasputin. Yusupov leaned forward and listened. Having heard the shot, the others came running down and burst into the room, only to find Yusupov kneeling on the floor next to Rasputin lying motionless in a pool of blood.

'Is he dead?' asked Pavlovich.

Yusupov stood up, his face ashen, but didn't reply.

Lazovert examined the body. 'He's dead,' he pronounced and closed Rasputin's eyes.

Thank God! thought Yusupov. 'We'll now go back to Rasputin's apartment as planned,' he said, taking control. He put on Rasputin's overcoat and cap. Yusupov, Pavlovich and Lazovert then drove to Rasputin's apartment. This was a naive precaution in case they had been followed by the police that night. It would show the police that Rasputin had been returned to his apartment alive and well in the early hours of the morning.

'Just give me a moment,' said Yusupov at the bottom of the stairs. 'Wait here. I want to take his coat and cap inside.'

A few minutes later, Yusupov returned, clutching a package under his arm.

'You look like you've seen a ghost,' said Lazovert.

'Haven't we all?' replied Yusupov. 'Let's go home and dispose of the body.'

Yusupov was the first to enter the cellar. He walked over to Rasputin lying on the floor and looked at him. *The monster is dead at last*, he thought. *The nightmare is over; we've saved Russia.*

Yusupov was about to turn away, when Rasputin opened his eyes and stared at him with hatred and contempt. 'Good God,' whispered Yusupov, fear clawing at his throat. '*It can't be!*' Then Rasputin got unsteadily to his feet, and howling loudly like some mortally wounded creature, rushed out of the room and then through a back door out into the snow-covered courtyard, leaving a trail of blood behind him. Having heard the commotion, Purishkevich came running down the stairs with a gun.

'He's out there,' cried Yusupov and pointed into the courtyard.

Purishkevich ran outside, trying to find Rasputin. Following the trail of blood, he found him crawling through the snow on all fours, shouting incoherently and foaming at the mouth like a man possessed. Purishkevich fired two shots, and then two more at close range. One bullet entered Rasputin's forehead and delivered the fatal wound.

Outside, the temperature had plummeted and a howling wind was rattling the windows like the breath of evil ghosts risen from the netherworld, coming to collect one of their own. Lazovert, Pavlovich and Sukhotin wrapped Rasputin's blood-covered body in a heavy woollen blanket, carried it to Purishkevich's car and quickly bundled it inside. Then Purishkevich drove through the empty, snow-covered streets to the Petrovsky Bridge. He stopped the car in the middle of the bridge, got out and opened the back door. They lifted out the heavy body and threw it into the icy waters below.

So ended one of the most bizarre chapters in modern Russian history. Instead of silencing an evil genius and saving the tsar and his empire, Rasputin's death only added to the legend and ensured that the mad monk from Siberia, who had foreseen his own violent end, would be remembered forever.

18

Kuragin chateau: 25 January 2017

'What are you doing?' asked Countess Kuragin. She walked up to Jack, who was sitting by the fire in the music room. His laptop was open and he was furiously typing notes. 'It's late.'

'A little research.'

'Oh?'

'You must admit, it was very generous of Aubert to let me take photos of everything in the strong box, including this here.' Jack held up the screen on his phone, showing an image of the spectacular enamelled gold egg that had taken his breath away the day before.

'I suppose it was.'

'I'm sure he must have broken a few rules.'

'Well, you are the heir, after all.'

'*Apparent*, perhaps, but not with all the necessary legal credentials, verified and presented to satisfy the lawyers. Not yet, anyway.'

'I still can't believe it, Jack. Was there really a Fabergé egg in that box?'

'It would appear so.' Jack found another photo on his phone that he had taken in the safe and pointed to the gold crest on top of the box – the Russian double-headed eagle with the crown. 'At the Pan-Russian Exhibition in 1896, the House of Fabergé was awarded the State Emblem by Tsar Nicholas II. It became that famous logo we all know and admire today. This is it here.'

'That fits,' said the countess.

'It does.' Jack pointed to his notes in front of him. 'But what worries me is there's no mention of a Fabergé egg that looks remotely like this one here in any of the official records I could find. All the eggs ever made by the House of Fabergé are carefully documented, and their history and present whereabouts meticulously recorded.'

'A lot could have happened during the firm's long history,'

remarked the countess.

'True. When you consider that the firm was founded in 1842 and began to create those famous Easter eggs in 1885, then yes, a lot could have happened, but still ... if this is truly an original Imperial Fabergé Easter egg, then surely there has to be some mention or record of it somewhere.'

'But what if it is one, regardless? It would be worth a fortune and make history. Have you considered that?' asked the countess.

'You mean one that got away and was missed during the Russian Easter egg hunt?' mused Jack. 'And then mysteriously resurfaced in France and was placed for safekeeping by Countess Bezukhova in the Amber Safe at the Ritz during the war? Sure. Pity we weren't allowed to open it and have a look inside.'

'And find the surprise?'

'Well, you can understand that, can't you?' said Jack.

'I suppose so.'

'To me, the real surprise is that it ended up in the safe at the Ritz in Paris, forgotten and waiting ... It's not something you just forget to collect and leave behind, is it?' Jack looked thoughtfully into the fire.

'The way it all began is really fascinating,' he continued, changing direction. 'The Imperial Easter egg tradition started with a simple, charming idea. Tsar Alexander III commissioned the House of Fabergé to create an egg as an Easter gift for his wife. Peter Carl Fabergé, the celebrated master jeweller, rose to the challenge and created something unique and spectacular that took Empress Maria Feodorovna's breath away: an enamelled gold egg that could be pulled apart to reveal a gold yolk, which in turn could be opened up to reveal a gold chicken that also opened up to reveal a tiny Imperial Crown with a miniature ruby egg suspended in the centre. That was the surprise when you opened the egg step by step. Each egg had to have a surprise inside, you see.'

'How wonderful. You *have* been doing some research.'

'That was the first Imperial Easter egg ever made,' continued Jack. 'It has a name like all the others that came after it. It's called the Hen Egg – not very original, I know – and is currently in the collection of oligarch Viktor Vekselberg. Do you know Vekselberg spent more than one hundred million dollars purchasing nine Fabergé Easter eggs?'

'Incredible! Do you know how many Imperial eggs were made?'

'Yes. Fifty in all, of which forty-three have survived. They all have names, like Resurrection, Apple Blossom, Winter, Napoleonic, Standard Yacht and so on. Much more interesting than Hen Egg, wouldn't you say?'

'Sure. I wonder if this one had a name?'

'Perhaps. The tradition began with Alexander III and then continued with his son, Nicholas II. Each year the tsar gave a Fabergé Easter egg to his wife, Alexandra, and one to his mother, the Dowager Empress Maria Feodorovna.'

'You are well informed.'

'Well, as the potential owner of one of these little beauties, I have to be, don't you think?' said Jack, smiling. He closed his little notebook, slipped the familiar rubber band around it, and looked at the countess.

'What could it be worth, do you think?' asked the countess.

'If it is an original, say, ten million dollars.'

'*What?* Are you serious?'

'Absolutely. The record for an Imperial Easter egg sold at auction was eight-point-nine million pounds. That was in 2007 for the Rothschild Egg.'

'Amazing!'

'And then there is the story about the Fabergé egg sold a few years ago at a US flea market for fourteen thousand dollars. It was one of the eggs given by Nicholas II to his wife, Alexandra, in 1887. Today, it could be worth as much as thirty-three million. As you can see, Easter egg miracles do happen.'

'The question here is this: is the Bezukhova egg in the Amber Safe a Fabergé original?'

'Yes, that's the multi-million-dollar question,' said Jack, laughing.

He pulled the little brass key out of his pocket and placed it next to his phone. 'And could this be the key to my future fortune?'

'Who knows?' said the countess. 'But don't forget, Easter miracles can happen, right?'

'Oh yes. You know I believe in miracles.'

'What about the letters?' asked the countess. 'Have you had a look?'

'Only briefly. The egg had priority.'

'Understandable, but still ...'

'All I can tell you about the letters at the moment is this: there are four. All very similar to the letter we found in the music box. Same handwriting, same salutation.'

'"My dearest little Snow Queen"?' said the countess.

'Yes, and all are signed "Alix" and have the same crest at the top.'

'More letters sent by Empress Alexandra to her dear friend Countess Marya Bezukhova, do you think?'

'Looks that way.'

'How fascinating. Did you read them?'

'Not yet. I want a clear head for that. I'll do it in the morning.'

'Good idea. What an exciting life you lead, Jack.'

'Not bad for an Aussie adventure junkie, you mean, about to inherit a fortune?'

'That reminds me,' said the countess, smiling. 'What about Mademoiselle Darrieux, your admirer? Have you given that some thought?'

'You mean about collaborating with her on another exciting chapter for both the Ritz history and the Petrova biography?'

'Yes. Well ...?'

'That's a tricky one. She's right in the middle of all this, and we owe her,' said Jack, turning serious. 'Without Adrienne, we wouldn't have found out about the safe, and the rest.'

'You're right. So, what are you going to do? *Collaborate?*'

'I'm thinking about it. She knows a surprising lot about Russian history, not to mention Madame Petrova and her life and times. And she's very well connected. All that could come in useful, especially with these new letters here.'

'You have made up your mind, then?'

'I suppose so. And you know what? I've really begun to like her ...'

'You don't say? Tight Valentino creations, big bosom, loud voice and even louder colours, and all?' teased the countess.

'She's fun, and smart.'

'Ah. Night cap?'

'Definitely!'

19

Alexander Palace, Tsarskoye Selo: 17 December 1916

News of Rasputin's murder spread like wildfire through St Petersburg. There was dancing and rejoicing in the streets, and total strangers kissed and embraced one another. The reviled monster who had been destroying Russia was dead.

The mood in the Alexander Palace, however, was quite different. Alexandra was devastated and refused to believe that her 'dear friend', as she used to refer to Rasputin, was dead. Her entire world had suddenly collapsed. As soon as news of the murder reached the palace, Alexandra withdrew to the mauve boudoir to pray.

The mauve boudoir in the Alexander Palace was the tsarina's private world where she kept her most precious possessions and had spent some of the happiest times of her life, surrounded by her family and her pets. This was the room where she entertained close friends and confidants, and where Rasputin had sat with her many times, holding her hand while they had prayed together.

During the day, two large windows flooded this space with natural light, making it airy and appear much larger than it was. At night, several strategically positioned electric lamps illuminated the room with a cosy, soft light that gave the lilac silk that covered not only the high walls, but every upholstered piece of furniture in the room, a warm glow, accentuating the mauve, which was Alexandra's favourite colour. The furniture was made of lemonwood, painted creamy-white and sculptured in the French *rocaille* style. All the bookcases and even the piano were painted to match. The centrepiece of the room was a beautifully crafted fireplace with shelving on both sides, full of photographs in Fabergé frames and choice pieces of the Empress's glass collection, radiating elegance and style.

On all sides, paintings crowded the walls. Everywhere one looked, paintings greeted the eye. One of them was a painting by

Nesterov of the Annunciation, given to Alexandra by her beloved husband in 1897. Other favourites were a portrait of her late mother by di Angeli, and portraits of Nicholas and her son, Alexei, whom she adored.

But the most precious item in the room as far as Alexandra was concerned, was an icon given to her by Rasputin as an Easter gift two years earlier. The reason it was so precious was because of what Rasputin had told her about it. The icon came from a monastery in Kazan, Rasputin had pointed out, and would protect her family, and in particular her ailing son, Alexei, as long as Alexandra kept it by her side. Exquisitely painted – tempera on wood panel with a silver-gilt riza, a metal cover protecting the icon – it dated from the thirteenth century and even had a name: *Kazanskaya Bogomater* – Mother of God of Kazan, or Madonna of Kazan.

Painted in a realistic manner and encased on a heavy-gauge, silver-gilt and repousse *oklad*, the icon was a head-to-shoulders version of the icon of the Theotokos Hodegretia. It showed the Infant Christ sitting on Mary's arm, His right hand raised in a gesture of blessing, and holding a book in His left hand. But the most striking feature of the icon by far was the fact that the Virgin Mary appeared to be weeping.

Alexandra lit the candle next to the icon and began to pray. For a moment she thought she could hear Rasputin whispering to her, his familiar voice seductively reassuring:

'When your heart is heavy, look at Kazanskaya Bogomater, and ask her for advice. When you are in danger, ask her for help. When Alexei is ill, kiss the icon and he will recover.'

Countess Bezukhova knocked and entered the tsarina's boudoir. As one of Alexandra's closest friends and confidantes, she had free access to her private apartment. For a while she just stood there, reluctant to intrude. Then Alexandra turned around, her pale face streaked with tears.

'Ah, here you are,' she said and pointed to a chair next to her desk. 'Please sit with me.'

'You sent for me?'

'I did.'

Bezukhova walked over to Alexandra and placed a hand on her shoulder. The comforting touch seemed to calm Alexandra, who was trying to compose herself.

'Something quite extraordinary has happened,' began Alexandra, wiping away the tears.

'What?'

'Providence has sent me something ...'

'Oh? What?'

Alexandra pointed to a bundle of papers on the desk in front of her. 'This here,' she said.

'What is it?'

'Before I tell you, let me explain how, and by whom it has been sent.'

Bezukhova nodded, but didn't reply.

'I received a letter this morning from Felix Yusupov.'

Bezukhova looked at Alexandra, surprised. 'Felix? But he was involved in the murder ...'

'He's denying it. He sent me a letter; here.' Alexandra handed her friend a letter.

'"Your Imperial Majesty, I hasten to obey the command of Your Majesty and to report what occurred in my house last night",' Bezukhova began to read aloud. '"It will be my aim, in doing so, to clear myself of the dreadful accusation that is being made against me ..."'

Bezukhova finished reading the letter in silence and handed it back to Alexandra. 'Do you believe this?' she asked, incredulous. 'This is fantasy, surely.'

'The investigation is in its early stages. We don't know what happened,' said Alexandra.

'But Felix was involved and so was Dmitri. The whole of St Petersburg is talking about it.'

'It would seem so. And I have already told Niki that both must be punished severely if they had anything to do with Grigori's death. But how do we explain this?' Alexandra pointed to the bundle of papers on her desk.

'I don't know what to think,' said Bezukhova, shaking her head.

'Let's take a closer look. According to Felix, Grigori rang him last night and invited him to come to see the gypsies. That's unusual to begin with. Felix agreed. When he got there, Grigori was lying in the snow, dying. He had been shot.'

'Does this make sense to you?'

'It's in the letter.'

'And just before he died, Grigori pleaded with Felix to do something for him. A last wish of a dying man?' asked Bezukhova.

'Yes. That's the kind of man he was: unpredictable and different. He asked Felix to go straight to his apartment before it was too late, and retrieve something precious.' Alexandra reached for the bundle of papers in front of her and held it up. 'This here. He told Felix where to find it. Apparently, it was in a box under Grigori's bed.'

'*And deliver it to you?*'

'Yes, as a parting gift.'

'Amazing! And Felix went there to retrieve it?'

'You read the letter – he did. Shortly after Grigori died.'

'And he just left Grigori lying there? *Dead?*'

'Apparently so. He didn't want to become involved in the murder.'

'Do you believe this? And what are these papers anyway? Felix doesn't tell us anything about that in his letter.'

'Perhaps he didn't know.'

'You think so?'

'Could be. It took me some time to figure out what I was looking at. As it turned out, the papers are a musical score for a symphony.'

'*A what?*'

'Music. Composed by one of Russia's greatest composers, Pyotr Ilyich Tchaikovsky.'

'You are joking, surely! He's been dead for years.'

'I know, but I already had the papers examined. This is an original score written by Tchaikovsky and dedicated to Niki's father, Tsar Alexander III. All in Tchaikovsky's handwriting and signed by him just before he died.'

'And Grigori never mentioned this to you?'

'No. You know what he was like.'

'How did he get it?'

'No idea. Lots of people gave him things.'

'What are you going to do about this?'

'I will send the letter to the minister of justice.'

'And the symphony?'

'Belongs to me. The letter doesn't refer to it.'

'Not as such, but—'

'It's a private matter,' interrupted Alexandra. 'And for now, this stays strictly between us.'

'But this is too important,' said Bezukhova. 'If this is indeed a symphony by Tchaikovsky, then surely it belongs to Russia!'

'It does. And Russia shall receive it. All in good time, but now is definitely not the time.'

'Perhaps not.' Bezukhova knew not to contradict Alexandra once she had made up her mind.

Alexandra turned to face the icon. 'Please hold my hand and pray with me,' she whispered, close to tears. 'My heart is heavy and I have to ask Kazanskaya Bogomater for guidance.'

Bezukhova reached for Alexandra's hand and kissed it. Then she knelt down beside her chair and together, they began to pray.

20

Frieda Malenkova's art collection: 26 January 2017

Malenkova liked order and routine. She spent the first few hours of her day in the crypt below her study, surrounded by her treasures. This was her private world of peace and inspiration where she did her best thinking. The crypt had been one of the main reasons she had purchased the old, abandoned church and decided to turn it into her residence. The isolated, remote location had been another. As soon as she had set eyes on the large underground chamber hewn out of virgin rock, she knew she had to own it. Suspended between the living and the dead, the crypt was the perfect place to house her art collection.

Malenkova, a strong believer in destiny, was convinced that the pieces in her collection had found *her*, not the other way around, and were communicating with her in ways only she could understand. In her mind, that explained the struggle, the risks and sacrifices involved in obtaining them, and justified the often ruthless and violent means involved. Down in the crypt, far removed from the distractions of the outside world, she was able to listen to what her treasures had to say, and plan her strategies and moves accordingly.

For the past hour, Malenkova had thought about nothing else but the Petrova letter, as she called it, and all the available information surrounding it, and she listened. This was a form of meditation that required total concentration. She was convinced that the words in the letter were reaching out to her like pieces of a perplexing puzzle, telling her things that were not recorded on the page, but hidden and just waiting to be discovered, and all she had to do was listen. As she moved awkwardly around the room crowded with paintings, sculptures and antiquities, past familiar bookcases full of first editions and manuscripts, and glass cabinets containing rare porcelain, silverware, vintage watches and jewellery, she became more and more excited as the letter began to whisper in her ear.

Then, all became clear. Malenkova knew exactly what she had to do next. She walked over to the intercom by the stairs and pressed the button.

Zuzanna answered. 'Has she arrived?' asked Malenkova.

'She has.'

'Please bring her down.'

Anielka had arrived half an hour earlier. She had not visited Malenkova's home before, and had communicated with her only by phone or through Zuzanna. The invitation had therefore come as a complete surprise and she was looking forward with great excitement to meeting the woman who had been her benefactor since her release, and had done so much for her.

Anielka had spent several years in a psychiatric prison hospital in Paris after she had savagely attacked a fellow inmate with a kitchen knife in the juvenile detention centre where she was serving time for assault. Before that, she had almost killed a man she claimed had tried to rape her. Because she was only seventeen at the time, the prosecutor reduced the more serious charge of attempted murder to common assault, and she was sent to an institution for rehabilitation.

For the first three months she was a model prisoner, then something happened in the kitchen that set her off. It had taken three guards to restrain her and take the knife out of her hand. Hysterical and screaming, she was sent for psychiatric assessment and ended up in hospital under the care of a psychiatrist whom Malenkova knew well.

Malenkova had recruited patients from psychiatric institutions before. Some of her best and most loyal operatives had been sourced that way. Vulnerable people who had been in institutions could be moulded and groomed to carry out difficult assignments in ways that were impossible to arrange in normal circumstances. Total dependence gave total control, and gratitude inspired loyalty, which was a powerful tool that could be used in many effective ways. This was something Malenkova had also learned from her father and perfected over the years.

Just before her release from hospital, Anielka – a girl of Polish background without family – was introduced to Zuzanna, also a Pole, by her doctor. The doctor received a generous fee from Malenkova for the introduction and the case notes. He told Anielka that she would be released into Zuzanna's care, thereby preparing the way for what was to come.

That was how the grooming had started. After that, Zuzanna looked after all of Anielka's needs and made her totally dependent on her. She then gave her small jobs to do, simple at first, but becoming more daring and complex over time. Anielka handled all of them perfectly and showed great initiative and imagination in carrying out the tasks. She seemed to enjoy her involvement and was always asking for more. She was also eager to please and wanted to show Zuzanna what she could do.

There was also another side to Anielka that had surprised her carers and supervising psychiatrists during her time in hospital. After a particularly violent outburst, Anielka had spent the night in isolation, locked in a room. When the nurse arrived in the morning and opened the door, she found the walls covered in extraordinary drawings, displaying a hidden talent that seemed at odds with Anielka's mental and emotional state.

After that, she was provided with proper materials and encouraged to draw and paint. She embraced this opportunity with consuming passion and spent most of her waking hours creating pictures. It was as if a window to her tortured soul had been opened, allowing her spirit to soar. The quality and originality of her work dumbfounded even art experts who were brought in to view her paintings. Gradually, Anielka's pattern of behaviour and persona seemed to change and the demons retreated, paving the way for a full recovery that eventually resulted in her release.

Anielka felt strangely aroused as she followed Zuzanna down the stairs leading into the crypt. Something about the house brought back memories of her childhood in Krakow.

Anielka's mind was a strange place. Exceptionally bright, charming and vivacious, she was a pathological liar who concealed her psychopathic inclinations and behaviour in incredibly imaginative ways that could fool even the most critical observer. In many ways, she was also an artist of mind games and deception.

Devoid of any feelings of remorse or guilt, she was capable of violent acts – including self-harm – so extreme, they would have shocked even a seasoned homicide investigator. If caught, she could lie her way out of a compromising situation in ways that could convince a jury and even a trial judge. Her stunning looks – especially her almost angelic face – were of great help here, as her appearance and manner seemed at odds with whatever she was supposed to have done.

Because of her looks, she attracted the attention of men wherever she went and she exploited this attraction ruthlessly because deep down, she hated men. She liked sex, often coupled with violence, because of the power it gave her over others. Without inhibitions or moral compass of any kind, she was prepared to engage in sexual activities that would have taught a debauched pervert a lesson or two. Her promiscuous sexual behaviour had been one of the main problems since her release, and had caused some hesitation in Zuzanna about using Anielka for certain assignments. However, as she got to know her better and Anielka became ever more trusting and dependent on her, Zuzanna realised that this very inclination could be used to great advantage in certain situations.

Malenkova was impressed the moment she set eyes on Anielka. The young woman had a presence that would instantly be noticed the moment she walked into a room. Apart from her looks, the way she walked, the way she held her head, all gave her an aura that was impossible to ignore. There was a certain seductive glamour and natural elegance about her that reminded Malenkova of a fashion model walking down the catwalk, oblivious of the admiring looks following her every step of the way.

Just like Celine, thought Malenkova. *Amazing.*

As soon as Anielka entered the crypt, her eyes went straight to the paintings lining the walls, surprise and excitement on her flushed face.

'Wow!' she cried out. 'Look at this.' Anielka walked over to one of the paintings – a 12th-century Chinese splashed ink painting by Liang Kai – and just stood there lost in thought.

She isn't even aware I'm here, waiting for her, thought Malenkova. Instead of being annoyed by this, Malenkova found it fascinating. To have found the art of the Chan Buddhist painter Liang Kai, one of Malenkova's favourites, so appealing, was remarkable, thought Malenkova. Liang Kai's work was well known for discarding accurate representation to enhance spontaneity. He did this in an attempt to represent the non-rational mind of the enlightened.

'What do you like about it?' asked Malenkova.

Anielka spun around, surprised. 'I'm so sorry,' she said. 'I didn't mean to be rude. It's just this painting ...'

Slowly, Malenkova walked over to Anielka, who towered over her. Her long blonde hair was a little dishevelled, which only accentuated her prominent cheekbones and cornflower-blue eyes.

'What do you like about it?' repeated Malenkova, watching Anielka carefully.

'Everything,' said Anielka without hesitation.

'Why?'

'Because this is exactly how I feel.'

It was a strange answer that nevertheless resonated with Malenkova. 'I am Frieda Malenkova,' she said, extending her hand. 'I have wanted to meet you for a long time.'

Instead of shaking the outstretched hand, Anielka just looked a Malenkova, tears in her eyes. Then she threw her arms around her and held her tight.

'What did I do to deserve this?' asked Malenkova, surprised by the spontaneous embrace. 'We haven't even met.'

'You deserve it, all right,' whispered Anielka.

'Why?'

'Because you saved my life.'

Malenkova smiled. This was the kind of loyalty and devotion she was always looking for. *Zuzanna is right; she's ready*, she thought. Then she took Anielka by the hand and guided her to the stairs. 'Come, let's go up to my study and get to know each other a little better. There are too many distractions down here, for you and for me.'

21

Frieda Malenkova's whiteboard: 26 January 2017

Malenkova stood in front of her whiteboard contemplating the new information provided by Anielka earlier, when Zuzanna walked in. She had just driven Anielka back to her flat on the outskirts of Paris and was in high spirits.

'What do you think?' was the first question she asked.

'You were right.'

'About what?'

'She's ready.'

'I agree. This girl thinks on her feet and can improvise. You have to admit, the way she handled the Ritz was outstanding,' said Zuzanna.

'Lucky she could step in at such short notice while you were in the States.'

'It was her first big assignment. Look at the results.'

As Mademoiselle Darrieux was their most promising lead, she had been under surveillance around the clock since the lunch at La Closerie des Lilas that had revealed so much. It was the way Malenkova collected information once she decided a matter was worth pursuing. She had focused on the key person in the matter and as far as she was concerned, that was Mademoiselle Darrieux.

'All right, let's have a look at what we've got,' said Malenkova and hobbled over to the whiteboard, which by now contained a lot of information, unfortunately much of it still with serious question marks attached. The investigation was in its infancy, but Malenkova was convinced she was on to something big. She had a sixth sense when it came to matters like this. Her finely honed instincts told her that every time she looked at the Petrova letter. And besides, just like her father before her, she thrived on a challenge that put much-needed excitement into her otherwise quite banal life dominated by routine and isolation, with only her art collection to sustain her.

'On twenty January, two weeks after that lunch at La Closerie des Lilas, Darrieux spent the weekend at the Kuragin chateau with Countess Kuragin and Rogan. We have no idea of the reason behind this, but three days later, they met again, this time at the Ritz. Aubert, the manager, whom Darrieux obviously knows well, was present. Curious don't you think?' said Malenkova.

'Sure, but thanks to Anielka, we now have some idea what that meeting was about,' said Zuzanna.

'Lucky you briefed her so well. As soon as I heard from our surveillance team that Darrieux was meeting Countess Kuragin and Rogan at the Ritz, I phoned Anielka and told her to go there straight away and find out as much as possible about that meeting.'

'And she did just that. Look what she came up with. First, she managed to get a table in the busy Bar Vendôme, close enough to Darrieux to observe what was going on, and she even overheard some of the conversation. Brilliant!' said Zuzanna, feeling proud of her protégé.

'Yes. I don't think you could have done any better. But what exactly did she see and what did she hear, and more importantly, what does it all mean?'

'Well, let's have a look,' said Zuzanna. 'To begin with, we have a small key. That must be significant because Rogan handed it to Aubert, who carefully examined it. Some kind of strong box was mentioned and Aubert talked about an old ledger. The question is this: is any of this relevant?' asked Zuzanna.

'I think I can help you there.'

'You can?' said Zuzanna, surprised.

'I read not only Darrieux' Petrova biography, but also her book about the Ritz during the war, cover to cover,' said Malenkova.

'*Scandal on Place Vendôme?*'

'Yes. There is a brief mention in the book about a safe, a very special one somewhere in the basement called the Amber Safe. It was installed in the 1920s.'

'How curious. And could this somehow be linked to our investigation?'

'Perhaps. Apparently, some of the high-profile guests staying at the Ritz during the war were allocated strong boxes for the duration of their stay. They kept their valuables in there, a bit like the room safes we have today. Remember what Anielka told us about what happened shortly after Rogan gave that key to the manager?' said Malenkova.

'They all got up and went to the lifts.'

'Correct. Anielka followed them and actually managed to get into the lift with them. That was smart,' said Malenkova. 'They went down to the basement together. Anielka even exchanged a few words with Aubert, who apparently couldn't take his eyes off her. She mumbled something about having caught the wrong lift. While she waited for the next one to take her back up to the foyer, she could see Aubert and the others go down some stairs to another level below.'

'Interesting, don't you think?' said Zuzanna. 'Where did they go, and why?'

'Sure is. But the next thing Anielka did was genius. She found a seat in clear view of the lifts and waited for Darrieux and the others to come back up. When they did, which was about twenty minutes later, she made eye contact with Aubert and smiled. She sent him a subtle signal, and it worked. By then she knew, of course, that he was the hotel manager. Can you remember what happened next?' asked Malenkova.

'All right, this is what I think happened,' said Zuzanna. 'Anielka was quite specific about it all: Darrieux, Countess Kuragin and Rogan went to L'Espadon, that posh restaurant, to have lunch, but Aubert excused himself and stayed in the foyer. As he was walking to the reception desk, he noticed that Anielka was still looking in his direction. As an experienced professional who's worked all his life in hospitality, he couldn't help noticing that Anielka looked decidedly exasperated and out of sorts. She had her phone in her hand and was shaking her head. Something was clearly bothering her. That's how she attracted his attention and gave him a reason to come over and talk to her. And that is precisely what he did, and it all went from there. How does that sound to you? Plausible? Brilliant, I say!'

Malenkova nodded. 'She played him like a pro. You can't be taught this. It comes naturally to special people who instinctively know how to do such things. Anielka is a natural, an asset, just like Celine ... was,' added Malenkova.

Zuzanna could hear the sadness in her boss's voice. For years, Celine, a former circus performer, had been Malenkova's star. Recruited just like Anielka after her release from prison, Celine had carried out several spectacular burglaries directed by Malenkova, targeting luxury hotels and billionaires. She was known by the police throughout Europe as 'The Ghost' because of her uncanny ability to break into hotel suites, open safes, and disappear with the loot without a trace. She was the ultimate cat burglar until one day in Monte Carlo, her career came to a sudden, tragic end. She lost her footing on the roof of one of the grand hotels during a rainstorm and fell six storeys to her death.

'She is. And she can make up plausible stories on the spot, convincingly,' said Zuzanna, pleased that Celine's name had been mentioned. To hear Malenkova compare Anielka to Celine augured well.

'She certainly can,' said Malenkova, who could remember every detail of Anielka's account of what happened that day. 'She told Aubert she was supposed to meet a friend, another fashion model, for lunch in L'Espadon, but unfortunately she didn't have a reservation and couldn't get a table because the restaurant was fully booked. How clever was that? *Fashion model?* She gave Aubert a perfect opening to come to her rescue, and that is exactly what he did.'

'By then he was hooked,' continued Malenkova. 'He escorted a very grateful Anielka into the crowded restaurant, spoke briefly to the maître d' and hey presto, a table for two materialised. He even gave her his business card and told her if there was anything he could do for her in the future, to call him. Unfortunately, she was too far away from Darrieux' table to overhear anything, but she could see that they had an animated conversation, punctuated by Darrieux' shrill laughter that could be heard "by everyone", she said.'

'You must admit it takes a very special, talented person to pull all this off. And let's not forget, Anielka is only twenty-four,' said Zuzanna.

'Very mature for her age, that's for sure. And confident.'

'So, what's next?' asked Zuzanna, well aware that Malenkova had most likely already worked out the next step. She was always well ahead of the game.

Malenkova pointed to the whiteboard. 'We need more information to tie all this together and make sure we are on the right track. There's just too much speculation here for my liking.'

'I agree, but how are we going to do that?'

'The best way to get accurate information is by going directly to the most reliable source available. This has always worked well for us in the past.'

'And what exactly would be that reliable source in all this?' asked Zuzanna.

Malenkova looked at Zuzanna, a rare, knowing smile spreading across her pudgy face. 'Mademoiselle Darrieux, of course; who else? For the moment, she's our best lead.'

'And how do you suggest we tap into that source?'

'That's easy. You have brought the answer to that question back from the States with you, my dear.'

'I have?'

'Oh yes, and it has a name.'

'What name?'

Fear, and as we both know, fear comes in many forms. But what I have in mind is perhaps the most potent of them all: *fear of losing face.*'

Zuzanna looked puzzled.

Malenkova walked over to her desk, sat down and poured herself a large cognac. 'Would you like one?' she asked.

'I think I need one.'

Malenkova poured another cognac and handed Zuzanna the brandy balloon, then sat back in her chair and raised her glass. 'Now, listen carefully; this is what I have in mind. Cheers!'

'Before you do, I have something for you. It's from Anielka; a gift.'

'Oh? What kind of gift?'

'Give me a second, I'll be right back.'

Moments later, Zuzanna returned with a large painting under her arm. 'This is for you,' she said, leaning the painting against the wall.

Malenkova walked over to it and studied it in silence. 'Extraordinary,' she said. '*She painted this?*'

'She did, and she wanted you to have it because it's a window into her soul.'

'That's remarkable, especially for someone of her age and background, with virtually no formal training. It reminds me of Liang Kai's work—'

'Discarding accurate representation to enhance spontaneity? I think you once told me,' said Zuzanna.

'Very good. If this is a window into her soul, God help us all.'

22

Shakespeare and Company, Paris: 1 February 2017

On the first Thursday of the month, at eleven am precisely, Mademoiselle Darrieux held court at *Shakespeare and Company*, the famous bookstore at 37 rue de la Bûcherie. There, surrounded by rows and rows of new and second-hand books, and adoring fans, she felt truly at home. Established in 1951, the bookstore was originally called 'Le Mistral', but in 1964, on the four-hundredth anniversary of William Shakespeare's birth, it had been renamed Shakespeare and Company. This was a tribute not only to Shakespeare, but to the earlier bookstore of the same name established by Sylvia Beach, an American, in 1919. That iconic store had been a favourite haunt of such luminaries as Hemingway, Ezra Proud, Scott Fitzgerald, James Joyce and many others, but was closed during the German occupation in 1941 and never reopened.

Locals and tourists flocked to the store to chat with Mademoiselle Darrieux about her books and, if they were lucky, have their picture taken with the famous author as she signed one of her books for them. For someone who loved the limelight and being the centre of attention, this was author heaven.

Apart from selling new and second-hand books, the store was well known as an antiquarian bookseller of rare editions, and for housing aspiring writers and artists on the premises in exchange for helping out in the store. It also had a free reading library open to the public. Since opening its doors in 1951, thousands of helpers had slept on the premises in beds wedged between bookshelves, surrounded by the genius of literary giants haunting the store at night.

Mademoiselle Darrieux sat at a small table at the entrance to the reading library, directly under the sign of the shop's motto: *Be Not Inhospitable to Strangers Lest They Be Angels in Disguise.*

Zuzanna waited until Darrieux had signed a few books before making her approach. Wearing a headscarf and dark glasses, and holding a copy of Madame Petrova's biography in her hand, she looked like Sophia Loren in Vittorio De Sica's classic film *Yesterday, Today and Tomorrow*.

'It is such a pleasure to meet you,' said Zuzanna and put her copy of *The Darling of Swan Lake* on the table in front of Darrieux. 'At last.'

'Oh? Have you been planning this for some time?' asked Darrieux and looked up at the woman standing in front of her.

'Oh yes, I am definitely a fan. My favourite is *Scandal in Place Vendôme*. I have read it several times; fascinating.'

'Several times, you say? That's quite something. I don't think many of my readers would be doing that. What do you find so fascinating about the book?' asked Darrieux, trying to make conversation. She reached for her fountain pen and unscrewed it.

'The Amber Safe.'

Darrieux looked up, surprised. 'Oh? There's only a very brief mention about that in the book. Why do you find it so fascinating?'

'It's such a romantic idea, don't you think? All those celebrities during the war keeping their jewels in there. One can't help wondering ...'

'Wondering? About what?'

'If the safe is perhaps still there today? In the Ritz?'

Darrieux felt her face flush as she remembered her visit to the Amber Safe with Aubert only a few days ago. *How strange*, she thought and opened the book in front of her. 'To whom shall I make this out?' she asked, changing the subject.

'Oh. Armand Baudin, please,' said Zuzanna, watching Darrieux carefully.

Darrieux froze and stared at the page, her hand shaking. She hadn't heard that name mentioned in years. *A terrible coincidence*, she thought, taking a deep breath. *Nothing more.*

'Would you like me to spell it for you?' continued Zuzanna cheerfully. 'And would you mind putting RIP after the name, please?'

Oh my God! thought Darrieux and looked at Zuzanna. *It can't be!* 'Who are you?' she whispered.

'A stranger, but definitely not an angel in disguise. Who I am is not important. What is important is this: who are _you_?'

Zuzanna paused to let this sink in. 'Is it Maurice Moreau, or perhaps Estelle Montplaisir?' she continued quietly. 'Could you help me with that?'

For a moment, Darrieux thought she would throw up and it took all of her willpower to compose herself. 'What do you want?' she stammered.

'Just write down your phone number and we'll have a chat about all this later, shall we? Now's not the time. Look, others are waiting to meet their favourite author. I better go.'

Darrieux scribbled her mobile number under her name in the book, and closed it.

Zuzanna picked up the book. 'Thank you so much,' she said. 'I can't tell you what this means to me. Ah, I almost forgot; this is for you.' Zuzanna placed a small envelope on the table in front of Darrieux. 'I'm sure you'll find this interesting,' she said, and then turned around and hurried out of the bookstore.

Curious, Darrieux opened the envelope, looked inside, and paled as she read the headline at the top of the Miami newspaper cutting: _Who is Estelle Montplaisir?_

23

Frieda Malenkova's study: 2 February 2017

Although it was quite late, Zuzanna knew that Malenkova, a night owl, would still be in her study. Zuzanna had called Mademoiselle Darrieux several times that day and had carefully prepared the way for what was to come. By revealing little by little what she knew about the celebrity author's colourful past, and by telling her exactly what would happen if full cooperation wasn't forthcoming, she had created an atmosphere of uncertainty and fear so powerful that Darrieux had been reduced to tears, and became almost hysterical on the phone. Zuzanna was a master when it came to subtle intimidation and knew how to remove any kind of resistance, or temptation to lie or deceive.

She told Darrieux that she had prepared a detailed dossier about her past, reaching all the way back to her childhood in Louisiana. She spoke about her absent mother and that shack on the banks of the Mississippi where Darrieux had grown up, beaten and abused by a brutal father who was always drunk. She spoke about the young male prostitute working in New Orleans and then mentioned the murder trial. Zuzanna even read extracts from the dossier to Darrieux and quoted the sources, all of which would be delivered to several Paris papers as material for one of the juiciest and most sensational scandals to appear in the society pages. It would rock the Paris establishment to the core.

Once Zuzanna was confident that Darrieux was facing certain ruin with nowhere to go, she showed her a way out. 'It doesn't have to be this way,' she consoled a teary Darrieux quietly. 'All you have to do is answer a few questions; truthfully, of course, because any kind of lie or deception would be most costly.'

By ten pm that evening, Darrieux was totally exhausted and prepared do almost anything to avoid a devastating scandal. Zuzanna had assembled a series of strategic questions she wanted Darrieux to answer. One by one, she had put the carefully crafted questions to Darrieux and recorded both her questions and Darrieux' answers.

'How did it go?' asked Malenkova, who had been expecting Zuzanna. She took off her glasses and looked at her PA.

'I think you are in for a big surprise,' said Zuzanna calmly. 'I've recorded everything. Wait till you hear this.' Zuzanna pressed a button on her device and sat back.

Malenkova listened in silence, the way she kept playing with her glasses the only sign of the excitement boiling within.

'Amazing,' she said at the end of the recorded conversation. 'I certainly didn't expect something like this. It sounds like something out of a movie.'

'It sure does,' said Zuzanna. 'I don't think she made it up.'

'Neither do I. But the question surrounding the true contents of strong box thirty-three remains.'

'You mean, is there really an original Fabergé Imperial Easter Egg in there, or is it something else altogether, blurred by speculation and wishful thinking?'

'Exactly. Until that is further investigated, which will certainly happen in due course once Rogan is given access to the box, we'll never know for sure, unless …'

Zuzanna smiled. She had seen Malenkova in action enough times to know how her mind worked. 'Unless what?' she asked.

'We get there before him.'

'Are you serious?' said Zuzanna, realising at once where this was heading.

'Absolutely.'

'How?'

'Once again, you have already given me the answer to that question.'

'You speak in riddles.'

'Simple really; vanity and sex.'

'Please tell me.'

'To control Mademoiselle Darrieux – that little social butterfly – and get all the information we need, we use vanity and fear of exposure. To get access to the Amber Safe and the strong box, we use a man who thinks with his dick. In short, we use sex.'

'Aubert?'

'Precisely.'

'And then what?'

'We put together the old team.'

'Emile Fabron, the safebreaker?'

'There's none better.'

'But he's retired.'

'We'll coax him out of it.'

'How?'

'One last job; for Celine.'

'Hm. Do you think he'll go for it?'

'I'm certain of it. Leave him to me.'

'You do realise what kind of risks we are taking here?'

'Of course, but consider this: if we pull this off, it could be our last big job. All we need is imagination and balls – and you and I have plenty of both. If that Russian Easter egg is authentic, well … Can you imagine what it could fetch on the dark web? Buyers would be falling all over one another to secure this rare little beauty. No questions asked,' said Malenkova, who could see this was the perfect opportunity to bow out of the game with a gold medal that had eluded her since the dreadful accident that had crushed her dreams.

'We would have to go to ground after this, that's for sure; you know that, don't you? All of us, and that includes Anielka. For a long time.'

'Money, lots of money, heals all and makes everything possible,' said Malenkova, quoting one of her father's favourite sayings.

Malenkova and Zuzanna worked through the night and into the early hours of the morning. Malenkova emptied almost an entire bottle of cognac and Zuzanna had several cups of strong coffee to keep her going, but by the time the first rays of a weak morning sun penetrated the grey winter sky, promising snow, they had put together a plan so daring it would have made a James Bond plot look pedestrian.

24

The tsar's study, Alexander Palace, Tsarskoye Selo: January 1917

In early 1917, cataclysmic forces were about to be unleashed in Russia, and talk of revolution was everywhere. The murder of Rasputin had been a catalyst, helping the centuries-old dam of oppression, poverty and antiquated feudal rule to burst with unprecedented violence, and at great cost to the nation. Yet inside the cocoon of the Alexander Palace, shielded from the realities of life outside, life went on almost as usual.

Rasputin's death had affected Alexandra deeply and she descended into a state of constant melancholy, yet her influence and control over her husband only became stronger and more pronounced. Acutely aware of the tsar's inadequacies and weaknesses, she saw it as her duty to step in and show strength and support. She took more and more control of matters of state and made several ill-advised decisions. This only accelerated the approach of the juggernaut of change hurtling irresistibly towards them, with catastrophic consequences that would soon sweep them brutally away into oblivion.

Despite Alexandra's very robust opposition, the perpetrators of the shocking murder had barely been punished. Grand Duke Dmitri Pavlovich was sent to the Persian front and Prince Felix Yusupov was banished to one of his family estates, where he continued to live a life of opulence and luxury. The other conspirators escaped punishment altogether. So strong was the support on the streets for the perpetrators, who were treated as liberating heroes, that the state didn't dare step in with more severe punishment and condemnation of a crime that was hailed as a patriotic deed.

Aware of his wife's grief after losing 'her friend', Nicholas decided to cheer her up a little with a special Easter present. He summoned Carl Fabergé, the famous jeweller, to discuss the matter.

Nicholas was sitting at his desk in his study, where he spent a lot of time during the day, when Fabergé was admitted.

'Good of you to come so promptly,' said the tsar and walked across the large room to meet his guest. 'I know how busy you are, especially this time of the year.'

'It is a pleasure and an honour as always, Your Majesty,' said Fabergé, taking a bow. 'The House of Fabergé is at your service.'

Nicholas pointed to a small table in the middle of the room. 'Tea?' he asked.

'Please; thank you.'

Fabergé had been to the tsar's famous study several times over the years, usually to discuss the designs of the Imperial Easter eggs that Nicholas was so passionate about. Every year, the tsar gave one to his mother, the Dowager Empress Maria Feodorovna, and one to his wife, Alexandra. This tradition had been started by his father, Tsar Alexander III, in 1885 and had continued ever since. Over the years, the spectacular eggs had become increasingly elaborate and extravagant, as each year Fabergé tried to outdo the one that had come before it.

Fabergé loved this room, especially the proportions and the polished timber ceiling, and the timber floor covered in precious Persian rugs. To the eyes of a designer, proportions were important and balance was the key to pleasing the eye – and the tsar's study had it all. The billiard table was in the right place and the tiled fireplace had enough prominence without dominating the room, as fireplaces often tend to do. There was a certain warmth and Edwardian charm in the room, often lacking in other more opulent rooms within the palace.

'I have asked you to come here this morning because I would like to discuss something personal and confidential with you,' began Nicholas as soon as tea had been served and they were alone.

Fabergé looked at the tsar sitting opposite with curiosity, but didn't reply. As an experienced man of tact who knew how to deal with royalty, he knew his place: when to speak, and when to remain silent and wait.

'Recent events have deeply affected the tsarina and I would like to present something to her this Easter that will make her grief easier to bear,' continued Nicholas. He didn't refer to Rasputin's murder as such, but Fabergé was well aware what Nicholas was talking about.

'I understand completely,' said Fabergé and took a sip of tea. The ice had been broken. 'Does Your Majesty have something specific in mind?'

'Yes. One of your spectacular Easter eggs.'

'I see.'

'Not to replace our current order for the two you are no doubt already working on,' the tsar hastened to add, 'but something quite different.'

Fabergé sat up, his curiosity aroused. 'An *additional* egg?'

'Precisely. Not just any egg, but one with quite a specific design and purpose, especially as far as the traditional surprise inside the egg is concerned.'

'We will do our best, Your Majesty.'

'I have no doubt about that,' said the tsar, smiling. 'But there are some special circumstances involved here.'

'In what way, Your Majesty?'

'Complete confidentiality. In short, no-one must know about this egg and its design. Under no circumstances can a single word about this egg and its purpose be allowed to get out and reach the public, especially during these difficult times. Am I making myself clear?'

'Perfectly, Your Majesty,' said Fabergé, finding it difficult to suppress his excitement.

'I knew I could rely on you. Now, let's go over to my desk and I'll show you what I have in mind.'

Fabergé followed the tsar to his desk.

'Consider this a special commission, a personal one from me,' continued Nicholas. 'There are three essential elements involved here that I would like to have incorporated into the design.'

'I understand.'

'First, the Easter egg will be presented by me to the tsarina, to commemorate the recent death of Grigori Rasputin,' said the tsar softly. The elephant in the room now had a name. 'The overall concept and design should therefore reflect this in a subtle way, but of course, that will be a matter for you.'

Fabergé nodded, but didn't say anything. The tsar then went on to describe the other features he wanted to have incorporated into the egg. Fabergé listened in silence as the tsar presented photographs by way of illustration of what he had in mind and became quite emotional about the subject. It was obvious that Nicholas had given a great deal of thought to the matter and it meant a lot to him, especially during these difficult times that seemed to threaten the very existence of the Romanov dynasty and the future of his family.

Taking a deep breath, Nicholas turned to face the window and looked pensively out into the snow-covered garden. 'The third and final element is something quite different and very personal,' he continued. 'I hope it can be incorporated into the design as the highlight, the ultimate surprise if you like.'

'What is it, Your Majesty?'

'Something very dear to the tsarina. She keeps it in her boudoir and never lets it out of her sight.'

'How interesting. Could I see it?'

'That may be difficult ...'

'I understand.'

'I have a photograph of it right here.'

Nicholas handed Fabergé a photo.

Fabergé nodded. 'Fascinating.'

'Will the photograph do?'

'For now, yes.'

'Not too difficult?'

'A challenge, certainly, but I'm sure we can do it. We could use diamonds and enamel.'

'Do you think you could somehow insert this into something, say, like a small crypt? Echoes of resurrection as the egg is being opened and the surprise revealed as the final destination that ties it all together? It is an Easter present, after all. Does that make sense to you?'

'Yes, it does. Very poetically put, Your Majesty, if I may say so. We have some very talented artists and designers who can capture the spirit of an Easter concept like that. I'm sure we can come up with something that will express what Your Majesty has in mind.'

'I was hoping you would say that,' said Nicholas, relieved. 'Now, that's about it, but please remember, confidentiality is paramount here.'

'I understand, Your Majesty,' said Fabergé, well aware of the explosive nature of the commission and what it represented. In the wrong hands, the egg could have devastating consequences, perhaps even destroy the Romanov dynasty and the Imperial family.

'Good man. Some more tea?'

'Yes, please.'

25

Hôpital Cochin, Paris: 3 February 2017

Jack had visited Dupree several times in hospital since that dreadful fire and had formed a special bond with the man who had not only lost his home and his only son, but almost his life as well. And all of this because of an old music box in need of repairs.

For quite different reasons, Jack and Dupree wanted to find answers to the same question: who was so interested in Madame Petrova's music box, and why? Dupree wanted to track down those responsible for taking away all that was precious to him in the twilight of his life, and Jack sensed there was a lot more behind Madame Petrova's music box and its mysterious contents than he had been able to find out so far.

The little key had taken him to the Amber Safe and strong box thirty-three with its astonishing contents, but in Dupree and the fire, Jack saw another, perhaps more important lead he had to follow up.

'How are you, mate?' said Jack as he walked into Dupree's room. He turned around to make sure that the nurse had left before slipping the small flask of whisky he had brought with him under the bedcovers. This was, of course, strictly forbidden and would have resulted in not only a stern reprimand from the nurse in charge, but most likely a total visiting ban in the future. Naturally, this made the little gift even more enjoyable and fun.

Dupree had made remarkable progress and was hoping to be discharged soon. The bandages had come off and his burns were healing. It had turned out that the burns had not been quite as serious as first thought and further recuperation could occur outside the hospital. With no home to return to, the more urgent problem for Dupree was where to go after his discharge, to begin the long climb back to good health.

'I had an interesting visitor earlier today,' said Dupree.

'Oh? Who?'

'An old friend from my days in the police. I've known him since he was a green rookie. Now he's the Prefect of Police, in charge of the Prefecture of Police right here in Paris; he's the big boss. He was appointed by the president himself last year and is responsible for the security of Paris, in collaboration with the military.'

'Wow! And he came here?' said Jack.

'Yes. He found time to visit me. Says a lot about the man, don't you think? It made a big impression here, I can tell you. Even the nurse, the strict one, is actually talking to me instead of just giving orders. I rang my friend a few days ago and asked for a favour.'

'What kind of favour?'

'Lying here during the past two weeks or so, virtually unable to move, often drugged and in pain, has given me a lot of time to think. I went through some of my old cases; you know, just thinking about them,' said Dupree. 'It was surprising how much I was able to remember. The mind works in strange ways when there are no distractions, don't you think?'

'I know what you mean. I do that all the time when I write. It's amazing what's hidden in the recesses of our mind and what can trigger an avalanche of memories.'

'Quite. One thing in particular kept rattling around in my brain. A name: *Le Fantôme*. Remember I told you that the woman who came to visit Philippe that night called herself Le Fantôme?'

'Yes, you did. Quite weird, I thought.'

'I knew I had come across that name before, but I couldn't quite remember when or how. Then the other day, the penny dropped.'

'Oh?'

'A few years ago there were a number of spectacular burglaries, not just here in France but in various parts of Europe.'

'What kind of burglaries?'

'High-end stuff involving celebrities and billionaires staying in luxury hotels. There was a pattern. This was all well after my time in the force. I had retired years before that, but the papers were full of it and my former colleagues were all talking about it. It was quite sensational.'

'In what way?'

'A cat burglar managed to break into hotel rooms, mainly late at night, evading all security, open the room safes and disappear with the contents without a trace, often while the occupants were asleep in their beds. Some heists were spectacular. One in particular involved a large amount of cash that a gambler had won at the casino in Monte Carlo. Not only did the cash disappear from the room safe – several hundred thousand euros, apparently – but also the wife's jewellery, worth even more. When the couple woke up the safe was open, and empty.'

'And the connection?'

'The papers had given the burglar a nickname: Le Fantôme.'

'The Ghost. Interesting. And you think there could be a link?'

'Perhaps. Not with the cat burglar as such. She fell to her death in Monte Carlo a few years ago and the burglaries stopped after that, but there were definitely others involved. She didn't work alone, for starters. She had an accomplice, a master safebreaker who could open any safe, however sophisticated, quickly and with only a few tools. Old school, but very effective. But there was more ...'

'Oh? What?'

'This is how the burglaries worked: The young woman broke into the hotel suites, often by abseiling from the roof or climbing up drainpipes, or scampering across ledges and balconies from other rooms higher up. She would then open the door from the inside and let in the safebreaker – often disguised as room service staff – who then went to work and quickly broke into the safe. After that they made their getaway, usually by abseiling to a waiting car.'

'Did the police find out anything further about the woman who died?'

'Yes, of course. She came from a family of French circus per- formers who regularly toured the country. They were trapeze artists. The father was a petty criminal who had done time for, wait for it, burglary.'

'You think the daughter followed in his footsteps?'

'All we know is she left the circus while her father was in jail and then disappeared for several years, until she was found dead in a hotel car park in Monte Carlo after a robbery gone wrong. Suddenly Le Fantôme had a name: Celine LeBlanc.'

'Is that it?'

Dupree reached under the bedcovers, pulled out the flask and took a swig of whisky. Then he looked at Jack and smiled. 'The Prefect brought me a file, a cold case directly related to all this. This is it here.' Dupree held up a bundle of creased papers, curling and yellow around the edges. 'It even had a name, but I'll tell you about that later.'

'It's good to have friends in high places,' said Jack, smiling.

'Sure is. Listen to this: there was a bigger, much wider investigation going on at the time; discreetly, behind the scenes so to speak. Apparently, there was a sophisticated network of underground art and jewellery dealers, fences if you like, who bought and sold stolen goods and even commissioned targeted break-ins on behalf of wealthy collectors, mainly in museums in Eastern Europe where security was lax and outdated.'

'How interesting.'

'It gets better. There was one particular fence operating right here in Paris who was the boldest of them all. The police suspected that LeBlanc and her accomplice had worked for that ring.'

'How did they make that connection?'

'Ah. Remember what my son said to me just before he died? Two words.'

'Yes, you told me: black widow.'

'Exactly.'

'And that could be relevant here?'

'Yes, because of this ...' Dupree opened the file and pointed to a page. 'There was one specific piece of information about these burglaries the public was never told about because it was considered a major lead by the police at the time.'

'What was that?'

'Each time, the burglars left something behind in the empty safe, like a signature, obviously to taunt the authorities.'

'Fascinating. What was it?'

Dupree took another swig of whisky and took his time, enjoying himself.

'You want me to die of curiosity before you tell me, is that it?'

'A black plastic spider.'

'*What?*' Jack almost shouted.

'And do you know what the operation was called?'

'Tell me?'

'Black Widow,' said Dupree, a triumphant little smile creasing his swollen cheeks. 'Celine LeBlanc was dressed all in black when she died. I suppose that inspired the name.'

'That's incredible!'

'Successful police work is always in the detail, *mon ami*. Little things can make all the difference.'

'And did Operation Black Widow have any success?'

'Unfortunately, no. After two years of running into blind alleys, the investigation was closed. The Paris fence was never found.'

'So, we now have two things of significance here that could be a link: Le Fantôme, and a Black Widow. Is that it?'

'Coincidence?' said Dupree. 'I don't think so. I think Operation Black Widow has just been revived, don't you?'

'Definitely! Let's drink to that.'

Dupree handed Jack the flask. Jack took a swig and handed in back to Dupree. 'I like cold cases,' said Jack. 'You know why? Because some of them can turn white hot overnight.'

'Do you think this could be one of them?' asked Dupree.

'Yes, I think so,' said Jack and then told Dupree about the Amber Safe, strong box thirty-three and what had been found inside.

Dupree listened in silence and then looked at Jack. 'That's why these guys were after that key; they must have known. Amazing!' he said, and handed Jack the empty flask. 'Better make it a bottle next time. I think we'll both need one.'

'That only leaves one more thing,' said Jack, changing the subject. 'You'll be leaving here in a couple of days.'

Dupree nodded, looking worried. 'I know ...'

'Where will you go?'

'That's the problem. I can't look after myself just yet, but they want me out of here. Hospitals, you know how it is.' Dupree held up his bandaged hands.

'That won't be a problem,' said Jack.

'What do you mean?'

'Countess Kuragin sends her regards. There's an old cottage in the grounds of the chateau that hasn't been used in years. The gardener and his family used to live there. It's yours. Tell me when you are ready to leave here and we can continue Operation Black Widow in earnest. What do you say?'

'Are you serious?' said Dupree, choking with emotion.

'Absolutely. And I can tell you, we have an excellent cook. I can vouch for her, mate. So tucker won't be a problem, and neither will the wine. You should see the Kuragin cellar,' Jack prattled on.

'You *are* serious.'

'What; you thought I was kidding, mate? No way! Call me when you are ready to leave and I'll pick you up – and with a bottle of whisky; promise.'

'You're on!'

26

The Ritz, Paris: 4 February 2017

Anielka admired herself in the mirror. 'What do you think?' she asked and turned to face Zuzanna. Dressed in an insanely short designer skirt, a tight, stylish jacket by Olivier Rousteing, a pair of thigh-high black boots that accentuated her long legs, and a houndstooth baker boy cap that gave her a sexy, coquettish air, Anielka looked like someone who had just stepped off the catwalk.

'Perfect,' said Zuzanna, satisfied. *Straight out of The Devil Wears Prada,* she thought. *What a transformation!* 'This is what a fashion model would wear when meeting someone for a late-night cocktail at the Ritz, wanting to impress, and tempt ... and that, my dear, is exactly what you will be doing tonight,' added Zuzanna. 'Monsieur Aubert won't know what hit him.'

Zuzanna had taken Anielka shopping in Saint-Germain in the afternoon. They had started with a coffee at Café de Flore and then strolled arm in arm through Rue Bonaparte and Rue Saint-Honoré before exploring the boutiques showcasing small Parisian designers. Impossible to ignore, Anielka had a natural elegance and flair that made heads turn wherever she went. When exclusive designer fashion was added to this, she became exceptional and that was exactly what Zuzanna had in mind for Anielka's meeting with Aubert. She was certain he would find her irresistible.

Zuzanna looked at her watch. It was almost time. 'Now, remember what we talked about this afternoon,' she said. 'You know what's riding on this, and you will get only one chance to pull this off. Once you step out of here, you're on your own. Understood?'

'Perfectly,' said Anielka, her face aglow with excitement. She was on a high after their shopping trip that afternoon, with several thousand euros spent on fabulous outfits and accessories she could only dream of, but would be wearing for this assignment. And then there was the great trust, especially by Malenkova, whom she adored.

Zuzanna handed Aubert's business card to Anielka. 'Call him now, and don't let them fob you off. It's a Saturday, so we know he's on duty. If you make it sound personal, I'm sure they'll put you through to him. He's a womaniser, remember?'

'Don't worry. I know all about womanisers and how they think. Leave it to me.'

Anielka called Aubert's number and was eventually put through to the front desk and told to hold on.

Aubert was talking to guests in the Bar Hemingway when the barman tapped him on the shoulder. 'Call for you, sir,' said the barman and pointed to the house phone. Aubert excused himself and took the call. 'Aubert, how may I help you?'

'You helped a lady in distress once already, Monsieur Aubert. Last week, with a table in L'Espadon ...' said Anielka, her voice husky and mysterious.

'Ah, the mannequin, I remember. How did it go?'

'The lunch was a great success, thanks to you. So much so in fact, that I would like to ask you for another favour. You did say ...'

'Yes, of course. What kind of favour?'

'It would be best if we could perhaps discuss this in person?'

'Sure. When?'

'Would later tonight be possible? It's quite urgent.'

'No problem. I'm here until at least three in the morning.'

'I'll be there within the hour.'

'Ask for me at the desk.'

'I will do that. Thank you, Monsieur Aubert. Until then ...'

Aubert put down the phone and smiled as he remembered the stunning young woman with the sexy voice, the dreamy eyes and those long legs reaching for heaven.

I wonder what she wants, he thought. *And what she may be prepared to do in return?* Aubert had been in situations like this many times and recognised all the signs. He signalled to the barman and ordered another Scotch. *God, I love this job*, he thought, as a ripple of excitement made the hairs on the back of his neck tingle.

Anielka arrived by taxi an hour later. Heads turned as she confidently crossed the crowded lobby wearing her short fur jacket, walked up to reception and asked to see Aubert. Smiling, Aubert appeared moments later, and gallantly kissed Anielka's hand. 'What a pleasant surprise,' he said. 'Let's go to the Bar Hemingway. We can talk there in private. It's my favourite place, I'm sure you'll like it; come.'

Named after the famous American journalist and Nobel Prize-winning author who had been a regular, this tiny bar, which only seated twenty-five, was arguably one of the most famous bars in Paris. Intimate, exclusive, with the atmosphere of a gentleman's club full of curiosities like hunting trophies, a collection of American police badges, books, a gramophone and even an old-fashioned typewriter, the iconic bar oozed masculine charm and excitement.

'According to our head barman, a cocktail is drunk three times: once with the eyes, once with the nose, and finally with the palate,' said Aubert. 'Let's see if he's right. I can strongly recommend the Serendipity, one of Colin Field's famous creations. Would you like one?'

'Absolutely,' said Anielka. 'As long as you will have one too.'

Aubert ordered two.

'Have you heard of Colin Field?'

Anielka shook her head.

'According to *Forbes* magazine, he's ranked the best bartender in the world. He invented several iconic drinks such as the Clean Dirty Martini, Highland Cream, the Picasso Martini and, of course, Serendipity, his signature drink. He prepared it for the first time right here in the bar on thirty-one December 1994, for Jean-Louis Constanza. As for the name, as soon as Jean-Louis tasted it, he looked at Colin and exclaimed "Serendipity",' Aubert prattled on.

'Fascinating,' said Anielka, crossing her legs and making sure she looked interested. Listening attentively to men when they talked about themselves or tried to impress, was an important part of her strategy. 'What's in it; do you know?' she asked.

'Eight fresh mint leaves, one and a half shots of Calvados, one and a half shots of pressed apple juice, and a quarter-shot of sugar syrup. First you shake these ingredients with ice, then strain into an old-fashioned, ice-filled glass and finally top with champagne.'

'Sounds amazing.'

'Tastes even better. So, how's the career going?' said Aubert, changing the subject.

'It's not easy breaking into modelling here in Paris, especially for someone like me. You need connections. As you know, I come from Poland.'

'You told me. Your accent ...'

'But that lunch last week – L'Espadon – turned into a bit of a breakthrough, thanks to you.'

'Oh? In what way?'

'The contact I was meeting here – an agent – was quite impressed ...'

'Impressed? Impressed by what?'

'I exaggerated a little, I'm afraid,' said Anielka, smiling. 'I did say that I knew the general manager here at the Ritz, and that's how I was able to arrange a table without having made a reservation weeks in advance. And it all went from there.'

Aubert laughed. 'Was that all? I'm glad I was able to help.'

'You certainly did. But as often happens with little fibs, they can easily get out of hand.'

'In what way?'

'As it turned out, the agency I was hoping to impress has tried in vain for some time to get permission for a photoshoot here at the Ritz ...'

'Oh? I see. We get many requests like that.'

'Then I'm sure you can also see where this is heading,' said Anielka, and placed a hand on Aubert's arm, her touch sending shivers of excitement tingling down his spine.

'To cut a long story short, it was made quite clear to me that should I be able to get permission for a fashion photoshoot here in the Ritz, doors would open for my career.'

'Ah. So, that's the favour?'

'It is, but there's more.'

Just then the barman came over and served two Serendipities.

'Well, let's drink to that then, shall we?' said Aubert, enjoying himself, and handed a glass to Anielka. 'To serendipity.'

'You mean to the unfolding of events by chance in a happy or beneficial way?' said Anielka, a coquettish look in her eyes.

'Something like that. Let's see where this takes us, shall we?'

'Absolutely. *A votre santé!*'

'*A votre santé,*' said Aubert as they touched glasses.

'This is delicious,' said Anielka. 'The barman is a genius.'

'You said there was more.'

'There is, I'm afraid,' said Anielka with a sigh, looking dejected. She realised that Aubert was watching her carefully and made sure she looked vulnerable. 'Somehow, there's always more.'

'Tell me.'

'Apparently, there is a very special place somewhere here in the Ritz. According to the agent I met here, it's mysterious and quite famous, with a long history dating back to the war.'

'Oh? What kind of place?' asked Aubert, feigning ignorance.

Anielka took another sip and looked at Aubert with those dreamy eyes full of promise. Well aware of the effect she had on men, Anielka knew exactly how to play her cards. It was always what wasn't said, but perhaps implied, that counted.

'The Amber Safe?' she said softly.

Aubert looked at Anielka, momentarily taken aback. 'Not many people know about that,' he said, suddenly alert.

'I had never heard of it myself, and I don't really know what it is, but the agent seemed to know a great deal about it. She said if a photoshoot could be arranged featuring the Amber Safe, well ...'

Aubert nodded but said nothing, the request having taken him completely by surprise.

Anielka took another sip. 'Does this Amber Safe exist?' she asked.

'It does.'

Anielka put her hand on Aubert's knee and looked at him intently. 'If I buy us another one of these delicious Serendipities, could I see it?'

'Perhaps.' Aubert put his hand on Anielka's knee and squeezed it gently, the gesture obvious.

'In that case, why don't we see if we can make these events unfold in a happy and beneficial way?' said Anielka seductively.

'An excellent suggestion, but the drinks are definitely on me.'

'You're on.'

Aubert ordered two more Serendipities and stood up. 'I'll be back in a moment. The keys to the safe are in my office,' he added. 'Don't go anywhere.'

'I wouldn't dream of it. How exciting! Don't be too long.'

As they approached the Amber Safe in the deserted basement – strolling arm in arm – Anielka could see a small table with an ice bucket, champagne and two glasses at the end of the dimly lit corridor.

'Here we are,' said Aubert, and began to play with the keys. 'No-one really comes down here much anymore. It's a forgotten corner of the hotel.'

'You are obviously a man of influence,' joked Anielka and pointed to the champagne.

'If I can't arrange something like this in my hotel, I shouldn't be in the job,' said Aubert and inserted a key into the lock. 'You are in for a big surprise,' he said, turning the key. 'Close your eyes.'

Anielka did as she was told. Aubert opened the heavy door, turned on the lights and stepped away.

'Now look. Welcome to the Amber Safe. One of the many secrets of the Paris Ritz.'

'My goodness, this is amazing!' said Anielka, barely trusting her eyes. 'This feels like stepping into a dream, not a safe.'

She pointed to the sparkling ceiling. 'And all this is amber?'

'It is,' said Aubert. Smiling, he carried the ice bucket and the two glasses into the room and placed them on the small table in front of the mirror.

Anielka looked at herself in the mirror and pirouetted slowly, her reflection almost surreal in the yellow-gold light. 'A photoshoot in here would be incredible ...'

Aubert realised the right moment had arrived to make a move. Experienced in matters like this, he knew it would be a mistake to let the opportunity pass. What he couldn't have known was that Anielka was thinking the same, but for entirely different reasons. Instead of being seduced, it was she who was calling the shots.

'What's incredible in here, right now, is *you*,' said Aubert and put his arms around Anielka's waist, pulled her towards him and kissed her gently on the mouth.

'I can feel that matters are unfolding in a happy and beneficial way,' said Anielka, pressing herself against Aubert. 'Serendipity. We are both rising to the occasion, don't you think?' she added, licking her lips with the tip of her tongue.

'And I don't even know your name,' whispered Aubert, kissing Anielka's neck.

'I'll tell you, but only if you don't stop.'

'I won't; promise.'

'It's Celine. Yours?'

'Louis.'

'Louis, do you think a photoshoot in here would be possible to give a budding Polish mannequin a start in the ferocious Paris fashion jungle?' whispered Anielka, and put her tongue into Aubert's ear.

'I would have to talk to my superiors about this and obtain their permission. The hotel's reputation, you understand ...'

'Completely. I'm sure you can be very persuasive.'

'I will do my best.'

'I'm sure you will, but let me harden your resolve, just in case ...'

'And how exactly are you planning to do this, Celine?' said Aubert, putting his hand up Anielka's skirt.

'I have my ways.'

'Care to show me?'

'Could be dangerous.'

'I'm prepared to take that chance.'

'Be careful what you wish for,' said Anielka and began to loosen Aubert's belt.

27

Frieda Malenkova's study: 5 February 2017

'Extraordinary,' said Malenkova and pointed to the whiteboard in front of her. 'And she did all that last night? *By herself?*'

'She did. All her initiative,' said Zuzanna. 'This girl can think on her feet. The photos were particularly clever, don't you think? All taken by Aubert on *her* phone! She said it was a game, a private photoshoot.'

'Private, all right.' Malenkova pointed to a series of photos pinned to the whiteboard showing a partially naked Anielka posing provocatively in front of the strong boxes. One in particular – a close-up of Anielka kneeling next to box thirty-three and wearing only a G-string – stood out.

'I have already shown this one to Emile,' said Zuzanna.

'And?'

'He said it told him everything he needed to know about the lock and how it operates. Provided he is given access to the safe, he said he could open the box easily within minutes, using only a few basic hand tools.'

'Just like the good old days, eh?' said Malenkova, clearly enjoying herself. 'I told you he wouldn't be a problem. I had a chat with him; he's ready to go. No doubt the money I promised him helped. I think he's almost broke.'

'That only leaves two things: permission for a photoshoot in the Amber Safe, and access to the safe for Emile,' said Zuzanna. 'Unless he can get in there, the job can't be done.'

'Quite.'

'Anielka came up with a few ideas already.'

'Oh? In what way?' said Malenkova.

'She's meeting Aubert again tomorrow.'

'A rendezvous in the Amber Safe?'

'Something like that. They've made it their secret love nest, would you believe? Kinky sex in the Amber Safe; her idea. Clever, eh?'

'Very.'

'Apparently, Aubert's on fire and ready to do almost anything to see her again. Hardly surprising. Just look at that body!'

'I bet. The girl's a genius and totally without inhibitions. While he's thinking with his you-know-what, she's thinking with her head and running rings around him.'

'Aubert said he'll have an answer for her regarding the photoshoot tomorrow,' said Zuzanna.

'We'll have to move quickly, then. The problem will be how to give Emile access to the safe so he can open the box. There's no way he can break into the safe without complicated power tools and oxy torches, which in this case just wouldn't be possible.'

Zuzanna smiled. 'Anielka has a few suggestions about that too ...'

'She does? Amazing! What kind of suggestions?'

'Leave that to me. Let's get permission for a photoshoot first. Everything hinges on that.'

'You're right. Anielka has done an outstanding job. I will call her.'

'Please do that. It would mean a lot to her. Do you know what she's doing right now?'

'Tell me.'

'Working out what to wear to tomorrow's meeting with Aubert. She's crazy about clothes. I think the clothes actually transform her personality. She becomes someone else, a different persona. I have seen nothing quite like it.'

'A complex character, for sure, but let's not forget she's a psychopath and therefore unpredictable, dangerous and capable of anything—'

'But very useful, and perfect for this assignment,' interjected Zuzanna.

'She's that, but only if you control her. In many ways, she's even better than Celine; far more ruthless.'

'You really think so?'

Malenkova nodded. 'I do. Just you wait and see.'

28

Mauve boudoir, Alexander Palace: Easter 1917

The end of the Romanov monarchy was swift and brutal and began on 8 March 1917 with mass demonstrations in St Petersburg against food rationing. The violent protests lasted for eight days and had an unstoppable momentum of their own. Armed confrontations with police and gendarmes further inflamed an already explosive situation, and on 12 March, mutinous forces in the Russian army sided with the revolutionaries, which accelerated the end of Romanov rule.

On 17 March, Tsar Nicholas II abdicated. This brought the Russian Empire and three hundred years of Romanov dynastic rule to an abrupt end and the former tsar – now referred to as Nicholas Romanov – and his family were placed under house arrest in the Alexander Palace at Tsarskoye Selo, just outside St Petersburg.

In a strange way, the abdication brought some temporary peace into the turbulent life of the former tsar, who had been incapable of dealing with the unprecedented challenges facing his rule and the cataclysmic changes overwhelming Russia.

Nicholas settled into family life and an uncertain future in the palace he loved and called home, with the wife he adored and the children he treasured. Wearing a simple military-style shirt and trousers, boots and his favourite forage cap, he went for long walks with his daughters in the grounds surrounding the palace, collected firewood and worked in the vegetable gardens, enjoying for the first time in his life a carefree existence without the heavy responsibilities of politics and state he had found so difficult to cope with.

Of course, this was but an illusion because Colonel Romanov, as the former tsar was now called, and his family were prisoners facing an uncertain future as Russia tried to deal with revolutionary changes affecting every corner of the vast country and threatening to tear apart the very fabric that had held Russia together for centuries.

In many ways, Alexandra found it far more difficult to accept the new reality that now ruled the lives of her family than Nicholas did. The abdication of her husband had affected her deeply and she blamed this catastrophe on his weaknesses and inadequacies of dealing with his God-given rights. She was also far more realistic as far as their new position and future were concerned, and could sense the dangers and uncertainties ahead.

Easter – *Pascha* as it was called in Russia – was the major religious celebration of the year and to many, it was far more important than Christmas. Based on powerful traditions deeply entrenched in the Russian psyche, Pascha was not only the celebration of the Resurrection of Christ, but a time of reflection that would cleanse the soul and bring peace, joy and hope for the future.

At Easter in 1917, dark storm clouds hovered over Russia and instead of hope and joy, hardship and fear dominated the lives of the masses trying to deal with unprecedented changes facing their country. The certainties of the past had been torn away and destroyed, leaving behind uncharted waters and the relentless forces of social change. Millions had died during the devastating war and the tsar had abdicated. Russia would never be the same.

Alexandra, by far the strongest member of the Romanov family, tried to hold family life together and keep it functioning as best she could. With her household drastically reduced this wasn't easy, as armed sentries were everywhere watching the family's every move. This caused an element of danger and unease in what should have been a safe haven.

Bezukhova approached her meeting with Alexandra with trepidation. As a loyal friend and confidante of the former tsarina, she had stayed by her side despite her husband urging her to leave Russia and join him in France, where he had lived since falling out with the tsar two years earlier. The tsar's abdication and the house arrest of the Romanovs had made Bezukhova's position untenable, and she had been instructed to leave the palace or face incarceration.

When Bezukhova entered the mauve room, she found Alexandra calm and composed. Both knew this would be their last meeting. Without saying a word, Alexandra walked over to her friend and embraced her, tears in her eyes.

'Parting is never easy, especially at times like this,' said Alexandra. 'You have been a loyal friend to me all these years and I will miss you more than I can put into words. But times have changed forever, and you can no longer stay here. You must join your husband in France while you can.'

'I know what you say is true, but that doesn't make this any easier.'

'No, it doesn't.' Alexandra pointed to a chair next to her desk. 'Please sit with me; I have some important things to tell you before you go. I would also like to ask you for a favour ...'

'Anything,' whispered Bezukhova, struggling to speak through her tears. The past few weeks she had been under considerable strain. Torn between her loyalty to the tsarina and her duty to her husband waiting for her in France, Bezukhova almost had a breakdown. In a way, the recent developments that no longer allowed her to stay by Alexandra's side had saved her from a difficult, heart-wrenching decision.

'Apart from anything else,' said Alexandra, 'this is Pascha, a time of hope and joy, and I would like our parting to reflect this rather than the difficult times we live in.'

Bezukhova nodded, feeling a little better.

'Needless to say, I will try to stay in touch with you. We can correspond.'

'I would like that.'

'At least for now, there are ways for my letters to reach you while the channels are open,' said Alexandra. 'As for the future, who knows? I have five children and a husband who has gone through very difficult times, ill-equipped to deal with them. We have to be careful when we write to each other. These are dangerous times. Our letters may be opened ...'

'I understand.'

'We should refer to subjects that may be sensitive in ways that others may not understand, but we will. We have done this many times before.'

'We have,' said Bezukhova, smiling.

'But enough of this,' continued Alexandra and reached for a blue box on her desk. 'Niki gave me this yesterday,' she said and handed the box to Bezukhova. 'As a special Easter present.'

'What is it?'

'Have a look.'

Bezukhova pointed to the gold double-headed eagle on the top of the box. 'Fabergé?'

'Open it.'

Bezukhova opened the box. 'A Fabergé Easter egg; magnificent!'

'It is. Niki commissioned it especially for me. You'll see why in a moment. Have a look.'

Bezukhova took the heavy gold egg carefully out of the box and placed it on the desk in front of her. 'Amazing!' she said as she admired the egg made of solid gold and decorated with garlands of diamonds and pearls mounted on a dark-blue-enamelled claw-foot stand.

'It's the surprise inside that's the surprise. Open it.'

'How?'

'The top half opens up if you press this diamond here.' Alexandra pointed to a large diamond.

Bezukhova pressed the diamond, the egg opened and she gasped. Inside the egg was a diamond-encrusted gold cross with the Romanov double-headed eagle on top. On one side of the cross was a miniature portrait of Rasputin in his usual pose – left arm at right angles, held in front of his chest – painted on an enamelled disc surrounded by diamonds. On the other side of the cross was a portrait of Alexandra.

'How extraordinary,' said Bezukhova. 'I know how much he meant to you.'

'But that's not all,' said Alexandra. 'There's more. Lift up the cross.'

As Bezukhova lifted the cross, the bottom half of the egg opened up, exposing what looked like a miniature crypt below. Inside the crypt was something Bezukhova recognised immediately. 'This is amazing,' she said. 'I've seen nothing quite like this before.'

'Neither have I,' said Alexandra.

'Martyrdom and resurrection,' said Bezukhova. 'A true Easter message.'

'Yes, but a very dangerous one. It was reckless of Niki to commission something like this, especially now. Another error of judgement. You can see that, surely, but it was made out of love.'

Bezukhova nodded and kept staring at the jeweller's masterpiece in front of her, its clear symbolism and direct link between Alexandra and Rasputin.

'If this were to be found in my possession, it could have disastrous consequences ... it could easily condemn me. As you know, I have many enemies and we are being watched all the time.'

'I understand.'

'That brings me to the favour I mentioned before,' said Alexandra and placed a hand on Bezukhova's shoulder.

'All you have to do is ask, you know that.'

'I would like you to take my Easter present with you to France and keep it safe for me. If we should meet again, you can return it to me then; if not ...' Alexandra paused, choking with emotion, 'I would like you to have it in memory of our friendship,' she whispered.

Unable to hold back the tears any longer, Bezukhova began to cry. 'I will keep it safe for you, I promise.'

Alexandra reassembled the egg, put it back in its box and handed it to her friend. 'Now please go, before my heart bursts.'

29

Amber Safe, Paris Ritz: 6 February 2017

Anielka looked impatiently at Zuzanna. It was almost time to go. An excited Aubert had asked her to meet him at the Ritz at eleven pm. He had hinted he had some good news. Anielka had changed her outfit twice already until, finally satisfied, she had chosen a creation by Tuomas Merikoski. His Paris-based Finnish label, Aalto, appealed to her because it combined Scandinavian minimalism with Parisian nonchalance. Raw, direct, sophisticated. But most important of all, the outfit reflected her mood and expressed exactly how she felt that night: mysterious and dangerous, like midsummer nights in the forests of Finland with echoes of a violent, pagan past ...

Zuzanna adjusted Anielka's hair. 'Here, let me look at you,' she said and stepped back. 'Perfect, especially the dark lipstick; like blood. Now, remember what I told you. We have to move quickly here. You will have to improvise. The best outcome would be if you could somehow arrange access to the safe for Emile while you are with Aubert in the Amber Safe tonight. Emile would only need a few minutes to open the security box. Celine was a master at doing things like this,' she added and watched Anielka carefully. She noticed the mention of Celine's name had its desired effect. Pleased with the reaction, Zuzanna was sure that Anielka would try to live up to expectations at all cost.

'And what am I supposed to do with Aubert?' asked Anielka.

'Drug him. One of the pills I gave you stirred into his drink should do it quickly.'

'And then what?'

'You call me and Emile will make his way to the safe in the basement. We've already had a trial run. He knows exactly where to find the Amber Safe and how to get to it unnoticed. Don't forget, he's a pro. He knows how to blend in and improvise.'

'I'll do what I can,' said Anielka and reached for her tiny designer handbag.

'I know you will,' said Zuzanna and kissed Anielka gently on the cheek, careful not to disturb her makeup. 'I will be waiting for your call.'

Looking like a fashion queen, Anielka stepped out of the taxi, her long legs showing off her wide-legged black pants, glossy black, embroidered jacket, red scarf and shiny red stilettos. With her long blonde hair carefully dishevelled to give her a sultry, straight-out-of-the-bedroom look, she once again turned heads as soon as she entered the lobby, like a visual magnet for the curious, always on the lookout for glamour.

Aubert's heart missed a beat when he saw Anielka come towards him, smiling alluringly. *She looks completely different*, he thought, as he remembered their passionate encounter in the Amber Safe two days earlier. *Magnifique!*

'You look ravishing,' said Aubert. 'Drink?'

'Absolutely.'

'I have a table waiting for us in the Bar Vendôme; come.'

As soon as they were seated, Aubert ordered champagne.

'I haven't been able to get the Amber Safe out of my mind,' said Anielka. 'It seems to have cast a spell over me.'

'Oh? In what way,' said Aubert, raising an eyebrow.

'Difficult to tell. Perhaps it wasn't the room as such, but something else ...' said Anielka. She reached under the table and walked the tips of her fingers gently up Aubert's thigh.

'You think so?'

'Not sure, but there's a way to find out, don't you think?'

'Could be exhausting,' said Aubert, trying to contain his excitement. 'I spoke to the Board, and ...'

Before Aubert could complete the sentence, Anielka stopped him by putting a finger on his lips. 'Not here,' she whispered. 'Tell me later. In the safe ... But first, let's have some champagne.'

Half an hour later, Aubert and Anielka made their way discreetly down to the basement. 'Are there security cameras down here?' asked Anielka as they stepped out of the lift.

'No. Why do you ask?' said Aubert, surprised.

'Because of this,' said Anielka. She stopped, put her arms around Aubert's neck and kissed him passionately on the mouth.

'No-one really comes down here,' whispered Aubert.

'Only us; perfect,' said Anielka, ticking off the first part of her assignment. Then she kissed Aubert again, took him by the hand and pulled him towards the Amber Safe.

'No champagne?' said Anielka, pointing to the safe door at the end of the deserted corridor. 'You promised!'

'Heads will roll,' said Aubert, annoyed. 'We'll have some later ...'

Could be a problem, thought Anielka, her mind racing.

As soon as they were inside the safe, Aubert pushed Anielka towards the mirror and began to undress her, his hot breath fogging up the glass behind her head.

After that, there was no stopping him, but Anielka had lost all interest in sex and seduction. All she could think of was how to drug Aubert. Everything depended on that, but there was no champagne and no glass. As Aubert became more and more aroused, Anielka became more and more annoyed and began to resist. It was evident that Aubert had had a lot to drink that evening and he was becoming increasingly demanding and aggressive.

'What's wrong?' he said, sensing Anielka's change of mood. Instead of the passionate surprise encounter of the other day, he could sense reluctance. 'Not what you expected?'

'Nothing like that.'

'Then what?' said Aubert. 'You want to know about the photoshoot, is that it? Is that what this is all about?' he asked, becoming angry. 'Are you trying to use me?'

'Of course not. Louis, you are *hurting* me!'

Without saying another word, Aubert spun Anielka roughly around, pinned her against the mirror and attempted to enter her from behind.

'*No!* Not that way!' shouted Anielka.

Ignoring her protests, Aubert didn't stop. Suddenly, something inside Anielka snapped as she remembered a similar situation on her fourteenth birthday, the first time she had been raped by her uncle.

Instead of resisting, she let Aubert have his way. 'See, I knew it,' hissed Aubert, his hot breath reeking of alcohol, tickling her ear. 'You love it, don't you, you slut!'

Taking a deep breath, Anielka searched for her handbag on the table next to her with her left hand. She found the bag and pressed the clip at the top. The bag opened and Anielka reached inside, the touch of cold steel calming her. Then she gripped the small but lethal switchblade knife – a Schrade Viper – and activated the assisted opening mechanism by pressing a button. Almost instantly, the razor-sharp spear-point blade leaped from its cover.

As Aubert loosened his grip, groaning and breathing heavily, Anielka raised her hand holding the knife and stabbed him in the side, penetrating his liver. Feeling excruciating pain, Aubert let go of Anielka and looked down, blood gushing from the deep wound.

'You cut me, you bitch!' he stammered and pressed his hands against the wound to stem the blood flow. As he turned away, Anielka cut his throat from behind with one clean stroke from right to left and stepped back as Aubert fell to his knees. She walked around to face him, careful to avoid stepping in his blood. He stared up at Anielka with glassy eyes, surprise and disbelief contorting his face. Then, making a gurgling sound as blood trickled down his chest, Aubert fell forward and his whole body began to convulse as he lay dying on the floor, his blood staining the Persian carpet.

Anielka bent down and calmly wiped the blade of her knife on Aubert's trousers lying next to him on the floor, and slipped the knife back into her handbag. Then she quickly dressed, reached for her phone and called Zuzanna.

30

Frieda Malenkova's crypt: 7 February 2017

It should be over by now, thought Malenkova and poured herself another cognac. *Something's wrong.* It was four in the morning and she had almost finished the bottle. Patience, self-imposed inactivity and waiting were the price for staying safely in the background, and leaving it to others to do the risky work. Yet it was only because of this discipline that Malenkova had been able to stay under the radar of the law and ahead of the cat-and-mouse-game with the authorities that she so enjoyed. These were the main reasons she was still in business after all these years and not behind bars.

To help her deal with the nerve-racking tension during an especially delicate and dangerous operation with so much riding on it, she withdrew to her crypt, her inner sanctum, and drew strength and inspiration from her art collection.

If we pull this off, it will be a masterpiece, she thought, *with enough money for several lifetimes. And as Dad always used to say, leave the table while you are ahead, and that is precisely what we shall do.*

Malenkova lifted her glass. 'Cheers,' she said and then sat back, closed her eyes and continued to listen to Bruckner's unfinished Ninth Symphony, her favourite.

Zuzanna knew exactly where to find Malenkova. She had decided against telling her over the phone what had happened, and opted instead to do it in person. At least that way, she could exercise some control over the dramatic turn of events, and the potentially catastrophic consequences.

For a long, agonising moment, Zuzanna stood at the top of the stairs and listened to the music drifting up from the crypt below, trying to steel herself for what was to come. Malenkova's violent outbursts were legendary, especially after she had been drinking. She could tolerate and forgive almost anything, except failure. And the challenge for Zuzanna was how to present what had happened that night as a triumph, instead of a failure. She looked at the blue box in her hand and smiled. If anything could make that possible, it was what was inside that box. Zuzanna took a deep breath and began to walk slowly down the stairs to face the music.

Malenkova saw a shadow move out of the corner of her eye and looked up. 'Ah, you at last!' she said with impatient anticipation in her voice.

Without saying a word, Zuzanna walked up to Malenkova and placed the blue box on the table next to the bottle.

Malenkova stared at the box through her thick glasses, a wave of familiar excitement welling up from somewhere deep within and making her heart beat faster. 'Is that what I think it is?' she said, pointing to the Fabergé crest on top.

'Open it and see.'

Malenkova reached for the box, her hands shaking, and slowly lifted the lid. To her surprise, all four sides of the box separated by themselves and fell apart, exposing the unique treasure within.

'Good heavens, *it is*!' she cried out, her voice quivering with emotion. '*We've done it!*' Then she reached slowly across and began to caress the top of the bejewelled egg with her fingertips. 'Have you opened it to find the surprise?'

'No. I left that for you to find.'

'How wonderful!'

'But before you do, there's something I have to tell you ...'

Instantly alert, Malenkova looked at Zuzanna.

'Is there a problem?' she asked, steel in her voice.

'Depends how you look at it.'

'Tell me.'

'Aubert is dead.'

'*What?* How?'

'Anielka killed him.'

Malenkova withdrew her hand and sat up. 'You can't be serious!'

'I am; deadly serious.'

'How?'

'She couldn't drug him, so she improvised.'

'*Improvised?* In what way?'

'She cut his throat. In the safe.'

'Good God!'

'You said yourself she was a psychopath. "Unpredictable, dangerous and capable of anything", I think is how you described her. And far more ruthless than Celine. I suppose now we know.'

'This changes everything,' said Malenkova, her mind racing.

'In what way?'

'Can you imagine what will happen now? All hell will break loose! That's what. And that could be a big problem for us.'

'Perhaps,' replied Zuzanna calmly. 'But that depends ...'

'On what?' said Malenkova curtly.

'On how well Emile and Anielka covered their tracks, and from what I've heard so far, they've done a remarkable job.'

'Oh? Tell me.'

'Anielka couldn't drug Aubert in the safe. The promised champagne didn't arrive. That only left her with one choice: abort the entire plan, or do something about this. She chose the latter.'

'So, she just killed him by cutting his throat?'

'Exactly. Then she rang me and told me all was ready for Emile.'

'Did she tell you about ...?'

'No. She sounded calm and in control and told me there were no CCTV cameras in the corridor downstairs leading to the safe. So, I sent Emile on his way.'

'And?'

'You know he's a pro. He was in disguise. Wearing a dinner suit and wig, he blended in perfectly.'

'And the body in the safe?'

'Didn't seem to bother him too much. He went to work immediately and opened the box within minutes. After that he said he "cleaned up".'

'What does that mean?'

'He wiped all the surfaces that could have been touched by Anielka. No fingerprints that way. He was wearing gloves, of course. He then removed the blue box, put it into his briefcase and left. He didn't spend more than twenty minutes inside the hotel. As I said, he's a pro and acted like one.'

'And Anielka?'

'She followed a few minutes later. As you can imagine, they didn't want to be seen together. I waited at the prearranged spot. They got into my car and we drove away. Simple as that.'

'How was Anielka?'

'Calm, but excited. She believes she did an excellent job. By killing Aubert, she has removed a big problem, she said. No witnesses who could identify her, or in any way help the police ... We did ask her to improvise, and she did just that.' Zuzanna pointed to the spectacular Fabergé egg on the table. 'A little extreme, perhaps, but without her and what she has done, we wouldn't have this.'

'What about the letters?' asked Malenkova.

Zuzanna had expected the question and was ready. 'Left behind in the rush, I'm afraid,' she said. 'The pressure, the dead body, confusion.'

'*What?* I thought we made it clear the letters were all part of it!'

Zuzanna shrugged. 'Shit happens.'

Instead of the violent outburst Zuzanna had expected, Malenkova nodded calmly. She was already a step ahead, trying to work out how to solve the problem. After careful analysis of the letter found in the music box, she was certain that the letters in box thirty-three held important clues about something big, perhaps even bigger than the Imperial Fabergé egg on the table in front of her. Unfortunately, those letters now appeared beyond reach, unless ...

'We have to move quickly,' said Malenkova.

'In what way?'

'I'm not worried about Emile. He knows how to go to ground and disappear for a while. We've seen him do it many times. It's a different story with Anielka.'

'What's on your mind?'

'We should do two things straight away. First, change her appearance, and then take her out of Paris.'

'I agree.'

'Change her hair; it's one of her most striking and recognisable features. You know, colour, length and so on. And then take her to my ski lodge in Grenoble and stay there for a while, and keep an eye on her. Destroy all the clothes she wore on all the occasions connecting her to the Ritz and liquidate her accommodation. Do it tonight; right now. If we are lucky and act quickly, you'll be out of town even before the body is discovered.'

'Excellent suggestion. I'll get onto it straight away,' said Zuzanna, surprised to be getting off so lightly. 'But I think we should praise Anielka for what she has done, don't you think? That way, we can use her again in the future.'

'Yes, you're right. We should do that. She's quite exceptional. We've never worked with someone quite like this before. I'll give her a call.'

'That would certainly do it. She's like a finely honed weapon. Handled correctly, she's capable of extraordinary things,' said Zuzanna.

'I agree. All of you have done an outstanding job. As for those letters left behind, the only one who knows what is contained in them is our Mr Rogan. According to Mademoiselle Darrieux, he has photographed all the pages, remember?'

'Correct. And in due course he may well receive the originals, but not the Fabergé egg,' added Zuzanna, smiling.

'But those letters could be even more important than the egg,' mused Malenkova, sensing another challenge.

Zuzanna looked at her, surprised. 'In what way?'

'Later. For now, we should use our Darrieux connection to find out as much as we can about those letters. I'll prepare a number of questions I want you to put to her in that regard. We must strike while fear will make her do all we ask. Who knows? This may change with the murder. A high-profile murder like this in the Paris Ritz of

183

all places, will be a sensation Paris hasn't seen for a while. If we handle this correctly, it could even work in our favour.'

Malenkova turned to face Zuzanna. 'I'm very proud of you,' she said. 'Now go and call me when you get to Grenoble.'

'Will do,' replied Zuzanna, relieved.

Malenkova watched Zuzanna walk up the stairs. Then she turned up the volume and continued to listen to Bruckner while she caressed the Imperial Easter egg on the table next to her like a lover, and looked forward to exploring the surprise inside at the end of the symphony.

31

Prefecture de Police de Paris: 7 February 2017

A cleaner discovered Aubert's naked body at six-thirty am and reported the matter to the duty manager. The duty manager rang the police immediately and closed off access to the basement. The police arrived twenty minutes later and took over. The officer in charge rang the Prefect of Police at home and reported the incident. Realising the enormity of the matter and its far-reaching consequences, not only for France but internationally, he personally took charge and appointed Marcel Lapointe, a senior commissaire of the Paris Brigade Criminelle, to head the investigation.

On his way to work half an hour later, the Prefect remembered his conversation with Dupree a few days earlier and the cold case file he had given to him. As he entered the prefecture, a large building in the Place Louis-Lépine on the Île de la Cité, he called Dupree.

'How are you, Claude?' asked the Prefect.

'Quite well, considering. Thank you,' said Dupree, surprised to hear from his illustrious friend. 'Countess Kuragin has been very generous. She let me use a cottage here at her chateau. I'm being well looked after.'

'Excellent. I need your help.'

'In what way?'

'We had an incident with potentially far-reaching implications.'

'Oh? What kind of incident?'

The Prefect then gave Dupree a brief outline of what had happened at the Ritz. 'That's all I know at the moment. I would like you to join the team. Interested?'

'*Are you serious?* In my condition?'

'It's your brain and experience I'm after ...'

'I'm in! Echoes of Le Fantôme and the Black Widow, you think?'

'Could be. Nothing happens in a vacuum and without a reason you used to tell us, remember? You always had some of the best instincts in the force when it came to matters like this.'

'Thank you! My recovery has just taken a giant leap forward.'

'I will send Lapointe to see you and keep you informed. Another former pupil of yours who's done well. Anything else you need, just call me. You have my number. We desperately need results here, and quickly!'

'I understand. I can't tell you what this means to me,' said Dupree, but the Prefect had already hung up.

32

Kuragin chateau: 7 February 2017

Jack was working in the conservatory as he did most mornings, when Countess Kuragin walked in with a pot of tea. 'Still working on those letters, I see,' she said. 'Tea?'

'Yes, please. They are absolutely fascinating.'

'In what way?'

'They are written in some kind of code. I'm sure of it.'

'Oh? What makes you say that?'

'Just listen to this: *"I am so glad you made it safely to France and took N's gift with you. Just as well, as our rooms were searched again yesterday. Very humiliating. Imagine if they had found it among my things? Instead of helping us, our friend would have done the opposite. I would have been condemned for standing next to him, separated only by the cross. N, too, would have been in trouble and pilloried for having arranged it all."* Strange, don't you think?'

'You think so? It's a personal letter between two close friends. They understand each other and know what is meant by references that may appear strange, perhaps even mysterious to an outsider, but make perfect sense to them because they refer to shared experiences.'

'Perhaps, but this is only the first letter. The others are even stranger and more complicated until it is almost impossible to work out exactly what is being said. It's all innuendo. If the former tsarina did in fact write these letters while she and her family were under house arrest in the Alexander Palace in 1917, then these letters are of great historical significance.'

'Never a dull moment in your life, that's for sure.'

'The weirdest letter by far is the last one, sent from Yekaterinburg in July 1918. The one we found in the music box.'

'Written the day before the Imperial family was murdered?' said the countess.

'Yes. The closer you look at it, the stranger it becomes, and quite desperate. There's a certain urgency in the language. It's like a final farewell.'

'Hardly surprising when you consider what happened.'

'True, but I believe there's a significant message buried in that letter, and it is in some way connected to the Fabergé egg.'

'What makes you say that?'

'I'm still working on it,' said Jack, sidestepping the question. 'But I sense that something really big is involved here. Some kind of far-reaching secret Alexandra wanted to protect, but at the same time share with her friend. It's absolutely fascinating!'

'You and your secrets! Following those breadcrumbs of destiny again?' said the countess, smiling.

'Something like that.' Jack sat back and looked intently at the countess. 'I have to ask myself, what could possibly have been so important, especially during those desperate times? By now, the Imperial family had been in captivity in Yekaterinburg for over two months. Cut off from the outside world and living in difficult, cramped conditions, watched over by guards. This is the day before the entire Romanov family is brutally murdered, perhaps by the very same guards.'

Jack shook his head. 'I think Alexandra had to get something off her chest before it was too late, and she did that by putting it all in this letter. This is no social chitchat between friends. This is something far more important, and it's all right here,' said Jack and pointed to the letter in front of him.

'You may be right.'

'And let's not forget, somehow this letter made it all the way to France.' Jack held up the letter like a trophy. 'From faraway Siberia during those turbulent times. This could not have been easy to arrange.'

'By the way, Claude just rang from the cottage,' said the countess. 'He would like to see us. He said it was important.'

Jack put down the letter and looked at the countess. 'He's an interesting man. Very good of you to put him up.'

'It's the least we can do, don't you think?'

'Still. Did he say what it was about?'

'No, but he did say it would be better if we heard it from him first, rather than read it in the papers.'

'How intriguing. Let's go and see him.'

Jack and the countess walked across to the Gatekeeper's Cottage on the other side of the moat. As they crossed the bridge and turned the corner, they could see a police car parked in front of the cottage.

'Interesting, don't you think?' said Jack and pointed to the uniformed officer standing at the front door. 'Do you think we're harbouring a criminal?'

'I hope not. Let's find out.'

'You are expected,' said the officer and opened the door after the countess had told him who she was.

Dupree and another man in his fifties sat at the kitchen table. 'Good morning, Countess, thank you for coming,' said Dupree. He nodded to Jack and stood up. The other man stood up as well. 'This is Detective Chief Superintendent Lapointe,' continued Dupree, making the introductions.

Jack looked at the man in front of him with interest. Shortish, powerfully built and wearing a heavy overcoat, he reminded Jack of *Maigret*, the legendary fictional Paris detective who featured in more than seventy novels by Georges Simenon, and became an iconic character and the subject of countless films and TV dramas. But most striking of all was the man's face. Radiating intelligence but also sadness and compassion, the eyes had seen a little too much brutality and violence, and the deep lines around the mouth and prominent chin suggested a determination to do something about it. *The only thing missing is the bowler hat and the pipe*, thought Jack. Then he saw the slouch hat and the pipe on the table, and smiled.

The countess extended her hand. 'To what do we owe the pleasure, Chief Superintendent, and so early in the morning? Is Claude under arrest?'

'Far from it, Countess, he just joined my team and will help us in the investigation.'

'Investigation?' said Jack. 'What kind of investigation?'

'We are investigating a murder.'

'Oh? Can you tell us about it?'

'Monsieur Aubert, the general manager of the Ritz, was found in the Amber Safe this morning with his throat cut,' said Lapointe calmly and reached for his pipe. 'Do you mind?'

Speechless, the countess just shook her head in disbelief and shock.

'Are you serious?' said Jack. 'What happened?'

'Forensics are at the scene right now, but it looks like a robbery—'

'*Robbery?*' interrupted Jack. 'What kind of robbery?'

'Strong box thirty-three has been broken into; professional job,' replied Dupree.

'And the contents?' asked Jack, feeling rather ill.

'Removed, I'm afraid, except for the letters,' said Lapointe.

'How could this have happened? In the Ritz of all places? There must have been hundreds of people in the hotel at the time.'

'We are working on it,' said Lapointe. 'I understand you have some photographs of the Fabergé egg, Mr Rogan, and a key to the box; is that correct?'

'Yes.'

'If I could have those that would be most helpful.'

'Of course. This is unbelievable.'

'The publicity surrounding this will be huge and it would be best if you could stay in the background, Mr Rogan. A prominent man like you could easily become the subject of innuendo and speculation, and therefore a distraction. Your involvement in this matter is unlikely to reach the press, and we should try to keep it that way. Better for all parties, don't you think? Claude here will keep you informed. That's all for the moment, thank you.'

Lapointe lit his pipe, signifying that the meeting was over. 'My officer outside will go with you and collect the key and the photographs. Now, if you would excuse us, Claude and I have a lot to discuss. It has been a pleasure meeting you both,' said Lapointe. 'Of course, we'll need statements. Not only from you, but also from Mademoiselle Darrieux.'

'Understood,' said the countess.

'We can do this here rather than in Paris. Less publicity that way.'

'That would be appreciated,' said Jack and followed the countess to the door.

33

La Closerie des Lilas, Paris: 7 February 2017

Mademoiselle Darrieux followed the maître d' confidently to her usual table like a true celebrity, and nodded to several regulars enjoying their morning coffee and croissants. Breakfast at La Closerie des Lilas twice a week was part of her routine, and she looked forward to being fussed over by the staff and, most importantly, being seen. To a woman living on her own who loved the limelight, these occasions were the lifeblood of her social life and the way she made sure of being noticed and talked about.

Her deliberately outrageous outfits turned heads and invited comment, albeit not all of them flattering. That didn't seem to matter because being talked about was the oxygen that sustained a socialite who craved attention. The painful alternative was to be ignored, and that was tantamount to social death. It had taken Mademoiselle Darrieux many years to climb the fickle and often unforgiving Paris social ladder and create a persona that was both respected and liked, despite her many eccentricities and very public foibles.

The thought of losing this or having her carefully cultivated reputation in any way tarnished, filled her with terror. Nightmares had haunted her restless sleep since that fateful encounter with the mysterious woman at Shakespeare and Company a few days earlier, and her heart filled with dread every time her phone rang. Despite having answered all the questions put to her by Zuzanna and providing all the requested information to the best of her ability, she felt vulnerable and unsafe. Fear of exposure dominated her life and the strain had begun to show.

Mademoiselle Darrieux paled when the waiter handed her the morning paper and she read the headlines on the front page: *Murder at the Ritz. A cleaner doing her rounds early this morning found the mutilated body of Louis Aubert, the general manager of the Paris Ritz, inside a walk-in safe in the basement of the hotel. His throat had been cut during a suspected robbery ...*

Her head spinning, Mademoiselle Darrieux felt suddenly ill. Curious heads turned as she dropped the paper on the floor, stood up and hurried to the bathroom like a woman being pursued by a dangerous stalker. She locked herself inside a cubicle and, breathing deeply, tried to calm herself. *My God! This is all my fault*, she thought. *Everything's connected. What am I going to do?* After making sure there was no-one else in the ladies, she came out of the cubicle and washed her face. When she looked in the mirror, she was shocked by the face staring back at her. *That's not me*, she thought. *This can't go on.* Feeling better, she called Countess Kuragin.

'Katerina, something terrible has happened,' Mademoiselle Darrieux blurted out as soon as the countess answered the phone.

'You saw the headlines?'

'Yes, unbelievable! I need your help.'

'You sound awful; where are you?'

'I think I am in danger,' said Mademoiselle Darrieux, ignoring the question. '*I have to see you!*'

'Sure. Where?'

'May I come to you?'

'Of course. When?'

'Now. Please?'

Driving her red Citroën, Mademoiselle Darrieux arrived at the Kuragin chateau two hours later.

'What's the matter, Adrienne?' said the countess taking her distraught visitor by the hand once she'd parked her vehicle. 'Let's go into the music room; come.'

As soon as Jack saw Darrieux, he knew something was seriously wrong. The dark rings under her eyes and the puffy cheeks with the usually impeccable makeup now smudged, made her look a lot older. Gone was the larger than life socialite with the raucous laugh and almost theatrical demeanour. Jack was looking at a frightened, middle-aged woman who appeared crushed and barely able to speak.

She's upset about the murder and the robbery, thought Jack. He walked over to the sideboard, poured a large brandy and handed it to Darrieux. She looked at him gratefully and gulped down the soothing liquor. 'Come,' said Jack, 'take a seat. You are among friends.'

'I know, and that's why I'm here. I have something very important to tell you that may shock you, but I have to get it off my chest.'

'As Jack just said, you're among friends, Adrienne,' said the countess.

Without saying a word, Darrieux reached into her handbag, pulled out a bundle of newspaper clippings – part of the dossier left behind by Zuzanna – and put them on the table in front of her.

'What's this?' asked Jack. 'Have a look,' said Darrieux. 'I know this will shock you, but the truth is the truth.' Darrieux burst into tears.

The countess put a comforting arm around her. 'Come now, Jack and I aren't easily shocked; isn't that right, Jack?'

'Absolutely,' said Jack, trying to sound cheerful. He picked up the bundle of papers and began to read, well aware that Darrieux was watching him carefully.

'You may change your mind in a moment,' said Darrieux quietly and wiped away a few tears. 'Can I have another brandy, please?'

This is amazing, thought Jack as he read about Darrieux' dreadful childhood in the Deep South, the abusive father and her life as a teenage prostitute in New Orleans. His eyes widened in disbelief as he read the article about Maurice Moreau and the murder trial, and how Maurice Moreau became first Estelle Montplaisir after a sex change, and then after spending some time in jail in Miami for a break and enter, became Adrienne Darrieux.

Slowly, Jack put the newspaper clippings back on the table and looked at Darrieux. 'I can see what you mean. Is that really you?' he asked quietly.

'It is,' sobbed Darrieux. 'That pitiful, despicable creature is me.'

'What's all this about?' asked the countess, frowning.

Jack handed her the bundle of newspaper clippings. Then he got up, walked over to the sideboard and poured two large brandies. 'I need one too,' he said, holding up his glass, and handed the other to Darrieux.

The tension in the room grew by the second as the countess read the articles about a dreadful journey filled with unimaginable hardship, pain and abuse, but resulting in an almost miraculous transformation that could only have been achieved by someone with exceptional courage, fortitude and strength of character, deserving admiration and respect.

The countess put down the articles, walked over to Darrieux and without saying a word, embraced her. It was a gesture of true friendship and support by someone who also knew hardship and pain, and what it took to overcome adversity.

'May I ask a question, Adrienne?' said Jack, sipping his brandy.

'Please go ahead,' said Darrieux.

'Why are you telling us all this; here, right now? Why are you baring your soul and opening painful old wounds?'

'Because unfortunately, there's more, and it's related to Aubert's murder and the robbery in the Amber Safe. It's all my fault, you see.'

'I don't understand,' said the countess.

'You will in a moment. Just listen to this.'

Now that the worst was out in the open, a composed and much calmer Darrieux talked about her encounter with the mystery woman during her book signing session at Shakespeare and Company, and what she had been asked to do to avoid exposure and a devastating scandal.

'So, that woman blackmailed you?'

'Yes she did, and I was naive and weak and caved in to her demands, until now. But the murder this morning changed everything. In fact, I just put an end to it all on the way here.'

'Oh? In what way?' asked the countess.

'The woman called again and asked for more information.'

'What kind of information?' said Jack.

'It was about the letters we found in the safe.'

Jack shot the countess a meaningful look. 'How interesting. What did you tell her?'

'I told her to go to hell and hung up.'

Pity, thought Jack. This had most likely shut down an important lead and sent that dossier on its way to the papers. *Poor Adrienne.*

'I admire your courage, Adrienne,' said the countess. 'And you definitely did the right thing coming here with all this. Now, before the police interview—'

'What police interview?' interrupted Darrieux, alarmed.

'The police have already been here, you see. Chief Superintendent Lapointe is in charge of the investigation and wants to interview all of us about the Amber Safe,' said Jack. 'Not surprising. We'll have to make a statement. I have no doubt he will be very interested in what you've just told us about that mystery woman and the blackmail. All highly relevant and perhaps a very important lead, thanks to you.'

'I suppose so, but none of that matters much to me right now. I am finished, that's for sure.' Darrieux pointed to the newspaper clippings on the table. 'Obviously, all of this will now become public very soon. You can imagine ... it will destroy me,' she added quietly. 'I will have to leave Paris and go into hiding. I couldn't bear the shame. I've been running away all my life; I just didn't think I would have to do it again.'

'Not necessarily,' said Jack, who had already been working on a plan to deal with Darrieux' predicament and, if possible, turn it into an advantage.

'What do you mean?' said Darrieux.

'I have an idea ...'

'This is classic Jack,' interjected the countess, smiling. She turned to Darrieux. 'Jack always comes up with something unexpected, you see, when there seems to be no way out. I've seen him do this many times, especially when his back was against the wall. He must have something up his sleeve.'

'You really think so?' said Darrieux, not daring to hope.

'I do,' said the countess. 'Jack, care to tell us about what you have in mind?'

'Later perhaps. I have to call a friend first and ask for her help.'

'What kind of friend?' asked Darrieux.

'An international celebrity; a famous rock star adored by millions. A woman, trapped in a man's body ...'

'Oh? And she could help *me*?' said Darrieux.

'I believe so,' said Jack. 'But we have to act quickly before it's too late.'

'That's very clever, Jack,' said the countess, who instantly realised where Jack was heading with this. 'Quite ingenious, in fact.'

'I need another drink,' said Darrieux, suddenly feeling a lot better.

'What I think we should do right now,' said Jack, changing direction, 'is to go and talk to Dupree. I have no doubt he'll be very interested to hear what Adrienne has to say about that mystery woman ...'

'Le Fantôme?'

Jack shrugged. 'Could be; who knows? This is all somehow connected.'

'I agree,' said the countess. 'Come, Adrienne, let me introduce you to a fascinating man who may well hold the key to cracking this baffling case.'

'How exciting! May I please use your bathroom, Katerina? I have to improve this wreck and touch up my lippy before we go.'

Two hours later, Jack called Isis in London. The retired rock star was sitting in a vintage barber's chair in her bespoke apartment on top of the Time Machine Studios overlooking the Thames.

'Am I calling at a bad time?' said Jack. 'You sound preoccupied.'

'Not at all. I'm having my hair done and sipping champagne. Pity you can't join me.'

This was typical Isis. The flamboyant megastar whose stellar career had come to an abrupt, tragic end during a rock concert in Mexico in 2011, was enjoying herself.

197

'That's all right then. Trying out a new hairstyle, perhaps?'

'How did you know? New colour in fact. Maurice here suggested it. We are working on it right now.'

'Most opportune, I'd say,' said Jack.

'In what way?'

'You could show it off in public and gauge the reaction … in Paris.'

'*Paris?* How come?'

'Because of what I'm about to suggest.'

'Sounds intriguing.'

Jack and Isis had shared a number of exciting adventures in the past, and had forged a close friendship over the years. Isis was always ready to drop everything and participate in one of Jack's unpredictable but never boring escapades.

'It is, but we haven't got much time.'

'What's new? With you, it's always urgent.'

'I suppose so, but this is definitely up your alley, mate.'

'Oh? In what way?'

'I would like to help a friend in need and you, my dear, are precisely the person whose help could make all the difference.'

'How interesting! What's it about?'

'I have to warn you, it would involve a public appearance,' said Jack, introducing the bait he knew would be hard for Isis to resist.

'A public appearance? How public?'

'Very. Would you mind?'

'*Mind?* I love public appearances; you know that!'

'You don't say?'

'You are not playing games, here …'

'Far from it. Could you come to Paris on Thursday?'

'Of course! Now tell me, what's this all about?'

'Well, this friend of mine is in a spot of bother, you see—'

'Hold on,' interrupted Isis, 'I need more champagne.'

34

Shakespeare and Company, Paris: 9 February 2017

As suggested by Jack, Mademoiselle Darrieux had quickly arranged a special book-signing session at Shakespeare and Company, her favourite bookstore, and told the press about it. She also informed her contacts in the media that she had a sensational announcement to make and that a world-famous celebrity would be in attendance. Intrigued, but somewhat sceptical because Darrieux was well known for her often outrageous exaggerations, the editors nevertheless sent a couple of junior reporters and photographers along, just in case there was something of interest in what Darrieux had foreshadowed. One TV station even sent a camera crew.

Isis and Lola had caught the early Eurostar from London to Paris. Jack and the countess picked them up at Gare du Nord and drove them straight to 37 rue de la Bûcherie. By the time the Kuragin vintage Bentley pulled up outside, a curious crowd had already gathered in front of the bookstore. Darrieux had arrived half an hour earlier, and was holding court inside and talking to fans.

'Look at that crowd,' said Jack. He pointed to the entrance and turned around to face Isis, who sat behind him. 'Now, remember to make a fuss as you get out of the car. They don't know you're coming and we want to make sure you are noticed.'

Lola, Isis's PA and personal pilot, began to laugh. 'Don't encourage her too much or there will be a riot here in a moment.'

'Don't you worry, darling, I do know how to make an entrance,' said Isis and adjusted her scarf. 'I do love crowds.'

For someone who craved the limelight and being recognised almost as much as Darrieux, making a surprise entrance, especially now in retirement, was a rare treat. When Jack had approached her two days earlier and explained what he had in mind and why, Isis had eagerly jumped at the opportunity.

'Here's the book,' said Jack and handed Isis a copy of Darrieux' *Scandal in Place Vendôme*. 'Remember, you will greet Adrienne like a long-lost friend, and ask her to sign it for you. That's how we kick this off; clear?'

'If you can get near her, that is,' said the countess, chuckling.

'Don't worry, I know what to do. I must say, I very much look forward to meeting this fascinating friend of yours you keep talking about. A fashion icon, I believe?' teased Isis and raised an eyebrow. 'Wasn't she the one who told you about the scandal of the crystal skull? It was the key to solving the puzzle in *The Hidden Genes of Professor K,* right?'

'It certainly helped,' said Jack, rolling his eyes.

'We'll have a literary morning; how wonderful,' said Isis.

'And a fashion show.'

Jack turned to Lola. 'I have a feeling these two will get on famously and dazzle the crowd.'

'No doubt about it,' said Lola. 'There's no stopping her now. She spoke of nothing else on the train.'

Two bored reporters stood in front of the bookshop, smoking, and looked across to see what all the fuss was about when the door of the Bentley opened and Isis got out.

'Who on earth is that?' asked one of them and reached for his camera.

Isis looked like she had just stepped out of a *Vogue* fashion spread. Wearing a stunning, if somewhat provocative, outfit by Jean-Paul Gaultier – the *'enfant terrible'* of Paris fashion and one of her favourite designers – Isis looked incredible in a black pantsuit reminiscent of the outfit worn by Madonna in her 1990 *Blond Ambition World Tour*.

The reason Isis had chosen that outfit was simple: Gaultier was well known for blurring gender divisions by bravely mixing women's and men's fashion in creative ways that stood out. Men wearing skirts and women in tuxedos were only some of the better-known examples the public at large was aware of. And so was Madonna's cone bra, revisited many times by such musical icons as Lady Gaga and Katy Perry.

Isis believed in always dressing for the occasion, and the outrageous gender-mixing Gaultier was definitely the perfect choice for the occasion that had brought her to Paris that morning. Those fortunate to be present would be treated to a performance they were unlikely to forget, and the lucky reporters in the crowded room were in for the scoop of their professional lives.

One of the girls at the back of the queue trying to get into the bookshop recognised Isis and began to scream. Others turned around and joined in. Within moments, Isis was surrounded by adoring fans who couldn't believe their luck to be unexpectedly standing next to their idol. Soon, Isis was participating in selfies, doing high-fives and shaking hands, as the two security guards Jack had hired began to clear a path into the store.

Inside, the excitement had already reached fever pitch as Isis and Jack made their way to the library to meet Darrieux.

'This is Jack Rogan, my biographer,' said Isis, pointing to Jack pushing through the crowd next to her. 'Many of you would know him as the author of such wonderful books as *The Disappearance of Anna Popov* and *The Hidden Genes of Professor K*. He too, will be happy to sign books for you. They are all available right here in the store. So, get your copies now. You don't want to miss out, do you?'

Isis turned to Jack. 'How am I doing?'

'Want to join my publicity team?'

'Love to; how exciting!'

She's a natural, thought Jack, looking for Darrieux. He spotted her signing books at her usual small table at the entrance to the reading library, and waved. An excited Darrieux waved back and stood up. *Good God*, thought Jack, *she's certainly outdone herself this time, but she's clearly sending a message here.*

Dressed in the latest butch chic style – a plain white shirt and thin black tie, a punkishly torn embroidered vest, baggy black trousers with echoes of Charlie Chaplin, and vintage riot grrl boots – Darrieux had unwittingly chosen the perfect outfit for the occasion by letting her instincts guide her. The outfit expressed who she was and how she felt. It was the Freemason's handshake of gay women, a code for her sexuality others of similar persuasion would instantly recognise and appreciate. And that was precisely what Isis did as soon as she set eyes on Darrieux.

'I *do* like your clothes, darling,' said Isis and embraced Darrieux like an old friend. 'Smashing. Wonderful to see you again.'

'And you,' said Darrieux, tears in her eyes. By now the photographers had fought their way to the front row and were furiously taking pictures of the outrageous celebrity pair embracing in front of them, to the delight of the cheering crowd.

After Darrieux had signed Isis's book, Jack the storyteller sensed the right moment had arrived to introduce the subject that had brought them all together in the first place: Mademoiselle Darrieux' 'coming out'. At a signal from Jack, Isis stood up and introduced him.

'Friends, there is a more serious side to our jolly meeting here today, and I will ask Jack Rogan, who is a much better storyteller than I will ever be, to let you know what this is all about. Jack?'

Jack held up his hand until the excited crowd fell silent. 'I feel privileged to stand here before you with two dear friends, Isis and Mademoiselle Darrieux, by my side. Isis's transgender journey is well known to millions of her fans and as most of you here would know, she struggled early in life with her sexuality and with the fact that she is a woman, trapped in a man's body—'

'I couldn't help it that I was born with a dick,' interjected Isis, to the delight of the cheering crowd, used to outrageous remarks like that from their idol.

'Be that as it may,' continued Jack, smiling, 'there is someone present here right now whose journey hasn't been as clear-cut and straightforward.' Jack turned to his right and pointed to Darrieux. 'In fact, that journey has been a remarkable struggle with many difficult

202

and tragic twists and turns. What you are about to hear, my friends, will surprise, perhaps even shock you, but please remember that it often takes great courage to face who we really are, and greater courage still, to share that with the world. And that, my friends, is precisely what Mademoiselle Darrieux is about to do right now. The time has come for her to tell you who she really is.' Jack stepped aside to let Darrieux come forward. 'Adrienne, you have the floor.'

Taking a deep breath, Darrieux began to tell her story just as she had done two days earlier in front of Jack and Countess Kuragin, in a calm and measured way. She told them about growing up in a run-down shack on the banks of the Mississippi, terrorised by a brutal father and how Maurice Moreau – the teenage boy-prostitute working in New Orleans – first became Estelle Montplaisir after a sex change, and then after some time in jail, Adrienne Darrieux.

By now, the bookstore had become as silent as a grave.

'There's a lot more,' continued Darrieux, her voice by now barely audible. 'I have prepared a dossier of newspaper clippings for the journalists present that will provide further information and detail about what I've just told you. But in a nutshell, this is me, the *true* me,' said Darrieux, and for a long, lonely moment, she just stood there, looking forlorn and dejected.

Then Isis, the consummate performer who knew that timing was everything, walked up to Darrieux, embraced her and, turning to face the silent crowd said, 'This is without doubt one of the most courageous things I've heard in years. You can be very proud of yourself, Adrienne.'

Then the room erupted in cheers and spontaneous applause as a tribute to a brave human being who had dared to bare her troubled soul in public and was prepared to face the consequences, however harsh, with humility and grace.

35

Frieda Malenkova's study: 10 February 2017

Malenkova pushed her breakfast tray impatiently aside and stared out the window. Usually she would have found the view across the valley to the snow-covered hills relaxing, but not that morning. The dense fog and the sensational headlines in the morning papers had seen to that.

Instead of attracting embarrassment and ridicule, Mademoiselle Darrieux and her sensational 'coming out' had become the toast of Paris. By meeting the threat of exposure head on, Darrieux had successfully turned a dark secret she had desperately tried to conceal for years, into a shining beacon of courage, admiration and social success. The fact that Isis, an international superstar and transgender social heavyweight had supported her in this in a very public way, had certainly given gravitas to Darrieux' surprising revelations and elevated her to new, unexpected heights in the social hierarchy of Paris life.

She could never have done this on her own, thought Malenkova. *Clever; quite brilliant in fact*, she grudgingly had to admit. After having carefully read the articles several times, she was left with no doubt who the architect of that masterstroke had been.

The friendship between Jack and Isis was common knowledge in social circles, and Isis had featured prominently in several of his books. The recent contact between Darrieux and Jack involving the Petrova music box, the Russian letter and the key to the strong box, was a direct link to what had happened at the Ritz. It was apparent to Malenkova that Darrieux must have confided in Jack and told him about Zuzanna and the blackmail.

And what better way to deal with blackmail than to remove the threat altogether? Malenkova asked herself. And that is precisely what had occurred in a rather spectacular and very public way. Malenkova couldn't suppress a crooked little smile, because what had just happened was precisely the kind of plan she would most likely have come up with to deal with a situation like that.

Malenkova reached for her pen and circled Jack's smiling face on the front page. The photo captured Jack standing between Isis and Darrieux as he was addressing the crowd in the library at Shakespeare and Company. *He's the one responsible for this,* she thought. *Look out, Jack Rogan, I'm coming after you!*

Feeling better, Malenkova put down the paper and called Victor Sokolov, one of her old contacts she had done business with in the past. Sokolov, who could trace his roots all the way back to the Mongols, was a Russian oligarch close to Putin and worth billions, who had made his fortune during the era of privatisation following the disintegration of the Soviet Union in the 1990s. As a young, savvy entrepreneur during Mikhail Gorbachev's unprecedented period of market liberalisation, he had begun his career by smuggling personal computers and jeans into the country and selling these sought-after goods on the black market for a huge profit.

By quickly learning the ropes of privatisation and with a few lucky breaks, he built a business empire out of nothing in record time by acquiring contested state property and making shady deals with former USSR officials. Rising quickly, he became the go-between, between the emerging market and the often corrupt but elected government officials trying to facilitate the Russian state's transition to a market-based economy.

Sokolov was still in bed with his mistress when his mobile rang. 'Frieda, what a pleasant surprise,' said Sokolov, and reached for his cigarettes on the bedside table. 'To what do I owe this honour?'

'Where are you?'

'In Scotland.'

'Ah, that castle. Is the restoration finished?'

'Restorations like this are never finished.'

'Do you get to read the papers up there?'

'Of course!'

'Then you would have noticed the story about the Fabergé egg in the Ritz ...'

'Ah. A spectacular murder in a weird safe, and a daring robbery. I thought you might have had something to do with that,' said Sokolov, laughing, and lit a cigarette. 'It has your fingerprints all over it. Was it you?'

'Perhaps.'

'I see. What's on your mind?'

'The item in question is absolutely spectacular and totally unique. Most likely the last Imperial Easter egg crafted by Fabergé: Easter 1917.'

'What makes you say that?'

'The surprise inside ...'

'There was nothing in the papers about that.'

'Of course not. No-one knows what it is.'

'Except you, of course.'

'Except me.'

'Can you tell me?'

'How about miniature portraits of the tsarina and Rasputin for starters? I can send you pictures if you like.'

'*What?* Are you serious? There's no record of such an egg.'

'No, there isn't, but are you surprised?'

'Is it authentic?'

'Absolutely! I can even provide provenance.'

'*Provenance?* What kind of provenance?'

'How does a letter written and signed by Alexandra herself sound?'

Inhaling deeply, Sokolov was hoping the nicotine rush would clear his spinning head. 'Do you realise what you are saying?'

'Absolutely. This is history! *Russian* history. That's why I immediately thought of you, Victor. Interested?'

'You know I am. What about price?'

'Difficult to establish in this case. Why don't we do what we did with *The Missing Little Shepherd?*'

'The Nesterov painting? Good idea.'

Rumours that Malenkova had *The Missing Little Shepherd* – a famous Russian painting – in her private collection, had begun to circulate a few years ago. Sokolov heard about it on the black-market grapevine and expressed interest in buying it. Because the painting had been the subject of a spectacular robbery, establishing a price that was acceptable to both parties turned out to be impossible. To overcome the impasse, Malenkova suggested the icon be put up for auction on the dark web to find out what the market was prepared to pay for a unique, stolen item with no guidelines as to value.

Sokolov was given the right of first refusal and once the bidding stopped, Malenkova and Sokolov commenced negotiations, agreed on a price and Sokolov bought the painting for two million pounds. It now had pride of place in the great hall of his castle in Scotland, next to other choice pieces of Russian art he had acquired over the years.

Sokolov was well known as an avid and shrewd art collector with deep pockets, who didn't ask too many questions, could outbid almost anyone else and was prepared to buy when other, more circumspect buyers might get cold feet and hesitate. For Sokolov, who craved respectability and recognition and had access to billions, collecting art – especially Russian pieces, preferably of historic significance – had become a passion. It was the way he tried to set himself apart from the despised 'kleptocrats', who had made their enormous fortunes by taking advantage of the vast price difference between old domestic prices and world market prices for such sought-after Russian commodities as oil and gas. The principle behind it all was simple enough: buy cheap and sell at a huge profit, look after those who made it all possible and remove obstacles that stand in the way. This accounted for Sokolov's ruthless streak and reputation as a very dangerous man not to be crossed, who would stop at nothing to get what he wanted.

'Give me a few days and I'll set it all up. Should create quite a stir, I imagine,' said Malenkova.

'It sure will. We probably know all the potential buyers anyway. There wouldn't be more than a handful, I imagine, who could come up with that kind of money and are prepared to take the risk. Especially in these circumstances.'

'It's a once-in-a-lifetime opportunity to acquire a piece of history,' said Malenkova, repeating her strongest point. 'That's rarely possible without risk.'

'You don't have to tell me; I know.'

'But that's not all, Victor, there's more ...'

'What do you mean?'

'I can't give you any precise details at the moment except for this: I believe there's something even bigger involved here that may surpass the discovery of the Fabergé egg.'

'Seriously? A hunch?'

'It's more than that.'

'Based on what?'

'More letters.'

'Alexandra?'

'I'm working on it; that's all I can tell you for now,' said Malenkova, evading the question.

Encouraged by the last set of answers provided by Darrieux to her quite precise and pointed questions, Malenkova had been left in no doubt that the letters left behind in the strong box held the key to something big and significant involving the tsarina and her friend, and that Jack was working on that very subject and trying to solve the puzzle.

'And you are telling me this because ...?' asked Sokolov.

'You and I may have to join forces to – how shall I put it? – get to the bottom of this and share the spoils. Interested?'

'Absolutely. A partnership? Sounds interesting.'

'It is, perhaps in more ways than you can possibly imagine just now. As you know, I have a good nose for things like this.'

'You sure have, Frieda,' said Sokolov, laughing. 'You sure have.'

Malenkova's ability to follow leads, uncover unlikely connections and possibilities and come up with spectacular discoveries and deals were well known in the underground art world, and therefore deserved to be taken seriously.

'Well, keep me informed,' said Sokolov. 'And please send me those pictures. I can't wait to see what Fabergé created as his final Imperial Easter masterpiece.'

'You won't be disappointed. Now, go back to your girlfriend.'

'How did you know?'

'I can hear her moaning next to you.'

'You don't miss much, do you?'

'I try not to. That's why I'm still in business,' said Malenkova and hung up.

36

Gatekeeper's Cottage, Kuragin chateau: 12 February 2017

Jack pushed a few crumpled sheets of paper littering the large kitchen table aside, and put down the bottle of Scotch he had brought across from the chateau.

'Looks like you'll be needing this,' he said and looked at Dupree. 'You have been a busy little detective. All I can see are police cars coming and going at all hours. One just left and it's almost midnight. Any progress?'

'A little, but not enough. As you know, the first forty-eight hours are critical. After that ...' Dupree shook his head and shrugged. He had set up his laptop on the kitchen table and was using the cosy kitchen as his makeshift office. He still had problems with his bandaged hands, but was rapidly improving. What he found frustrating and most difficult to deal with, was being unable to leave the cottage and follow the investigation in the field. He had never been a desk man, but that was precisely what he had become. Necessity was a cruel teacher.

Jack pointed to the mountain of files on the table. 'I can see Lapointe has kept his word, and you in the loop and definitely in the harness.'

'He sure has, and that's what keeps me going.'

Jack walked over to the Welsh dresser, took out two glasses and opened the bottle. 'Nothing new, then?'

'I wouldn't say that,' said Dupree and reached for a large photograph on the table in front of him. 'I am more than ever convinced that the Black Widow has made a comeback.'

'The mysterious predator in the shadows strikes again? What makes you say that?'

'If you pour me a big one, I'll tell you,' said Dupree and handed the photograph to Jack.

'*Good God!*' said Jack. 'Is that what I think it is?' He poured two large whiskies and handed one to Dupree. 'Cheers.'

'I couldn't tell you about this before. We kept it under wraps as a possible lead until now. That's why there was nothing about this in the press briefings.'

'I can understand that,' said Jack and gulped down his Scotch. 'That's how they found the ...?'

'Exactly as you see it.'

'Jesus. Who would do a thing like that?'

'Do what thing?' asked Countess Kuragin, who had overheard the remark. She closed the front door behind her and put the cheese platter she had brought across from the chateau on the kitchen bench. 'A late-night snack for hungry sleuths burning the midnight oil.'

Jack put the photograph back on the table and turned it over. 'Nothing important,' he said, brushing the question aside and trying to sound casual.

'Don't patronise me, Jack! I know you ... So, what is it?'

Jack looked at Dupree. Dupree shrugged. 'All right. But you may not feel like any cheese after this,' said Jack, looking resigned.

'That bad, is it?' said the countess.

'It is.'

'Go on.'

'Looks like the killer has left something behind in the strong box for us to find.'

'Oh? What?'

'It's gruesome.'

'Come on, Jack, I'm a big girl. Tell me.'

'The murderer cut off the victim's, how do you say?' said Dupree, trying to come to Jack's assistance. 'Just show her the photo!'

Without saying another word, Jack handed the photo to the countess.

'*Mon Dieu!*' she exclaimed. 'That must have hurt!'

'I doubt it,' said Dupree. 'He was well and truly dead by then.'

'So, after they cut poor Monsieur Aubert's throat and he bled to death, they cut off his penis and put it into the strong box? What an indignity! Is that what happened?'

'Looks like it,' said Dupree. 'But obviously there's more to it than that. My colleagues don't agree with me, but I'm convinced this is a signature.'

'The Black Widow?' said Jack.

'Yes, I believe so.'

'Making a comeback? Exchanging plastic spiders for ...'

'Could be. The facts speak for themselves.'

'Can someone please tell me what this is all about?' said the countess and began to peel back the foil covering the cheese platter. 'I can recommend the Roquefort-sur-Soulzon, boys; superb,' she said, making a point.

'The king of cheeses,' said Jack and reached for a cracker.

'Says who?' asked Dupree, edging closer.

'None other than the philosopher Diderot, my friend. And he should know. He clearly gave it a lot of thought.'

Munching happily, Dupree told the story about Le Fantôme, the dramatic death of Celine LeBlanc in Monte Carlo and the Black Widow cold case.

'So, that's what you two are doing in here late at night. Raking over shocking old cases like this?'

'Yes, but with good reason,' said Jack. 'I agree with Claude; it definitely looks like there's a connection here.'

'I wish you could convince my colleagues,' said Dupree, laughing. 'Perhaps this will help.' Dupree turned his laptop around. 'Here, let me show you. This just came in.'

'What's that?' asked Jack.

'As you can imagine, the Paris police is always closely monitoring the dark web. Routine. They came across this just a few hours ago. Here, have a look.'

'Good heavens!' exclaimed Jack and pointed to the screen. 'The Fabergé egg!'

'You're right, *it is!*' said the countess, leaning forward for a better look.

'The auction started at noon and as you can see, it has already created a lot of interest. The bidding is up to eleven million euros right now, and rising.'

'You mean this is real?' asked the countess.

'Absolutely. Someone is auctioning the Imperial Fabergé egg stolen from the Amber Safe on the dark web right now, in real time.'

'Seriously? How does this work?' asked the countess.

'Quite simple really, and virtually impossible to trace. Bidders access a secure site and place bids. Like us, they can see what other bidders are doing and place their bids accordingly. There's a time limit, here: noon tomorrow. The owner gets in touch with the highest bidder through another secure site and a code, and they complete the transaction. Simple.'

'And this actually works?' asked Jack.

'Yes. Payment is usually by bitcoin.'

'And delivery?'

'Depends on the circumstances, I suppose. Up to the parties. You won't see anything about that here.'

'And the police can't do anything about this?'

Dupree shook his head. 'This server is perhaps somewhere in Russia or China. Secure and beyond reach. We tried, but we can't crack it.'

'So, the parties could be anywhere?'

'Correct,' said Dupree.

'Great! There goes my inheritance,' said Jack. 'Eleven million and rising; bummer! I need another drink.'

'Poor boy. So close and yet so far,' said the countess and poured Jack another Scotch.

'Perhaps not all is lost,' said Dupree.

'What do you mean?' said Jack, feeling sorry for himself.

'The auction here is another clue that points to the Black Widow.'

'In what way?' said the countess.

'We came across something similar just before Le Fantôme fell to her death. An auction just like this one.'

'Oh? What was that all about?'

'It was the case of *The Missing Little Shepherd*. Another sensational Monte Carlo robbery.'

'Fascinating. Sounds like a thriller,' said the countess, slicing another piece of cheese.

'*The Missing Little Shepherd* is a Russian painting by Mikhail Nesterov. It's worth a fortune. A Russian count, a distant Romanov relative by the way, was gambling in the casino in Monte Carlo and losing heavily. In the end, he put up the painting to be allowed to continue. It was the poker game of the year. Everyone was talking about it. To cut a long story short, the count lost and the winner walked away with the precious painting.'

'And?' said Jack.

'The winner only had it for a few hours, then his luck ran out too.'

'What happened?' asked Jack.

'He took the painting back to his hotel room. During the night, Le Fantôme struck and by the time the lucky winner woke up the next morning, *The Missing Little Shepherd* was gone.'

'Incredible. What a story!' said the countess.

'A few days later, *The Missing Little Shepherd* surfaced again. It was being auctioned on the dark web. Just like the Fabergé egg here right now. I think the bidding reached two million pounds. After that, nothing. We didn't solve the case.'

'Interesting,' said Jack. 'The similarities are striking but, of course, Celine is dead.'

'I know. But I don't think the Black Widow is. She has a new Fantôme, *a new Celine*, that's all. A much more dangerous one as we've seen; a killer.'

'You really think so?'

'I do. All of my instincts are pointing in that direction.'

'What about the investigation?' said the countess. 'Did you find anything at the Ritz? Any clues? Such a public place, surely ...'

'Dozens of people have been interviewed about that evening. There was a formal dinner at the hotel that night for over a hundred surgeons from all over the world. All dressed in dinner suits. And there's a real problem with security cameras,' said Dupree.

'In what way?' said Jack.

'Guests in hotels of this calibre don't like CCTV, certainly not in the bars and dining areas, not even the corridors. Privacy issues. The hotel knows this and the cameras are positioned accordingly, and at times even turned off altogether.'

'Not helpful,' said Jack.

'Definitely not. As you can imagine, we looked at many hours of material.'

'What about Aubert? There must have been a woman involved. The circumstances ...'

'Quite. Again, a dead end. Aubert mingled with guests every night. He spoke to many women and shouted drinks all over the hotel like the captain of a ship. It was his job and he was quite a ladies' man. The staff couldn't tell us anything specific, except for one particularly stunning young woman who was briefly seen with Aubert that night.'

'Anything?' said the countess.

'Not really. Descriptions vary and nothing on CCTV. However, there's one image that has caught our attention: this one here.' Dupree reached for another photo on the table and held it up. It showed a grey-haired man in a dinner suit walking towards the exit at one twenty-five am.

'What about him?' said Jack. 'All the men look the same; dinner suits.'

'Look at his bag. Here's a close-up.'

'A surgeon brought his medical bag to dinner?' said Jack.

'Exactly. Not what you would expect, is it? We think this is the safebreaker leaving the hotel. What he's carrying is a tool bag, not a medical one.'

'With my eleven-million-euro Easter egg inside?'

Dupree nodded. 'Could be. But that's the end of the good news.'

'No identification possibilities?'

'Unfortunately, no. You can hardly see his face and we are sure he's wearing a wig.'

'Very brazen,' said the countess.

'Classic Black Widow,' said Dupree.

'Where to now?' said Jack and poured himself another Scotch. 'Another dead end, you think?'

'Not necessarily.'

'How come?' said the countess.

'These guys do trip up. Mistakes happen. It may be ever so subtle and hardly noticeable, but it happens, and I intend to be there when it does. I'm convinced we are dealing with the same operators who, it shames me having to say this, did business with my son that started it all, burned down my home and killed him. I am very sorry it has come to this, but it's all connected. Surely you can see that?'

'I can, as a matter of fact,' said Jack. 'I feel the same way. Be damned if someone will cheat me out of my inheritance and get away with it!'

'Let's drink to that,' said Dupree and awkwardly raised his glass.

37

Celebration lunch at La Closerie des Lilas, Paris: 13 February 2017

'We really have to leave right now if we want to make it to lunch,' said the countess as she walked into the conservatory. Wearing her full-length Russian fur coat and stunning silver fox hat she had worn to Madame Petrova's open-air funeral, Countess Kuragin was certain to turn heads wherever she went.

Bleary-eyed and tired, Jack sat in his usual chair, glued to the screen of his laptop. He had stayed up all night following the auction on the dark web and feeling sorry for himself. 'Wow! This should give even Mademoiselle Darrieux a run for her fashion money,' he said, turning around.

'You think so?' said the countess, pirouetting slowly.

'The bidding has reached a staggering nineteen million euros with a few hours still to go. Unbelievable!' said Jack, shaking his head. 'More information about the notorious Easter egg has been released during the night, no doubt to create more interest and drive up the price, and it seems to have worked. Quite spectacularly, in fact.'

'In what way?'

'Well to begin with, the mysterious Imperial Fabergé egg has now been given a name – *Rasputin*. That alone created a flurry of activity, which reached fever pitch when these pictures were posted. Here, have a look.'

Jack called up images of the surprise inside the exquisite master-piece, showing miniature portraits of Rasputin and Alexandra, separated by a gold cross.

'So, that was the surprise inside,' said the countess. 'How fascinating.'

'It sure is, and it pushed up the bidding by two million straight away. And then there are other dazzling close-ups of the magnificent workmanship and the spectacular gems used in the design. Someone knows what they are doing; teasing the bidders and loosening the purse strings. Very clever. And to think this could have been mine ...'

The countess put her hand on Jack's shoulder. 'Don't forget, a man had to die for this, in a most cruel way ...'

'You are right,' said Jack, to whom money and material things had never been important, and closed his laptop. 'That does put everything into perspective. This is a world of slippery crime, not fair commerce, and we don't play within those circles or by their rules. Let's go and have that celebration lunch with Mademoiselle Darrieux. I could certainly do with some laughter.'

'That's the way,' said the countess, pleased to see a change in Jack's dark mood. 'We'll take the Bentley.'

'Of course. Arriving in style, especially the way you're dressed. We can't disappoint Adrienne, can we? Especially now that she has become the toast of Paris.'

'And don't forget, you too are a Paris celebrity now. Rubbing shoulders with Isis on the front page. You are certain to be asked for an autograph, Jack,' teased the countess, smiling. 'Make sure you have a pen ready.'

Jack stood up and waved dismissively. 'I envy Isis.'

'In what way?'

'She had the good sense to return to London straight away before the media storm.'

'Come on, it won't be that bad.'

'You think so? Let's go and face the circus.'

Darrieux sat at her usual table surrounded by fans and curious diners, keen to get a glimpse of the colourful celebrity the whole of Paris had been talking about for days.

'Ah, here they come now,' said Darrieux, pointing to the entrance as Jack and the countess swept into the room. Applause erupted as Darrieux kissed first the countess, and then Jack on both cheeks.

This is like some bizarre play, thought Jack, trying to put on a brave face. *The Princess and the Aussie Drover.* In the commotion, he didn't even notice Darrieux' dazzling outfit she had carefully chosen for the occasion, and gratefully accepted a glass of champagne from the sommelier making a fuss. He asked the diners standing around like eager spectators watching a Cirque de Soleil performance, to kindly return to their tables.

Her face flushed and bursting with excitement and, Jack feared, at any moment out of her tight-fitting designer dress, Darrieux was in her element. 'I am so glad you could make it,' she gushed, holding up her empty glass to be refilled. 'I thought it was only befitting we should celebrate here, where it all began.'

'A lot has happened since our lunch on the day Jack showed you the music box letter,' said the countess, trying to make conversation.

'You can say that again,' mumbled Jack. 'Not much left to celebrate, and to think that was only a month ago.'

'The auction, of course,' said Darrieux and turned to face Jack. 'I heard. How awful.'

Jack shrugged.

'Are the police doing something about it?' Darrieux asked.

'Apparently, there isn't much they can do. We are dealing with a very brazen and sophisticated crime here. Unfortunately, dark web auctions are beyond law enforcement reach in this country.'

'I'm so sorry. Then let me cheer you up a little. I have some good news.'

'What about?' asked the countess.

'The questions Jack left with me a few days ago, which I promised to follow up with my contacts,' said Darrieux, sounding conspiratorial.

'You have answers already?' said Jack, looking interested. 'I could do with some good news.'

Within seconds, the outrageous, flamboyant socialite had once again turned into the serious author and researcher Jack had come to admire and respect. 'I have more than that,' she said quietly.

'Let's hear it.'

'I got in touch with an old acquaintance of mine, Konstantin Vasiliev, a Romanov specialist and handwriting expert. He lives in

St Petersburg and has helped me with research before. His knowledge of the final years of the Romanov dynasty, Rasputin and the Russian Revolution is astonishing.'

'The letters?' said Jack.

Darrieux nodded. 'I emailed him sample pages. One from each of the five letters.'

'The music box letter and the four in the safe?' interjected the countess.

'Yes. It didn't take him long to get back to me. He was very excited because according to him, the letters are authentic. Even without sighting the originals, he has no doubt that the handwriting belongs to Alexandra.'

'That's great!' said Jack and sat back. 'At least now, we have a reliable starting point and can dig deeper.'

'As for digging deeper,' said Darrieux, enjoying herself, 'I have more.' She pointed to her empty glass as the waiter walked past, and waited until he had refilled it and left the table.

'All the letters are incredibly significant because they follow the journey of the Imperial family all the way from the Alexander Palace to Yekaterinburg, their final, tragic destination.'

'Oh? How interesting,' said the countess.

'It's more than that; it's *history*! The first of the four letters in the safe was written shortly after the tsar abdicated and the Imperial family was placed under house arrest in the Alexander Palace at Tsarskoye Selo. Nicholas abdicated on fifteen March 1917. The letter was written in May 1917, two months later. The second letter is dated twelve July 1917, and was also sent from the Alexander Palace. After that, things become really interesting.'

Darrieux paused to catch her breath and took a sip of champagne.

'In what way?' asked Jack, hanging on Darrieux' every word as the pieces of the puzzle that had taunted him were slowly beginning to fall into place.

'The third letter was written in October 1917, and was sent from Tobolsk. You may not know this, but the Romanov family was moved from the Alexander Palace to faraway Tobolsk in Siberia in August 1917 for political and safety reasons, and lived in the Governor's Mansion in relative comfort until April 1918. After that, their lives changed for the worse and things began to go rapidly downhill.'

'In what way?' asked Jack.

'Rebellious Red Guards from Omsk – the regional capital – fighting with rival groups, civil unrest, political turmoil, the lot. As a result, it was decided to move the Romanovs again, further east from Tobolsk to Yekaterinburg, the capital of the Ural region, where they were eventually murdered in July.'

'How absolutely fascinating,' said the countess.

'Wait, it gets even better,' said Darrieux. 'The fourth letter is rather short and was obviously written in a hurry. It was sent from Tyumen and is dated twenty-eight April, just before the family boarded a requisitioned train to take them to Yekaterinburg. By now, the family had been split into two groups because young Alexei was too ill to undertake the arduous one hundred and fifty-kilometre journey by horse-drawn carriage from Tobolsk to Tyumen to catch the train. The river was still frozen, you see, and the ferries couldn't go. So, Alexandra went ahead with Nicholas and their daughter Maria, while Alexei and the other daughters remained behind until Alexei improved and they would be able to make the journey.'

'Incredible,' said Jack.

'You can see now how important it is to read and interpret these letters within the historical context and geographical background in which they were written,' said Darrieux. 'Without that, it is impossible to be accurate and get the true meaning. Without the history to fill in the gaps, these letters would be like a coat with huge holes in it.'

'I can see that,' said Jack.

'Konstantin agrees with you, by the way,' continued Darrieux, 'that there appears to be something big, something very personal and important involved here as far as Alexandra was concerned. Something that must have troubled her deeply because she refers to it, albeit obliquely, in all of the letters. And it is clear from the content that Bezukhova must have known what it was about. There is a common theme here, culminating in a desperate plea in the last letter, the one sent from Yekaterinburg. Now surely, that must be significant.'

Jack nodded, deep in thought. He had come to a very similar conclusion after trying to make sense of the cryptic passages, pondering their meaning over and over.

'Konstantin was particularly interested in the music box letter. The date is incredibly significant.'

'It was written the day before the Romanov family was murdered in the Ipatiev House,' said Jack.

'Exactly, and that has a direct bearing on the other questions you asked.'

'In what way?'

'Konstantin wanted to examine the entire letter before giving an answer. So, I emailed it to him. I hope you didn't mind.'

'Of course not,' said Jack. 'We have to get to the bottom of this.'

'You had specific questions about the possible meaning of certain words and phrases used by Alexandra, remember?'

Jack nodded.

'Well, Konstantin was able to suggest certain interpretations straight away. For instance, the reference to "our dear friend" definitely refers to Rasputin. There are countless examples in other correspondence and court records about this. The entire Romanov family often referred to Rasputin as "our dear friend".'

'Excellent! That ties in with the surprise in the Fabergé egg,' said Jack. 'You have seen it?'

'I have,' said Darrieux. 'The miniature portraits of Alexandra and Rasputin that have caused such a stir. I saw them on the Net; unbelievable.'

'And now the egg even has a name – *Rasputin*,' said Jack.

'Hardly surprising in the circumstances. All the famous Imperial Easter eggs have names. But there's more ...'

Darrieux turned to Jack, her face flushed. 'I can't begin to tell you how grateful I am for what you've done for me, Jack,' she said, tears in her eyes. 'You saved my life.'

'No, you saved your own,' said Jack. 'Isis and I just paved the way, and perhaps provided just a little encouragement,' he conceded, smiling.

'Very generous of you to say so, but we both know that's not the case. Without you, my life and reputation would be in tatters by now, and I wouldn't be sitting here.'

Jack looked at Darrieux and was wondering where this was heading.

'It therefore gives me great pleasure to be able to repay you, albeit in only a small way,' said Darrieux, her voice barely audible.

'What do you mean?' said Jack, surprised by her formal tone.

'I found something in the interviews I recorded with Madame Petrova.'

'Oh? What?'

'Something that could have a direct bearing on the hidden message we believe is buried in that final letter. A clue that could be the key to making sense of it all.'

'Seriously?'

'You know what it's like when you are lying in bed late at night, exhausted, but unable to go to sleep, going over certain things time and time again, because you feel you've missed something?'

'I know that feeling,' said Jack, laughing, 'just too well, I'm afraid.'

'That's exactly what happened to me the other night. Suddenly, I remembered something. It's only a brief comment by your great aunt. We were sitting in her apartment in the retirement home next to the piano. It was a beautiful, sunny morning, and she was telling me stories about her mother, Countess Bezukhova, and her time at the Alexander Palace and her friendship with Alexandra during those difficult times. That's when she mentioned it.'

'Mentioned what?'

'It's all about memories dealing with something quite remarkable when you look at it more closely.'

'Can you be more specific?'

'It's about Felix Yusupov and the Rasputin murder.'

'What about it?' said Jack, looking puzzled.

'There was this letter, you see.'

'What letter?'

'Yusupov wanted to explain his part, or the lack of it would be a better way to put it, in Rasputin's murder, but Alexandra refused to see him. So, what did he do? He sent her a letter instead.'

'And this is relevant because ...?'

'Apart from the circumstances surrounding the sensational Rasputin murder, Yusupov raised something else that could be hugely important in light of these letters we've just discovered and are trying to interpret.'

'What was it?' asked the countess.

'Madame Petrova was very clear about this. As you know, she had an exceptional memory about things that happened a long time ago. And on that sunny morning, she was particularly lucid. She remembered her mother giving her a detailed account of the contents of that letter. Apparently, Yusupov was very specific about something rather curious. He claimed that Rasputin had entrusted something important to him just before he died, and that he had asked him, no, *pleaded* with him, to deliver it to the tsarina as a parting gift.'

'Do we know if it was actually delivered?'

'Apparently it was, and Yusupov was trying to use this to ingratiate himself with Alexandra and to extricate himself from a difficult situation—'

'How interesting. Do we know what kind of gift we are talking about here?' interjected Jack.

'Unfortunately, Madame Petrova couldn't remember what it was, or perhaps her mother didn't tell her, but she did remember her mother telling her that Alexandra actually showed it to her, and that it was something of great historic significance that belonged to Russia and its people. And whatever it was had a name: *Mat' Rossiya*, Mother Russia. Now, surely that's significant, isn't it, because two of the letters specifically mention Mat' Rossiya?'

Darrieux paused to let this sink in.

'That's true, but is that it?' asked Jack.

Darrieux shrugged. 'Regrettably, yes, for now,' she said.

'Oh no. Another dead end?' said Jack, looking exasperated.

'Not necessarily. I mentioned all this to Konstantin and his reaction was quite remarkable.'

'In what way?'

'He became very excited. As soon as I mentioned the Yusupov letter, it triggered something in Konstantin. Apparently, such a letter exists and has survived in the Romanov archives. It has been studied extensively over the years and has been the subject of much speculation. Konstantin even remembered actually seeing the letter and indicated that he would follow it up.'

'How?' asked Jack.

'He said to leave it with him. A former colleague of his, a retired professor, is an expert on Rasputin. It may take some time because his friend has been quite unwell lately and lives in some kind of home for the elderly somewhere in the country. And let's not forget, they are both in their eighties. But it's certainly an encouraging lead, don't you think?'

'It sure is that,' said Jack. He reached for Darrieux' hand and squeezed it. 'Thank you, Adrienne, I really appreciate this. It's often the little things we come across that trigger something obscure, which somehow ends up making all the difference. These are the dominoes of history that tumble once you push the first one, until the curtain is lifted and all becomes clear. We make a good team.'

'Jack's right about that,' said the countess. 'I've seen him turn small, insignificant clues into surprising results. It's all about instincts and the courage and conviction to follow them. And Jack has all of that in abundance.'

'His books are full of it,' said Darrieux, beaming. 'Let's hope this is one of those occasions and I may be privileged to play a small part in it.'

'I'm sure you will,' said Jack, feeling better.

38

Le Club Barrière Paris: 16 February 2017

Zuzanna arrived at the exclusive Club Barrière Paris in 104 Avenue des Champs-Élysées, a well-known casino popular with high rollers, just before midnight. She knew exactly where to find Malenkova and went straight to the room where Malenkova's favourite game – L'Ultimate Poker – was in full swing. The game, a variation of tradi-tional poker, offered players something new and exciting. Instead of playing against one another, the game gave players the opportunity to beat the bank, represented by the croupier.

There were four players left at the table, surrounded by curious onlookers watching the game as it was about to reach its climax. The mountains of chips on the table told Zuzanna that the bets had been huge, and the stakes worth thousands of euros.

From time to time, Malenkova, who rarely left her home, treated herself to a night of gambling, usually after a successfully concluded deal involving lots of money. It wasn't unusual for her to take a hundred thousand euros in cash to the casino and gamble through an entire night, and well into the early hours of the next day. These occasions were a rare breakout from her self-imposed, almost monastic existence, and provided a much-needed release from the monotonous routine that dominated her life.

However, there was another, quite different reason for these highly charged sessions. Malenkova did some of her best and most creative thinking when under extreme pressure, albeit self-imposed. She also made some of her best gambling decisions at the same time. Gambling and taking risks were in her blood. It was about instinct, gut feeling and self-control, and Malenkova, a highly skilled and disciplined player, had plenty of all three.

When looking at the plain, middle-aged woman in the simple black dress staring at her cards through thick glasses, one could have been forgiven for underestimating her, as many players meeting her for the first time often did to their detriment.

The game was reaching its high point as the croupier began to turn over his cards one by one. Suddenly, there was deathly silence in the room as the players began to compare their hands to that of the bank's. Malenkova, her pudgy face inscrutable, was the last player to show her cards. None of the other players had a better hand than the croupier, and it seemed certain the bank would win again.

Slowly, Malenkova put her cards on the table one by one, to reveal a run of five cards of the same suit – a straight flush – and a ripple of envious excitement eased the atmosphere in the room. Not only had Malenkova recovered all her initial stakes, but her winnings amounted to fifty times her wager: two hundred thousand euros in total.

Zuzanna walked up to Malenkova. 'Congratulations! That was amazing,' she said. 'Your lucky day.'

'And yours too,' said Malenkova, struggling to stand up.

Zuzanna helped her and handed her the walking stick. 'Oh? In what way?'

'I transferred a million euros into your bank account today; your bonus. An early Easter present.'

'Are you serious?' said Zuzanna, looking incredulous.

'Absolutely. Victor and I concluded the Fabergé deal shortly after the auction and today is payday. Fifteen million euros.'

'Fifteen? How come? The auction reached nineteen million.'

'Let's go over to the bar and I'll explain.'

Malenkova gave the croupier a thousand-euro tip and assisted by Zuzanna, she walked awkwardly over to the bar and ordered a bottle of cognac.

'I must say, I was surprised when you told us to return to Paris so soon after the assignment. Isn't that risky? No doubt there's a good reason for this?' said Zuzanna, sipping her cognac.

'There is. You'll understand why in a moment. As you know, I did say this would be our last assignment. That's why the large bonus, but now there's more. Much more.'

'I'm a little overwhelmed,' said Zuzanna, 'and I don't quite know what to say, but thank you for your generosity.'

'You earned it. There's been a change of plans.'

'I suspected that. In what way?'

'You did as I asked? With Anielka, I mean?' said Malenkova, ignoring the question.

'Yes, of course. We drove back from Grenoble and went straight to the accommodation you arranged for Anielka in Montmartre. A bedsitter in the artist quarter. She's there right now, working on her new persona, just as you asked. By the way, the change in her appearance is remarkable. The short black hair has transformed her, but she's as striking as ever.'

'Excellent! How did she take it?'

'Very well. Her reaction was exactly as you predicted. In fact, she embraced the idea of reinventing herself. I told her there was another important assignment waiting for her, and all because she had done so well in the previous one. I must say, your phone call made all the difference. She was very excited about your praise and show of confidence in her. She didn't stop talking about it for days, but not once did she mention the murder. She behaved as if it never happened. Strange, don't you think?'

'Not really. Classic psychopathic behaviour. I was hoping that would be the case, because Anielka is the key to what I have in mind.'

'Can you elaborate?'

Malenkova paused, poured herself another cognac and looked pensively across to the gambling tables. 'You know I don't like to be defeated, but that recent, very public declaration by Darrieux was a defeat, no doubt about it, albeit a temporary one. We thought she would do our bidding, provide us with information and keep dancing to our tune. Not so. What she did was a very clever move that took the wind out of our sails. Quite humiliating.'

'You're right, it did that,' conceded Zuzanna.

'Unfortunately, what that means for us right now is this: that crucial source of information is no longer available to us, but I am a fighter. I don't give up easily, and there's always another way.'

'I don't understand,' said Zuzanna. 'You just sold the Rasputin egg for a fortune and said this would be our last assignment. Does any of this therefore matter?'

'Oh yes, it does.'

'Why?'

'Because Victor and I have made a deal.'

'What kind of deal?'

'As you know, I'm convinced there's something really big involved here, much bigger than the Imperial Fabergé egg we just sold. That was only the sideshow, the main event is still to come.'

'What makes you say that?'

'Instinct mainly, and all the little snippets of information we've gathered so far, most recently through Darrieux about Rogan and what he's up to. He, too, can sense it, I'm sure of it, but of course, he's much better positioned at the moment than we are to make progress and solve this mystery.'

'The letters?'

'Yes, and especially the letters we unfortunately left behind in the safe, which Rogan has access to and is working on right now. You do remember what Darrieux had to say about that during your last conversation with her?' said Malenkova.

'Yes, of course. She was very clear about this: Rogan had certain specific questions he wanted her to follow up for him. No doubt through her contacts, and we know she's very well connected, especially in Russia.'

'Quite, and all those questions point in one direction: the final days of the Imperial family, more specifically Alexandra and what she was so desperately trying to tell her friend in that farewell letter from Yekaterinburg.'

Malenkova paused and took a sip of cognac.

'That's the key to all this,' she continued. 'And after having lost the Fabergé egg in such dramatic circumstances, Rogan will be more determined than ever to pursue this. From what I've found out about him so far, he won't let go until he's found all the answers, trust me.

And I intend to be standing right next to him when he does. Fascinating, don't you think? A puzzle worth pursuing.'

'And how, may I ask, are you planning to do this?'

A rare smile spread across Malenkova's face. 'With Victor's help,' she said quietly.

'I see. So, what about that deal you made with him that is worth four million?'

'I'll tell you when he gets here.'

'*Gets here?* Who?'

'Victor. It's payday, remember?' Malenkova looked up and waved. 'Here he comes now.'

So, that's why we're all here, thought Zuzanna. She had been wondering about that. She watched the elegantly dressed man wearing a dark, pinstriped suit and silk tie walk confidently towards her. In his sixties, shortish, but powerfully built, with a shock of fair hair and a craggy face dominated by prominent cheekbones and restless, slanted eyes that appeared a little too close together, the man radiated power and danger.

'Frieda, I hear you had quite a win,' said Sokolov and embraced Malenkova. 'And I'm not talking about the auction. I believe you know Martin Charpentier?' Sokolov pointed to the elderly man standing next to him.

'Of course,' said Malenkova. 'No-one knows more about Fabergé than Martin. We've done business in the past.'

She's doing the handover here, right now, thought Zuzanna. *Brilliant!*

'So, why don't we get business out of the way first, and then we can have a quiet chat?' said Sokolov.

'Good idea. This is my assistant,' said Malenkova, introducing Zuzanna.

After politely shaking Zuzanna's hand, Sokolov turned around and spoke briefly in Russian to a huge man – obviously his body-guard – standing behind him. 'Ivan will find a quiet corner for us and make sure we are not disturbed,' said Sokolov, smiling. 'Drinks any-one?'

Used to being in control, Sokolov had taken charge of the situation.

Once they were seated at a table at the back, well away from others and out of view of the CCTV cameras trained on the gambling tables, Malenkova opened her tote bag, pulled out a small, soft leather pouch and, without saying another word, placed it on the table in front of Charpentier. 'It's all yours, Martin,' she said and sat back.

For a long, tense few minutes, Charpentier peered inside and, without taking it out of the pouch, slowly ran his fingertips over the jewel-encrusted egg like a physician exploring the body of a patient. Those sensitive fingertips transmitted information accumulated over a lifetime of studying Fabergé masterpieces all over the world, to a brain that had carefully processed all the intricacies and details of the unique designs and craftsmanship that constituted an authentic Fabergé piece. When it came to authenticating such a piece, Charpentier's word was final and accepted not only by collectors, but by auction houses, museums and insurers alike.

After what seemed an agonisingly long time during which no-one said a word, Charpentier put the pouch back on the table, looked at Sokolov and nodded.

'Thank you, Martin, there's no need to detain you any longer,' said Sokolov breezily. Aware that he had been dismissed, Charpentier stood up, nodded to Malenkova and Sokolov, and left.

'Aren't you going to have a look?' said Malenkova.

'Not here. There will be plenty of time for that later. I'm flying back to Scotland straight away. I don't like Paris.'

'It must be nice to have your own plane,' said Malenkova with a mock sigh.

Sokolov reached for his phone and made a call. 'Done,' he said, and slipped the phone back into his pocket. 'Should be in your account by about ... now. If the boys in the Virgin Islands have done their job, that is,' he added, laughing. 'We agreed fifteen, right? Care to check?'

Malenkova nodded and turned to Zuzanna. 'Would you mind?'

Zuzanna reached for her phone, called up Malenkova's Swiss bank account details and nodded. 'Fifteen, just arrived.'

'Congratulations, Victor,' said Malenkova. 'You won't regret this.'

'I hope not. Let's drink to that,' said Sokolov, and handed the pouch to his bodyguard.

Ivan poured Sokolov a shot of vodka from the bottle he had ordered earlier, and handed the tumbler to his boss.

Nostrovia! said Sokolov and held up his glass.

Nostrovia! said Malenkova and gulped down her cognac, the warm, burning sensation tingling down her throat, making her feel more alive than she had felt in months.

'Now, tell me what you have in mind,' said Sokolov and handed the empty glass to Ivan, who dutifully refilled it at once.

Two hours later, Malenkova and Zuzanna sat in the back seat of the hired limousine taking them home. Sokolov had left earlier because he didn't want to be seen leaving with them.

'What a fascinating man,' said Zuzanna. 'And boy, can he drink! A whole bottle of vodka in an hour without any signs of even the slightest intoxication.'

Malenkova laughed. 'That's Victor,' she said. 'The only intoxication he knows is money and power, but don't be deceived by his charm. This is a dangerous man, believe me. I've seen him in action. Do you know what Sokolov means in Russian?'

'No, tell me.'

'Bird of prey. The name says it all.'

'Do you trust him?'

'Only his greed, and that is always reliable.'

'I'm sure you're right.'

'If I'm right about Rogan and the letters,' said Malenkova, pensively, 'and what they mean, then the rest of this saga will play out in Russia. I'm sure the answers are to be found there and nowhere else. And that's when we need Victor and his connections.'

'Is that why you gave him a four million discount?'

'Four million, you say?' said Malenkova, raising an eyebrow. 'Not really. The genuine bidding stopped at fifteen or so. Let's say I "encouraged" the final bids. I have a few well-heeled friends who owe me a favour ... or two.'

Zuzanna shook her head, amazed. 'You fixed—'

'No, I *bought* a partnership,' continued Malenkova. 'Because without Victor, I don't think we can do this. And if we find a pot of gold at the end of this rainbow, he and I will share it fifty-fifty. If there's nothing there, we walk away. That's the deal. There aren't many men like Sokolov around who would go for something like that. You need balls of steel and an ego as big as Kilimanjaro to go through with something like this and I can assure you, Victor has plenty of both.'

'You still haven't told me how we can possibly deliver what you promised him,' said Zuzanna.

'You mean having a source close to Rogan that will provide us with all the information we need to know to crack this?'

'Precisely. Wasn't that a little hasty?'

'Hasty? I don't think so. Ambitious? Perhaps, but that all depends ...'

'On what?'

'Anielka.'

'*Anielka?* In what way?'

'How well she carries out her next assignment.'

'What's on your mind?'

'Celine and Count Orsini. Monaco. Just after you started.'

'*You can't be serious!*'

'But I am.'

'Celine pulled that off because there were special circumstances.'

'There are always special circumstances.'

'Are you seriously suggesting that Anielka could pull off something like that?'

'I am, and we are already working on it. *The new persona?*

'What, the cute, impoverished Polish art student living in a bedsitter in Montmartre, trying to make her way as a serious artist in Paris?'

'Precisely. I have read all of Rogan's books and most of what has been written about him on the Net. I think I know enough about the man to make this work.'

Zuzanna looked at Malenkova. 'You never cease to amaze me,' she said, shaking her head.

'The prize always belongs to the bold and the brave prepared to take risks. Big ones. And what I have in mind here is about as big a risk as you can take. I have no doubt Victor will like it and that's all that matters for now. But something tells me we haven't much time. We have to move fast.'

'How fast? How much time have we got?'

'Couple of days, that's all.'

'But we'll need time to prepare?'

'I have done most of it already. Rogan's movements are very predictable. He's a man of routine, just like me. We know all we need to know. All you have to do is prepare Anielka for her new role, that's it. Do you think you can do that?'

'Yes, I think so. She's very keen.'

'Good. This is something big, I tell you. I can feel it in my bones,' said Malenkova, sounding excited. 'And if we pull this off, we'll make history. That's why Victor is so interested in this. That's what's in it for him.'

'And you; what's in it for you?' asked Zuzanna.

Malenkova took her time before giving her answer. '*Feeling alive,*' she said quietly, and watched the raindrops march along the fogged-up car window like tiny beads of coloured glass.

39

Kuragin chateau: 18 February 2017

Jack put on his bomber jacket and scarf and picked up the countess's car keys that were usually kept on a small table near the front door.

'What a glorious morning,' said the countess. 'Love that mist. Are you going out?'

'Just the usual. Into the village to get the paper.'

'Could you get a few croissants from the baker?'

'Sure, but I may be a while. You know how Pierre loves to chat.'

'You don't mind, admit it, especially when he offers you a morning Armagnac under the table.'

'You know me too well,' said Jack, laughing, and headed for the door.

Jack started up the BMW, drove across the moat, turned right and followed the quiet country lane leading to the village. He opened the car window to let in the fresh morning air, took a deep breath, and turned on the radio. As he came around a blind corner and the road straightened up again, Jack noticed someone waving frantically in the distance. Jack rarely met anyone along that lonely stretch of road surrounded by fields, especially not on a Saturday morning.

'Here he comes now,' said Zuzanna, adjusting her binoculars. She stood on the crest of a small hill nearby and watched the car approach. 'He's slowing down,' she said into the speakerphone in the breast pocket of her jacket.

Malenkova was listening intently on the other end of the line. She knew the next few minutes were critical. After that, she was confident the situation would take care of itself and have a momentum of its own.

Half an hour earlier, Zuzanna had helped Anielka stage a roadside accident, right down to a dented fender that blocked the front wheel and incapacitated the scooter. At the same time, they added a few superficial injuries: a little cut to the forehead, a bruised elbow poking through holes in the jumper, and torn jeans with a bleeding knee.

Something's wrong, thought Jack and slowed down. As he came closer, he could see a scooter lying on its side in a ditch by the roadside. A tall young woman in a short red coat stood next to it, waving and looking distressed. She was pressing what looked like a handkerchief against her forehead. Jack stopped the car and got out.

'Are you all right?' he said, looking concerned.

'Thank God you came along! I'm freezing,' said Anielka.

'What happened?'

'I lost control over there on the ice; that was it. I must have been lying in the ditch here for a while ...'

'Let me have a look,' said Jack. 'Nothing broken; that's good. Nasty cut, though. Look at you, you are shivering.'

Jack went back to the car, opened the boot and took out a blanket. 'Here, let's put this over your shoulders. That's a start. What on earth are you doing out here? This lane isn't going anywhere.'

'I must have taken a wrong turn.'

Jack opened the passenger door. 'Sit down in there,' he said, 'and I'll have a look at your knee.'

What a stunner, thought Jack, finding it difficult to take his eyes off Anielka's face as he carefully tore away the bloodstained denim and examined her knee. 'I've seen worse. You won't need an ambulance, but let's get you cleaned up. You can't stay here; you'll freeze to death. And that thing isn't going anywhere.' Jack pointed to the scooter. 'I live just up the road.'

He's very good looking, thought Anielka, sizing up Jack as he got to his feet. *Love that voice and his accent.* 'Thank you,' she said. 'I could kill for a hot drink.'

'Coming up,' said Jack.

'Could you get my stuff? *Please?* I can't afford to lose it.'

Jack walked over to the scooter and picked up a small leather bag that must have been strapped to the luggage rack, but had come off during the crash. Then he saw something else lying on the ground next to the scooter. 'What on earth is that?' he said. He picked up a strange-looking contraption and held it up.

'That's my easel. It unfolds. I can show you.'

Jack shook his head. 'You're a painter?'

'Yes. The light was so beautiful this morning, so I took off.'

Amazing girl, thought Jack. He put the bag and the easel into the boot and got into the car. 'I'll get someone to pick up your scooter later,' he said. 'Let's go and get you that hot drink.'

'She's in,' said Zuzanna. 'Just as you predicted. He just turned around and is heading back.'

'Excellent,' replied Malenkova. 'I think we can safely leave the rest up to her, don't you?'

The countess heard a car pull up in the front and looked out the kitchen window. *Back already?* she thought. *Can't be.* Then she saw a young woman get out of the car with blood on her cheek. The countess took off her apron and hurried upstairs and outside.

'This is Alina,' said Jack. 'She had a small accident.'

'You didn't run her off the road, I hope?'

'Nothing like that,' said Jack and put down the leather bag and the easel by the door.

'I am Katerina,' said the countess. 'Here, let me have a look at you. He's always going too fast.'

Anielka looked at the countess gratefully, her large, cornflower-blue eyes reflecting the sunlight and giving her angelic face a special glow.

'It was my fault,' she said. 'There was some ice on the road, and my scooter ...'

God, she's gorgeous, thought the countess. *One of those rare creatures who has it all. I would kill for those eyelashes.* 'Come, let's go upstairs and get you out of these wet clothes,' she said and took Anielka by the hand.

'She could do with a hot drink, and so could I,' Jack called out.

'Go down into the kitchen and put on the kettle. We won't be long. I was just making some muffins.'

The countess and Anielka returned twenty minutes later. Despite a loose black tracksuit top with NYPD emblazoned on the front and a matching pair of baggy pants that were far too short, tucked into ugg boots, Anielka looked stunning. The bandaid above her right eye gave her a rakish look that was accentuated by her prominent cheekbones and short hair combed straight back in pageboy style.

'Tea, coffee or hot chocolate?' said Jack. 'And my nose tells me the muffins won't be long,'

'What a wonderful place,' said Anielka as soon as she stepped into the kitchen. 'And a samovar on the table! My grandmother had one just like that in her kitchen, only smaller.'

'Where was that?' asked the countess.

'In her home in Zakopane in the Tatra Mountains. An old wooden cottage with a huge stone fireplace. I grew up there.'

'You are Polish?' said Jack.

'Yes. I was born in Krakow. My mother was Polish, my father Lithuanian.'

'How interesting,' said the countess. 'And you now live in France?'

'Yes, in Montmartre. I only arrived a week ago.'

'Why Montmartre?' said Jack.

'Many of my favourite painters lived and worked there. Picasso, van Gogh, Matisse, Renoir and, of course, Toulouse-Lautrec. I am hoping that some of their genius is still there, waiting to be discovered. And besides, I love the bohemian atmosphere of the place.'

'Makes sense,' said Jack. 'I love the place too.'

'But this isn't my first visit to France,' continued Anielka, inventing her past on the run. 'I worked here as an au pair. I fell in love with Paris then and have wanted to come back ever since. I'm hoping to go to art classes.'

'You are an artist?' said the countess.

'I paint and draw a little.'

'My daughter is a painter. She lives here with her son. She has a studio at the back. You must meet her.'

'I'd love to!' said Anielka. *A studio of her own?* she thought.

'Here's your hot chocolate,' said Jack and put a large mug in front of Anielka. 'That should improve things.'

Anielka looked at the countess. 'Thanks for the clothes and your hospitality.'

'You are welcome. The clothes belong to Anna. She's not quite as tall as you, but it'll do the job.'

'Look, here comes Claude,' said Jack, pointing out the window. 'Must have smelled the muffins.'

Moments later, Dupree entered the kitchen. 'You did say eleven,' he said. 'Smells wonderful. Oh, I see you have visitors.'

'Come in Claude, this is Alina,' said the countess.

'I found her by the side of the road this morning,' said Jack cheerfully. 'She had a little accident.'

'Monsieur Dupree lives in the cottage,' continued the countess. 'You passed it on your way in. He was involved in a terrible fire a short time ago. His home in Montmartre burned to the ground.'

'I am so sorry,' said Anielka.

Dupree held up his bandaged hands. 'As you can see, I am in rehabilitation,' he said.

'Claude used to look after all of our clocks here in the chateau,' said the countess. She opened the oven door and pulled out a tray of muffins, filling the kitchen with a mouth-watering aroma of toasted almonds and cinnamon. 'Ready.'

'As you can see, your timing was perfect, Alina,' said Jack. 'More chocolate?'

Dupree kept watching Anielka. Years of policing and dealing with stressful situations and violence had given him a unique insight into the criminal mind and a finely honed sense of detecting danger. And what he could feel radiating from the young woman with the angelic face sitting opposite, was raw danger. At first, he tried to shake this off as nonsense, but the feeling kept returning with stubborn persistence, and instead of fading, it became more urgent and pronounced.

After Anielka had finished her second mug of hot chocolate and devoured three muffins, the countess put the last two on a tray with a cup of tea. 'Come, let's take this to Anna,' she said.

Dupree excused himself and said that he was expecting Lapointe with some news.

Anielka turned to Jack sitting next to her on the bench. 'Where can I find my bag?' she asked. 'I would like to show Anna my drawings.'

'I'll show you; come.'

Anna spent most of her time in her studio – a converted conservatory at the back of the chateau – alone, and painting. Since her ordeal in outback Australia and her dramatic rescue seven years ago that had almost cost her life, her condition had stabilised, but she had never fully recovered. Now in her early thirties, Anna had become an accomplished artist and her work was sought after by several galleries in Paris and beyond. Inward-looking and shy, with virtually no social skills, she had withdrawn from the outside world and expressed herself through her art. Since Tristan, who was the only one who could really understand her and reach her emotionally, had moved to Venice, Anna had become even more of a recluse.

As soon as Anielka entered the sun-drenched studio full of paintings, she felt a wave of excitement. Ignoring Anna, who stood next to her easel by a large window overlooking the garden, Anielka went from one painting to another, totally engrossed in what she saw.

Anna was watching her carefully. As Anielka came closer, a feeling of dread and fear began to claw at Anna's stomach that she hadn't felt in years, and she began to tremble. *Pity Tristan isn't here*, she thought. *I wonder what he would make of this?* Anna looked away, trying to ignore the demons assaulting her from all sides. *Danger. She exudes danger!*

'You painted all these?' said Anielka. 'Amazing!'

As soon as Anna turned around and looked into those cornflower-blue eyes, the demons retreated, and the fear fell away.

The spell was over, leaving only the striking beauty of the young woman in front of her.

'Yes, I did,' said Anna and put down her brush. 'Mum tells me you paint?' said Anna.

'I do, but compared to this ...'

Anna pointed to the sketchpad under Anielka's arm. 'May I have a look?'

'Sure.' Anielka handed Anna her sketchpad.

Anna opened the pad and stared at the first page. Then, taking her time, she began to turn the pages, one by one, her breathing becoming heavier by the moment.

'This is fantastic!' she whispered. 'I wish I could draw like that. Where did you study?'

'I didn't. I'm self-taught, I suppose.'

'That's even more amazing. And your paintings? Are they like this?'

'No, they are very different. I draw what I *see*, but I paint what I *feel*.'

'That's a real talent. Very few can do that,' said Anna. She pointed to a small table and two chairs by the window and took Anielka by the hand. 'Come, sit with me, we have a lot to talk about.'

Jack looked at the countess standing next to him by the door. They had watched the curious exchange with interest. 'We should leave them to it; what do you think?' said Jack quietly.

'I agree. This will be good for Anna. Let's go.'

Jack and the countess were sitting in the music room, drinking coffee, when Anna and Anielka walked in. The two artists had spent several hours in the studio, talking. By now it was almost dark outside and it was beginning to snow.

'Can Alina please stay the night?' asked Anna, unusually animated.

'Sure,' said the countess. 'It's too late to drive back to Paris anyway, and besides, look at the weather.'

'I don't want to impose,' said Anielka. 'But we lost track of time, I'm afraid.' Anielka turned to Jack. 'Anna told me about what

241

happened in Australia, and how you rescued her. I had no idea you were a writer!' she lied.

'He is that,' said the countess, smiling, 'and a lot more.'

Anielka shook her head, a troubled look on her face.

'What's wrong?' said Jack.

'I'm a little overwhelmed by what has happened today,' said Anielka and looked at Jack, her blue eyes sending a ripple of excitement through him that he hadn't felt in years.

'Could be that bump on the head,' said Jack, laughing. 'We've taken your scooter to a garage in the village. They'll repair it as soon as they can. I'll drive you back to Paris tomorrow and we'll take it from there. What do you say?'

Anielka reached for Jack's hand and squeezed it. 'That would be great, thank you.'

'It's all settled then,' said the countess. 'But you'll have to put up with my cooking for dinner. I gave cook the weekend off.'

'I think we can manage that,' said Jack. 'Anyone for more coffee?'

40

Quasimodo: 19 February 2017

Zuzanna joined Malenkova for breakfast in the dining room. It was six o'clock in the morning and still dark. This was most unusual because Malenkova wasn't an early riser. But what was an even bigger surprise was the reason for this early meeting: Malenkova was planning to go out, and Zuzanna had been told to have her car ready. For someone who lived in almost monastic isolation, a spontaneous decision like this was totally out of character.

Malenkova's housekeeper was serving breakfast when Zuzanna walked in. Zuzanna, who lived in a cottage nearby, had only left Malenkova's house a few hours earlier, after a very excited Anielka had phoned them with an update.

'Toast?' asked Malenkova and pointed to a basket covered with a serviette.

'Thank you. This is a little unexpected. Where are we going?'

'Visiting an old friend of mine.'

'Oh? Who?'

'Quasimodo.'

'The hunchback of Notre Dame? I didn't know he was still alive.'

'He's the best in the business.'

'What kind of business?'

'Forgery, and he will only deal with me personally.'

Zuzanna reached for the marmalade and spread generous lashings on her toast.

'And only this early in the morning?'

'No. There's another reason for that. Could you please pass the butter?'

For a while, Malenkova and Zuzanna munched in silence, until curiosity got the better of Zuzanna.

'It's about Anielka, isn't it?' asked Zuzanna.

'It is. It's about what she told us last night.'

'Oh?'

'Look, she got so much further with this than we could have hoped for,' said Malenkova.

'True. She met Rogan, he took her back to the chateau, she met the countess and was asked to stay the night. It doesn't get any better.'

'My point exactly. Rogan even showed her the Petrova music box, would you believe? Things will move very quickly now.'

'What do you mean?'

'This investigation has only one way to go. I had another look at the Petrova letter last night. It all points in one direction.'

'And what direction is that?' said Zuzanna.

'*Russia*. The answers we are looking for are to be found in Russia, and I have no doubt Rogan knows this.'

'So, what's next?'

'We've told Anielka to stay close to Rogan. I believe she can do this. Just look at the girl. From what I've been able to find out about Rogan, he will not be able to resist her. It's what comes next that worries me.'

'And what's that?'

'He's likely to go to Russia to follow the trail. That's what I would do. And I want to make sure that Anielka is able to go with him. Otherwise ...'

Zuzanna looked at Malenkova, amazed, and shook her head. 'You really think that's possible?'

'Yes, and that's why we have to move fast. I want to make sure everything is in place before she gets back to her flat later today.'

Zuzanna knew better than to ask questions. She put her serviette down on the table and looked at Malenkova. 'When do you want to leave?'

'Right now. Let's go.'

By the time Zuzanna pulled up in the deserted square in Montmartre, it was getting light and the houses were beginning to melt out of the darkness. It was also drizzling and bitterly cold. Two stray dogs were curled up in one of the driveways, trying to keep warm, and the view up to the familiar dome of Sacré-Coeur was obscured by dense fog drifting up from the Seine.

'Bleak, isn't it?' said Zuzanna and parked the car.

'It's early and it's winter. And besides, bohemian neighbourhoods like this are always bleak in the morning. Late nights come at a price: garbage bins overflowing with trash and empty bottles. I used to live not far from here after the Berlin wall came down in '89,' said Malenkova, looking dreamily across the square.

'I didn't know that.'

'Two years I spent here. It was tough going at the beginning, but I made some of my best contacts in the Paris underworld during that time. Emile was one of them. Come, let me introduce you to another.'

'Quasimodo?'

'Yes. Like Emile, he too is retired now, except when friends ask for a favour and pay handsomely for it,' said Malenkova, smiling and pointing to a small house on the other side of the square. 'He lives just over there; has done so for as long as I've known him.'

'But that's where Anielka—'

'I know. That's where I lived for two years. Same flat.'

'Is that why you chose that place?'

'I like dealing with people I know and can trust. Quasimodo owns the house. He rents out a flat at the back and one on the first floor, my old place, which has just become the new home of a young art student from Krakow called Alina.'

'You are full of surprises,' said Zuzanna, shaking her head.

'I like it that way. Surprises keep people on their toes. When I used to live here, Quasimodo's father was still alive. Now, he was an interesting character; a master forger. He spent several years in the penal colony of Cayenne—'

'French Guiana, Devil's Island?' interjected Zuzanna.

'Yes.'

'Like *Papillon?*'

'A bit like that, but unlike *Papillon*, he didn't have to escape. He was released in 1953, the year the prison was closed down, and returned to Paris a free man. He bought this house – no-one knew where the money came from – married his girlfriend, and a few years later Quasimodo came along.'

'Quasimodo? Can't be his real name, surely.'

'He's always been Quasimodo. You'll see why in a moment.'

When the door finally opened, the first thing Zuzanna saw was the head of a huge dog, growling at her. Before she could step back, a small hand reached out from behind the door and pulled the dog away.

'Come in and close the door,' said a voice. 'Enzo won't harm you once you're inside.'

'I hope he's right,' mumbled Zuzanna and held the door open for Malenkova. 'After you.'

'Coward,' said Malenkova and hobbled inside. 'I've met Enzo before. He's harmless.'

Quasimodo was a dwarf. Not quite as tall as the dog sitting next to him, barrel-chested with broad shoulders, a twisted spine and very short legs, he had a normal-looking head that seemed out of proportion with the rest of his deformed body.

'Good to see you, Frieda,' said Quasimodo as he looked up at Malenkova and shook her hand. 'It's been a long time. Come, let's go to the back.'

Malenkova didn't introduce Zuzanna.

As Quasimodo turned around, Zuzanna noticed the hump and smiled as the tiny man moved along the corridor with surprising agility, followed by his faithful dog.

The room at the back looked like something out of a doll's house. The chairs and the lounge were low to the ground, having been custom-made for Quasimodo. Zuzanna helped Malenkova sit down, which wasn't easy.

'I stopped apologising years ago,' said Quasimodo, pointing to the furniture, and climbed onto one of the chairs. His dog settled down next to him.

'No need,' said Malenkova. 'We are here to do business, not to drink tea. How did you go?'

'Finished.' Quasimodo pointed to the table in front of Malenkova. 'Have a look.'

Malenkova picked up what looked like a passport and examined it carefully. 'Perfect,' she said and handed it to Zuzanna. 'What do you think?'

'Amazing.'

'And the rest?' said Malenkova.

'All done. Driver's licence, everything you wanted.'

'Always a pleasure doing business with you, my friend, and thank you for arranging the flat.'

'Your old place. You are welcome. She's quite a girl. Now, if I were twenty years younger ...'

Zuzanna looked at Quasimodo, surprised.

'Look at your faces,' said Quasimodo, laughing raucously. *'It's a joke.'*

'She is that,' said Malenkova, ignoring the remark. 'In more ways than you can possibly imagine. And now, thanks to you, Anielka Kowalski has become Alina Dabrowski.'

'Keeping the first name similar is clever,' said Quasimodo. 'That's where most new identities slip up, but not with you, Frieda, eh?'

Malenkova opened her handbag, pulled out a wad of banknotes and put them on the table. 'Twenty thousand, as agreed,' she said. 'And please keep an eye on the girl. You know how to reach me.'

'With pleasure.'

'I can see Enzo is getting restless,' said Malenkova and began to stand up. 'Before we go, I would like to have a look at the flat upstairs before Alina gets back.'

'Sure, I'll get the keys.'

'And, of course, we haven't been here,' said Malenkova.

247

'Of course not,' said Quasimodo. 'Just like the old days, eh?'

'I wish.'

The stairs leading up to the flat were on the outside of the building and Malenkova had to stop several times to catch her breath.

'Well done,' she said as soon as they stepped into the compact bedsitter and looked around. 'That's exactly what I had in mind.'

'Thanks,' said Zuzanna.

Consisting of one long, narrow room with a tiny kitchen area and two tall windows facing the square, the small flat only had enough space for a large bed, a dressing table, a sofa and a wardrobe. A bathroom without windows was at the back. However, the most striking feature of the flat was the paintings covering the walls, giving the room a bohemian, arty look.

'With a bit of luck, she'll bring Rogan up here to show him her paintings as you suggested, and if she does, everything has to look authentic. A student pad doubling as a studio: untidy, full of girl stuff, canvasses and paintbrushes. Chaos, but oozing seductive charm.'

Malenkova paused, and pointed to the windows. 'The easel and the tubes of paint over there near the windows are a nice touch,' she said. 'Don't forget, Rogan's a writer and an experienced private investigator with an eye for detail. He would notice straight away if something was out of place or didn't quite fit, and ask himself why that was so. I would do the same.'

'What do you think of the paintings? Remarkable, aren't they?'

Malenkova walked over to the small side table next to the bed and put the passport and the driver's licence into the top drawer. 'I feel better now,' she said. Then she turned around and looked at the paintings.

'Amazing,' she said. 'She has a unique talent. I'm sure Rogan will be impressed. Excellent. We've set the trap. Now let's hope he takes the bait. Let's go.'

41

Montmartre: 19 February 2017

'My little flat's just over there,' said Anielka, and pointed across the deserted square, the cobblestones glistening in the rain. 'That's home for now. It's tiny, but I love it. Come, let me show you.'

Jack parked the BMW in front of Quasimodo's house, unaware he was being watched from inside. Malenkova and Zuzanna had left two hours earlier, satisfied that everything was exactly as it should be. Jack turned up his collar, took Anielka's bag and easel out of the boot and followed Anielka up the stairs, oblivious of the rain hitting his face.

'Let me get you a towel,' said Anielka as soon as Jack stepped inside. Jack put the bag and the easel down by the door and looked around. His eyes went straight to the paintings covering the walls. *Extraordinary*, he thought as he remembered what Anielka had told him about her paintings the night before: 'I draw what I see, but I paint what I feel.' *Anna and Alina have a lot in common; no wonder they got on so well.*

'What do you see, Jack?' asked Anielka and handed Jack a towel.

Taking his time, Jack wiped his face and then dried his hair. *What I see and what I feel here, are two different things*, he thought. Jack realised he had to choose his words carefully because these paintings were very personal.

'On the way here you told me that your paintings were a window into your soul. A few years ago, Anna told me something similar,' began Jack, and handed the towel back to Anielka.

'What do you *see*, Jack?' asked Anielka again, urgency in her voice. 'Tell me!'

'Anna was close to death when I found her in the remote Australian outback, not expected to live, and she had a small baby with her. It is almost impossible to imagine what she's been through

249

during the years she was missing, yet she survived. She never talked about it, not even to her mother. She put it all into her paintings. That's how she communicated; still does. That's why her work is so remarkable.'

Jack pointed to the large painting on the wall in front of him. 'I can see the same thing is happening here,' he said quietly, but didn't explain how he felt. The painting shocked him with its expression of extreme violence, anger and raw pain.

For a while there was silence in the room, the rain drumming against the windowpanes the only sound. Then slowly, Jack turned around and looked at Anielka standing behind him, afraid that he may have offended her. 'What's wrong?' he asked. 'Come here.'

Anielka was crying, her beautiful face reflecting pain. Jack put his arms around her and began to gently stroke her wet hair. 'What's wrong?' he repeated quietly, the warmth of her body pressing against his, sending a ripple of excitement to a long-forgotten corner of his private memory castle.

'You've seen it straight away,' whispered Anielka and looked at Jack, her cornflower-blue eyes now tinged with sadness.

'Seen what?'

'The dark side. You've been there, and so has Anna.'

'I don't know what—'

Anielka put a finger on Jack's lips and brushed her lips against his cheek, her hot breath tickling his nose. 'Shhh, not now, later,' she whispered and pulled away. 'Now, let me buy you that lunch I promised you. There's a lovely bistro just around the corner. The food is excellent and the wine cheap, but here in France, even the cheap wine is good, right?'

'Let's do that,' said Jack, surprised by Anielka's sudden change of mood, but also relieved, because he could sense the situation was quickly spinning out of control.

'I better get changed,' said Anielka and began to undress.

'I'll wait outside.'

'No need. I won't be a moment.'

Anielka threw her clothes on the bed and then opened her wardrobe. 'This will do,' she said and held up a pair of fresh jeans and a crumpled blue sweater that had seen better days. 'What do you think?'

'It will do just fine,' said Jack, shaking his head. *Super sensitive about her paintings, yet totally without inhibitions; remarkable,* he thought, admiring Anielka's athletic body as she got dressed.

'I hate ironing,' said Anielka. 'Let's go.'

After a delicious bouillabaisse followed by coquilles St Jacques, washed down with an excellent chablis, Jack got a little carried away and ordered a bottle of Beaujolais and some cheese. Relaxed, and fascinated by the exciting young woman sitting close to him, he drank a little too much as he listened to Anielka telling him what it had been like growing up in Poland as a teenager after her mother had died, with only her grandmother looking after her.

Anielka, a natural liar, knew instinctively how to create a plausible picture of a past that was pure fantasy and fiction, but would appeal to a romantic like Jack. She also knew that men loved to talk about themselves.

'But that's enough about me,' she said and put her hand on Jack's, and then took another sip of wine. 'It's definitely your turn. Katerina told me you grew up on a cattle station in Australia; is that right?'

'It is.'

'What was it like?'

'Hot, dusty, lonely and full of hardship,' said Jack, looking dreamily out the window. 'Especially during a drought, and a drought could last for years. That's when the cattle began to die and the bank manager came knocking.' Anielka listened intently as Jack told her about growing up in outback Queensland as a boy, where the nearest neighbour was two hours' drive away, and the nearest town further still. As Jack told Anielka more and more about himself, he unwittingly created an air of intimacy that played straight into Anielka's hands.

By the time they left the restaurant, it was late afternoon and getting dark. As Jack was heading for his car, Anielka stopped him. 'There's no way you are going to drive back to the chateau,' she said and grabbed his arm.

Jack looked at her, surprised.

'In this rain? After two bottles of wine and a cognac? I had my accident, be damned if I'm going to let you have one, too. After all you've done for me? And besides, we haven't finished talking about my dark side.'

'What do you mean?'

Anielka linked arms with Jack and gave him a quick peck on the cheek. 'Come upstairs and I'll show you,' she said in a seductive voice.

Looking a little worse for wear, Jack arrived back at the chateau just after eleven the next morning. Bleary-eyed and with a grey stubble sprouting on his chin and, of course, wearing the clothes from the day before, he had hoped to go to his room and freshen up before meeting the countess.

'Must have been some lunch,' said the countess and raised an eyebrow. She had seen the car pull up and was waiting for Jack in the foyer. 'Not like you to stay out all night like this.'

Jack had called the countess the night before and told her he would be staying in Paris because of the weather and because he'd had a little too much to drink, but didn't otherwise elaborate.

'I have something for you,' said Jack, ignoring the remark. 'It's in the car. I'll get it.'

Jack returned moments later carrying a painting. 'A thank-you present from Alina.' Jack placed the painting on top of a chest and stepped back. 'What do you think?'

'Incredible. Not what I would have expected from a young woman like her. And so different from her drawings.'

'We must show it to Anna.'

'Of course. Was Alina painting all night?' teased the countess.

Jack shook his head, but didn't reply.

'I thought not. You are a big boy, Jack, and it's none of my business, but you are a dear friend. She could be your daughter.'

'I know. All I can tell you is, I haven't felt like this in years.'

'Understandable. I saw the way she looked at you at dinner. The girl had made up her mind by then.'

'What about?'

'What do you think?'

'Come on ...'

'Jack, you are very naive when it comes to matters like this; trust me, I think this girl has a plan.'

'What makes you say that?'

'Intuition and experience.'

'What kind of plan?'

'Don't know. I just don't want you to make a fool of yourself and get hurt.'

'I'm happy to take that risk.'

'I know she's young, gorgeous and clever, but consider this ...'

'What?'

'If it's too good to be true, then, it's most likely too good to be true!'

'Isn't that a little cynical?'

The countess shrugged, and kept looking at the painting. 'Quite dark, don't you think?' she said, changing the subject.

'In that, I have to agree with you.'

'Be careful, Jack; that's all I'm going to say.'

'I'm used to living dangerously,' said Jack, his eyes sparkling.

'I know that but this is different, trust me. Not the kind of danger you're used to, or know how to deal with,' added the countess quietly. 'This is fire of a different kind.'

'Ah, well—'

'You are going to see her again, I suppose?'

'Yes, tomorrow. We are going to the Louvre,' said Jack cheerfully.

'How romantic. A lovers' outing followed by another long lunch, perhaps?'

'I hope so.'

'You know what you are, don't you?'

Jack shrugged. 'A middle-aged incorrigible rascal, punching above his weight?' he said, a smile creasing his face.

'You forgot *infuriating*.'

'Yes, that too.'

'Do you want some breakfast?'

'Oh, yes please. I'm starving!'

'I thought so; come.'

42

Gatekeeper's Cottage, Kuragin chateau: 20 February 2017

'I saw the light was on in the kitchen. You're up early,' said Jack as he stepped into the cottage. 'Coffee smells good.' It was still dark outside and dense fog hovered above the frozen pond like a shroud.

'You are chirpy this morning,' said Dupree. 'It wouldn't by chance have something to do with that stunning young woman you found by the roadside the other day?' Dupree raised an eyebrow and looked a Jack.

'News travels fast around here,' said Jack, looking a little sheepish.

'It sure does, my friend. Katerina must have said something to François, who said something to cook, who mentioned it to me last night. So, there you have it.'

'Indeed,' said Jack, but he didn't elaborate.

'I couldn't sleep last night,' said Dupree. 'You know when something keeps rattling around in your head and just doesn't want to let go?'

'I know that feeling just too well,' said Jack. He reached for the plunger on the kitchen table and poured himself a cup of coffee. 'How did your meeting with Lapointe go the other day?'

'As you can imagine, he's under a lot of pressure from all sides.'

'Understandable. A sensational murder like this in the heart of Paris – the Ritz of all places – doesn't come along too often, does it?'

'Everyone's screaming for results, especially the hungry news-hounds. Even the President has weighed in, putting more pressure not only on Lapointe and his team, but on my friend the Prefect as well. In fact, he just spoke to me a short while ago. He was up all night, too.

'Any progress?'

'Depends what you mean by progress; that's the problem. Lapointe is a first-class officer: meticulous, hardworking, highly respected.'

'But?'

'He's a traditionalist. His methods are very set in their ways and predictable. I fear this case needs more.'

'A little imagination and thinking outside the square, perhaps?' suggested Jack.

'Exactly. I did mention my hunch to him—'

'About the Black Widow?'

'Yes. He wouldn't have any of it. He thought the idea was absurd.'

'But you don't think so, do you?'

'No, I don't, and that's what the Prefect and I discussed just before you came in. We spoke about Lapointe and his methods.'

'And did your friend listen?'

'He did. In fact, he did more than that.'

'In what way?'

'He said I should follow my instincts and pursue my own line of inquiry, irrespective of what Lapointe may think or do.'

'That's great, isn't it?'

'It is and it's certainly unusual. I've been given a free hand, but I'll have to be careful.'

'In what way?'

'Not to step on toes, but with the Prefect behind me—'

'I like it,' Jack cut in. 'Congratulations. This is my kind of inquiry.'

'I know, and you of all people will understand where I'm going with this.'

'You've found something?'

'Perhaps. We have two, possibly three leads at the moment. A hair, a limp and a strange man in a casino.'

'Intriguing.'

'Lapointe and his team came up with two. One is a long shot of my own. Based on gut feeling; a hunch.'

'And that's what kept you up all night?'

'Yes.'

'Care to tell me about it?'

'Sure. Come over here.'

Dupree pulled his laptop across and called up the CCTV footage of the man in the dinner suit leaving the Ritz at one-thirty am on the night of the murder. 'Here, watch carefully,' said Dupree. 'What do you see?'

'Well, I see a white-haired, elderly man – quite distinguished-looking – in a dinner suit walking towards the exit. He looks like all the other men in the foyer. I believe they were all surgeons leaving after a conference dinner.'

'Correct. What else?'

'Then, of course, there's that case he's carrying. We discussed this before, because one wouldn't expect a dinner guest to be carrying such an item and it didn't look like some kind of medical or doctor's bag. It just didn't fit and you thought it could perhaps be a toolbox of sorts.'

'Correct again, but what else do you see? Think outside the square. Watch carefully. I'll play it again.'

Jack bent down for a closer look. 'The man is walking with a slight limp. It's hardly noticeable, but it's definitely there.'

'*Bravo!*' said Dupree. 'Exactly! And that's what's kept me up all night.'

'Why?'

'Because I remembered something.'

'What?'

'A case, a long time ago.'

'What kind of case?'

'A bank robbery, here in Paris about thirty years ago. We had a tip-off and caught the gang in the act. One of them, a notorious safebreaker, got shot in the leg as he tried to get away. He did time, of course, and walked with a limp after that. He was in and out of jail for a number of years, but eventually disappeared.'

Jack looked at Dupree, impressed. 'That's certainly thinking outside the square. And do we have a name for this man?'

'Not yet. I just mentioned this to the Prefect. He will send me the relevant files across. As I said, it's a long shot, I know.'

'Perhaps, but definitely worth pursuing.'

'The Prefect thought so, too.'

'And the other two leads?' said Jack.

'One's a forensics classic. A hair was found under one of the victim's fingernails, and it's not one of his own. It's a tiny piece, but it was possible to extract a DNA sample.'

'Belonging to his attacker?'

'Could be. Lapointe is following this up right now. It's the most promising lead he has at the moment.'

'And the third?'

'That's an interesting one. It came from quite a different direction and could be connected to the theft of the Fabergé egg and the auction on the dark web that followed.'

'In what way?'

'As you can imagine, our airports and customs monitor arrivals all the time, using facial recognition and other sophisticated methods. Mainly terrorism related.'

'Sure. So?'

'A few days ago, a private jet arrived here in Paris from Edinburgh. Nothing unusual about that, but who owns it and travelled on it that day was of interest, especially to customs.'

'And who was that?'

'Victor Sokolov, a shady character on our watchlist. He's a Russian billionaire who lives in the UK.'

'And this could be relevant?'

'It could.'

'In what way?'

'For several reasons. To begin with, Sokolov is an avid art collector, and apparently owns a few Fabergé Imperial Easter eggs—'

'Of course! I saw his name on the register,' interrupted Jack excitedly. 'He owns three! Worth millions.'

'Exactly. But wait, there's more. We have a number of popular casinos under surveillance here in Paris. Facial recognition picked up Sokolov a few hours after his arrival, entering a casino on the Champs-Élysées.'

'Interesting.'

'But more interesting still is the fact that he only stayed for two hours and, listen to this, *didn't gamble*!'

'So, what was he was doing there?'

'Meeting someone, I'd say. Casinos are favourite meeting places for people like that. After leaving the casino he went straight to the airport and flew back to Scotland. He only stayed in France a few hours. Strange, don't you think? And look at the timing. This happened just four days after the dark web auction. Coincidence? I don't think so.'

'Do we have any idea whom he might have met?'

'Lapointe is looking into it right now.'

'Well, at least that's something.'

'It is. When it comes to more traditional stuff like this, he's excellent.'

'But not good with more creative lines of enquiry,' said Jack.

'No. That's apparently my department.'

'And could I perhaps be of some assistance in that department?'

'I certainly hope so. If you can tear yourself away from your new girlfriend, that is,' said Dupree, chuckling.

Jack shook his head and gave a cheeky smile, but didn't reply.

'Look, Jack, it all began with that letter in the music box I discovered, right?'

'Correct.'

'And then Philippe ...'

'Yes.'

'And it all went from there. The visit from that mystery woman—'

'Who called herself Le Fantôme. And the fire?' said Jack.

'Exactly. And again later, a woman made contact with Mademoiselle Darrieux.'

'The same one, you think?'

'Quite likely.'

'And asked pointed questions about what I was up to. And it's all to do with the Petrova letters.'

'That's the key to all this, isn't it?' said Dupree. 'The common theme. And then came that brazen break-in and the Aubert murder and finally, the auction. This is all connected; it's obvious.'

'I agree,' said Jack.

'The same person or persons are behind this, no doubt about it.'

'And I am determined to find out who they are,' said Jack.

'So am I. Our reasons may differ, but the ultimate aim's the same.'

'It is. So, why not join forces?' said Jack. 'And see where all of this takes us?'

'I thought we already had,' said Dupree and closed his laptop. 'More coffee?'

43

Montmartre: 20 February 2017

Jack drove into the square just after noon and parked the car. The traffic had been heavier than usual and he was late. Anielka stood at the window and watched him get out of the car. *At last, she thought*, relieved. Anielka realised the first date was always a little unpredictable, especially with a complex man like Jack. After that, she would feel more comfortable and in control.

Jack hurried up the stairs, two at a time, and knocked on Anielka's door. Anielka opened the door and looked at him with hurt in her eyes. 'I thought you'd changed your mind,' she whispered and then threw her arms around him, pulled him inside and covered his face with kisses.

'I must try to be late more often,' said Jack, a little overwhelmed by the enthusiastic welcome.

'Shut up,' said Anielka and pushed Jack towards the bed.

'I thought we were going to the Louvre?'

'Art can wait. I don't know about you, but I can't,' said Anielka. She took off her top and gave Jack a gentle shove. He lost his balance and fell backwards onto the bed. Laughing, Anielka climbed on top of him and began to unbutton his shirt.

By the time they finished making love, it was almost two o'clock and it was too late to go to the Louvre. 'I'm starving,' said Anielka and nestled against Jack, the warmth of her body and the touch of her skin making his heart beat faster, conjuring up long-forgotten feelings of youth and wonder he hadn't experienced in decades. 'Same bistro for a late lunch; what do you think?'

'Good idea.'

'Can you stay the night?'

'Could be a problem.'

'What do you mean; why?' asked Anielka, trying not to sound alarmed.

'Tell you later. But first I have something to show you. Come.'

'What is it?'

Jack got out of bed, took Anielka by the hand and, without saying a word, pulled her up and guided her towards the window. 'There,' he said and pointed down into the square.

'What am I looking at?'

'Your scooter, silly. Can't you see it?'

'You had it repaired! How thoughtful of you! Where is it?'

'Right there, next to my car.'

'That's not my scooter. Mine is grey, not red and shiny.'

'I think you're wrong. We had it repainted.'

'You're having me on! That's a joke, right?'

Jack burst out laughing.

'You bought me a new one!' said Anielka and ran to the door. 'I want to have a look!'

'Better put something on first or you'll die of cold, or shock your neighbours and get arrested.'

Anielka stopped and turned around. 'How sweet of you,' she said, a tinge of sadness in her voice. 'No-one has done anything like this for me before.'

'No big deal,' said Jack, who had arranged with a dealer in Paris to have the new scooter delivered that morning. He reached for his trousers. 'The other one was a wreck.'

Anielka took the trousers out of Jack's hands and threw them on the floor. 'The scooter can wait and so can lunch, what do you think?' she purred and pushed Jack back onto the bed.

'I really have to go,' said Jack as they strolled arm in arm back to the flat after dinner. He had told Anielka about Madame Petrova and the strange letter found in the music box she had left him. He also spoke of the remarkable chain of events that had followed, and explained why he had to find out what it all meant.

As they entered the square, Anielka stopped next to a lamp post and looked at Jack. 'Is that why you can't stay the night?' she asked.

'It's more complicated than that. I have to go to Russia in a few days.'

'To *Russia?* Why?'

'To follow those breadcrumbs of destiny I told you about,' said Jack and gently stroked Anielka's hair.

'Where in Russia?'

'St Petersburg, to begin with. After that, who knows?'

'*St Petersburg?* The Alexander Palace, Catherine's Palace, the Hermitage! Oh, Jack, I've dreamt about visiting the Hermitage since I was a little girl. Can you imagine, all those treasures in one place?'

'It sure is an amazing city. I've been there before.'

Anielka looked at Jack, her eyes full of longing and wonder. 'Oh Jack, take me with you! *Please.*'

'You want to come with me?'

'Oh yes, please! I could help you find those "breadcrumbs of destiny".'

Jack burst out laughing. 'Are you serious?'

'Of course I am. Can't you see? It's meant to be!'

'It's not quite that simple, you know. You need a valid passport, visas—'

'I have a passport,' interrupted Anielka. 'It's upstairs!'

'I'll think about it.'

'You can't leave without me, Jack,' said Anielka. 'You've ignited a flame and I can't put it out. It will consume me if you don't take me with you.'

'Well, we can't let that happen, can we?' said Jack and gently kissed Anielka on her forehead.

PART III
THE WEEPING MADONNA OF KAZAN

44

Ipatiev House, Yekaterinburg: 16 July 1918

7:00 am

Alexandra opened her eyes, terrified. Covered in sweat and breathing heavily, she tried to sit up, but fleeting images of the frightening dream just wouldn't go. Alexandra could still see the troubled face of the Madonna. She could also see that the Madonna was weeping. Alexandra closed her eyes, trying desperately to banish the remaining fragments of the dream, and sat up. After a while, she opened her eyes and looked at the icon on the small table by the window as the first rays of the morning sun reached hesitantly through the dirty window like comforting fingers, caressing the heavy silver-gilt frame, and making the jewels on the riza sparkle with hope and the promise of a new, better day. Feeling calmer, Alexandra got out of bed, slowly walked over to the window and knelt down in front of the icon. Bowing her head, she began to pray and asked Kazanskaya Bogomater for guidance.

10:00 am

Privacy was impossible in the crowded quarters on the first floor of the house occupied by a family of seven, a doctor, Alexandra's maid, a cook and Nicholas's valet, all watched over around the clock by leering, uncouth guards. Once the chaotic, banal routine of the morning had settled down somewhat, Alexandra retreated to the bedroom she shared with Nicholas and Alexei, and began to write a letter to her friend, Countess Bezukhova:

I had a terrible dream last night. Kazanskaya Bogomater was looking down on seven open graves from above, and weeping. I woke up, terrified, and with a sense of foreboding making me tremble, I began to pray. I asked for guidance, and Kazanskaya Bogomater showed me the way, but I fear that something dreadful is about to happen to us.

Alexandra put down her pen and looked pensively out of the window, unable to banish the dark premonition clawing at her heavy heart. *This may well be my last letter to you, my dear friend,* she wrote, *as my only contact with the outside world is a kind nun from a convent nearby, who brings us food.*

4:30 pm

Sister Natalya arrived from the Novo-Tikhvinsky Convent with a basketful of food for the family, as she did most days. Yakov Yurovsky, a rough, vulgar man in charge at the Ipatiev House, stopped her at the front door, lifted the serviette covering the basket and examined the food. 'Very nice,' he said and helped himself to several large portions, which he piled on a wooden plate. 'You can go upstairs now.'

For several weeks, Sister Natalya, a simple, pious woman in her forties, had brought food for the Imperial family from the kitchens of the convent. This was tolerated by the guards despite orders that any kind of contact between the prisoners and the outside world was strictly forbidden. The reason for this forbearance was simple enough: Yurovsky enjoyed the tasty food from the convent, which was a welcome change from the meagre, boring rations issued to the guards. Besides, contact with a nun didn't seem to be a threat.

'I have to talk to you before you go,' whispered Alexandra after Sister Natalya had emptied her basket and put the food on the table. 'Come.'

Alexandra ushered Sister Natalya into her bedroom, careful not to attract the attention of the guards in the corridor outside who watched the family's every move.

'You have been a wonderful friend to us,' said Alexandra and placed her hand on Sister Natalya's arm. 'You have shown us kindness and compassion during these difficult times, and for that I am grateful.' Sister Natalya nodded, surprised by the intimacy of the moment, and looked at her former empress. 'With a heavy heart, I have a great favour to ask of you,' continued Alexandra, her face troubled. 'It may involve danger, but I have no-one else I can turn to, and I fear that time is running out.'

'What kind of favour, Your Majesty?' asked Sister Natalya, barely able to speak.

Alexandra pointed to the little table by the window. 'It involves that icon over there, and a letter,' she said, tears glistening in her eyes.

Midnight

Yurovsky put his hand on the pistol in his pocket and walked slowly upstairs. It was time to wake the family. Aware of the gravity of moment, he stood quietly in front of one of the bedroom doors, collecting his thoughts. Then, taking a deep breath, he knocked.

Dr Eugene Botkin, the family physician who had accompanied the Romanovs into exile, answered the door.

'Apologies for the intrusion,' said Yurovsky. 'There's unrest in town. For the protection of the family, we have to move everyone downstairs. It's no longer safe up here should there be shooting in the streets outside.'

Botkin nodded. For days, artillery fire had been rumbling in the distance and was coming closer. An anti-Bolshevik White Army had joined forces with thousands of former Czech prisoners of war on their way home, and was closing in on Yekaterinburg. A showdown appeared imminent.

'Please get everybody ready; there isn't much time,' added Yurovsky. 'I'll wait here.'

Dr Botkin went inside to wake the family and explain the situation.

17 July, 1:00 am

It took the family forty-five minutes to get ready. The first one to step out into the dark corridor was Nicholas. Dressed in a simple military shirt and trousers, boots and a forage cap, the former emperor was carrying a sleepy Alexei who, weakened by chronic haemophilia, was unable to walk. Alexandra came out next, followed by her daughters Olga, Tatiana, Marie, and Anastasia, the youngest.

All wore dresses without hats or shawls, and Anastasia cradled her pet King Charles spaniel, Jemmy, in her arms.

After the daughters came Dr Botkin and the three faithful servants who had shared the former Imperial family's imprisonment since their house arrest in the Alexander Palace the year before.

'We'll go down into the basement,' announced Yurovsky, leading the way down the stairs and out into the courtyard. Without saying a word, everyone followed him across the courtyard and then downstairs into a small room at the corner of the house.

As Alexandra entered the stark, claustrophobic basement room without any furniture, the feeling of dread that had so troubled her the night before returned, only this time it was stronger and more urgent. 'No chairs? May we not at least sit?' she asked, turning to Yurovsky.

'Wait here,' said Yurovsky and left the room. He returned moments later with two chairs. Alexandra, who suffered greatly from sciatica, sat down in one, and Nicholas put Alexei into the other. The daughters stood behind the chairs.

Aware of what was about to happen, Yurovsky began to give instructions. 'You stand here, and you over there,' he said until his eleven charges were spread out across the room in two rows.

'What's the meaning of this?' asked Alexandra, her voice hoarse.

'I have been instructed to take a photograph of you all,' said Yurovsky, 'because some of my superiors in Moscow believe you may have escaped.'

Alexandra looked at Nicholas and made eye contact. Nicholas shook his head, but said nothing. It was the way he had approached every crisis in his troubled life.

Yurovsky stepped back and looked around the dimly lit room. The four former grand duchesses stood behind their mother's chair, Dr Botkin and the three servants stood behind Nicholas in a bizarre tableau of impending death. Satisfied, Yurovsky turned around, opened the door and barked some instructions. Instead of a photographer, eleven men armed with revolvers crowded into the room, their faces flushed with excitement and the alcohol they had consumed.

1:15 am

Yurovsky stood in front of Nicholas, the silence in the room electric. He held a piece of paper in his shaking right hand, from which he began to read:

'In view of the fact that your relatives are continuing their attack on Soviet Russia, the Ural Executive Committee has decided to execute you,' pronounced Yurovsky in a shrill voice.

Nicholas placed his hand on Alexei's head and turned to face Alexandra, looking bewildered. *'What?'* he called out, refusing to believe what he had just heard.

In a hurry and slurring his words, Yurovsky repeated the order from the Ural Executive Committee. He then reached into his trouser pocket, pulled out a revolver and shot Nicholas in the chest, killing him instantly. The ice was broken and the brutal killing of the last tsar and his family had begun.

The eleven excited men standing behind Yurovsky began to fire, cursing and shouting obscenities. Each had been allocated a specific target and was aiming for the heart. Because there was little space in the crowded room and the noise from the gunshots deafening, the shooting was chaotic. Alexandra tried in vain to make the sign of the cross just before she died in her chair. Olga, who stood behind her, tried to do the same, but was killed by a single shot through the head.

Alexei lay on the floor, mortally wounded, but still alive. One of the men kicked him in the head, but the former tsarevich was still moving. Yurovsky stepped forward and shot the boy twice in the ear. The killing frenzy continued.

Demidova, Alexandra's maid, crawled along the back wall, bleeding. The executioners attacked her with bayonets until her mutilated body, cut more than thirty times, lay still in a pool of blood.

1:45 am

Yurovsky held up his hand, the acrid gunpowder smoke making him choke and his eyes water. The room fell silent and the men, many of them covered in blood, stood aside. Slowly, Yurovsky went from body to body, checking pulses. Satisfied there were no signs of life, he ordered sheets to be brought down from the bedrooms. One by one, the bodies were wrapped in the sheets, carried outside and thrown into the back of a waiting truck.

Just before the bodies were covered by a tarpaulin, one of the men discovered Anastasia's little spaniel, its head crushed, in the courtyard. Laughing, he carried it outside. The truck was already moving away, but the man ran after it and hurled what was left of the little dog into the back of the truck.

This senseless, pathetic act concluded one of the most brutal chapters in Russian history, which would leave an ugly stain on the soul of an entire nation and haunt it for generations to come.

45

***Carpe Diem*, Paris: 22 February 2017**

It was still dark outside, but Jack was already sitting at his desk in the conservatory. He was working on his itinerary for the upcoming St Petersburg visit, when his phone rang. It was Dupree calling from the Gatekeeper's Cottage.

'His name is Emile Fabron,' said Dupree, sounding excited.

'What are you talking about?'

'The safebreaker from the bank robbery. I got the files last night.'

'The long shot you mentioned the other day? The man with the limp?'

'Exactly.'

'And this is helpful?'

'Yes.'

'Why?'

'Because he's still around.'

'Do you know where you can find him?'

'Yes. He lives on a houseboat.'

'Where?'

'In Paris.'

'What's on your mind?'

'Let's pay him a visit.'

'All right. When?'

'What are you doing right now?'

'Getting my coat.'

Moored at the end of Canal Saint-Martin near the Bassin de la Vilette, the largest artificial lake in Paris, the *Carpe Diem*, a converted tugboat, had seen better days. Years of neglect had given rust, peeling paint and rotting timber a free hand. A dense fog hovered about the still water of the canal, wrapping the dilapidated vessel in what looked like grey cotton wool and giving it an almost ghostlike appearance; a Flying Frenchman of the Seine.

'Do you think someone could actually live on this?' said Jack.

'Let's find out,' replied Dupree and slowly walked across the rickety gangplank, careful not to lose his balance.

'Hold it right there!' a voice called out from somewhere near the wheelhouse at the stern. 'Stop!'

'Is that you, Emile?' said Dupree, certain that Fabron had a gun.

'Who wants to know?'

'Last time we met you were lying in front of a bank you had just robbed, with a bullet in your leg.'

'*Dupree?* You've got a nerve coming here. What do you want?'

'A chat.'

'What about?'

'How to avoid a possible murder charge through a little cooperation.'

'What are you talking about?'

'May we come in?'

'You're not even with the police anymore. You're retired.'

'But still doing the odd job here and there, just like you, Emile.'

'Do you have a warrant?'

'No. But when Chief Superintendent Lapointe gets here, he will certainly have one. Only by then, it may be too late.'

'Too late for what?'

'I'll tell you.'

'Better come in, then.'

The inside of the tugboat looked surprisingly comfortable and well appointed.

Wearing an apron over a pair of flannel pyjamas, Fabron, a short, bald man in his sixties, stood in the galley, his eyes fixed on a frying pan.

'Smells good,' said Jack, and let his eye roam around the spacious interior that had been modified to create one large living space.

274

Under the untidy chaos of crumpled newspapers, empty bottles, dirty plates and a washing basket full of worn clothes waiting for attention, the place reflected the lifestyle of a man who had known hard times, but didn't care.

'State your business and leave me alone,' said Fabron. 'As you can see, I'm cooking breakfast.' Fabron picked up a half-empty bottle of brandy, splashed some into the pan, took a swig and burped.

'It's hard to imagine you in a dinner suit,' said Dupree. He called up the CCTV recording of the limping man walking through the foyer of the Ritz on his iPad, placed it on the table in front of him and turned the screen towards Fabron.

Jack could see that Fabron was watching out of the corner of his eye.

'And you came here after all these years just to show me this?' he said, laughing.

'That's you, isn't it?' continued Dupree, undeterred. 'Walking through the Ritz. You broke into one of the strong boxes in the safe in the basement and stole what was in it. Wig suits you. Makes you look younger.'

Fabron took the pan off the cooktop, turned off the gas and began to laugh.

'You think this is funny?'

'It is. For some reason I can't possibly imagine, you are accusing me of some fancy robbery I'm supposed to have committed, *in disguise?*' Fabron pointed to the screen. 'Are you seriously suggesting that this is supposed to be me? Come on—'

'No doubt you noticed the limp and the bag?'

'Is that all you have? If so, I will not be the only one laughing. You can't even see the guy's face. The prosecutor will be laughing too, at you. For the record, that's not me leaving the Ritz and I don't know anything about a robbery. Now, get out and let me eat my breakfast.'

'Being accused of robbery will be the least of your worries,' continued Dupree quietly. 'There was a dead man in the safe with his throat cut.'

'So, now it's murder as well? You should hear yourself.'

'I don't believe you killed the man. Not your style, but Lapointe may think otherwise when he gets here and pulls this place apart. All I want is some information.'

'What kind of information?'

'Who hired you?'

'I already told you, I know nothing about this. This is harassment. Now piss off!'

'Remember Le Fantôme and the Black Widow?'

'Ancient history. What's that got to do with this?'

'You tell me.'

Fabron shook his head and didn't reply.

'I believe the Black Widow is back in business and hired you. Yes, it's only a hunch – for now. But you know how these things go. A hunch can quickly turn into the real thing, and you could find yourself in the frame, not only for a robbery but for murder, as well. Once Lapointe starts to dig, who knows what he will find, eh?'

Fabron frowned at Dupree. Jack noticed a flash of fear and uncertainty race across Fabron's stern face. It only lasted an instant, but Jack recognised the telltale sign.

'For the last time, leave me alone and get out. You've got nothing on me!'

'Very well, Emile,' said Dupree and turned to leave. 'I thought you were smarter than that. The Fabergé egg sold for nineteen million the other day, and you took all the risks. What did they pay you? Peanuts, I bet.'

Dupree put his business card on the table. 'Call me if you change your mind. I can help you if you help me, but don't wait too long. Once Lapointe gets his teeth into this—'

Fabron waved dismissively.

Dupree opened the door, stopped and turned around to face Fabron. 'I didn't say that the man in the recording was *leaving* the Ritz; you did. Actually, he was on his way out, but there's nothing in the footage to suggest this. Curious, don't you think?' With that,

Dupree picked up the iPad and stepped outside into the cold followed by Jack, who closed the door behind him.

Dupree turned up his collar and looked at Jack. 'Your impressions?' he said.

'Gut feeling?'

'Always the best.'

'What I saw on Fabron's face was fear when you raised the possibility of a murder charge.'

'I saw it, too. When we stepped on board it was just a hunch; now I'm actually convinced he's involved. I just can't prove it yet.'

Jack nodded and opened the car door. 'Interesting character,' he said, 'but I don't think he's a killer.'

'Neither do I. He was without question one of the best safebreakers of his time. Did fifteen years and has nothing to show for it. You saw the way he lives. I think that's why he took the job.'

'Are you going to tell Lapointe about this?'

'No. At least not yet. As Fabron correctly pointed out, we have nothing. No concrete evidence. I've raised the Black Widow with Lapointe before. He dismissed the idea and thought it was absurd. If I was to raise it again, he would laugh and think I was past it, and lost my marbles.'

'Well, we've at least rattled the cage,' said Jack.

'That we have done. And you never know; a rattled cage can soon lead to panic. All we can do for now is wait.'

Even before Dupree and Jack stepped off the boat, Fabron had called Malenkova and told her about the visit. She listened patiently and tried to calm him down. Then she rang Zuzanna.

'I just had a call from a very worried Fabron,' said Malenkova, looking pensively at one of her paintings on the wall of her study. It was the painting Anielka had recently given her as a gift.

'Oh? What did he want?'

'He just had a visit from Dupree and another man. I think it could have been Rogan. We know Dupree lives at the chateau and is working informally on the case.'

'That's interesting.'

'It's more than that; we have a problem. They showed Fabron CCTV footage of a man in a dinner suit leaving the Ritz after the robbery, and suggested it was him.'

'How on earth did they come up with this so *soon*?'

'Don't know, but we have to take this seriously. Obviously they don't have anything concrete, or they would have come in, guns blazing, and made an arrest.'

'I agree.'

'Fabron's afraid the police will be back. He wants to disappear immediately and has asked for more money.'

'What's on your mind?'

'When is Anielka supposed to go to Russia with Rogan?'

'Any time now. They are waiting for the visas to come through. Why do you ask?'

'There's something I want her to do before they leave. *Straight away!*'

'What?'

'I'll tell you when you get here,' said Malenkova and hung up.

Feeling better, she sat back in her chair, pressed the button on her remote and continued to listen to Bruckner's Symphony No. 3, dedicated to Richard Wagner. It was another of her favourites that never failed to inspire her.

46

The body on the houseboat, Paris: 23 February 2017

Chief Superintendent Lapointe arrived at the Gatekeeper's Cottage just after eleven am and rang the bell. Dupree closed his laptop and answered the door.

'Unannounced and in person?' he said. 'Must be important. Coffee?'

'Yes, thank you,' said Lapointe and followed Dupree into the kitchen. 'I owe you an apology.'

'Oh? What for? And you came all this way to tell me?'

'There's a good reason for this.'

'Oh?'

'A jogger saw a body lying on the deck of the *Carpe Diem* early this morning.'

'Fabron?'

'Yes.'

Dupree looked at Lapointe, shocked, his mind racing.

'I know you went to see him yesterday,' continued Lapointe, sipping his coffee.

'How——?'

'It's my business to know,' interrupted Lapointe. 'You taught me that.'

'Do we know what happened?'

'It's interesting ...'

'In what way?'

'I thought you could help me with that. That's why I'm here.'

'Please explain.'

'I would like you to see the body in situ before it's moved.'

'*That* interesting?'

'It is. Shall we go? We can talk on the way.'

'Would you mind if I asked Jack Rogan to come with us? He might be able to help.'

'By all means. After all, he was with you yesterday.'

Lapointe's police car pulled up close to where the *Carpe Diem* was moored. The whole area had been cordoned off and the two police officers standing guard at the gangplank saluted as the chief superintendent approached.

'I told them to leave the body exactly as it was found,' said Lapointe as he stepped on deck. 'First impressions count. You taught me that, too. Forensics can wait.' Lapointe pointed to the wheelhouse. 'The body is just over there.'

'Good God!' said Jack. 'He's wearing a wig!' For a moment he stood quite still and stared at the body. Fabron was lying on his back in a pool of blood, with something long and lethal-looking embedded in his chest.

'That's a whaler's boarding knife,' said Lapointe.

'Correct,' said Dupree, his eyes fixed on the body. 'Extremely sharp. A boarding knife is a double-edged sword blade at the end of a short wooden pole, just like this one. It was used by whalers for cutting a hole in the whale's carcass for the blubber hook.'

'Only here, it was used to cut a deep hole in Fabron's chest,' said Lapointe. 'The blade went right through his body and, as you can see, is still embedded in the wooden boards, effectively pinning him to the deck.'

'What a way to go,' said Jack.

'He didn't die instantly,' continued Lapointe.

'What makes you say that?' asked Dupree.

Lapointe took a step forward and pointed to Fabron's outstretched right arm. 'Because of this. Come closer and have a look.'

Dupree turned to Jack. 'What do you make of this?' he asked.

Jack crouched down for a closer look. 'Good heavens, I think he made some kind of mark with his index finger here, in his own blood. A letter? It looks like an X.'

'Yes, it does,' said Dupree. 'I wonder what it means.'

Lapointe nodded in agreement.

Jack stood up. 'An accusing finger pointing to something, but what?'

'Looks that way,' said Dupree. 'He's sending us a message, and so is the killer: the wig. The killer is effectively identifying Fabron as the man in the CCTV footage. Fabron's our Ritz safebreaker, no doubt about it.'

'How bizarre,' said Jack.

'Not quite as bizarre as a severed dick in a strong box, don't you think?' said Dupree. 'This is another signature. The killer is teasing us.'

'We searched the boat,' said Lapointe. 'Nothing of interest except for a leather case full of tools, just like the one in the CCTV footage.'

'No phone? No laptop or iPad?'

'No. Fabron didn't have a phone account in his name; we checked. He must have used disposable phones. He was a pro, after all, but it's all gone, together with any other incriminating clues. The place had a thorough going over before we got here. Neat job.' Lapointe turned to the Forensics team waiting near the wheelhouse. 'Okay boys, you can go ahead now.'

Dupree had another close look at the body. 'Very theatrical, wouldn't you say? The body, the setting, the murder weapon. What do you make of it, Jack?'

'Let's go inside and have a chat,' said Lapointe and opened the door to the cabin.

'Your impressions, please, gentlemen,' said Lapointe. He reached into his pocket, pulled out his pipe, and lit it. 'What does this crime scene tell you?'

'It tells me that Jack and I were on the right track,' said Dupree.

'How so?' asked Lapointe.

'The first clue was the limping man in the CCTV footage. That pointed the way to Fabron and this boat. Jack and I confronted him yesterday and showed him the CCTV footage. We did that to flush him out, if possible. We wanted to create fear and uncertainty, and it seems to have worked. Perhaps a little too well, bearing in mind what happened—'

'And what do you think did happen here?' interrupted Lapointe.

'I think Fabron contacted his employer as soon as we left the boat, and reported the visit and the CCTV footage,' said Jack. 'I'm sure he didn't realise that this sealed his fate. He had just signed his own death warrant. The person or persons in the shadows realised he had to be silenced quickly, before the police returned, and that's exactly what happened.'

'But that's not all; we have more. A lot more,' said Dupree. 'First, extreme violence and a dramatic setting, just like in the Aubert murder. Then we have another grim signature: the wig. I'm sure it was put on after death. Deliberately left behind for us to find, linking Fabron to the Ritz robbery. It's the same wig as the one in the CCTV footage. What does all this tell us?'

'The two murders are not only linked, but were most likely committed by the same killer,' said Jack. 'And I think that killer is a woman.'

Lapointe nodded, enjoying the familiar tobacco rush as he drew on his pipe. 'I agree, but what about the X? A dying man doesn't make a mark in his own blood as the last thing he does in this life without a good reason. It has to be significant, but what does it *mean?*'

'He's obviously trying to tell us something,' said Dupree.

'I think I know what it is,' said Jack quietly.

Dupree looked at him, surprised. '*You do?*'

'Yes. I don't think it's an X, but an hourglass that *looks* like an X.'

'Why do you say that?' asked Lapointe.

Jack took his time before giving an answer. The storyteller in him wanted to let the suspense grow. 'Because the hourglass is a well-known symbol for the Black Widow. *Latrodectus hesperus* is the most venomous spider in North America. The female is much bigger and more powerful than the male and devours its mate. It has what *looks* like a red hourglass on its rump: an X.'

For a long, tense moment there was total silence as the small tobacco cloud drifting from Lapointe's pipe filled the cold cabin with a pleasant aroma of dry autumn leaves and roasted chestnuts.

'Excellent work, gentlemen,' said Lapointe. 'Thanks to you, our investigation has just taken a big step forward. We must catch that spider before she devours another victim. You two make a good team.'

'No, we three make a great team, Chief Superintendent,' said Jack. 'I have no doubt we can't crack this case without you.'

47

The phone call from Zuzanna, Paris: 23 February 2017

'How is she?' asked Malenkova and activated the speaker mode on her iPhone.

'Excited and cheerful,' said Zuzanna.

'Where are you?'

'Shopping.'

'A reward?'

'A bit like that, but she does need some casual clothes for the trip. Something an impecunious art student would wear, not a fashion model. Warm stuff. Russian winter, you know.'

Malenkova reached for the violin-shaped box on her desk, helped herself to another Mozart Ball and began to slowly peel off the wrapping. This was a treasured ritual – a moment of anticipation she always enjoyed. A delicious combination of dark chocolate, nougat and marzipan, *Mozartkugeln*, as they were known in Austria, were Malenkova's favourite sweets.

'Tell me again exactly how she killed him,' said Malenkova and took a small bite, savouring the marzipan at the centre.

'She improvised.'

'Oh? How?'

'We arrived at Emile's boat just after eleven. He was, of course, expecting me with the money, but was a little surprised when both of us turned up.'

'Understandable.'

'I asked him to take me through the CCTV footage Dupree had shown him. While he was talking about that, Anielka walked around the cabin. She was particularly interested in a collection of whaling paraphernalia hanging on the walls. One item in particular seemed to fascinate her. She asked Emile about it and he walked over to her and explained what it was.'

'What was it?'

'A sword-like whaling knife with a wooden handle and a long blade; very sharp. I knew what was going through her mind. We had agreed that Emile would be killed outside and not in the cabin, as we had work to do; you know, search the place. She would cut his throat from behind, just as she had done with Aubert, quick and deadly effective—'

'Yes, yes,' interrupted Malenkova impatiently. 'I am interested in how she *actually* killed him.'

'As I began to put the money on the table, I pretended to hear footsteps outside. This spooked Emile, and he immediately went outside to investigate. He had a gun. I told Anielka we would do it now, and followed him outside.'

'Then what happened?'

'He walked around the deck for a while and then came back, shaking his head. It was completely dark and foggy. You couldn't even see the embankment. I stood in front of the open cabin door, watching him. As he came closer, Anielka pushed past me. She was holding the whaling knife with both hands and lunged at Emile. She ran him through with it. I saw him staring at her, surprised. The gun fell out of his hand and he fell backwards. I think he was dead before he hit the deck. He didn't make a sound. There was a lot of blood; that's about it. We left him where he fell and went inside to search the place.'

'What about that wig you told me about earlier?'

'That was Anielka's idea. We found it among Emile's stuff in the cabin. She wanted to leave something behind, just like Celine used to do. It seemed important to her, and I couldn't see any harm in it. In fact, I thought this would add an element of intrigue to the entire matter. Just like the you-know-what in the strong box.'

'I see. And Anielka? How did she seem afterwards?'

'Excited. On a high, but controlled. She didn't hesitate for a moment. I think she enjoyed all of it. She's a killing machine with finesse.'

Classic psychopathic behaviour, thought Malenkova. 'Very good,' she said and took another Mozart Ball out of the box. 'This was the last test before we let her go out on her own. Do you think she's ready?'

'I do.'

'So do I. Now tell me about Rogan and the trip, and what she's found out about his project so far.'

'They are booked on a flight to St Petersburg tomorrow afternoon.'

'How's Rogan?'

'Besotted. She's got him wound around her little finger, just as you predicted.'

'Good. What about the project?'

'He's working closely with Darrieux. She put him onto a Romanov expert in St Petersburg. That's the main reason for the trip. Rogan's already made arrangements to meet him.'

'Excellent. What about communications?'

'As you know, I stayed in Anielka's flat last night. We went over all this and set up a protocol. She will call me on my secure phone, report in regularly and we will only speak Polish, which Rogan doesn't understand. She will call me *babcia*, grandmother, her only relative she's close to.'

'You thought of everything. What about Dupree and Chief Superintendent Lapointe?'

'Dupree and Lapointe are working on this case together. Rogan, too, is involved.'

'A good reason to get Anielka out of town and under the radar, don't you think? The best place to hide a book is in the library, no?'

'Sure is.'

'Now with a second murder on their hands, the investigation will step up a notch, that's for sure.'

'I think it already has. The crime scene was swarming with police this morning. Dupree and Rogan were there and so was Lapointe, of course.'

'How do you know?' said Malenkova.

'I have my ways,' came the cryptic reply.

'I'm impressed. I'll call Anielka before she leaves.'

'Please do that. She's devoted to you and eager to please.'

'I know. Now go and buy her something nice,' said Malenkova and hung up.

Malenkova put the lid back on the box of sweets and looked pensively out the window. Zuzanna made her feel uneasy. It certainly wasn't the first time, but as the project had become more complex and demanding, the feeling had become more frequent and pronounced.

Why would a young woman with her abilities be content to do my bidding and take such huge risks? she asked herself. Compared to Zuzanna, Anielka was an open book. To Malenkova, this didn't make sense, and when something didn't make sense, her warning antenna went into overdrive. *She's almost too efficient, and certainly too independent,* she thought. And that usually meant only one thing: a plan, an agenda. But what plan? And why?

Malenkova reached for the remote on her desk and selected a Deutsche Gramophone recording of Bach cantatas. When she felt anxious or uneasy, she liked to listen to Bach. Somehow, his music — especially the cantatas — seemed to relax her and focus her thinking. She pressed the button, hoping the ethereal music would allay her fears and banish her dark thoughts. She was wrong.

48

Peter and Paul Cathedral, St Petersburg: 25 February 2017

February is one of the coldest months in St Petersburg. Heavy snow had fallen during the night, and by morning it had turned the star-shaped island fortress on the Neva River into a winter wonderland that was at odds with its violent past. Used by the Bolsheviks as a notorious prison and place of execution, the original citadel founded by Peter the Great in 1703 had gradually been turned into a museum, and was now the centrepiece of the State Museum of the History of St Petersburg. It was minus three degrees and an icy, bone-chilling wind was blowing across from the Gulf of Finland.

Jack was running late. He turned up his collar and regretted not having brought gloves and a warmer jacket as he hurried across the cobblestoned square towards the Peter and Paul Cathedral in the middle of the island. To avoid the tourist crush, he had taken a very excited Anielka to the Hermitage Museum well before it opened and promised to link up with her later in the day. That had taken longer than expected and catching a taxi on that bleak morning hadn't been easy.

I hope he's still there, thought Jack. He had phoned Konstantin Vasiliev the day before to arrange a meeting. To his surprise, Vasiliev had declined an invitation to lunch and suggested instead they meet at the cathedral where the Romanovs were buried, because what he had to tell Jack was directly related to that solemn place.

Jack thought the old man in the shabby army coat, wet ushanka hat and leaning on a walking stick was a beggar, and almost walked past him when the man asked: 'Mr Rogan?'

Jack stopped and looked at the man. 'Mr Vasiliev?'

'Please call me Konstantin. Let's go inside. It's warmer among the dead than out here among the living.'

Jack had read a lot about the cathedral and its extraordinary history, but nothing could have prepared him for the emotional impact of the rows of white marble tombs greeting him as soon as he stepped inside.

'Have you been to the cathedral before?' asked Vasiliev.

'No; my first time.'

'Then let me show you around. There are forty-one tombs in here. It's quite a history lesson. Almost all the Russian emperors and empresses are right here, from Peter the Great to Nicholas II.'

Vasiliev walked up to a simple white sarcophagus surrounded by a low wrought-iron enclosure and pointed to the gilded bronze cross on top of the heavy lid, and the double-headed Russian eagle on each of its four corners.

'This is the tomb of Peter the Great,' said Vasiliev. 'He was first placed to rest in the Alexander Nevsky Monastery in 1725, but was moved here a few years later. And that one over there belongs to Catherine the Great, who died in 1796 after a long rule of thirty-four years. As you can see, all the sarcophagi are made of white marble except those two over there.' Vasiliev pointed to a pair of magnificent sarcophagi crafted out of semi-precious stones, standing a little apart from the others. 'The grey-green Altai jasper tomb belongs to Alexander III, and the pink Ural rhodolite one is the tomb of his wife, Maria Alexandrovna,' continued Vasiliev. 'But the most relevant tombs as far as you are concerned, of course, belong to Nicholas II and his family. They are all in the Chapel of St Catherine the Martyr over there. Come, let me take you to them.'

Vasiliev walked over to the chapel entry on the right-hand side of the cathedral. 'We can't go inside. We are only allowed to look through the open double doors. There's a barrier. Nicholas and his family are separated from all the others, even in death. They've only been here since seventeen July 1998, eighty years exactly after their murder. It was an amazing ceremony, very moving. I was there. So was Boris Yeltsin and numerous members of the Romanov clan.'

'Why did it take so long to bring them here for burial?'

'That's quite a story. Perhaps for another time. For now, we should focus on your story. Those extraordinary letters you found recently, no?'

Jack nodded.

'Adrienne sent me copies. I have no doubt that all the letters are authentic. Written by Alexandra. Her handwriting is unmistakable, but you already know that.'

'Adrienne told me. She also told me that you were following up something else with a colleague of yours, an expert on Rasputin?'

'Yes, the Yusupov letter and something else Adrienne mentioned in passing about your great aunt, I believe—'

'Madame Petrova,' interrupted Jack.

'Yes, and her mother, Countess Bezukhova. It's a little gem. One of those innocuous pieces of information you come across from time to time like a shiny pebble on a beach. Easy to miss, but with potentially far-reaching implications, if you know what it means and what to look for.'

'Oh? In what way?'

Vasiliev reached into his coat pocket and pulled out a crumpled piece of paper. It was a copy of the music box letter Darrieux had sent him. 'My friend and I have carefully examined this letter and analysed its content. There are several fascinating parts to it, which I will now talk to you about.'

'Would you like to go somewhere else to discuss this, a little more private? A restaurant perhaps; a hot meal, a little vodka?' suggested Jack.

Vasiliev looked at Jack with sad eyes. 'Look at me. I'm but a shadow of what I once was. I'm past fancy restaurants and vodka. I live in a tiny, damp flat in one of those decaying concrete blocks left over from the Soviet era you saw on your way in from the airport. I've been a scholar all my life, but my generation has fallen through the cracks of Glasnost, Perestroika, and the new Russia. I'm one of the forgotten people who no longer matter.'

Vasiliev paused and looked pensively into the Chapel of St Catherine, a dreamy look on his wan face. Then he took off his steel-rimmed glasses and began to polish them on his threadbare shirt cuff.

'No, I wanted to talk about this *here*,' continued Vasiliev softly, 'near the graves of those most affected by all this, especially Alexandra.'

Jack nodded, a shiver of excitement racing down his spine. He recognised all the signs: another great story was in the making and hurtling towards him in a most unexpected way. He pulled the little notebook and pen he always carried with him out of his pocket and looked expectantly at Vasiliev.

'If what I'm about to tell you should turn out to be true and not just academic conjecture,' said Vasiliev, 'then having played a small part in it would be my crowning achievement as a scholar, and I will go to my grave content in the knowledge that I've made a difference.'

'Heady words,' said Jack quietly.

'Perhaps. It's all about Alexandra, Felix Yusupov, Rasputin and Mat' Rossiya. But before I tell you about that, I want to show you something fascinating.'

Vasiliev held up the crumpled piece of paper and pointed to the top right-hand corner of the letter. 'Can you see this here?' he asked.

'Yes. I haven't noticed that before.'

'What does it look like?'

'A tiny Star of David and a heart?' ventured Jack.

'Exactly. And do you know what this is and why it is here?'

'No idea.'

'This is a *signature*.'

'Are you serious?' said Jack. *It can't be, surely,* he thought, feeling the fine hairs on the back of his neck begin to tingle.

'Absolutely, and quite a famous one at that.'

'Do you know whose?'

'Yes. The Postmaster of Treblinka.'

'As in the Nazi concentration camp?'

'Yes.'

'David Herzl?' said Jack, smiling.

Vasiliev looked stunned. 'How can you *possibly* know this?' he whispered.

'I've seen this "signature" before. Five years ago in Switzerland. We were investigating the authenticity of a painting stolen by the

Nazis in the Warsaw Ghetto in 1943. A Monet. It turned out to be a forgery. It was signed by a David Herzl with a tiny Star of David and a small heart hidden in the painting, in a lily pond of all places. The Star of David stands, of course, for David, and the small heart for Herzl, which means heart in German.'

Vasiliev continued to look at Jack with an expression of astonishment and disbelief.

Jack paused and ran his fingers through his hair. 'Only *that* David Herzl was a master forger from Warsaw, not a postmaster from Treblinka,' he added pensively. 'But it has to be one and the same man, surely.'

'How extraordinary!' said Vasiliev. 'But I shouldn't be surprised. Everything about this matter so far has been extraordinary. As if it were all preordained.'

'I sensed that too, right from the very beginning.'

'Serendipity, or something deeper perhaps?'

'I would call it one of my breadcrumbs of destiny,' said Jack.

'"Breadcrumbs of destiny", eh? I like that. Let's follow those breadcrumbs. Who knows? They may just show us how Alexandra's letter, written the day before she and her family were murdered in Yekaterinburg, found its way to Countess Bezukhova in France many years later. If we crack that, your destiny-crumbs may even lead us to Mat' Rossiya. And I know just the man who may be able to help you with that.'

'You do? Who?'

'Sandor Kun. He wrote a book about David Herzl: *The Postmaster of Treblinka.*'

'Amazing. Do you know where I can find him?'

'Yes. In Budapest. I can give him a call if you like. We've worked on projects before, but there's a problem ...'

'What kind of problem?'

'Kun is quite eccentric. He lives like a recluse in Szentendre, a small village close to Budapest, and rarely leaves his home. He has withdrawn from the world.'

'That's unfortunate. Do you think he would agree to see me?'

'Do you play chess?'

'Yes; why do you ask?'

'Kun has two passions in life: chess, and thermal baths, of which there are several in Budapest. They help him with his arthritis.'

'I see. Are you saying a chess game and a hot bath could coax him out of isolation?'

'Leave it with me. I'll do my best.'

'Another breadcrumb of destiny?' said Jack, smiling.

'Looks that way.'

'And Mat' Rossiya? Do you know what that's all about?' asked Jack, carefully watching Vasiliev.

'Perhaps. I only know part of the story. A lot of it is rumour and speculation, but it packs quite a punch.'

'I'm listening.'

The Hermitage had just closed its doors, the crowds were leaving and Anielka was waiting for Jack at the entrance. It was almost dark and it had just started to snow again when Jack's taxi pulled up.

Jack opened the back door from the inside. 'Sorry it took so long. Get in; we may just make it,' he called out.

'Make it? Where to?' said Anielka. She got in and kissed Jack on the cheek.

'Nevsky Prospect.'

'What's Nevsky Prospect?'

'The Champs-Élysées of St Petersburg. The place where you can find all the right boutiques.'

'We are going *shopping*?'

'We are.'

'Shopping for what?'

'Something nice for you to wear tonight.'

'How exciting! You certainly know the way to a girl's heart. Are we going somewhere special?'

'We are.'

'Are you going tell me?'

'It's a surprise.'

'I love surprises,' said Anielka and snuggled up against Jack in the back seat. 'You are spoiling me!'

Jack looked at his watch. It was almost time to go. He poured himself another Scotch and closed his notebook. 'Are you ready? We have to leave in a minute,' he called out.

Anielka had spent almost an hour in the dressing room of their large hotel suite. 'Won't be long,' she replied.

Moments later, Anielka appeared in the doorway. 'What do you think?' she said, striking a classic *Vogue* pose.

Jack looked up. 'Wow! I had no idea that a little black designer dress could look like *that*. Ravishing!'

'I've never worn a Valentino before,' said Anielka, scrutinising herself in the mirror. 'Where are we going?'

'A visit to St Petersburg wouldn't be complete without a visit to?'

'Where?'

'The ballet, of course! Come, we mustn't be late.'

Named after the Empress Maria Alexandrovna, wife of Alexander III, the stunning Mariinsky Theatre – known during the Soviet era as the Kirov – was only a short taxi ride from the hotel. A generous tip slipped into the pocket of the concierge earlier that day had secured two of the best seats in the theatre that had once been the leading music venue of nineteenth-century Russia. In terms of musical history, it had no equal. Musical greats like Tchaikovsky, Glinka and Rimsky-Korsakov had wowed discerning audiences with their timeless masterpieces since the theatre opened its doors in 1860.

'This is like a fairytale,' said Anielka as they crossed the sumptuous foyer packed with mainly foreign visitors. 'What's on tonight?'

'Swan Lake; what else?' said Jack, soaking up the electric atmosphere of relaxed anticipation in the packed theatre as they took their seats in a coveted dress circle box.

Then suddenly, the lights dimmed, the hum of excited voices ebbed away and the orchestra began to play, introducing the first act of the timeless story: a magnificent ball at the royal court, celebrating Prince Siegfried's twenty-first birthday.

For a while, Jack allowed himself to be transported by Tchaikovsky's stirring music and the magic unfolding on stage, watching the wonder reflected in Anielka's beautiful face next to him.

Tchaikovsky. This is no coincidence, thought Jack as he remembered the amazing story Vasiliev had told him that afternoon about Mat' Rossiya. *This is destiny at work!*

Jack closed his eyes, trying to concentrate on the music, but Vasiliev's words wouldn't leave him alone.

'These letters written by Alexandra are history, especially the last two. They are the only tangible evidence I'm aware of that support Yusupov's extraordinary claim. For years, he maintained that Rasputin had presented Alexandra with a lost symphony by Tchaikovsky as a farewell gift just before he died,' Jack heard Vasiliev say over and over in his mind.

Could Mat' Rossiya really be a piece of music? Jack asked himself. A lost symphony by one of Russia's greatest composers? Is that what Alexandra was telling her friend about in the letters? Was that a desperate attempt to save a masterpiece by a musical genius that belonged to Mother Russia? *Incredible!*

Jack opened his eyes and watched Siegfried take aim with his crossbow. But before he could shoot, the Swan Queen turned into a beautiful woman.

As Tchaikovsky's sublime music reached a climax, the questions Jack had been asking himself all afternoon, surfaced again with alarming clarity: Could Alexandra have been like the cursed Princess Odette? Could her death in the Ipatiev House have been her only means of escape from Lenin, the dark sorcerer, and his power? Jack took a deep breath. Was meeting her tragic, brutal end the only way to preserve her love for her family and her country? Could Mat' Rossiya, Tchaikovsky's lost symphony, be her legacy? A precious parting gift to Russia and the world? Then came the big, final question: *What if the symphony really does exist? Just waiting somewhere to be discovered, and Alexandra's letters are showing us the way?*

With his head spinning, Jack closed his eyes again and made a promise to himself: he would follow those breadcrumbs and do whatever it took to find out if that was so.

49

The chess game at the Gellért, Budapest: 27 February 2017

The day before

An early riser, Jack was sitting at a small desk by the window. He hadn't slept much. The turbulent events of the previous day, especially his meeting with Vasiliev, had kept him up most of the night. Outside, it was still snowing and there was ice on the windows, obscuring the view down into the busy St Petersburg street choking with morning traffic.

Deep in thought, Jack kept staring at his open notebook, trying to make sense of all the hurried entries. Then he picked up his pen and underlined a name: Sandor Kun. *I hope Konstantin can arrange that meeting*, thought Jack, playing with his pen. *Everything depends on that.*

Anielka tiptoed up to Jack from behind and put her arms around his neck. 'You're up early,' she said and kissed him on the cheek. 'What are you doing?'

'Going over my notes from yesterday. As I told you, it was a big day with a few unexpected surprises. I would almost call it a breakthrough, but it all depends ...'

'On what?'

'Tomorrow.'

'Great. While you were out meeting mysterious strangers, I had one of the best days of my life.' Anielka kept playing with Jack's hair. 'A visit to the Hermitage – the museum of my dreams – followed by a magical evening at the ballet, and not to forget, shopping in between. I still have to pinch myself.'

'I'm glad you had a good time. I did warn you that I would be quite busy and preoccupied on this trip, and not all of it would be fun or of interest to you.'

'Well, so far, you're not doing too badly. Before we talk about tomorrow, what are we doing today?'

Jack put down his pen and looked at Anielka. 'We are flying to Budapest,' he said, smiling.

'*What?* Are you serious?'

'Absolutely. I'm hoping to meet someone … important.'

'One of those breadcrumbs of destiny you keep talking about?'

'Something like that. Have you been to Budapest?'

'No.'

'Then you are in for a real treat. Budapest is one of my favourite cities in Europe. Breathtaking, especially at night with all the lights. The Parliament, Buda Castle with the Fisherman's Bastion, the Chain Bridge and all those churches, lit up like a magic stage full of history and imposing buildings. Echoes of a glorious past, but also of struggle and suffering.' Jack was getting quite excited.

'And then there are the amazing thermal baths. So many of them,' he continued. 'The Gellért, the Széchenyi Baths and my favourite, the Rudas. Many of them date back to Roman times and the Turkish occupation. The Rudas is a Turkish bath, which still has its original sixteenth-century Ottoman cupola and octagonal pool. Fascinating. There's so much there to see. You won't be disappointed, I promise. We are staying at the Hotel Gellért, a classic. A grand hotel and spa complex from way back. You'll love it, I know.'

'With you, I'm never disappointed,' purred Anielka. 'When's our flight?'

'In the afternoon.'

'Then there's no rush, is there?'

'No. It's still early.'

'But not too early for a little fun. You know what they say, too much work …'

Anielka took Jack by the hand and pulled him gently towards her. 'That was a magic evening, thank you,' she said. 'I loved the ballet, and *that dress*! Very sweet of you. But now it's definitely my turn.'

'Your turn? In what way?'

'To spoil *you* a little; come,' said Anielka. She let go of Jack's hand, a coquettish smile on her face, and began to walk slowly towards the open bedroom door, seductively exaggerating the sway of her hips.

Jack and Anielka were seated in the hotel lobby waiting for their taxi to take them to the airport, when the concierge walked up to Jack.

'This was left for you earlier, sir,' he said and handed Jack a small parcel wrapped in coarse brown paper.

'Expecting something?' said Anielka and looked over Jack's shoulder.

'No. I have no idea what this is.'

'Why don't you open it and see?'

Jack unwrapped the parcel, looked inside and smiled. 'It's a book,' he said. '*The Postmaster of Treblinka* by Sandor Kun.' Inside the book was a brief note:

It was a pleasure talking to you yesterday. Sandor will meet you at the Gellért tomorrow at 11:00 am. I told him you like chess. Keep following those bread-crumbs. Who knows where they will take you?

Konstantin

The next day

Just before eleven am, Jack walked down the imposing staircase of the Gellért Hotel to meet Kun as arranged. Outside it was freezing, and large chunks of ice were floating down the Danube, promising doom for anyone foolish enough to get in their way. He stopped briefly on each landing and admired the beautiful stained-glass windows depicting the ancient Hungarian legend of a magic stag, and prepared himself for what he knew would be a critically important meeting, perhaps even a watershed moment in his investigation.

The large foyer wasn't busy. The foul weather had kept most of the early morning regulars away. *That must be him,* thought Jack, and walked over to a well-dressed, elderly gentleman standing near the doors with a folding chessboard under his arm. 'Mr Kun?' said Jack, extending his hand.

'Yes. How did you know?' replied Kun in perfect English.

'The chessboard gave you away.'

'Ah. Have you been to the baths before, Mr Rogan?'

'Not to the Gellért baths, no. I've only admired this grand establishment from the outside.'

'Then let me be your guide. You're in for a treat; come.'

Kun, a sprightly man in his seventies, moved with surprising agility for a man of his age. 'You know this is one of the biggest natural spring-water bath complexes in Europe,' he said, leading the way to the change rooms. 'It is famous for its spectacular Art Nouveau design. There are ten pools of various sizes and temperatures we can choose from. The place is a maze and very popular with locals like me. I used to come here twice a week and spend the whole day in here. Meeting friends and playing chess.'

'Budapest is very lucky to have something like this,' said Jack. 'I love the stained-glass windows and the beautiful tiles. And, of course, the old-world charm of the place.'

'May I suggest we have a swim first in one of the warm pools, followed by a sauna? Always a good start. After that, we can relax in the comfortable recliner chairs upstairs in the gallery and have a game of chess. What do you say?'

'I'm in your hands.'

Kun was playing White. His opening move was e4. Jack responded with c5.

'Ah, the Sicilian Defence. Excellent move,' said Kun. 'So much has been written about this, especially by grandmasters like John Nunn and Jonathan Rowson. They attributed the popularity of this defence to its combative nature because it begins the fight for the centre of the board.'

'It does. A good friend of mine, a wonderful chess player who could play entire games from memory, told me to always open in this way. Apparently, a quarter of all games use the Sicilian.'

'Correct, and seventeen per cent of all games between grandmasters begin in that way.'

'And it is an excellent way to explore the strength of your opponent, especially if you are not familiar with his strategies and way of thinking,' said Jack, his eyes sparkling.

'Very good,' said Kun, enjoying himself, and moved his knight to f3. 'Let's see if that's right.'

The game progressed quite rapidly after that, and Jack lost after putting up a valiant fight.

'I read your book about the Postmaster of Treblinka on the plane yesterday,' said Jack, introducing the subject that had brought them together.

'Konstantin told me about your intriguing encounter with David Herzl and his work,' said Kun, setting up the chessboard for the next game. 'What an amazing coincidence.'

'It must be the same man, surely, but I thought Herzl was killed in the Warsaw Ghetto uprising in April 1943?'

'Not so. He was captured and the Germans sent him to Treblinka. They needed him, you see. That's what saved him, and his ability to adapt.'

'Was it his talent for forgery?'

'In a way, yes. He was an outstanding painter, but he was also a pragmatist who found imaginative ways to survive. The Germans had looted artworks all over Europe; amazing stuff. In their usual, efficient way, they had set up a whole department dealing with this, and were actually restoring some of the more valuable masterpieces before sending them to Berlin.'

'Is that what Herzl was doing?'

'Yes. He actually had a studio in Treblinka and was working with art experts to restore paintings right up until the end of the war. He was exceptionally good at this, and that gave him privileges.'

'He survived Treblinka?'

'Yes. He was one of the very few who did, and so did his diary.'

'I understand that was the inspiration for your book?'

'Yes. It's an extraordinary record of what happened inside the death camp.'

'Where's the diary now?'

'In Prague. I gave it to the Jewish Museum. As a contemporaneous record, it is invaluable.'

'I can see that. So, how did David Herzl, a master forger restoring stolen paintings for the Germans inside a notorious concentration camp, become the Postmaster of Treblinka, helping fellow inmates make contact with relatives and friends on the outside?'

'Ah. I knew you would ask that. As I mentioned before, Herzl was a pragmatist, a survivor. His unique situation in the camp gave him certain opportunities.'

'What kind of opportunities?'

'The most important and most valuable was contact with the outside world.'

'Seriously?'

'Yes. Concentration camps like Treblinka were strange places. Officials came and went all the time, delivering and collecting paintings. They also provided him with the materials he needed to carry out his delicate, highly specialised work. A lot of it arrived by post, the *Feldpost*, a very efficient military organisation of the Wehrmacht that became the general postal authority of the occupied territories like Poland. As part of his work, Herzl had access to this postal service and often wrote directly to suppliers, ordering materials and corresponding with curators and other art experts with questions relating to his restoration work.'

'Fascinating,' said Jack. 'But how is this relevant?'

'You'll see in a moment. Another game?'

'Sure.'

50

Frieda Malenkova's study: 27 February 2017

Malenkova hobbled awkwardly across to the whiteboard, reached to the top and pinned up another page of Jack's diary notes. Then she stepped back and stared at the board. By now, the crowded board was covered in pieces of paper, photographs and her own handwritten notes. To the uninitiated it would have looked like a disorganised jumble of ideas and connections, but nothing could have been further from the truth. To Malenkova it was a highly organised, invaluable aide-memoire that helped her focus on what mattered, and see what was often hidden under the crushing weight of the irrelevant and misleading.

'You must admit, she's doing a great job,' said Zuzanna. She had just downloaded the information Anielka had sent through on her iPhone from Budapest: three pages from Jack's latest diary notes she had photographed that evening while Jack was in the shower.

'That's not our problem. She's doing great. The problem is how to read and interpret Rogan's notations. He does exactly what my father used to do. He jots down ideas and connections with key words, abbreviations, or symbols. He obviously does that when he's in a hurry, while talking to someone, or thinking about things on the run. It's his own personal shorthand only he fully understands. I suspect this is done for two reasons: to save time, and to keep the information private.'

Zuzanna pointed to the whiteboard. 'Not all that different from what you are doing right here,' she suggested, smiling.

'I suppose not, but the interpretation problem remains.' Malenkova took a deep breath. 'Let's have another look at all this and see what we've got.' Malenkova walked back to her desk, poured herself another cognac and sat down, facing the whiteboard.

'Rogan travelled to St Petersburg to meet Vasiliev, a retired scholar. A Romanov expert. The meeting was arranged by Darrieux, who clearly knows him well and has worked with him in the past. Vasiliev and Rogan discussed the Petrova letter – and that's when things become really interesting.'

'In what way?'

'Why did Darrieux refer Rogan to Vasiliev in the first place, and why was it necessary for Rogan to meet with him in person? I think we now know part of the answer. Rogan's diary notes Anielka sent through the other day tell us something about that.'

Malenkova reached for the copy of the Petrova music box letter on her desk and held it up. 'It was all about two things: the meaning of Mat' Rossiya, and the Herzl signature on the top here.' Malenkova pointed to the top right-hand corner of the page.

'But that's the end of the good news, for now,' she continued. 'We are no closer to unravelling the meaning of Mat' Rossiya—'

'Except for this,' interjected Zuzanna. She walked over to the whiteboard and pointed to one of the pages – Jack's notes from his meeting with Vasiliev in the cathedral in St Petersburg.

'Is MR music by T as claimed by Y?' Zuzanna read aloud. 'What do you think this means? Could MR refer to Mat' Rossiya?'

'Quite possibly, but as for the rest?'

'There will be more clues later,' said Zuzanna. 'I'm sure of it. Mat' Rossiya is at the heart of all this. So much is clear from the letter.'

'Agreed. The second thing, the Herzl signature, has opened up a new line of enquiry: a book – *The Postmaster of Treblinka* – and a trip to Budapest to meet Sandor Kun, the author. That happened today. Fortunately, Rogan's notes give us a little more information about this.'

Malenkova paused and took a sip of cognac.

'What I find particularly fascinating is Rogan's thought process,' she said. 'Again, it reminds me of my father.'

'In what way?'

'When Rogan's jotting down ideas in a hurry – mainly when he's with someone – he uses abbreviations, symbols, key words and the like, as he has done with Mat' Rossiya. But from time to time, he transcribes his shorthand, and expands on the subject. This is done later when he has time to reflect and digest the information, and even then, he often just scribbles something in the margin, like here.' Malenkova pointed to the page dealing with the Kun meeting at the Gellért earlier that day.

'Fascinating. Rogan is definitely following a specific trail here, his "breadcrumbs of destiny" Anielka told me about yesterday when I spoke to her,' said Zuzanna.

'An interesting concept for sure, and very telling. It tells me a lot about the man and his way of thinking. Principally, Rogan's a man of intuition who is not afraid to follow his instincts, even if at times this defies logic or common sense. I do the same, only he calls it following breadcrumbs of destiny. I call it following your gut feeling.'

Malenkova put down the letter and reached for her iPad. 'I have already downloaded Kun's book. Fascinating stuff. I just can't see the full picture at the moment, but I am sure Rogan and Kun can. They have agreed to meet again tomorrow, no doubt to discuss this matter further.'

'But Rogan does give us a clue,' said Zuzanna. 'It's about this Petrova letter here. I believe the reason he's so interested in the Postmaster of Treblinka is this: he wants to find out how a letter written in 1918 made it from Yekaterinburg to Countess Bezukhova in France, and was finally delivered sometime during the war. Twenty-five years after it was dispatched. Where was the letter hiding all this time, and how did it finally find its way to France? How did it get there, especially during those turbulent times, and who delivered it? And why?'

Malenkova reached for the cognac bottle.

'I'm sure Kun's book holds the key to all this,' she said. 'The Postmaster of Treblinka may be able to help us here, even after all these years.'

'You really think so? Someone who lived in a Nazi concentration camp during the war?'

'Yes. There must be some clue buried in there somewhere, and Vasiliev was aware of this. That's why he sent Rogan to Budapest to meet Kun. It's the only explanation that makes sense.'

'I can see that, but why do you think Rogan's so interested in all this?' said Zuzanna, shaking her head.

'I'll tell you, and it's very clever. By somehow tracing the letter back to its source, he's trying to piece together its journey. Why? Because he believes this may lead him to Mat' Rossiya and Kazanskaya Bogomater, whatever they may be.'

'All right. Let me play the devil's advocate here for a moment,' said Zuzanna. 'If all is as you suggest, why is Rogan going to such extraordinary lengths to piece all this together in the first place?'

'You know the answer to that as well as I do. Because he believes, like we do, that something really big, something of great importance, is in play here. Something that Alexandra was desperately trying to protect—'

'But at the same time, desperately wanted to tell her dear friend about, before it was too late,' Zuzanna interjected. 'Something to do with Mat' Rossiya and Kazanskaya Bogomater, you think?'

'Absolutely. And I believe it's all contained in this one line: *'Is MR music by T as claimed by Y?* Once we know the answer to that, we'll be a lot closer to unravelling this mystery,' said Malenkova and reached for her glass.

'And thanks to you,' said Zuzanna, 'we have just the right person on the inside to help us with that: *Anielka.*'

'You are right. To Anielka,' said Malenkova and raised her glass.

51

A Rigó Jancsi at the Café Gerbeaud,
Budapest: 28 February 2017

Jack was early. He arrived at the famous Café Gerbeaud on Vorosmarty ter just before ten am, sat down at a small marble table by the window and ordered coffee. Established in 1870, this iconic establishment with its timeless, elegant interior had been the haunt of writers, politicians and artists for almost one hundred and fifty years, and had weathered two world wars, Russian occupation and the bloody 1956 uprising. It was a haven of Hungarian social life that had welcomed such distinguished guests as the composer Franz Liszt, and Empress Elizabeth, Queen of Hungary, who was particularly fond of the wonderful ice-cream creations, which she pronounced 'the best ice in Pest'.

To keep Anielka entertained, Jack had sent her shopping in nearby Vacy Street, with its high-end stores and exclusive boutiques, which he knew would amuse her for a while.

After several chess games at the Gellért – most of which Jack lost – Jack and Kun had agreed to continue their conversation the next day, as Kun had to leave early to catch the train back to his village. Jack had suggested they meet at the Gerbeaud, his favourite café in Budapest. This was eagerly embraced by Kun, who was enjoying Jack's company and was already looking forward to another one of his rare visits into town.

Inspired by Jack's enthusiasm and the intriguing content of the music box letter, Kun had promised to bring along some material he believed could be useful in assisting Jack in his quest.

'I'm sorry I'm late,' said Kun. 'Budapest trains.' He shrugged, took off his overcoat and sat down. 'No sweets?'

'I didn't want to start without you.'

'Ah, then let me remedy this at once.' Kun signalled to a waitress walking past and ordered two Rigó Jancsi in Hungarian.

'What's a Rigó Jancsi?' asked Jack. 'I understood that much. As for the Hungarian language, it's diabolically difficult. I only ever order coffee.'

'It is,' conceded Kun. 'That's why it's always a good idea to take someone like me along. It's a Finno-Ugric language like Finnish, Estonian and Lappic. Magyar is quite unique in Europe, and yes, very complicated. If you want to experience the real Budapest, you need a guide.'

'I'll keep that in mind,' said Jack, enjoying the banter.

'A Rigó Jancsi is a traditional Hungarian chocolate cake dating from the Austro-Hungarian Empire'. Kun smacked his lips. 'Delicious, you'll see. It's cube-shaped and has a touch of rum and vanilla in the filling. It also has quite a history.'

'Oh? Everything here in Budapest seems to have quite a history.'

'But this one is delightful. Let me tell you. The cake will taste so much better after you hear this: it's all about a Hungarian–Belgian love story.'

'How fascinating.'

'Rigó Jancsi was a famous gypsy violinist. Young, handsome, full of bravado and flair. He toured all over Europe with his own orchestra towards the end of the nineteenth century. One day in 1896, he was playing in a restaurant in Paris and was asked to come to one of the tables to play a solo to show off his extraordinary skills. That's when he met Clara, the beautiful young wife of a Belgian duke. Enchanted by Jancsi's music and charm, she immediately fell in love and eloped with him, disguised as a gypsy. They lived together for ten years in various countries and squandered a fortune. She was the daughter of an American millionaire, which no doubt helped. During one of their visits to Budapest, Jancsi ordered a chocolate cake for Clara. She loved the cake, and the shrewd proprietor immediately named it after Jancsi. The Rigó Jancsi was born—'

'What a wonderful story,' interjected Jack.

'Unfortunately, this whirlwind romance didn't last. It came to an abrupt end when Clara met an Italian waiter and exchanged the violin for a bowl of pasta,' said Kun, laughing. 'Ah, here come our Rigó Jansci now. Let me know what you think.'

'Will do.'

'Speaking of remarkable love stories,' continued Kun, enjoying his Rigó Jancsi, 'I have another one for you that happens to be relevant to what we are about to discuss. I also have a surprise for you.'

'Oh?'

'It's about David Herzl—'

'The Postmaster of Treblinka?'

'Yes.'

'And the surprise?'

'Before we talk about that, I must tell you about the love story, because the two are connected.'

Jack reached for his notebook, opened it, and put it on the table next to the empty Rigó Jancsi plate, which he had scraped clean right down to the very last morsel.

'I told you yesterday that Herzl survived the Warsaw Ghetto uprising, was taken by the SS to Treblinka and put to work,' said Kun.

'Yes, restoring stolen paintings for the Germans.'

'Correct, but what I didn't tell you was that he had an assistant, a beautiful young Hungarian woman called Ilona. She, too, was a talented painter. They fell in love, and it was she who came up with the idea.'

'What idea?'

'To introduce a little ray of sunshine and hope into the death camp.'

'How?'

'Because of his work, Herzl had free access to the Feldpost, the general postal authority established by the Wehrmacht in the occupied territories.'

'You told me.'

'It all began with a small, desperate request.'

'What kind of request?'

'One of Ilona's friends in the camp asked her if she could perhaps smuggle a letter out of the camp and send it through the Feldpost to her parents in Prague. She offered a valuable diamond ring as payment. When Ilona first mentioned this to Herzl, he dismissed the idea as absurd, but Ilona persisted. To cut a long story short, Herzl and Ilona managed to establish a sophisticated, underground postal network – involving people both inside, and outside the camp – to facilitate the sending and receiving of letters through the Nazi Feldpost.'

'Seriously?'

'Yes. It even had a name. It was called the Ballroom of Hope.'

'Strange name.'

'It is. They all knew they were dancing with death. If discovered, well, you can imagine ...'

'How macabre.'

'Hope often is.'

'You're right.'

'It was an ingenious set-up using contacts and bribes that went undetected right up to July 1944 when Soviet troops overran the camp. Despite risking their lives, Herzl and Ilona were among the few survivors.'

'Amazing.'

'But what is even more amazing is *this*,' said Kun. He opened his briefcase and put a bundle of papers on the table in front of him.

'What's this?'

'It's a copy of Herzl's diary. As I told you, the original is in the Jewish Museum in Prague. Another coffee?'

'Yes, please. I could certainly do with one. This is an incredible story.'

'Wait, it gets even better,' said Kun and began to sort through the pages in front of him. 'As part of his secret diary, which he must have kept carefully hidden, Herzl kept a meticulous record—'

'A record? Of what?' interjected Jack, sensing that something significant was about to be revealed. The butterflies in his stomach told him so.

'Herzl kept a record of all the letters he managed to smuggle out of the camp. Dates, names and addresses.'

'Why on earth would he have done that? Surely, if caught ...'

'I was wondering about that, too, but there's a simple explanation. This ingenious postal service was a two-way street. Not only did letters get out, there were quite a few replies as well, all addressed to Herzl. Using his records, he could then identify the intended recipient and pass on the replies. All part of a secret, underground postal service right under the noses of the SS. The Ballroom of Hope. Brazen, yes. Desperate, certainly, but surprisingly effective.'

'And this diary was like a dance card with death?'

'Sure, if the SS had found out about this ...'

'Unbelievable!'

'The bribes involved were huge, and this was what kept the wheels turning. Each letter cost a small fortune, but when you have nothing to lose ... A diamond on the way to the gas chamber is worthless.' Kun shook his head and looked sadly at Jack. 'Self-interest and greed in the middle of unimaginable slaughter, bringing a little hope, perhaps even joy, to the condemned.' Kun paused and looked at Jack. 'You must be wondering why I'm telling you all this.'

'The thought had crossed my mind,' said Jack, smiling.

'It's because of this here.' Kun held up a piece of paper. 'I went through all this stuff last night because I remembered something.'

'What?'

'A name.'

'What name?'

'Countess Bezukhova.'

'*What?*' Jack almost shouted. 'Show me!'

Kun handed Jack the piece of paper. One entry at the top of the page had been underlined: 12 June 1943. Countess Bezukhova. After the name was an address in France, and another name, obviously the sender.

For a while Jack stared at the piece of paper, his mind racing.

'Are you suggesting that in June 1943, a letter was sent from Treblinka to Countess Bezukhova in France?' he asked quietly.

'It looks that way.'

Jack reached into his pocket and pulled out a copy of the music box letter and put it next to the piece of paper on the table. 'This one here?'

Kun nodded. 'The Herzl signature at the top confirms it. Apparently, all the letters dispatched by Herzl had these markings at the top. A couple of letters with the same Star of David and the little heart have survived and are in the museum in Prague. But there's a further clue.'

'Oh? What kind of clue?'

'Here, the sender: *Pavel Ustinov*.'

'What about him?'

'Pavel Ustinov was a Trawniki guard, a Russian prisoner of war captured by the Germans during Operation Barbarossa in December 1941. Trawniki guards helped the Germans run the camps. They were all former Soviet Red Army soldiers who received special training in a facility at Trawniki outside Lublin.'

'How do you know all this?'

'It was part of my research for the book. Pavel Ustinov was an important link in Herzl's underground Treblinka postal network, and ultimately helped save Herzl and Ilona when the Russians liberated the camp. They wouldn't have survived without him.'

'Incredible.'

'He was a decent man. He also saved dozens of others. When the Germans decided to dismantle Treblinka and shoot all the remaining prisoners, Ustinov didn't participate and instead managed to hide many of them and keep them alive, including Herzl and Ilona, until the Russians arrived and liberated what was left of the camp—'

'Let me get this right,' interrupted Jack. He put down his pen and looked at Kun. 'Are you suggesting that this Russian prisoner of war sent the Bezukhova letter from Treblinka to France through the German Feldpost in 1943?'

Kun held up the Herzl diary page with the entry. 'According to this, yes. And the letter here in front of us is proof that it actually arrived.'

'German efficiency in the middle of a devastating war?'

'Looks that way. The Wehrmacht was incredibly well organised.'

'I have to find out more about this Pavel Ustinov,' said Jack, circling the name in his notebook. 'Do you think that's possible?'

'Yes. Ustinov was one of the few who showed some humanity and compassion, and actually saved lives, at great risk to himself. Almost a million Jews were slaughtered in Treblinka. It was a killing machine. One of the worst. There's a lot of material about him in the museum in Prague. He was known in the camp as the Golem of Treblinka.'

'Golem of Treblinka? How curious. Why?'

'I will let someone else who knows a lot more about this than I, tell you,' said Kun, smiling.

'Who?'

'A good friend of mine: Avigdor Stein.'

'This story is becoming more fascinating by the minute. Who is Avigdor Stein?'

'He's the curator of the Jewish Museum in Prague. He helped me with my book.'

'And he might be able to help me, too?'

Kun nodded. 'I think so. I spoke to him already. He has a lot of information about Pavel Ustinov in his museum that may be useful to you.'

'Should I go and talk to him?'

'Definitely!'

More breadcrumbs of destiny, thought Jack, shaking his head. He pointed to the bundle of papers on the table. 'How did you manage to get hold of this diary?' he asked quietly.

'It was left to me.'

'Oh? By whom?'

'Ilona Kun. My mother.'

52

Chief Superintendent Lapointe visits Malenkova, Paris: 28 February 2017

Sitting at her desk in the study, Malenkova was enjoying her second cup of strong morning coffee. She was going over the latest messages sent by Anielka from Budapest, when her maid knocked and walked in.

'Chief Superintendent Lapointe is outside, Madame. He would like to see you.'

'Oh? Did he say what it was about?' said Malenkova, her mind racing.

'No. Shall I tell him to leave, or come back later?'

'No! Just give me a moment and then show him in.'

Malenkova cleared her desk, pushed the whiteboard into a closet, and surveyed the room. Satisfied that nothing incriminating was lying around, she poured herself another cup of coffee.

Well aware that Lapointe was heading the investigation into the two sensational murders, Malenkova was wondering what had brought the chief superintendent to her doorstep. She was also aware that the best way to deal with the police was polite cooperation without giving anything away. Hiding or delay were not an option in a situation like this. On the contrary, Malenkova viewed this as an opportunity to gather valuable intelligence and, if possible, deflect attention away from her.

'Enter!' Malenkova called out when her maid knocked.

'Chief Superintendent Lapointe and a colleague, Madame,' said the maid and stepped aside.

'Apologies for the early intrusion, Madame, and thank you for seeing me,' said Lapointe, extending his hand. 'This is Claude Dupree, a colleague of mine who is assisting me with my enquiries.'

Dupree, here? How astonishing, thought Malenkova, composing herself and trying not to look alarmed.

'How can I be of assistance, gentlemen?' she said and motioned towards a Chesterfield and two leather chairs in the corner of the large room. 'Please take a seat.'

Dupree looked at Malenkova with interest, sizing up the fascinating, portly woman leaning on a walking stick in front of him. *Not what I expected. Could this be the Black Widow, or are we mistaken and jumping to conclusions?* he thought, as he remembered the meeting with Martin Charpentier, the Fabergé expert, the day before. What Dupree had found particularly interesting was not the little that Charpentier did say about Malenkova, but what was left unsaid.

After Fabron's spectacular murder, Lapointe had changed direction and focused his investigation on the Black Widow cold cases, as initially suggested by Dupree. He had also followed up the curious Victor Sokolov visit to Le Club Barrière on 16 February, as a possible lead. Further examination of CCTV footage obtained from the club had led him to Martin Charpentier, who was seen talking to Sokolov and a mystery woman. This in turn had resulted in a visit to Charpentier's antique shop and a robust interrogation, pointing the way, albeit obliquely, to Malenkova.

'This shouldn't take too long,' said Lapointe, preferring to stand. 'I believe you know Martin Charpentier?'

'I do,' said Malenkova, the question taking her by surprise. 'I've done business with him in the past. Why do you ask?'

'Recently?'

Malenkova was about to reply, but her finely honed instincts told her to take her time and be careful. She could sense danger signals radiating from the little man in the ill-fitting overcoat standing in front of her like a caricature straight out of a 1950s detective movie. *He refused to take a seat*, she thought. *A bad sign. He knows about the meeting with Sokolov! I almost walked into a trap!'*

'I saw him a few days ago, quite by chance actually,' said Malenkova, casually. 'Won't you take a seat? May I offer you some coffee?'

She's good, thought Lapointe, watching Malenkova carefully. 'Where?' he asked.

'Club Barrière. It was a chance meeting. I hadn't seen him in years. He was there with someone else.'

Lapointe reached into his pocket, pulled out a photograph and handed it to Malenkova. 'With this man?' he asked.

Malenkova looked at the photograph. It showed Sokolov sitting next to Charpentier. It also showed her, but only partially, and only from the back.

'Yes. That's Victor Sokolov, a former client of mine. Is he in trouble?'

'And is that you sitting next to him with your back turned towards the camera?' asked Lapointe, ignoring the question.

'Yes. As I said, it was a chance meeting. We were all in the club at the same time. I had a rare winning streak and we were celebrating. Now, would you like to tell me what this is all about, Chief Superintendent?'

'I am investigating two recent murders and the theft of a precious artefact, a Russian Imperial Fabergé Easter egg.'

'How fascinating. And you think Martin and Victor are somehow involved? That's absurd!'

'Is it? Charpentier is a well-known Fabergé expert who has spent time in jail, and Sokolov – a man with a dubious reputation – owns several Russian Imperial Easter eggs worth millions, and one such egg was recently stolen from a safe here in the Ritz. Involving a brutal murder.'

He knows nothing and is obviously fishing, thought Malenkova. Otherwise, he would have come with a search warrant, or worse still, made an arrest. She knew Charpentier must have kept his mouth shut. With Victor involved, that was hardly surprising. You didn't cross that man and get away with it. *This copper is trying to scare me, hoping I make a mistake. Well, I don't scare that easily!*

'And you are telling me all this because ...?'

'The stolen Fabergé egg was recently auctioned on the dark web,' said Dupree, 'and you are – how shall I put this? – an art dealer known for her creative ways.'

'I still don't understand. What has all that to do with me?' Malenkova said, going on the attack. 'You barge in here early in the morning, Chief Superintendent, unannounced, asking questions about some heinous crimes I know absolutely nothing about, and making veiled insinuations. I cannot help you!'

'But you already have, Madame,' said Dupree, smiling.

'What do you mean?'

Dupree raised his bandaged right hand and pointed to a painting on the wall behind Malenkova's desk. He didn't say anything, but kept watching Malenkova carefully. It was the striking painting Anielka had given her just a month earlier.

Malenkova paled. 'I think you better leave, gentlemen,' she said, steel in her voice. 'And next time, please make an appointment and I'll make sure I have my lawyer present.'

'As you wish, Madame,' said Lapointe and headed for the door.

'You obviously know a lot more about art than I do, Madame, but even well-paid lawyers can't silence a painting when it speaks,' said Dupree, and followed Lapointe outside.

'What was all that about?' asked Lapointe as they got into the waiting police car.

'The painting?' said Dupree.

'Yes.'

'Did you see her reaction?'

'I did. A flash of fear? You must have touched a raw nerve.'

'It's always about the little things; that painting ... it took me some time to work out where I'd seen something very similar just recently – no doubt by the same artist – and what that could mean.'

'And this could be helpful?'

'Oh yes. I don't believe in coincidences. It's all about a striking young woman and the infatuation of a friend of mine. Something about that young woman has bothered me from the moment I met her.'

'You are full of surprises, Claude. A connection, you think?'

'Perhaps. For now, it's just a gut feeling, a long shot, but you know how these things go. And besides, I have no doubt that Malenkova is involved. The question is how and to what extent.'

'I agree. You and your gut feelings, Claude; legendary stuff.' Lapointe reached for his pipe. 'I still remember your lecture about "the art of subtle connections", and "how to listen to what is not being said".'

'Ah, that,' said Dupree, smiling.

'I've never forgotten it. Some of our most spectacular break-throughs have begun in that way. Could this be another one?'

'Who knows?'

'Care to tell me about that young woman?'

'Buy me a coffee and a croissant, and I will.'

'You're on. I know just the place.'

After Lapointe and Dupree had left, Malenkova called Sokolov.

'We have a problem, Victor,' said Malenkova.

'Serious?'

'Could be.'

'What kind of problem?'

'I just had a visit from the police.'

'Oh? What about?'

'They know about our meeting. They spoke to Charpentier.'

'How much do they know?'

'Not much, for now. I don't think Martin told them anything important, for now ...'

'Leave him to me.'

'There is more.'

'Oh? What?'

'Anielka.'

'But she's doing a great job!'

'That's not the problem.'

'Then, what is?'

'She can't be allowed to come back to France.'

'Why?'

'I'll tell you.'

53

Old Jewish Cemetery, Prague: 2 March 2017

Jack turned up his collar and, braving the snow and the icy wind blowing up from the river, crossed the Old Town Square. As the Jewish Quarter wasn't too far away, he'd decided to walk.

Jack and Anielka had arrived by train from Budapest the night before, and Anielka was still in bed, sleeping in. As he walked past a chestnut vendor in front of a church, Jack stopped and bought some from the old woman, her face barely visible behind a thick woollen scarf. The aroma of roasted chestnuts drifting across from the brazier was irresistible and reminded him of Christmas in the Alps. And besides, the hot paper bag warmed his stiff fingers as he made his way through the deserted streets to the Old Jewish Cemetery to meet Avigdor Stein.

Stein had been quite specific about the meeting Kun had arranged the day before. Jack was to meet him in the cemetery at nine am, at the grave of Rabbi Judah Loew ben Bezalel, a famous sixteenth-century scholar. When Jack asked Kun why, Kun had replied with only one word: Golem.

Apparently, the grave was easy to find as it had a distinctive headstone that was one of the most striking and well preserved in the entire cemetery. According to Kun, this was typically Stein, who was quite eccentric and well known for his odd behaviour. As the curator of the Jewish Museum, he was also known as one of the most knowledgeable scholars of European twentieth-century Jewish history, especially the Holocaust, the *Shoah*.

Jack had given himself plenty of time to get to the cemetery, as he didn't want to be late and keep Stein waiting in the freezing cold. The Old Jewish Cemetery in Prague's crowded Jewish Quarter in the middle of town with its twelve thousand headstones – many of them broken and covered in moss and ivy – dated back to the fifteenth century. Because Jewish customs strictly forbid the removal of graves, and due to limited space in a cemetery that had outgrown its needs centuries ago, it has been estimated that more than a hundred thousand bodies have been buried there through the ages – in some places stacked ten deep on top of one another.

During the Nazi occupation, all traces of Jewish culture, including synagogues and cemeteries, were systematically erased in all the occupied countries, with relentless German efficiency. The reason the Old Jewish Cemetery and the Jewish Museum, with its thousands of precious historic artefacts, were spared by the Nazis was due to a dark, sinister plan: the establishment of an 'Extinct Race Museum' in Prague. The exhibits on display in this museum would tell future generations the story of an extinct culture and race, wiped out by superior Aryans.

Jack stopped at the walled entrance, looked at the plan of the cemetery he had downloaded earlier on his phone, and began to orientate himself. He could feel a cold chill racing down the back of his neck as he walked along the solemn rows of graves. He was looking for a large, ornate sand-coloured headstone decorated with a lion, belonging to the sixteenth-century rabbi of Prague. A morning mist hovered above the headstones like a shroud, making the long-forgotten reminders of generations past and lives long forgotten, look monotonous and confusing.

Just as Jack thought, *I'll never find this,* a tall, dark shape melted out of the mist. As he came closer, the shape morphed into a man standing motionless next to a headstone at the end of the row. Wearing a long black coat and black hat, the man looked like a Hebrew sentinel guarding the domain of the dead.

'You are much younger than I expected,' said Avigdor Stein in perfect English, his long white beard, sidelocks and prominent nose giving him an almost biblical look. 'But then, you are from Australia, I hear.'

'Please don't hold it against me,' said Jack, giving Stein his best smile.

'You must be wondering why I have suggested we meet here, among the dead, on this bleak morning.' Stein pointed to the striking headstone next to him.

'I was wondering about that, but I believe it has something to do with a golem.'

'Ah, Kun must have told you. Yes, that's correct, and there's no better place to talk about a golem than right here, next to the grave of the man who created the most famous golem narrative handed down through the ages.'

'Judah Loew ben Bezalel, the enigmatic, sixteenth-century rabbi of Prague,' said Jack, who had done some late-night research on the intriguing subject.

'Correct, and do you know what a golem is?'

'As I understand it, a golem is an anthropomorphic – that is, a being in human form created entirely from inanimate matter, like clay or mud.'

'Very good,' said Stein, impressed. 'Even some of my more gifted students couldn't have expressed this better. According to Jewish folklore, a golem is a changeable metaphor with endless symbolism. It can be a Jew, or gentile, man or woman. It can signify war, isolation, even despair, but also hope, generosity and compassion.'

'Fascinating,' said Jack, finding the scholarly explanations a little confusing.

'And you must be asking yourself what all this has to do with Pavel Ustinov, right?'

'Yes.'

'Pavel Ustinov was known as the Golem of Treblinka. To understand why, one has to delve into the famous golem narrative of rabbi Loew, who was known as the Maharal, and is buried right here. According to legend, the Maharal created a golem out of clay taken from the banks of the Vltava River—'

'And brought it to life,' interjected Jack, 'by using ancient Hebrew rituals and incantations to defend the Prague ghetto from pogroms.'

'Very impressive, Mr Rogan, you are well informed. The Holy Roman Emperor Rudolf II wanted to kill or at least expel the Jews living in Prague, and the Maharal created a golem to protect them from that fate.'

'And is that why Pavel Ustinov was called the Golem of Treblinka; because he wanted to protect the Jews in the death camp from extermination?'

'Yes, that was definitely part of it, but there's more. Come, let's go to the Klausen Synagogue; you would have passed it at the cemetery entrance. It's a lot warmer in there and we can talk about Pavel Ustinov, the famous Golem of Treblinka. Follow me.'

Jack felt a strange sense of excitement as he followed Stein up the stairs.

'We have some of the finest Hebrew manuscripts here,' said Stein. 'And exhibitions tracing Jewish traditions and customs reaching back to the Middle Ages. Everything the Nazis wanted to erase, but couldn't.' Stein stopped in front of a door and searched for the key in his coat pocket. 'The synagogue is a museum now; very popular. We have thousands of visitors from all over the world.'

Stein found the key, unlocked the door and opened it. 'Come in. This is my world.'

'Wow!' said Jack as he stepped into the crowded room. Shelves filled with dozens of leather-bound books, manuscripts, and all kinds of strange religious artefacts lined the walls. An intricately carved antique oak desk, covered with open books, notepads, photographs and an old typewriter, faced a large window overlooking the cemetery below.

'This is amazing,' said Jack, admiring the view down into the snow-covered cemetery with its thousands of headstones. 'It looks so different from up here.'

'It does,' said Stein and took off his heavy overcoat. 'Like a well of souls with thousands of voices. When I sit up here and look down, there are moments when I can actually hear them, calling out to me. They help me unlock the secrets of ancient manuscripts, even letters penned a long time ago, or precious ritual objects like these here.'

Stein pointed to a crate on the floor. 'These items were found quite recently near Krakow, where the Nazis destroyed a synagogue during the war. A secret hoard hidden from the barbarians, preserved for posterity. Please take a seat.'

Jack noticed that Stein was dressed in traditional Hasidic garb: an old-fashioned, black three-piece suit, *gartel*, and, of course, the customary black hat. He had come across this before in Borough Park, Brooklyn, and recognised it at once as the traditional attire of an Orthodox Jew.

As Jack sat down next to the desk, he could see a copy of Madame Petrova's music box letter on top of a neat bundle of papers.

Jack pointed to the letter. 'And could you hear those voices when you read this letter here?' he asked. 'Did they call out to you?'

'Ah, *that* letter.' Stein took a seat at the desk and carefully picked up the letter. 'This is an extraordinary document,' he said, ignoring the question and staring dreamily down into the cemetery at something only he could see. 'I would love to have the original here in our collection. A letter written by Empress Alexandra, the last tsarina, the day before she was murdered.'

'Is that the only reason the letter is extraordinary?'

'No. There's more; a lot more.'

Jack was carefully watching the expression on Stein's face. 'There is?' he asked. 'And what might that be?'

'It's extraordinary because it tells us so much, and I'm not talking about the actual content as such. That's for others to delve into.'

'Oh? What then?'

'I am interested in the letter's *journey* from the Ipatiev House in Yekaterinburg in 1918 to Treblinka, and from there to the home of Countess Bezukhova in France in 1943, in the middle of the war. This is an astonishing story worthy of investigation.' Stein turned around to face Jack. 'I understand this is what you are interested in as well, Mr Rogan, albeit for perhaps different reasons.'

It was clear to Jack that Stein had given this subject a lot of thought and was familiar with not only the historical background, but also with many other intricate aspects of the letter that only a scholar of his experience and standing would notice.

'That's correct. I am trying to trace the letter back to its origin—' said Jack.

'Because that may help you unravel the mystery surrounding Mat' Rossiya and Kazanskaya Bogomater?' interjected Stein. 'And perhaps even lead you to those treasures entrusted into the care of the Protectress of Russia by Alexandra?'

Jack nodded.

Stein held up the letter and began to read: '*If this letter does reach you, my dear friend, you can assume that both of my treasures are out of harm's way, and in the care of the Protectress of Russia.*'

'Exactly,' said Jack. 'And we now know that the letter *did* in fact reach Countess Bezukhova. I believe the two people who can help me unlock the secrets hidden in this letter are David Herzl and Pavel Ustinov.'

'The Postmaster of Treblinka and the Golem of Treblinka. This is quite a story,' said Stein and put the letter back on the desk. 'You already know all there is about Herzl. Kun would have told you. After all, he wrote a whole book about this subject. You know, of course, that David Herzl was his father, and Ilona Kun his mother?'

'He told me. But I don't know what happened to them after the liberation of Treblinka.'

'Ilona was Hungarian. They went back to Budapest. Sadly, Herzl was very ill by then and died shortly after. Ilona was pregnant and gave birth in her parents' home in Szentendre. Kun still lives in the same house.'

'That leaves us with Pavel Ustinov,' said Jack. 'And I was hoping that you would be able to help me with—'

'The Golem of Treblinka? Yes, I believe I can.' Stein reached for another letter on his desk and held it up. 'It all began with this,' he said. 'A letter sent from Treblinka I, the labour camp, through the Wehrmacht Feldpost, would you believe. It found its way into our museum a few years ago. Here, have a look at this.'

Stein showed Jack the letter.

'The same Herzl markings at the top: the Star of David and a small heart,' said Jack, becoming excited. 'Incredible!'

'It is. We call it the Treblinka postage stamp. The letter was sent by Roza Finkl in August 1943, to her mother here in Prague. We know all about this letter because it is recorded right here in Herzl's diary.'

Stein held up a page of Herzl's original diary. 'Roza paid for posting the letter with a ring given to her by her late father, a rabbi. It was the bribe that made it all possible.'

'Movingly sad,' said Jack. 'But at the same time beautiful in a way.'

'It is. Extreme brutality rubbing shoulders with acts of kindness and compassion in a death camp. We are extremely fortunate to have documents like these to give us a little glimpse into the lives of those who endured that horror, and didn't lose their humanity. But I didn't show you this letter to talk about Roza. Sadly, she didn't survive; she was only nineteen. I am showing you this letter because of one particular reference that has a direct bearing on what you are looking for. This passage here. I'll translate it for you.'

Jack pulled his little notebook out of his pocket and looked expectantly at Stein.

'*There is one kind man here in the camp, a Trawniki guard called Pavel,*' Stein began to read. '*He brings us extra food and sings beautiful Russian songs at night. He's a Russian prisoner of war, a huge man with a bushy beard. He reminds me of the Golem of Prague that Papa used to tell us so much about, only kinder.*'

Stein put down the letter and looked at Jack. 'This is just the beginning. I can tell you a lot more about the Golem of Treblinka that you will find interesting.'

'Obviously my breadcrumbs of destiny have brought me to the right place,' said Jack, smiling.

'What a wonderful phrase,' said Stein. 'Who knows? Perhaps it is a golem reaching out of the past that you need to answer your questions, Mr Rogan.'

'Perhaps. Let's find out, shall we?'

54

The Golem of Treblinka,
German-occupied Poland: August 1943

Treblinka. Just whispering the name would have made those who knew what happened in the death camp tremble with loathing and fear, because the name alone conjured up images of mass murder, unspeakable horrors, and brutality on a scale almost impossible to imagine. Between July 1942 and September 1943, 925,000 Jews were exterminated at Treblinka as part of a relentless killing machine created by Operation Reinhard.

David Herzl sat in a small room allocated to him as his 'studio' in one of the barracks in Treblinka I, used to house the 'Trawniki men'. The Trawniki were Soviet prisoners of war trained by the SS as auxiliary police guards, deployed as part of the 'Final Solution' to guard the forced-labour camps.

Herzl was trying to catch the last of the fading afternoon light to help him restore the halo of a Madonna. He preferred to work during daylight, as it was almost impossible to get the colours right otherwise. The harsh light from the single lightbulb dangling from the ceiling was not conducive to meticulous restoration work involving priceless masterpieces.

'What do you think?' said Herzl and stepped back from the canvas.

'Perfect,' replied Ilona, his assistant. 'Giotto would be pleased. You are a genius.'

Herzl took Ilona by the hand and drew her towards him. 'This is surreal,' he said. 'Here we are in this shabby little room in the middle of a concentration camp where hundreds are killed every day, surrounded by works of genius worth millions. Look over there, a Raphael, and there on my bed, a van Gogh and a Klimpt. All looted from who knows where, and damaged along the way by ignorant thugs.'

'Patiently waiting here for a little restoration to return them to their former glory, by *you*.' Ilona gave Herzl a peck on the cheek. 'Just think how fortunate we are—'

'Useful, would be a better way to put it,' interrupted Herzl, well aware that it was only his talent that kept them both alive. He had even survived the Warsaw Ghetto revolt in May, only because of his reputation as a master forger. Instead of being shot with all the others, he had been spared and was sent to Treblinka for 'special duties'. 'As long as we are useful, they'll keep us alive.'

'Hush,' said Ilona and placed a finger on Herzl's lips. 'Don't question fate; it's bad luck.'

'I know, yet here we are, getting preferential treatment and more food than we can eat. While out there, they are starving on the way to the slaughterhouse. It's obscene. I wish I could do something.'

'You *are*.'

'The letters?'

'Yes. They mean a lot more than a little extra food. A lot more than you realise. Hope is priceless, and communicating with those we love, precious.'

'You think so?'

'I know so. You should have seen Roza's face when I told her that her letter had been dispatched and was on its way to her mother in Prague.'

Herzl began to chuckle. 'Delivery with compliments of the Feldpost,' said Herzl, who got huge satisfaction out of the unique arrangement he had on the go right under the noses of the SS. It gave him a little power and self-respect.

For several weeks now, he had been able to smuggle letters written by fellow prisoners out of the camp as part of his own correspondence to order materials, or consult art experts throughout the Reich in connection with his work. These letters were never questioned by those in charge, as the '*Restorierer*', as Herzl was known, was under the personal protection of SS Captain Theodor van Eupen, the commandant of the Treblinka labour camp. Treblinka II, the horrific killing centre, was located a mile away in the forest, and had a different commandant who reported directly to Operation Reinhard.

Whatever Herzl asked for, Herzl got. His work was that important, and van Eupen, who considered himself something of an art connoisseur and frequently visited Herzl, used it to impress his superiors in Berlin. They welcomed the regular deliveries of priceless art treasures from Treblinka, meticulously restored by Herzl, and praised van Eupen accordingly.

Herzl and Ilona sat on Herzl's bed, holding hands. Outside it was already dark, and they were listening to the Trawniki singing soulful Russian songs full of sadness and longing, when there was a knock on the door. Herzl got up, opened the door and looked at the mountain of a man standing outside.

'I hear you speak Russian,' said the man, his voice deep and melodious.

'I do. What is it you want?'

'I've come to warn you,' said the man, lowering his voice.

'Warn me? What about?'

'The letters ...'

'I ... I don't know what you mean,' stammered Herzl, feeling sick.

'May I come in?'

Herzl stepped aside and let the man enter.

'We are safe in here as long as they are singing outside,' said the man, recognising the fear in Herzl's restless eyes. In the camp, fear was never far away. Life could be snuffed out in an instant, and for no apparent reason.

Ilona stood up and looked at the huge man, who almost filled the room with his presence. His curly beard and unkempt hair gave him a wild look, but his voice was seductively gentle, and seemed at odds with his powerful physique and threatening appearance. *He has kind eyes*, thought Ilona as she kept watching the man's body language.

Herzl pointed to the only chair in the room. 'Please sit.'

'There are whispers,' said the man.

'What kind of whispers?' asked Herzl.

'That you are smuggling letters out of the camp.'

Herzl looked at Ilona and locked eyes with her. She too, understood Russian.

'Don't worry, you are safe for now,' continued the man. 'Roza is a friend. I give her extra food when I can.'

So, that's her guardian angel, thought Ilona, who knew Roza well. *Her golem. He certainly looks like one.*

Used to dealing with the unexpected, Herzl realised there was no point in playing a charade of denial, and instead decided to find out what had brought the man to him, alone, and at this hour. 'Why are you doing this?' he asked, taking a dangerous leap into the unknown. 'Why the warning?'

'Because I need your help, and I can help you in return. In short, we can help each other.' With that, the man began to relax.

'Please explain.'

'My name is Pavel Ustinov. I'm from Yekaterinburg. Do you know where that is?'

Herzl nodded.

'I was captured by the Germans during the battle for Moscow at the end of 1941 and have been a prisoner of war ever since. I was trained as a Trawniki guard by the SS in a camp outside Lublin last year. And now, here I am.'

'Why are you telling me all this?' asked Herzl.

'Because I need your help,' repeated the man.

'What kind of help?'

'You can help me fulfil a promise.'

Herzl looked at Ustinov, surprised. 'I don't understand. What kind of promise?'

'A promise I made a long time ago to someone who was kind to me when I was in need. I grew up in an orphanage inside a convent in Yekaterinburg.'

'What kind of promise?'

'The nun who took me in when I was a starving little boy and looked after me, was dying just as the convent was being closed down by the Bolsheviks in 1920. I was twelve. She handed me a letter and asked me to guard it with my life because it was very precious.'

Ustinov paused and ran his thick fingers through his unruly hair, painful memories clouding his craggy face. 'She also asked me to deliver it, whatever that may take, and I promised to do just that,' said Ustinov, his voice barely audible. 'Then she died in peace,' he whispered.

'What kind of letter?'

'I don't know. It's in a sealed envelope with a name and address on it.'

'But that was twenty-three years ago,' interjected Ilona. '*You kept the letter all these years?*'

'I did. There's no time limit on a promise. I had it on me all the time. On the battlefields, in the prison camps, in the field hospital, always. In fact, I have it with me right now.'

Ustinov reached into his shirt pocket and pulled out a crumpled envelope. 'This is it here.'

'May I see it?' said Herzl.

Ustinov handed him the letter.

'Hmm. It's addressed to a countess in France. How interesting.'

'I don't know if I will ever get out of here alive, and I can't stop thinking about that promise. It's keeping me awake at night. I'm afraid that time is running out.'

'You are taking a big risk coming to me with this,' said Herzl.

'Roza said I can trust you. And besides, aren't we all taking big risks here every day? I have nothing left to lose, except this letter here.'

'I understand.'

'Do you think you could smuggle it out of the camp and send it to the countess in France through the Feldpost?'

Herzl looked at Ilona. She nodded ever so slightly.

'I suppose I could.'

'I cannot pay you like the others. I know that substantial payments are needed to make all this work, both here inside the camp, and outside.'

'You are well informed. You know how these things work in here. Yes, substantial bribes are needed to make this possible, but even then, the risks are great. And there are no guarantees. Anything can happen to the letter along the way.'

'Trying is better than doing nothing. I am happy to take that risk. While I cannot pay you, I don't come empty-handed.'

'What do you mean?'

'I can offer you something more valuable than payment.'

'Oh? What?'

'Protection. I have influence among the guards and they look up to me. I can make sure your secret stays safe, a blind eye is turned when needed, and no questions asked. The SS are lazy and leave the work to us. How does that sound?'

'Too good to be true. What do you think, Ilona?'

'I think with Pavel's help we could perhaps even expand our little operation, and you could become the Postmaster of Treblinka,' said Ilona, a sparkle in her eyes.

'Did you hear that, Pavel?'

'I did. I think Ilona's right. I am a prisoner in here just like you two, not expecting to live. If we can make a little difference in this hellhole and bring a little hope and sunshine into a few lives, like you did with Roza, then please count me in.'

'All right,' said Herzl and held out his hand. 'Leave the letter with me.'

'Thank you. I can't tell you what this means to me. You won't regret this,' said Ustinov, tears in his eyes. 'I better join the others outside, or they'll wonder where I am. The next song is my turn, and besides, I play the balalaika.'

55

Anna's Studio, Kuragin chateau: 3 March 2017

Hands folded behind his back and deep in thought, Dupree stood in front of the painting Anielka had given Countess Kuragin as a thank-you present after her overnight stay at the chateau.

'Cook told me I would find you here,' said the countess as she walked into Anna's studio, looking for Dupree. 'Dark, isn't it?'

'It's more than that. It's scary. Would you say this painting was unique, say, in style, composition and execution?'

'Absolutely. Anna certainly thinks so, and she's an artist with an eye for such things. According to her, it's unique. She called it genius. Why do you ask?'

'Because I saw one just like it a few days ago.'

'Are you sure? Where?'

'In the home of a fascinating woman who Lapointe and I went to visit the other day as part of our enquiries. It was hanging in her study.'

'How interesting. Is she a suspect?'

'Too early to tell, but I think she's definitely involved. At least in the recent sale of the Fabergé egg on the dark web. She's certainly keeping the right company for that. And then there was something else about her ...'

'What?'

'*Danger.* Despite her controlled manner, the woman exuded danger.'

'And the painting could somehow be relevant here?'

'Possibly, and that's what scares me.'

'Why?'

'Because if I'm right, it could have catastrophic consequences for someone we are both very fond of.'

'What are you talking about? Who?'

'Jack.'

'Are you serious? In what way?'

'I'll tell you, but you must promise me to keep this to yourself for the time being.'

'Of course.'

'Because at the moment, it's just a hunch. Have you ever wished that something you suspected wasn't true?' asked Dupree, changing direction.

'Yes. When Anna went missing. Why do you ask?'

'Because I am going through something similar right now. I can't get this disturbing painting out of my mind. It's even haunting me in my sleep.'

'Why?'

'Because reason and common sense tell me that if there are *two* such paintings, both of which are so unique in style and character, that can only mean one thing—'

'That both have been painted by the same artist?' interjected the countess.

'Exactly. And that's what worries me.'

'Why?'

'Because of what that could mean. I have had an uneasy feeling about Alina from the very beginning,' said Dupree. 'As you know, I only met her briefly once – in your kitchen on the morning of her accident.'

'Funny you should say that. She made me feel uneasy, too.'

'What prompted that, do you think?'

'The way she interacted with Jack. To me it looked like—'

'What?' interrupted Dupree, watching the countess carefully.

'She had a plan ...'

'My God. *That's it!*'

'What do you mean?'

'Throughout my entire career, I've been dealing with various manifestations of the criminal mind, and it has almost always been the little things that turned out to be the major clues. The little bits discovered quite by accident, like a gesture, a turn of phrase, or a slip of the tongue accompanied by a smile that didn't fit.' Dupree paused, and took a deep breath. 'We have to get to the bottom of this quickly, before it's too late!'

'What are you talking about?'

'Jack went to visit Alina on several occasions. He even spent the night with her, right? Do you know where?'

'She has a small flat somewhere in Montmartre.'

'Do you have an address?'

'No. All I know is they had a long lunch in a restaurant close by.'

'Do you know the name?'

The countess shook her head. 'Why don't you just call Jack and ask him?'

'*No!* I would have to explain the question, and I can't do that. Not yet.'

'Wait a minute. Jack bought her a new scooter and had it delivered to where she lives as a surprise.'

'*What?* When?'

'The day after he stayed the night with her.'

'What kind of scooter; did he tell you?'

'Yes. He wanted to surprise her and make it something special—'

'*Think!* This is important!'

'I believe it was a Vespa. Yes, that's it. A Vespa. We even joked about it.'

'Katerina, you are wonderful!' said Dupree. 'It shouldn't be too difficult to track down the dealer. I'll ask Lapointe to get onto it straight away.'

'You haven't told me yet why this is so important.'

Dupree bit his lip and looked at the countess with concern. 'Once we've found the flat and examined it, I'll know more.'

'You are scaring me, Claude. You owe me an explanation! What is it you are so frightened of?'

'I suppose you're right. But not a word to anyone, for now.'

'Promise.'

'If my hunch turns out to be correct, then Alina could be ...' Dupree paused, searching for the right words.

'What?'

'Somehow involved in all this.'

'What? *The murders?*'

'It's possible.'

'My God! What are you saying? *Are you serious?*'

'Absolutely.'

'But that would mean that Jack is travelling with—'

'A very dangerous woman, yes.'

'We must warn him!' said the countess.

'Not yet. We have to be sure first. Jack would never believe us without proof.'

The countess nodded. 'You're right. But he could be in danger.'

'Quite possibly. Even more reason to make absolutely sure we are right about this.'

'Anna saw it, too,' said the countess.

'Saw what?'

'As soon as she set eyes on Alina, right here in the studio, a feeling of dread came over her, she told me. She's very perceptive about matters like that, especially since her ordeal in Australia. She even gave it a name. I completely dismissed this at the time, but now ...?'

'What name?'

'Evil.'

'The pieces of the puzzle are beginning to fall into place,' said Dupree. 'All we need now is to see the whole picture.'

'Are you suggesting that coming here was no accident? That she *wanted* to get close to Jack; is that it? So, she staged one? The accident, I mean.'

'Yes.'

'But why?'

'If my hunch turns out to be correct, then Alina is working for the Black Widow and travelling with Jack to find out all she can about his investigations in Russia. This is all about that letter. The letter that killed Philippe,' said Dupree, sadness clouding his eyes. 'This definitely fits a pattern, a very dangerous one.'

'This is monstrous!'

'Perhaps, but it is also very clever. Just think of Mademoiselle Darrieux and what happened to her. And whoever was capable of that, and those two murders, is capable of anything. Someone's playing a very ruthless game here.' Dupree paused, and looked intently at the countess. 'I have to go, and please, not a word to anyone! The sooner we resolve this, the sooner we can warn Jack.'

'Where are you going?'

'To get proof!'

56

Frieda Malenkova's study: 4 March 2017

'You said it was urgent,' said Zuzanna. 'I came as soon as I could.'

'Sit down. We have a problem,' said Malenkova.

'What kind of problem?'

'I had a call from Quasimodo.'

'Oh? What about?'

'He just had a visit from the police. He sounded very agitated.'

'Understandable. What did they want?'

'They asked him about a red scooter parked in his driveway and wanted to know to whom it belonged. At first he thought it was some kind of traffic matter, but of course, there was more to it; a lot more. Remember Rogan bought Anielka a new scooter just a few days ago?'

'You told me. How weird.'

Malenkova raised an eyebrow. 'It sure is. A chief superintendent doesn't deal with petty traffic matters.'

'Lapointe?'

'Yes. Dupree was with him. They are obviously following some kind of lead and are looking for Anielka.'

How is that possible? asked Zuzanna, her shrill voice the only sign of her alarm.

'Don't know. At least Quasimodo kept his mouth shut. He gave nothing away.'

'Can you trust him?'

'Yes. He has more to lose than we do at this stage. Self-preservation is a strong motivator, and Quasimodo is a survivor. All he told the police was that a young woman, an art student – and of course, he gave them Anielka's new false name – was renting his flat on the first floor for a couple of weeks. A casual arrangement. Paid cash.'

'What happened then?'

'The police searched the flat. Apparently there were many of them, and they took some stuff away—'

'Could have been Forensics,' interjected Zuzanna.

'That's what I thought.'

'What could they have been looking for, do you think?'

'Don't know, but there's obviously some kind of connection here. First, Fabron, then Charpentier, followed almost immediately by a visit to me here. And now Quasimodo. This is no coincidence. Lapointe is following a specific trail, and the trail is somehow leading to Anielka, for now. After that, who knows?'

What Malenkova didn't tell Zuzanna was the curious comment Dupree had made about Anielka's painting as he was leaving. She was still trying to work out the meaning of that baffling statement, and if it could possibly have been some kind of clue.

'Where does this leave us?' asked Zuzanna.

'As long as Anielka stays out of their reach, I think we are safe. I cannot see how they can link us to her, or they would have done so already and come knocking. Worst-case scenario, they suspect that I had something to do with the sale of the Fabergé piece. They know I met with Victor. My reputation ... You have been very careful and have followed my instructions?' said Malenkova, changing direction.

'Sure have.'

'Good. I already told Victor that Anielka cannot be allowed to return to France.'

Zuzanna looked impressed. Malenkova was clearly in control of the situation and, as usual, a step ahead of the game. Instead of allowing events to overwhelm her, she already had a plan about how to meet the problem head on.

'And he can arrange that?'

'Yes. He will take care of it. He's well connected in Russia ...'

'I see. And what about us? You must admit, Lapointe and Dupree have made impressive progress in such a short time, and are a potential threat.'

'They have, and they are,' conceded Malenkova, who appeared to be enjoying herself. Zuzanna knew that Malenkova thrived on a challenge and needed the thrill of danger to keep her motivated. To her, danger and excitement were the oxygen that sustained her spirit. 'We have to be prepared and get ready—'

'Ready for what?'

'To disappear, of course. I've prepared for years for an eventuality just like this. When you take something to the wire, you must accept the consequences. When the stakes are high, so are the risks. And with Anielka out there and two sensational murders, the stakes were always going to be about as high as they can get.'

'*Disappear?* What do you mean?'

'Quasimodo prepared false papers for me years ago. The photo may be a little outdated by now, but it'll do. I have a bolthole in the Caribbean, ready and waiting with all the money I can possibly need. I can close up shop here and vanish within the hour without a trace. Even someone like Lapointe wouldn't be able to find me,' said Malenkova, laughing. 'You can come with me, if you like. Or would you perhaps prefer to make your own arrangements?' said Malenkova, sounding almost flippant.

'Are you serious? You are prepared to abandon all this?'

'Of course. We are only temporary custodians of stuff like this. But let's not panic. I think we are quite safe here for now, and I certainly don't want to abandon our project in midstream. Especially now that Anielka is doing such an excellent job, and Rogan seems to be making good progress.' Malenkova pointed to the whiteboard. 'Here. Have a look.'

Malenkova pointed to the last two pages from Jack's notebook Anielka had sent through from Prague the night before. 'He seems to have traced the music box letter to this mysterious Postmaster of Treblinka in the concentration camp in Poland. This was in 1943.'

'And then there's this strange Golem of Treblinka creature,' said Zuzanna, who had studied the entries the night before, 'who seems to have something to do with the letter.'

'Quite. That's why Rogan went to Prague and met with Stein. Once again, it is virtually impossible to make sense of his cryptic entries, except for this ...'

'What?'

'The Novo-Tikhvinsky Convent in Yekaterinburg. He's on his way there right now. I've already spoken to Victor about the convent. He has some kind of expert looking into this as we speak, and will have someone on the ground in Yekaterinburg to keep an eye on Rogan and what he's up to.'

'Impressive. Can you trust Victor?'

'You asked me this before. Not really, but as long as we need each other, all's well: allies of necessity. And at least for the moment, we do need each other. That's why I don't want to leave here too soon and give up our advantage.'

'What advantage?'

'Anielka. At least for now, we get all the latest information firsthand from her direct. Victor depends on us for that. Even the best experts can't help him without that. For that reason, we need Anielka by Rogan's side for a little longer.'

Malenkova looked pensively at something on the whiteboard. 'Until we know what this is all about, it's our best option,' she said and pointed to the whiteboard.

'And after that?'

Malenkova shrugged. 'Common sense tells me,' she continued, 'that some of the answers to this intriguing puzzle will be found in Yekaterinburg. After all, that's where the letter originated from, and that's where Alexandra was murdered. If there's anything left to find, that's the place to start looking for it.'

Malenkova paused and looked at Zuzanna.

'And my gut feeling tells me that something really big is involved here,' she said, 'and Rogan knows that too. That's why he's following his breadcrumbs of destiny, and Anielka is standing right there next to him, watching.'

'Makes sense. So, what's our next move?'

'We keep calm, we don't panic, but get ready to leave if necessary.'

'And Lapointe and Dupree?'

'As long as we keep them away from Anielka, we're safe.'

'And Victor?'

'We keep an eye on him and use him. Just as he is using us.'

'This is a dangerous game.'

'Would you have it any other way?' said Malenkova, chuckling.

57

Finbar Castle, Scotland: 4 March 2017

Perched on a narrow, rocky headland in Aberdeenshire overlooking the sea, the fortified, fourteenth-century medieval castle had played a prominent role in Scottish history. Bought as a ruin by Sokolov, it had taken more than ten years to restore the stunning complex standing high above the brooding sea like a proud, defiant reminder of warring clans defending their honour and their precious lands. With no expense spared, the restoration had so far cost more than thirty million pounds and was still ongoing.

Sokolov sat in front of a huge stone fireplace in the wood-panelled library where he kept the most precious pieces of his eclectic art collection. Rows of rare, leather-bound books dealing mainly with Russian literature and history, rubbed shoulders with paintings by Nesterov, Repin, Vrubel and Kandinsky. Priceless objets d'art like his four Imperial Fabergé Easter eggs and mysterious, centuries-old icons, were displayed on a painstakingly restored seventeenth-century Spanish harpsichord that had survived the Spanish Civil War and the Lisbon earthquake, and had a voice so pure it would have made a virtuoso weep with joy.

Sokolov was admiring his latest acquisition, the Rasputin Fabergé egg that had cost him fifteen million euros.

'Do you think I paid too much, Dmitri?' said Sokolov, and picked up the egg. 'Malenkova is a cunning old crow, you know.'

'You are not seriously asking me that, are you? We both know you cannot put a price on history. And this in the palm of your hand right here is history; our Russian history.'

'You are right, of course,' said Sokolov and looked affectionately at his friend. Sokolov and Dmitri Aldar, a former KGB agent in his sixties, had been close friends for a long time. Both had grown up in Ulaanbaatar in Mongolia and joined the Soviet Army as impoverished young men looking for a better life. Dmitri went on to work for the KGB, but a disillusioned Sokolov left the army in his early thirties and went to live in Moscow where he drifted aimlessly from one boring, menial job to another, until the disintegration of the Soviet Union in 1991 provided him with the opportunity of a lifetime: he became a young entrepreneur and made a fortune during the era of privatisation, and ended up a billionaire.

The disintegration of the Soviet Union had also brought about the dissolution of the notorious KGB, and Aldar found himself adrift, without the career he had thrived on. A few years later, he made contact with his old friend Sokolov, who offered him a job. Aldar became the young tycoon's trusted right-hand man in charge of security and 'sensitive' projects. Aldar's KGB experience and many contacts among USSR officials and former KGB operatives were invaluable, and had accelerated Sokolov's meteoric rise as one of the most successful and ruthless 'kleptocrats' of his day.

One of Aldar's greatest assets was his appearance, which he had carefully cultivated. Diminutive in stature, quietly spoken, with thinning hair and a deceptively disarming manner and charm, it was easy to be lulled into complacency and underestimate him. Yet under this almost mundane and ordinary facade resided not only a razor-sharp mind, but also one of the most ruthless tacticians who would stop at nothing to achieve his objectives, however brutal or devious.

In many ways, Sokolov and Aldar complemented each other and were the perfect combination: a brilliant entrepreneur, and a ruthless tactician and enforcer to back him up, remove obstacles and pave the way.

Sokolov sat back and reached for the bundle of papers on the cushion next to him. They were copies of Jack's notebook pages sent by Anielka to Zuzanna. Sokolov and Aldar had carefully analysed the entries, followed Jack's journey, and had tried to decipher the often-cryptic clues hidden among the pages. Sokolov quickly leafed through the pages and held up the one he had received earlier that day.

'Rogan's on his way to Yekaterinburg to visit the Novo-Tikhvinsky Convent,' said Sokolov. 'What do you make of that?'

Taking his time, Aldar lit a cigarette and let the smoke curl towards the ceiling before giving an answer. 'I think he's getting close,' he said thoughtfully.

'What makes you say that?'

'Pavel Ustinov.'

'The weird Golem of Treblinka?'

'Yes. He grew up in the convent as an orphan under the care of the nuns. He was there in 1918 when Nicholas and his family were murdered, and he brought the letter entrusted into his care with him to Treblinka. After all those years. That certainly means something.' said Aldar.

'And then sent it from there to Countess Bezukhova in France. Extraordinary, don't you think?'

'It is.'

'What do you know about the convent?'

'The Novo-Tikhvinsky Convent was founded in the eighteenth century. It was huge. Until the revolution it was the biggest convent in the Ural. It was like a small town with six churches, numerous workshops, and accommodation for hundreds. It was closed in 1920, and then used as Soviet offices and for military administration.' Aldar paused and looked pensively at the exquisite Fabergé egg in front of him.

'The convent was reopened in 1994,' he continued, 'and has had a big revival since. Nuns are flocking back and several of the churches are being restored right now. Monastic life has been reintroduced and traditions revived, especially canonical iconography. Nuns are now painting icons again, embroidering priestly vestments, and are singing Byzantine chants in the churches. The place is flourishing.'

'You seem to know a lot about this.'

Aldar shrugged. 'My job.'

'I think Malenkova is in trouble,' said Sokolov, changing direction.

'So do I. Is that a problem?'

'Only if our line of communication is interrupted, or stops altogether at this critical time. And that depends to a large extent on Anielka.'

'The beautiful, dangerous killer travelling with Rogan?' said Aldar.

'Yes. The ruthless young siren who has bewitched him and made him blind to all but her charms. It's an old story,' said Sokolov, chuckling.

'I do love human weakness. It opens so many doors. That, too, is an old story.'

'It is, and it makes people vulnerable. Malenkova is vulnerable right now, and her weak spot is Anielka. She doesn't want her to return to France. Too dangerous, she says, and it's quite obvious why.'

'Because Anielka could lead the authorities to her. The French police must be frantic by now. Malenkova fears exposure. So, the question is how do we take advantage of this, right?' said Sokolov.

'Exactly. I think we should take over before something goes wrong here and it's too late—'

'And the hidden treasures mentioned in Alexandra's letter are lost forever?' said Sokolov, a cheeky little smile playing on his face.

'Something like that,' said Aldar. 'In a situation like this, control and timing are everything. Spoils to the victor, right? We've come this far; we might as well see it through properly. Treasure, or no treasure. And who knows? Someone like Anielka could be an asset if handled correctly.'

'And how do you suggest we should approach that?' asked Sokolov.

'I think I should go to Yekaterinburg straight away. I want to be there when Rogan makes a breakthrough, as I believe he will. And you can tell your friend Malenkova that angel face will not return to France. That should give her some peace of mind.'

'How will you make sure of that?'

'Leave it to me,' said Aldar, smiling.

'I'll get the plane ready. You can leave in the morning.'

'Looking forward to it,' said Aldar and lit another cigarette.

'This is right up your alley, isn't it?'

'We'll see ...'

58

Novo-Tikhvinsky Convent, Yekaterinburg: 5 March 2017

Jack entered the huge, labyrinthine complex of the Novo-Tikhvinsky Convent and hurried past the recently restored cloisters and the St Ignatius Hermitage where the sisters and nuns resided. Glancing briefly at the map in his hand, he turned left and then walked towards the workshops, where traditional silk embroidery and iconography were making a comeback. This revival ensured that the ancient skills handed down from generation to generation were not forgotten.

It was still quite early and a pale morning sun was hiding behind a blanket of thick fog, making it difficult to find even the imposing three-domed cathedral dedicated to Grand Prince St Alexander Nevsky, where Jack was due to meet the abbot.

Wearing a heavy black woollen cloak and a conical fur hat, Abbot Serapion was waiting for Jack on the steps of the cathedral. His long white beard made him look like a Russian saint about to bless the faithful. In a way, he reminded Jack of Avigdor Stein, who had waited for him in the Jewish Cemetery a few days earlier. How Stein had managed to arrange the meeting was still a mystery, but Stein seemed very well connected, and apparently knew the abbot well. They had exchanged documents and information about Pavel Ustinov, the Golem of Treblinka, who had grown up in the orphanage run by the convent. An Orthodox Jew and an Eastern Orthodox Russian monk, united by scholarly pursuits.

Since meeting Vasiliev in St Petersburg, Jack had felt like a pilgrim of destiny being irresistibly swept along by forces beyond his control towards something momentous waiting for him somewhere in a distant, uncertain future.

Along the way, he had already met several helpers, each one holding an important piece of the puzzle. First there was Vasiliev, who had pointed the way to Kun in Budapest, who in turn had

346

referred Jack to Rabbi Stein in Prague. As Jack walked towards the abbot, he sensed that the most important piece of the perplexing puzzle, which could lift the veil of the past and perhaps complete the elusive picture, was waiting for him on the steps of the cathedral.

'We have been waiting for you for a long time,' said the abbot. He spoke perfect English, but with a heavy Slavic accent. 'Avigdor has told me a lot about you and your quest. Please follow me; there is something I would like to show you.'

Instead of asking for an explanation, Jack took off his hat and tried to make sense of the strange welcome as he followed the abbot into the cathedral. Inside, the cathedral was cold and empty. Shafts of pale morning light reached hesitantly through the dirty windows, like ghostly fingers exploring long-forgotten treasures.

The abbot stopped in front of a side altar and turned to face Jack. 'It was right there, until 1920, when the convent was closed by the Soviets, and the cathedral abandoned.' The abbot pointed to an empty pedestal in the middle of the altar, illuminated by one of the pale shafts of light from above, looking like an accusing finger pointing to a grievous wrong. 'We have been looking for it ever since and praying for its return.'

'What was there, abbot?' asked Jack.

'Something holy and precious.'

'Please tell me, *what was it?*'

'Kazanskaya Bogomater, the Holy Protectress of Russia,' said the abbot and bowed his head.

Good God! Alexandra's letter! thought Jack, his head spinning. 'Can you tell me more?' he whispered.

'Not here, not now. Please come back tonight, and you shall meet the Guardians and the Seeker. They will answer all your questions, and all will be revealed.'

Jack didn't notice the little elderly man sitting in the hotel foyer, watching him carefully as he walked past. Aldar put down his paper, stood and followed Jack outside. For the sake of convenience, Jack had deliberately chosen a hotel close to the convent and decided to walk. Anielka had reluctantly stayed behind, watching TV and ordering a room service dinner. To placate her, Jack had promised to take her sightseeing the next day.

Outside, it was dark and bone-chillingly cold, and it had begun to snow again. Jack turned up his collar and hurried towards the convent. As he approached the cathedral, he could see the abbot waiting for him on the front steps with a lantern in his hand.

'Come; it isn't far,' said the abbot and began to walk away from the cathedral.

I wonder where they are going? thought Aldar, trying to stay in the shadows.

The abbot pointed to a small church that had obviously missed out on restoration. It looked as if it had barely survived a bomb attack during the war and been left to languish ever since.

'Here we are,' he said and walked to the back of the derelict building. He stopped in front of a small wooden door and knocked. The door opened almost immediately. The abbot greeted a bearded man dressed in black, and walked inside.

'Be careful, the steps are steep and slippery,' warned the abbot as he began to walk slowly down a set of narrow, winding stairs leading into the darkness below.

That's it for now, thought Aldar, realising that any further surveillance was pointless. *Luckily, he writes everything down.* Aldar lit a cigarette, turned around and began to walk back to the hotel.

Just before they reached the bottom of the stairs, Jack could hear chanting, the ethereal harmonies making the fine hairs on the back of his neck tingle. The abbot stopped at the bottom and turned around. 'We are almost there,' he said, and held up his lantern. 'The one wearing the red hat is the Seeker, the others are the Guardians. Come.'

As they moved deeper into a large, vaulted chamber opening up in front of them like a cave, the chanting grew louder and Jack could see candlelight. Six monks, all dressed in black, their faces concealed behind black veils attached to their *kamilavkas* – the traditional cylindrical flat-topped hat – stood in a semicircle in the middle of the chamber. Illuminated entirely by candles sending crazy shadows dancing up the wet, moss-covered walls to the lofty ceiling above, the chamber looked like the gateway to a strange underworld guarded by a contingent of pious monks. Mesmerised, Jack watched the abbot take a bow. The chanting stopped, and the monks bowed in silent reply. The one wearing the red hat – the Seeker – stepped forward and turned towards Jack.

'Welcome,' he said in broken English. 'We have been expecting you. It has been foretold, and now it has come to pass. This is a day of great joy, because it heralds the return of Kazanskaya Bogomater.' The monk paused and took a bow.

'You must forgive me, but I don't follow,' said Jack, also taking a bow.

The Seeker pointed to the abbot. 'Would you please tell our friend here the legend of Kazanskaya Bogomater and what it means to us.'

The abbot nodded and turned to face Jack. 'Kazanskaya Bogomater – Mother of God of Kazan, or Our Lady of Kazan in English – is a precious, holy icon that was brought to Russia from Constantinople in the thirteenth century. It soon rose to prominence within the Russian Orthodox Church and became the much-revered protector of the city of Kazan.'

The abbot paused, looked at the Seeker and nodded. The Seeker raised his right hand and the chanting continued, only softer this time, and merged with the abbot's deep voice as he continued to tell the story. To Jack, it sounded like some eerie Gregorian chant, reaching out of a distant past.

'In 1438, the icon disappeared from the pages of history, and was miraculously recovered unharmed one hundred and forty years later, after a fire had destroyed most of Kazan. According to legend, the Virgin appeared to a girl named Matrona in a dream, and showed her where the icon had been hidden to save it from the Tartars. The icon was recovered, and for the next three hundred and twenty years it resided in the Convent of the Theotokos in Kazan. During this period, a number of miracles were attributed to Our Lady of Kazan, which included protecting Russia from invasions. After that, she became known as the Holy Protectress of Russia and was revered throughout the country.'

The abbot paused again and looked at the Seeker. 'I think the rest of the story should be told by you, Seeker, as you know it much better than I.' The abbot bowed again and stepped back.

'During the night of twenty-nine June 1904, thieves broke into the convent and stole the icon,' began the Seeker slowly. 'The thieves were eventually caught and initially maintained that the icon had been destroyed and its precious frame sold. However, one of the thieves told a different story. When he was about to throw the icon into the fire, he noticed that the Virgin had changed her appearance: she was weeping. Overcome by remorse, he could no longer destroy the icon and instead took it to a remote convent in Siberia. The authorities didn't believe him, declared that the icon had been destroyed and refused to investigate the matter further.'

The Seeker stared into the distance for a moment, then resumed.

'The alleged destruction of the icon was considered a sign by the Orthodox Church that great calamities were about to befall Russia. Sadly, that is exactly what happened. Revolutions tore the country apart, cities were destroyed and a devastating war killed millions. All of these disasters were attributed to the wanton destruction of the Holy Protectress of Russia.'

The Seeker paused again and looked at Jack. 'You must be wondering what all this has to do with you, and why we've brought you here and are telling you this.'

Jack nodded.

'You will why see in a moment,' continued the Seeker. 'This is where the matter rested until nineteen June 1918, the day after the tsar and his family were murdered in the Ipatiev House not far from here. On that day, Sister Natalya – a nun from this convent here who had taken food to the Imperial family during their incarceration – approached the abbot and showed him an icon entrusted to her care by Empress Alexandra, and asked for his advice. The abbot recognised it at once as Kazanskaya Bogomater, stolen from the Convent of the Theotokos in Kazan in 1904. When he examined the icon more closely, he noticed that the Virgin appeared to be weeping. For the next two years, the holy icon was on display here in the cathedral. Just before the convent and the cathedral were closed down by the Soviets in 1920, the icon was taken to the Tikhvin Assumption Monastery near St Petersburg for safekeeping. It remained there until 1941, when the Germans occupied Tikhvin for a month during World War II and looted the monastery. Kazanskaya Bogomater, now known as the Weeping Madonna of Kazan, was taken back to Germany together with other treasures, and disappeared. The Guardians and I have been looking for it ever since.'

The Seeker looked in Jack's direction.

'That's quite a story,' said Jack once the chanting had stopped. 'I would like to ask you some questions, if I may.'

'Please, go ahead,' said the Seeker.

'You said earlier that you had been expecting me for a long time. What did you mean by that?'

'Do you believe in destiny, Mr Rogan?'

'Is this question part of your answer?' said Jack, finding it difficult not to smile.

'Yes, it is, because certain things are preordained and will happen regardless of our actions.'

'You are right. And are you suggesting that what has brought me here, is just such a case—?'

'We *know* it is! The Seeker before me was a hundred and two when he died. Many years ago, he had a vision: Kazanskaya Bogomater was taken by a stranger out of her beloved country, and a stranger would bring her back, and we believe, Mr Rogan, that you are that stranger.'

351

'What makes you say that?'

'You are here, are you not? You are a seeker just like me, following the trail of Kazanskaya Bogomater. Isn't that enough? But, of course, there is more.'

'Can you tell me?'

The Seeker nodded. 'We know that Rasputin retrieved the icon from the monastery in Siberia and gave it to Alexandra, so that Kazanskaya Bogomater could watch over the tsarevich and keep him safe. We also know about the Yusupov letter and Yusupov's extraordinary claim, and your interest in that matter ...'

The Seeker waited to let this sink in and show Jack just how well informed he was.

'All of us here standing before you are scholars who have dedicated our lives to investigating every possible lead, every clue, anything that could help us find the icon,' continued the Seeker, 'and return it to Russia. The main reason we have been unsuccessful so far is due to an unfortunate mishap of history: no-one knows what the original icon actually looks like. Strange, don't you think? There are many descriptions and much speculation, but not a single, reliable image has survived. There are many copies out there – clumsy imitations would be a better way to put it – created by charlatans both here in Russia and abroad, claiming to be the real thing. Can you see the dilemma?'

'I can. And you believe that I can help here?'

'Yes, I do; we all do,' replied the Seeker without hesitation. 'If somehow we could find out exactly what the original icon looks like, find an image, a copy that is true to the original to guide us, then I have no doubt that this would lead us to the holy icon because as sure as night follows day, Kazanskaya Bogomater is somewhere out there, just waiting to return home.'

'What makes you so sure?'

'Faith.'

The Seeker raised his hand again, and the eerie chanting resumed. To Jack, it sounded like a prayer this time. He closed his eyes and let the stirring melodies carry him away. *If we could somehow find out exactly what the original looks like,'* Jack heard the Seeker say over and over, *'this would lead us to the holy icon.'*

Then something happened: a flash of inspiration exploded in Jack's brain. He remembered a certain passage in one of Alexandra's letters he had discovered in the Amber Safe. Jack opened his eyes, reached into his coat pocket and pulled out his little notebook.

The Seeker watched Jack intently as he opened the notebook and began to look for something. *Here it is,* thought Jack and quickly ran his eyes over the passage he had remembered.

Jack looked at the Seeker and smiled. 'Speaking of destiny and faith,' he said, 'something you said just a moment ago, may have just shown us the way. I just remembered something that could help us find the holy icon.'

'What have you remembered?' asked the Seeker, surprised.

'A passage from a recently discovered letter written by Empress Alexandra to her friend, Countess Bezukhova. It was sent from Tobolsk in October 1917. Allow me to read the passage to you.'

The chanting stopped and all eyes were on Jack.

'*I pray daily to Kazanskaya Bogomater,'* Jack began to read, *'and she gives me comfort and strength. You, too, can of course do the same, as her image is the wonderful surprise waiting below Faberge's ingenious Easter cross.'*

For a while there was silence in the chamber. Then the Seeker asked, 'Do you know what this means, Mr Rogan? Could you please explain it to us?'

Jack ran his fingers through his hair and took his time before replying. The storyteller in him was trying to find the best way to articulate something that he himself was having trouble coming to grips with.

'I believe an image of the Weeping Madonna of Kazan does exist. It is to be found inside an Imperial Fabergé Easter egg commissioned by Tsar Nicholas and given to his wife in 1917.'

'How do you know this?'

'I have seen the Fabergé egg. Just recently.'

'You have *seen* the image of …?' said the Seeker.

'No, but I am sure it's there.'

'How can you be sure?'

'Because of this letter, and because certain things are preordained and will happen regardless of our actions.' Jack looked at the Seeker. 'And because like you, I too believe in destiny,' he added softly.

'Do you know where to find this mysterious Fabergé egg with the surprise under the Easter cross?'

'The journey is far from over, but after what I've just witnessed here tonight, everything seems possible. Yes, I believe I do.'

'And should you find this image, what will you do?' asked the Seeker.

'I will keep searching for the icon.'

'And if you should find it, what will you do with it?'

'I will return it to where it belongs. The Weeping Madonna of Kazan will come home, and that pedestal in your cathedral will be empty no more. That, I promise.'

'I have no reason to doubt your words, Mr Rogan,' said the Seeker. 'After all, it was foretold.'

By the time Jack made it back to his hotel, it was quite late and Anielka was already in bed, asleep. For the next two hours, Jack wrote down everything he had witnessed that evening while the impressions were still fresh in his mind, and his memory clear. He was afraid that by the morning, he would cast most of it aside as something he must have experienced in a dream.

59

Tikhvin Assumption Monastery, Tikhvin: 1941

SS Major Axel Wolfbauer was on a mission. Tall, blue-eyed, with wavy blond hair, he was the pin-up boy of classic Aryan good looks and arrogant Nazi superiority. When he heard that the town of Tikhvin – two hundred kilometres east of St Petersburg – had been taken, he immediately called one of Hitler's adjutants at the Berghof on the Obersalzberg, Hitler's Alpine fortress-villa near Berchtesgaden. The purpose of the call was to advise the Fuehrer that he was making arrangements to go to the Tikhvin monastery as soon as possible, to investigate something they had discussed on numerous occasions.

The reason for this urgency had nothing to do with military or strategic considerations, but touched on something quite different. Something personal and secret: Hitler's fascination with the occult.

To a scholar like Wolfbauer, who was an acclaimed expert on esotericism and the paranormal, the Tikhvin Monastery of the Dormition of the Mother of God had special significance. It was generally believed that this was the place where the famous icon of the Theotokos of Tikhvin was being kept after the Soviets had closed down the monastery. Always on the lookout for significant artefacts, Wolfbauer was eager to find out if that was in fact the case and, if possible, bring it back to Germany.

But that wasn't all. There was another, more important reason for the hasty visit. Rumours had circulated for years that another, even more important icon was being kept at the monastery. It was the precious Kazanskaya Bogomater, transferred to the Tikhvin monastery for safekeeping just before the Novo-Tikhvinsky Convent in Yekaterinburg was closed down in 1920. The reason Wolfbauer was so interested in that icon was not because of historic or spiritual reasons, but because it was reputed to have occult powers that had protected Russia from invasions in the past.

According to legend, military commanders through the ages had successfully invoked the help and protection of the Virgin Mary through this icon. Hitler, who was a great admirer of past military commanders like Pozharsky and Kutuzov, was eager to get his hands on that icon. He believed this would weaken Russian resistance and morale, and enhance the strength of his own forces to help him conquer Russia.

For these reasons, Wolfbauer realised that securing the icon and presenting it to Hitler would be a major coup, especially during such a critical time in the Russian campaign. If successful, this would further enhance his already considerable influence and standing within the Fuehrer's inner circle.

Wolfbauer had risen to prominence within the SS with the publication of his book, *Dawn of the Superman,* which almost overnight became the Aryan Nazi bible. Himmler embraced the book and made it compulsory reading for every member of the SS. He also introduced the handsome young officer to Hitler, who saw in him the personification of the Aryan male discussed in the book.

Because the arguments put forward by Wolfbauer echoed Hitler's own personal views and obsession with the occult, in particular astrology, Hitler and the young major had many discussions about this subject. Hitler had shrewdly appropriated Christian ideas and symbolism, like the Holy Grail and the Spear of Destiny, and openly spoke of the coming of a new Messiah. The Nazi propaganda machine then took over and carefully planted the idea that Hitler could be the chosen one, who would lead the German people into a glorious future and forge a Reich that would dominate the world, and last a thousand years. This was enthusiastically embraced by the masses, and the cult of the Fuehrer was born.

Soon Wolfbauer became Hitler's confidant, with special powers and permits that allowed him to roam freely through occupied territories in search of artefacts of spiritual importance and with mystical powers that could be used to further Hitler's plans and standing.

This opened doors for Wolfbauer wherever he went, without too many questions being asked, and ensured the cooperation of those in charge. He was often compared to Albert Speer, Hitler's architect, who translated Hitler's vision into monumental buildings on a scale never seen before. In a way, Wolfbauer was doing the same, but in a more subtle way, using the occult to spread and refine Hitler's ideology and cult.

The monastery had seen better days. Years of neglect, especially after the Soviets had closed it down in 1920, had taken their toll. Founded in 1560 and constructed as a fortress because it was close to the Swedish border, it had endured several wars and was looted by Polish troops in 1610, and subsequently occupied by Swedish forces.

The only inhabitants now were a small group of monks who acted as caretakers and lived in the ancient cells of the monastery next to the belfry, and depended on the charity of peasants living nearby to survive. It was this group Wolfbauer went to see as soon as he arrived. A captured Russian officer who spoke German acted as translator.

Wolfbauer looked like a conquering god as he strutted arrogantly into the refectory in his imposing black SS uniform, radiating authority and instilling fear. Two heavily armed soldiers walked behind him and stood guard in the doorway. The bearded monks, many of them wearing rags instead of habits, watched with apprehension as Wolfbauer stopped in front of them, lit a cigarette, and let the tension grow.

Used to conducting interrogations and overcoming resistance and lack of cooperation, he decided to come straight to the point.

'I understand that the icon of the Theotokos of Tikhvin is kept here in the monastery,' said Wolfbauer. He paused for effect and let the cigarette smoke curl towards the vaulted ceiling. 'I would like to see it,' he added quietly. 'Now!'

One of the monks, apparently the eldest, stepped forward and took a bow. Realising that resisting the young officer was pointless, he decided that subservient cooperation was the safest option. 'The holy icon is kept in a crypt under the altar of the Church of the Dormition,' said the monk.

'Is that the large five-domed church I passed on the way here?'

'Yes, it is.'

'Take me to it!'

The old monk nodded and began to walk towards the exit. The other monks fell in behind him and followed him outside.

This was easy, thought Wolfbauer. He dropped his cigarette on the stone floor and stubbed it out with the tip of his boot. *The next part may not be.*

After walking along a maze of narrow underground corridors and down winding, candlelit stairs that would have confused all but the initiated, they came to a heavy, iron-studded wooden door. The old monk took a large key out of his habit, unlocked the door and stepped into a small chamber. The other monks followed him inside and formed a protective semicircle around a stone sarcophagus standing in the middle.

Illuminated by a single candle on top of the heavy marble lid, Wolfbauer could see a beautiful icon resting on a blue velvet cushion next to the candle.

The old monk pointed to the icon. 'This is the icon of the Theotokos of Tikhvin,' he said. Then he stepped forward, bent down, and kissed the icon.

Slowly, Wolfbauer walked around the sarcophagus without taking his eyes off the stunning icon, its gold riza reflecting the candlelight and making the Madonna's halo sparkle. *Impressive,* he thought, *but not what I'm looking for.*

Wolfbauer stopped in front of the old monk and looked at him with his piercing, ice-blue eyes. It was time to introduce the real reason he had rushed to Tikhvin. He was hoping it wasn't too late and the monks hadn't already removed, or safely hidden, the treasure he was after.

'Thank you for showing me this,' said Wolfbauer. 'But this is not why I have come here.' He paused to let this sink in. 'I believe you are the custodians of *another* precious icon, placed into your care by the abbot of the Novo-Tikhvinsky Convent in Yekaterinburg twenty years ago. That's correct, isn't it?'

'I don't know what you are talking about,' said the old monk, his voice quivering with apprehension and fear.

'But I think you do,' said Wolfbauer, his voice emotionless like the cold steel of his dagger attached to his belt. 'I am talking about Kazanskaya Bogomater, Our Lady of Kazan, who turned into the Weeping Madonna of Kazan after she had been stolen from the Convent of the Theotokos in Kazan in 1904,' continued Wolfbauer quietly, 'and was brought here for safekeeping in 1920 after she had been recovered.' He was showing the old man just how well informed he was. A tried and tested strategy he had used many times. By revealing precise details about a small part of the whole story, he gave the impression he knew a lot more than he did. This usually created an air of uncertainty and fear, eventually resulting in capitulation by those he tried to intimidate and control. But not so on this occasion. The old monk shook his head and stood there in silence. Defiant.

'I see,' said Wolfbauer. 'I will ask one more time: where is the Weeping Madonna of Kazan?'

The old monk didn't reply.

'Have it your way.' Wolfbauer picked up the burning candle, held it up and looked at the old monk. 'This is on your head. I hope you can live with it, old man,' whispered Wolfbauer, and held the burning candle against the exposed wooden parts of the icon. The monks looked on in horror as the flame began to lick the serene face of the Madonna – threatening to ignite it – and candle wax began dripping onto the velvet cushion like tears.

'*No! Stop!*' shouted the old monk and held up his hands.

Smiling, Wolfbauer withdrew the candle.

The old monk said something to his brethren and pointed to the sarcophagus. The monks stepped forward. First, the old monk lifted the icon and the cushion off the sarcophagus and placed it carefully on the ground. Then he gripped the edge of the stone lid with both hands. The others did the same and began to slowly turn the heavy lid, creating an opening big enough to be able to see inside.

Looking defeated, the old monk let go of the lid and pointed into the sarcophagus. 'Kazanskaya Bogomater,' he said, sadness in his voice, and stepped aside.

60

Berghof, Obersalzberg, Berchtesgaden: 1941

Hitler stood in front of the sprawling picture window in the conference room of the Berghof – his Alpine fortress on the Obersalzberg in the Bavarian Alps near Berchtesgaden – and looked pensively across to the Untersberg, one of his favourite mountains. Usually, this spectacular yet familiar view seemed to calm him, but not this time. Operation Barbarossa, the invasion of the Soviet Union, was going badly.

The largest invasion force in military history had failed to achieve its objective and had stalled. A furious Hitler, who had spent weeks at the Wolfsschanze, his headquarters in East Prussia, directing the campaign, needed some time to think, away from his generals and the depressing reports of huge casualties and setbacks. And the best way to do that was to spend a few days in his beloved Berghof, a comfortable Bavarian chalet where he felt at ease, and spent more time during the war than anywhere else.

Hitler's adjutant knocked and entered. 'Major Wolfbauer has arrived,' he said. 'Shall I show him in?'

'Please do, and bring us some tea.'

Moments later, Wolfbauer entered, stood to attention by the door and saluted. To be granted a private audience with the Fuehrer in the Berghof was a rare honour. Hitler looked at Wolfbauer and smiled. *Give me a thousand men like him and I could conquer the world*, he thought.

'How was Tikhvin?' asked Hitler.

'Eventful, Mein Fuehrer. Ancient walls and secretive monks were guarding a great treasure I have been trying to find for a long time.'

'And have you?'

Wolfbauer pointed to an embossed leather case under his arm he'd had specially made for the icon. 'I have,' he said.

'Some good news at last. My generals are imbeciles; men without vision who do not understand that you cannot build a Reich without struggle and sacrifice. You cannot have a glorious future without blood. We sent three million men into battle together with six hundred thousand motorised vehicles – an unheard-of number – to conquer the western Soviet Union and clear the territory of Slavic people and populate it with Germans. My *vision!* *Lebensraum* for Germany. But my generals don't seem to understand. All I hear are their excuses; nothing but excuses!'

Wolfbauer listened in silence as Hitler became progressively agitated. His monologues and tirades were legendary and could last for hours.

'Look at the Russians. They know what sacrifice means. They are dying by the hundreds of thousands, yet still they are coming. Relentless waves of primitive people armed with only the most basic weapons, and my generals cannot crush them. What is it these Russians have that we don't? What do you think, Herr Major?'

Wolfbauer took his time before replying. 'Faith?' he ventured. 'I have seen it firsthand.'

Hitler nodded and looked thoughtfully out the window. 'Faith, you say? We believe in destiny; that's stronger, surely! No matter,' he said and turned around. 'What have you got for me?'

'Something we've discussed before, Mein Fuehrer.' Wolfbauer placed the leather case carefully on a table by the window and opened it. 'The legendary Weeping Madonna of Kazan,' he announced and stepped back.

'*You found it!*' Hitler walked over to the table and looked at the icon in the leather case. Then he lifted it out of the case and held it up.

'Magnificent,' he said, admiring the intricate, yet unusually solid silver-gilt frame. 'Tell me about it.'

'The icon is very old and has a remarkable history. It dates from the thirteenth century and was brought to Russia from Constantinople.'

Wolfbauer then gave a brief outline of the icon's history he had carefully prepared earlier. He only touched on the highlights because he didn't want to overwhelm the Fuehrer with too much historic detail he wouldn't be interested in. What Hitler really wanted to know was not so much the history of the icon, but its reputed spiritual power and the reason it had been venerated throughout Russia for centuries. In short, he wanted to know if it could be useful to him.

'One of the main reasons the icon has occupied such a prominent position within the Russian Orthodox Church for such a long time,' said Wolfbauer, sounding more and more like the pedantic academic he was, 'and has enjoyed such popularity and is, to this very day, considered the Holy Protectress of Russia is this …'

Hitler was listening with interest. He put the icon back on the table, ran his fingertips over the heavy frame and looked expectantly at Wolfbauer.

'Numerous miracles have been attributed to the icon over the centuries, but none were more significant and are now firmly embedded in the national psyche than those linked to military matters.'

Wolfbauer paused to let this sink in because he knew from previous encounters with the Fuehrer that this was the subject of particular interest to him.

'Famous Russian military commanders like Dmitri Pozharsky and Mikhail Kutuzov attributed their success in repelling invasions by superior forces, to the intervention of the Virgin Mary. Both commanders had prayed in front of the icon and asked for help.'

Hitler nodded, deep in thought, but didn't interrupt.

'Keeping Russia safe during the Polish invasion of 1612, the Swedish invasion of 1709 and, most importantly, Napoleon's invasion of 1812 and repelling the invaders was all attributed to the intervention of Kazanskaya Bogomater, the Holy Protectress of Russia—'

'And do you think they are praying to her now and asking for help and protection?' asked Hitler.

'I questioned the monks at the monastery about that and the answer was *yes*. They seemed genuinely shocked when I took possession of the icon and told them I would take it back to Germany.'

'How did they react?'

'They looked terrified.'

'Do you know why?'

'Yes. They said if the icon were to leave Russia, great calamities would befall the country. Apparently, that has happened before.'

'In what way?' demanded Hitler, becoming excited.

'In 1904, the icon was stolen from the Convent of the Theotokos in Kazan and disappeared for a number of years. This was seen as a sign, heralding coming disasters. The Revolution of 1905, Russia's humiliating defeat in the Russo–Japanese War, and the millions of deaths during World War I that followed, were all attributed to this.'

'Interesting ...' said Hitler. 'Not all weapons require bullets. Do you know I spent some of my happiest times here on the Obersalzberg? It was right here in the Berghof that many of my great projects were conceived and ripened,' reminisced Hitler. 'This is where I had my best moments of inspiration.' He looked dreamily at the icon on the table. 'Could this be another one of those moments, I wonder?'

Hitler again looked out the window, searching for the answer in the timeless beauty of the mountains. *Perhaps the Madonna has changed sides?* he mused. *And all we have to do to break the Russian spirit is to let Russia know this has happened.* Then he turned around and faced Wolfbauer.

'You have done Germany a great service, Herr Major,' he said. 'I know I can always rely on you. You are not like my generals. Quarrelling weaklings, all of them! But enough of that.'

Hitler pointed to a settee and two leather chairs. 'Come, let's have some tea, and you must tell me more about that monastery and those monks.'

'Thank you, Mein Fuehrer,' said Wolfbauer, glowing with pride. Such praise from Hitler was rare.

61

The countess turned restlessly in her bed, unable to get back to sleep. It was still dark outside and too early to get up. For the second night running, bad dreams had haunted her sleep. Instead of fading away, Dupree's disturbing suspicions regarding Alina that in some strange way mirrored her own, had become stronger and had even invaded her sleep. Dupree had been very tight-lipped about the police visit to Alina's flat the day before and what, if anything, had been discovered. This had only heightened her apprehension.

The countess was slowly drifting back to sleep when her phone rang. Drowsy, she reluctantly reached for her mobile on the bedside table and answered it. It was Dupree.

'I am sorry to disturb you this early, Katerina, but I have something here that can't wait.'

'Do you know what time it is?'

'Yes; it's almost six. I just had a phone call from Lapointe.'

The countess sat up, instantly awake, a shiver of fear tingling down her back. 'What about?'

'Alina.'

'What about Alina?'

'Some things are better discussed face to face.'

'I'll be right over.'

'I'll put on some coffee.'

Wearing her gardening gumboots and a fur coat over her dressing gown to keep warm, the countess hurried across to the Gatekeeper's Cottage. Dupree was waiting for her at the door and opened it. 'Come in. I've rekindled the fire and the coffee is almost ready,' he said.

'Thank God for that; it's freezing.'

The countess walked over to the fire to warm her hands. Dupree joined her moments later and handed her a mug of hot coffee.

'You look worried,' said the countess, sipping her coffee.

'With good reason, I'm afraid.'

'Are you going to tell me, or are you going to kill me slowly with suspense?' said the countess, trying to introduce a little levity into the tense situation.

'I find myself in a very difficult position,' began Dupree.

'How so?'

'I've just been told something in absolute confidence I am strictly forbidden to share with anyone at this stage, because it could seriously jeopardise our investigation.'

'Yes?'

'On the other hand, our friendship ...'

'I understand,' said the countess and put her hand on Dupree's arm. 'You are facing a loyalty dilemma, right?'

'Very perceptive of you.'

'Yet you've asked me to come here at this hour?'

'Yes, because I have already made up my mind.'

'To tell me?'

'Yes.'

'You've discovered something!'

'Yes.'

'*Please tell me!* I haven't slept a wink since our talk the other day. And then the raid on top of it ...'

'It's bad news, I'm afraid; very bad.'

'Come on, Claude, *tell me!*'

Dupree took a deep breath and stared into the fire. 'One of the most promising pieces of evidence in the Amber Safe murder was a single strand of hair found under Aubert's fingernails. It was enough for a reliable DNA sample.'

'Jack told me.'

'Forensics had a close look at Alina's flat the other day and secured enough material to extract DNA. From a toothbrush and a comb, and a few other things.'

'And?'

'They compared the samples.' Dupree turned to face the countess. 'A perfect match.'

'What are you saying?'

'The person who was present in the Amber Safe when Aubert was murdered, and the person living in that flat in Montmartre, are one and the same.'

'Alina,' whispered the countess, looking shocked. 'Does this make her the murderer?'

'Most probably.'

'My God; *Jack!*'

Dupree nodded.

'What does all this mean? Where does that leave us right now? *What are we going to do?*'

'That's the second dilemma; the more serious one.'

'What do you mean?'

'Consider this: if we ring Jack now, confront him with the evidence and warn him about Alina, he may do something rash and put himself into greater danger than he probably already is. We know what Alina is capable of. Profilers have done a comprehensive analysis of the two murders. A textbook psychopath pattern.'

'What are you telling me?'

'If cornered, she'll kill him without hesitation, and they are sure she has a minder.'

'What; someone who pulls the strings and tells her what to do?'

'Yes.'

'Someone like the Black Widow you've been talking about?'

'Exactly. It all fits.'

'The woman you met the other day?'

'Could be. She had one of Alina's paintings in her study.'

'Is that all?'

'No, there's more.'

'Tell me.'

'A lifetime of intuition and gut feeling when it comes to the criminal mind and how it works.'

'*Mon Dieu!* What do you suggest we do?'

'We have to think this over carefully. Jack did say he was about to come back after Yekaterinburg.'

'Yes. Apparently, the visit to the monastery was very successful and has shown him the way,' said the countess.

'There's an arrest warrant out for Alina. Her real name is Anielka, by the way. As soon as she enters Europe, she'll be arrested. That's why I was told to keep all this to myself, for now.'

'I understand, but if Jack finds out that we knew about Alina all along and didn't tell him, what do you think he—?'

'That's the third dilemma,' Dupree cut in. 'We have to be very careful here, and there isn't much time. You know Jack much better than I. What do *you* think we should do?'

'Jack is a straight-up-and-down kind of guy. A wonderful friend who would give you his last shirt. His friends are his life, and he treasures friendship above all else. You know what I mean.'

'I do.'

'I think he would want to know. He would expect us to tell him, but there's a wild card here.'

'What kind of wild card?'

'He's totally infatuated with Alina. I've not seen him like this before.'

'In love?'

'Not sure. That's why I'm hesitating. I don't know how he will react, and what he will do if we tell him. Extreme emotions can do strange things to a man; I've seen it. And if we don't tell him, I don't know what impact that would have on our friendship, which I treasure. Jack's family; I would give more than my last shirt to shield him from all this.'

Dupree nodded.

'I have to think about it, Claude.'

'I understand, but don't take too long. This wheel is turning very quickly.'

'Do you really think she would hurt Jack?'

'Without hesitation.'

62

Church of All Saints, Yekaterinburg: 6 March 2017

Anielka propped herself up on her elbows and looked at Jack lying next to her, sound asleep. After a while, she kissed him gently on the forehead. Jack opened his eyes and looked at her.

'What time did you come to bed?' asked Anielka.

'Quite late.'

'How did it go?'

'I wrote everything down before I came to bed.' Jack reached for his notebook on the bedside table and opened it. 'When I think about it now, it seems like a dream, but the words here tell a different story.'

'Would you like to talk about it?'

Jack closed his notebook on the bedside table and looked at Anielka. 'Perhaps later. Today, I want to show you something quite extraordinary. Something very moving that is related to what I found out last night. I promised, remember?'

'This is our last day, then?'

'Yes. We are going home tomorrow. I think I've found out everything I can here. The rest is waiting somewhere else.'

'Do you know where?'

'I think so, but it won't be easy.'

Anielka shook her head. 'You and your stories, Jack,' she said and ran her fingers playfully through his hair. 'And your adventures.'

'I did warn you.'

'You did. Shall I order some breakfast?' said Anielka, changing the subject.

'Let's do that. I'm starving!'

'What's new?'

'Where are we going?' asked Anielka, snuggling up to Jack in the back of the taxi. The morning traffic was heavy and progress slow. Dirty

369

slush covered the busy streets of the bustling city that had become one of Russia's most important economic centres after the Soviet era, giving it a gloomy, monotonous, Siberian winter look. Founded in 1723, Yekaterinburg was known as the 'window to Asia'.

Jack pointed ahead. 'It's just over there.'

'A church?'

'Yes, but not just any church. This one has quite a story.'

'You don't say.'

'The most extraordinary thing about this church is where it stands,' continued Jack, undeterred, 'and what it signifies. It's all about a big wound, and healing.'

'Oh? It looks new, but it's quite beautiful with its golden domes, don't you think?'

'It is. It was consecrated in 2003 – eighty-five years after the former tsar and his family were murdered – to commemorate that horrific event. Here we are. Come, I'll tell you all about it.'

'Its full name is the Church on Blood in Honour of All Saints Resplendent in the Russian Land,' said Jack as they entered the church, crowded with visitors, many of them lighting candles and paying their respects at the altar.

'What did you mean: "it's all about a big wound and healing"?' said Anielka as she looked around the imposing interior of the spacious church, decorated with elaborate mosaics, icons and paintings.

'This church was erected where the infamous Ipatiev House used to stand. Tsar Nicholas, his wife Alexandra and their five children spent seventy-eight days imprisoned in that house before they were brutally murdered in its basement in the early hours of seventeen July 1918.'

'How horrible.'

'The house itself was demolished in 1977 and for a number of years the vacant site lay abandoned, until Nicholas and his family were canonised as Passion Bearers. After that, the Church decided to build a memorial in honour of the murdered Romanovs. Construction began in 2000.'

'Amazing.'

'Do you see that cross over there?'

Anielka nodded.

'It marks the exact location where the Imperial family was killed. That's the big wound I was talking about, but it's slowly healing. Healing can only begin once you face the demons of the past, and this entire complex here is about just that.'

Jack walked over to the cross and stood in front of it, his head bowed in silence. He was contemplating the dramatic events of the night before, when he thought he could hear the solemn chanting of the Guardians in the background as the Seeker asked: 'Do you believe in destiny, Mr Rogan?'

'I do,' whispered Jack. *Perhaps it was foretold after all*, he thought. *And I am that stranger who will bring the holy icon back to Russia and find Alexandra's Mat' Rossiya*. Without realising it, Jack was standing on the very spot Alexandra had died, her heart ripped apart by bullets, just before she could complete the sign of the cross with her shattered right hand.

While Jack stood in front of the cross, deep in thought, Anielka could feel her phone vibrating in her coat pocket. She pulled it out and looked at the screen. It was a message from Zuzanna: *Call me. Urgent!*

'You look like you've seen a ghost,' said Anielka as they left the church.

'Perhaps I have,' said Jack, shaking his head. 'Now, let me buy you some lunch. After all, it's our last day.'

'Where are we going?'

'A classic Russian restaurant called Pashtet, which means pâté in Russian, the house speciality. A friend recommended it. Very popular. The interior looks like a Russian *dacha*. I made a reservation.'

As soon as they entered the busy restaurant, Anielka excused herself and went straight to the ladies to call Zuzanna.

'You said it was urgent,' said Anielka. 'I called as soon as I could.'

'Where are you?'

'In a restaurant having lunch.'

'Can you talk?'

'Sure, I'm in the ladies. We are coming home tomorrow.'

'I know. That's why I'm calling. Please listen carefully. This is important.'

'Oh?'

'The police have been to your flat and searched the place—'

'*Why?*' interrupted Anielka.

'Not sure, but it sounds serious. Your landlord, Quasimodo, was taken in for questioning yesterday. You can't come back to France; too dangerous,' said Zuzanna, dropping the bombshell.

'What do you mean? How—?'

'Just listen to me! Frieda has taken care of everything. A man will meet you in your hotel tonight. His name is Aldar; he's Russian. I'll text you his number.'

'Are you serious? What about Jack?'

'You walk away and leave everything behind. Just bring your passport, phone, wallet, the stuff in your handbag. Nothing else. You got that?'

'Sure, but—'

'No buts, Anielka! This is serious! You must do exactly as I tell you, clear?' You have to slip out of your room unnoticed and call Aldar. Tonight! He'll meet you in the foyer.'

'Yes, but where am I going; with that guy, I mean?'

'He will take you out of Russia to a safe place. You can trust him. Frieda arranged it. We are depending on you! And one more thing. Copy Jack's notes from yesterday before you leave. Understood?'

'Sure. I'll do that when he's in the shower, as usual.'

'Now go before you are missed. We'll talk again once you are safely out of your hotel,' said Zuzanna and hung up.

'I've ordered *pashtet*, the speciality of the house, for an appetiser,' said Jack as Anielka sat down next to him. 'After that, we could try some *pelmeni*, dumplings filled with minced meat, a traditional Russian dish. The wine is passable,' Jack prattled on. 'Would you like some?'

'Yes, please,' said Anielka, her mind racing as she tried to get her head around what Zuzanna had just told her.

63

Kuragin chateau: 6 March 2017

Countess Kuragin was in the music room, drinking tea, when Dupree walked in, breathless and looking agitated. 'I think we've had a breakthrough,' he said.

'We have? Tell me.'

'Lapointe's methods are paying off.'

'In what way?'

'He found a connection; a very telling one.'

'Traditional methods carry the day? The plodder without imagination has found a bone?' teased the countess.

'It would appear so. It's all about Alina's landlord in Montmartre.'

'Tell me.'

'His name is Renee Duval, known in the Paris underworld as Quasimodo, a notorious forger who has done time in jail.'

'And that is significant?'

'By itself, perhaps not, but who he shared a cell with for several years certainly is.'

'Who?'

'Emile Fabron.'

'The Ritz safebreaker murdered on the houseboat?'

'The very same. Lapointe brought Duval in for questioning this morning. When he told him about Fabron's murder and hinted that he could be next, and why, Quasimodo began to sing like a bird in the belfry of Notre Dame.'

'And what was that song about?'

'What do you think?'

'The Black Widow?' ventured the countess.

'Very good. My hunch was right. The person who rented the flat for Alina was none other than Frieda Malenkova, the woman with Alina's painting in her study whom Lapointe and I visited the other day.'

'Extraordinary! Congratulations.'

'There's more. There's another woman involved here. Duval doesn't know her name, but from what he told us about her, she could be the woman who visited me when—' Dupree paused and began to choke.

'The fire?' said the countess. 'Le Fantôme?'

'Yes. The same woman who blackmailed Adrienne. It's all coming together.'

'Seems that way.'

'So, what's next?'

'We have to close the net. Slowly and carefully. Lapointe is very good at this, thorough and patient. He's putting everything in place right now. But first, we must arrest Alina.'

The countess nodded. 'Where's Duval now?'

'Still in custody being questioned. Lapointe wants to keep him there at least until we arrest Alina.'

'I understand.'

'Did you make that call?' asked Dupree, watching the countess carefully.

'I did. Just before you walked in.'

'How did it go?'

'I'm not sure,' said the countess, looking troubled.

'How come?'

'He was devastated. I could feel his confusion and pain. At first, he refused to believe me. He insisted I must be mistaken and dismissed the allegations as absurd. But when I took him through the facts, the DNA, the irrefutable evidence, I think he came around ...'

'You did tell him how crucial it was that he kept it to himself; not a word to Alina? No confrontation?'

'I did.'

'And you told him that she would be arrested as soon as she set foot in France?'

'I did that, too. I also have his flight number. They are booked on an Aeroflot flight arriving tomorrow afternoon at Charles de Gaulle.'

'How did he take that?'

374

'As I said before, I don't know.' The countess pointed to Madame Petrova's music box on the mantelpiece. 'And to think it all began with this, and that letter you found. Extraordinary.'

'It is. Ripples in a dangerous pond, and it's far from over.'

'I'm worried about Jack,' said the countess.

'Why?'

'He sounded like ...'

'What?'

'A broken man. I could hear his pain, his crushing disappointment. Still can.'

'I'm sorry, but—'

'I know. Perhaps I shouldn't have told him.'

'*No!* I'm sure you did the right thing, Katerina. Friendship demanded that.'

'I suppose you are right, but what about love?'

'What about it?'

'Perhaps love demanded something else.'

'What?'

'Silence. In any event, it's too late now. He knows; and who knows what he will do? Something like this is beyond reason. Emotions take over. I've seen that, and so have you.'

'I have.'

'Jack's a very passionate man. Very sensitive and emotional when it comes to matters like this.'

'I've noticed. Let's hope they get on that plane tomorrow and we can arrest Alina, or should I say Anielka. She's a lethal weapon. At least then, we can take care of Jack once the spell is broken.'

'I have a bad feeling about this, Claude. I won't sleep a wink tonight,' said the countess.

'Neither will I,' said Dupree. 'Let's keep our fingers crossed.'

One hour later, Malenkova received a text message from Quasimodo. He was still in custody, but had been allowed to make one phone call.

Malenkova paled when she read the message. It consisted of only three words: *Lapointe knows. Run!*

375

64

Yekaterinburg: 6 March 2017

Jack sat by the hotel room window overlooking the foggy street below, and once again went over his notes from the day before. 'I think we should stay in tonight,' he said. 'Early start tomorrow.'

'Good idea,' said Anielka, licking her lips. 'I'm tired. It's been a long day, but an interesting one. That church was amazing. Very moving.'

She looks preoccupied, thought Jack, trying desperately to come to terms with what the countess had told him on the phone earlier. Deep down, he still refused to believe it, but the facts, if true, were overwhelming. *Could she really be that monster? Has she come along only to spy on me? I have to know!* Then he thought of something he could do to find out.

Anielka sensed Jack's unease and walked over to him. 'You look troubled,' she said and looked over his shoulder. 'What's wrong? Is it about yesterday? Your meeting with the abbot?'

'No. As I told you, that went remarkably well. I would almost call it a breakthrough. I'm just trying to put it all together before my memory plays tricks on me.' Jack pointed to the last few entries in his notebook. 'If I'm right, then this could hold the key.'

'The trip was worth it, then?'

'Illuminating and eventful. In more ways than I could have possibly imagined.'

'I'm glad to hear it,' said Anielka, a little alarmed not by what Jack had just said, but by the way he looked at her when he said it.

Jack closed his notebook, put it on the table and turned to face Anielka. 'That's it for now,' he said, 'I'll take a shower.'

Jack stood up and walked slowly to the bathroom. *If what Katerina told me is true, then she won't be able to resist*, he thought, hoping desperately that he was wrong.

Instead of closing the bathroom door, Jack left it slightly ajar. He could just see his notebook on the table by the window. Then he turned on the water in the shower, returned to the door, and watched.

Anielka went to the dressing table by the bed and picked up her handbag. Turning around, she walked calmly over to the desk, put the bag on the chair and took out her phone. Then she opened Jack's notebook and began to photograph the last few pages.

Jack gasped as the implications of what he was witnessing began to sink in. Powerful, mixed emotions welled up from somewhere deep within him, clawing at his heart. Disbelief, disappointment and betrayal were soon replaced by humiliation and anger for having allowed himself to be deceived by a callous killer.

Slowly, Jack opened the bathroom door and began to walk towards the desk, hoping in vain that what his eyes were telling him wasn't true. As he came closer, Anielka could see a shadow moving out of the corner of her eye and turned around.

'What are you doing?' asked Jack, carefully watching Anielka. He saw the surprise on her face, and a flash of guilt and alarm in her wide-open eyes that could only mean one thing: she had been caught.

'I'm just taking a picture of your last entries here,' said Anielka, trying to sound casual as she was desperately searching for an explanation.

'Why would you do that?' said Jack, coming closer.

'Because I want to understand what you are doing. I want to be part of it. When you talk to me about your work, I feel so stupid, so left out. I thought if I could read your notes on my phone, I could, you know ... understand. Don't be cross, darling, I only—'

'This doesn't make sense! Please give me your phone,' said Jack, steel in his voice.

He knows, thought Anielka. The shower was still running, yet here he was. Fully dressed. How could this have happened?

'Please give me your phone,' repeated Jack and held out his hand.

By now, Jack was standing directly in front of her. She could sense the seething anger in him, and see hurt and danger in his eyes.

Feeling threatened and cornered, she had nowhere to go. Then Jack grabbed her wrist.

'You are hurting me; let go!' shouted Anielka.

'Your phone. *Give it to me!*' hissed Jack. 'No more charades!'

Then something snapped in Anielka and the demons lurking inside her took over. She reached into her handbag with her free hand and searched for her knife. When she touched the cold steel and activated the opening mechanism of the deadly switchblade knife, she felt calmer and back in control. As Jack tightened his grip and kept squeezing her wrist, Anielka raised her hand holding the knife, and stabbed him in the chest.

Jack let go of her wrist and staggered backwards. 'What have you done?' he stammered. Then, pressing both hands against his chest, he fell to his knees and looked at Anielka, pain and disbelief contorting his face. Anielka stepped forward and was about to cut Jack's throat to finish him off, when suddenly the demons began to retreat and all she could see was the accusing sadness in Jack's eyes.

Anielka dropped the bloody knife, as long-forgotten feelings of remorse cast aside the demons whispering '*kill, kill!*' For a few moments, Anielka stared at Jack lying on the floor, blood oozing out of his chest wound. Then she turned away and dialled the number Zuzanna had given her earlier.

A man answered almost immediately. 'Are you ready?' he asked.

'Yes.'

'Come downstairs. I'll meet you in the bar.'

As soon as Aldar saw Anielka walking towards him, he knew something was wrong. 'I am Aldar,' he said. 'Frieda and Zuzanna sent me. I've been expecting you.'

'I think I've killed him,' Anielka blurted out.

'*Keep your voice down!* What are you talking about?'

'Jack attacked me and I stabbed him. I think he's dead.'

'Where did this happen?'

'Just now, in our room.'

Used to dealing with pressure and the unexpected, Aldar evaluated the situation. 'Listen carefully. This is what I want you to do.'

Anielka nodded, reassured by the calm voice addressing her.

'Go back to your room, take his wallet and his phone. Clear?'

Anielka nodded again.

'And most important of all, take his notebook and come back down straight away. Leave everything else exactly as it is and leave the door to your room open. Understood? Now go!'

As Anielka walked back to the lifts, Aldar ordered another Scotch and rang his driver.

A few minutes after Aldar and Anielka had left the hotel, a maid walking along the corridor on Jack's floor noticed that one of the doors was left open. First she knocked, but when there was no reply she opened the door and looked inside. At first she thought the man lying on the floor must have had some kind of medical episode, but when she walked over to him and saw the blood, she began to scream.

PART IV
MAT' ROSSIYA

65

Fuehrerbunker, Berlin: 30 April 1945, *Walpurgisnacht*

Hitler was preparing to die. His evil empire had collapsed, and the Third Reich was about to pass into history. It was 30 April, *Walpurgisnacht*, a night of carnal feasting with witches and demons in German folklore. It was the night when evil forces roamed the land and bonfires were lit to ward them off as part of pagan rituals dating back to pre-Christian times.

The Fuehrer had dictated his final message and had his favourite dog, Blondi, poisoned. In his message he advised his generals that the defence of Berlin was over, and that he would kill himself rather than surrender. The Russians were closing in on the Chancellery, and it was only a matter of hours before they would break into the bunker. The iconic building, a symbol of Nazi power, had been under relentless Russian artillery fire throughout the night. The Russians were now very close. They had reached the Tiergarten and were shelling the nearby Potsdamer Platz.

Hitler stepped out of his private quarters deep down in the bunker under the Chancellery, to make his final farewells. Slowly, he walked along the crowded dining passage and shook hands with loyal members of his entourage. Everyone present knew the end was near. When he came to Wolfbauer, he stopped and looked at his favourite SS officer.

'It has been a pleasure knowing you, Herr Major,' said Hitler and held out his hand. Wolfbauer stood to attention and shook hands with the Fuehrer.

'It has been a privilege to serve you, Mein Fuehrer,' said Wolfbauer, his eyes misting over.

'Pity the icon couldn't work its magic, although I am convinced that was only because of disloyalty and betrayal, especially by Goering and Himmler, and, of course, my generals. No matter; it's too late now. I have left something in my room for you,' continued Hitler, lowering his voice. 'When I am dead and my body has been removed, I want you to go in there and get it. Take it with you. I don't want it to fall into Russian hands. Understood?'

'*Jahwohl*, Mein Fuehrer,' said Wolfbauer and clicked his heels.

Hitler nodded, turned around, and retired to his rooms.

Bormann, Goebbels and a few others stood in the passageway outside Hitler's quarters, waiting, the tension almost unbearable. Standing in the shadows behind them, Wolfbauer waited too, only he was on a mission. He would carry out the Fuehrer's last wish to the letter.

At three-thirty pm, a shot was heard. Bormann and Goebbels hesitated for a few moments, and then entered the Fuehrer's rooms. Hitler had shot himself in the mouth and lay on a sofa – his face disfigured – blood dripping from a huge wound. Eva Braun lay next to him. She had taken poison.

After the bodies had been wrapped in army blankets, they were carried up to the garden, dropped into a shell hole, and had petrol poured over them. Hitler's valet then ignited the petrol and set the corpses on fire.

Bormann and Goebbels stood to attention and raised their right hands in a Nazi salute as the flames engulfed the remains of one of the most evil dictators the world had ever seen. Behind them stood Wolfbauer, doing the same, but he didn't stay. While the others were still watching the flames, mesmerised, he hurried back down into the bunker and went straight to Hitler's quarters.

Wolfbauer closed the door behind him and looked around the deserted room. It didn't take him long to find what he was looking for. The leather case with the icon was on a table next to the sofa on which Hitler had killed himself. Wolfbauer opened the case, looked inside and smiled. He would make sure that Kazanskaya Bogomater would not fall into Russian hands. Then he closed the case and hurried out of the room, smelling of cordite.

66

Paris Charles de Gaulle Airport: 7 March 2017

Lapointe looked at the indicator board and smiled. The Aeroflot flight from Yekaterinburg had just landed. 'Well, Claude, this is it,' he said, and turned to Dupree standing next to him. 'You were right all along.'

'Everything in place?' asked Dupree.

'Sure. We can stay here and let the boys do their job. They are all in place and chomping at the bit to make an arrest.'

'Seniority is a wonderful thing, don't you think?'

'It has its moments. We'll take her straight back to HQ for questioning. We'll take Rogan along as well, of course. You can sit in on the interviews, if you like.'

'I would appreciate that, thanks. What about Malenkova?'

'Interviews first. She isn't going anywhere in a hurry. We have to play this by the book. The more we have to link her to the murders, the stronger our case. I don't want some fancy lawyer throwing a spanner in the works because we jumped the gun.'

Dupree nodded. Playing things by the book was one of Lapointe's strong points, and the reason he was so popular with the prosecutors. The power of patience.

Moments later, a young officer walked up to Lapointe and saluted.

'We have a problem, Chief Superintendent,' said the officer, looking decidedly flustered.

'What kind of problem?'

'They are not on the flight.'

'*What?* Are you sure?'

'Absolutely, sir.'

A fuming Lapointe had said barely a word during the drive back to HQ. He was trying to get his head around the disaster and had stormed straight into his office after their arrival, to make enquiries. He had left Dupree in the waiting room and asked him to call Jack on his mobile and try to make contact.

Half an hour later, Lapointe came out of his office and walked over to Dupree.

'I couldn't raise him,' said Dupree. 'I tried several times, but—'

'I'm not surprised,' said Lapointe and lit his pipe.

'Oh?'

'Rogan's in intensive care in hospital in Yekaterinburg, lucky to be alive.'

'What on *earth* happened?'

Lapointe shot Dupree a meaningful look. 'He was stabbed last night in his hotel room.'

'Alina?'

'What do you think?'

Dupree shrugged.

'The Russian authorities seem to think it was some kind of robbery, but we know better, don't we, Claude?'

'Do we know where she is?'

'No. Disappeared without a trace.'

'Merde!'

67

Frieda Malenkova's crypt: 7 March 2017

'I came as soon as I could,' said Zuzanna. 'You are leaving?' She stopped at the top of the stairs and looked down into the crypt below. 'What happened?'

Malenkova had called Zuzanna earlier and told her to prepare to disappear – urgently.

'Quite a lot,' replied Malenkova. She stood in front of an open wall safe and was stuffing money into a leather portmanteau. 'I think this is the end of the road – for us, I mean – at least for now.'

'How so?'

'Rogan's dead. Anielka killed him. She's out of control. Dmitri has taken her out of Russia.'

'*What?* Are you serious? What happened?'

'Don't know. But there's more,' said Malenkova, putting the last bundles of cash from the safe into the bag. 'Quasimodo just sent me a message from the police station. He's in custody, being interrogated. Lapointe knows about our connection to Anielka, and it's only a matter of time before he comes with a warrant. I want to make sure that when he does, the nest is empty. That's about it, and I strongly suggest that you do the same. There's little time. The only reason he isn't here right now pulling the place apart is because Anielka's disappeared. On the run, he thinks. And as we know, she's the centrepiece of his case. He must be furious.'

Malenkova chuckled as she closed her bag. It was obvious to Zuzanna that she was enjoying herself and thriving on the challenge and the adventure of it all. 'I've activated my exit plan. By the time Lapointe gets his act together, I will be long gone.'

'I ... don't ... think ... so,' said Zuzanna slowly.

'What are you talking about?' said Malenkova, frowning.

Slowly, Zuzanna turned around and lifted up a large metal canister. Then she unscrewed its top and began to pour its contents over the balustrade down into the crypt below.

What are you doing? shouted Malenkova. 'I can smell petrol!'

'You can, because it is. I've waited for a long time for this,' said Zuzanna calmly, and continued to empty the canister. Then she took a box of matches out of her pocket and held it up. 'Your life in my hands; at last!'

'What are you talking about?'

'Let me tell you a little story,' began Zuzanna. 'We have to travel back in time a bit. It's 1987. You are working for your father, the notorious Stasi Major General in East Berlin. You are his assistant, helping him with particularly sensitive cases—'

'What nonsense is this?' interrupted Malenkova in a shrill voice.

Zuzanna held up her hand. 'Bear with me. This won't take long. Does the name Professor Gero von Babenberg ring a bell? He was a university lecturer teaching modern history in Leipzig, and was considered an enemy of the state because of his views and outspoken manner.'

'Never heard of him.'

'But you and your father had a file on him as thick as a telephone book, reaching into every corner of his life, both personal and professional.'

'I don't understand. Where is this going?'

'You sabotaged his career and undermined his reputation. You hounded him mercilessly. You even managed to recruit his son, who became your most valuable informer. It was a coup – *your coup* – and you were even commended for it and promoted. Do you remember now?' said Zuzanna, becoming emotional. 'Turning his son against him was the final straw that destroyed him. He took his own life in 1987.'

'Why are you telling me all this?' shrieked Malenkova.

'Because Professor Babenberg was my father!' Zuzanna paused and stared at Malenkova.

'After the Berlin wall came down and the hated Stasi came crashing down with it,' continued Zuzanna, 'I made a promise. I promised myself that I would hunt down the perpetrators who destroyed my father.'

'This is insane! I know nothing about this. You are mistaken.'

'*Liar*! When the notorious Stasi files became public and the archives were opened and access was given to the people, I went to work. It took some digging and some time, but I finally found the files. *Your* files!'

This is serious, thought Malenkova as the enormity of her predicament became clear. She was trapped in an enclosed, underground space with only one exit, barred by a fanatical madwoman consumed by vengeance. Suddenly everything made sense and fell into place. As Zuzanna became more agitated, Malenkova inched closer to the open safe. She always kept a loaded Glock in there. An old habit from her Stasi days.

'It took me some time to find you, but I did. And now, here we are. You and me. The day of reckoning has arrived!'

'You are mad!'

'I don't think so. I have assembled a dossier about you with enough evidence to send you to jail for the rest of your life. I was going to send it to Lapointe, but events have obviously overtaken us. You are too slippery and too cunning to be caught. Always staying in the shadows and letting others do the dirty work has paid off. I can see that now.'

'Calm down, Zuzanna, and *think*! We can come to some arrangement here. Let's be reasonable about all this. It was a long time ago, a different world!'

'Perhaps for you, but not for me! After the wall came down, my mother and I went back to her native Poland. I am using her maiden name. There was nothing left for us in Germany. She died a few years later, a broken woman.'

Slowly, Malenkova reached into the wall safe behind her without taking her eyes off Zuzanna standing at the top of the stairs like a fury, and kept feeling for the gun.

'They call you the Black Widow, but you are much more than that. You are an evil witch without a conscience who sold her soul to the devil long ago. And do you know what they used to do with witches? *They burned them alive!* And that is precisely what will happen to you now,' shouted Zuzanna. She took a match out of the box and held it up. 'One spark is all it takes.'

Zuzanna was about to light the match when Malenkova found the gun in the safe. Holding it tight, she withdrew her hand, took aim and fired. The bullet hit Zuzanna in the shoulder. She lost her balance and staggered backwards. The box of matches fell out of her hand and hit the floor.

'Or one *bullet*,' shouted Malenkova, and fired again. The second bullet hit Zuzanna in the chest. As she sank to her knees, she could just see the box of matches lying tantalisingly close directly in front of her on the landing. Crawling towards it on all fours and ignoring the excruciating pain, she tried to reach the box, but her fingers wouldn't obey as her vision became blurred.

Malenkova hobbled closer to the stairs to improve her aim, and lifted the gun again.

Mustering all of her remaining strength, Zuzanna managed to reach the box of matches with her outstretched hand. The box was half open. She picked it up with one hand – her fingers shaking – and pulled out one of the matches with the other. Drifting in and out of consciousness, she could see her father's smiling face looking down on her from above.

'For you, Papa,' she whispered, and lit the match just as Malenkova pulled the trigger. With half her face blown away, Zuzanna fell forward, and tumbled down the steep stairs.

Moments later, the crypt erupted and drowned in a sea of flames.

'What's that?' said Dupree and pointed to a plume of smoke as the police car turned into the lane leading to Malenkova's house.

'The place is on fire!' said Lapointe. 'That's all we need!'

The area in front of the house was a hive of activity. Two fire engines were parked in the driveway with hoses criss-crossing the path leading to the open front door. A dozen firemen were working furiously to put out the flames, which by now had engulfed the entire roof.

Lapointe jumped out of the car and walked over to one of the firemen. 'What happened?' he asked.

The fireman pointed to a woman standing next to one of the fire engines. She had a blanket wrapped around her shoulders and was crying.

'That's the housekeeper over there; she called us,' said the fireman. 'According to her, the fire started somewhere in the basement. There were two women down there when it happened.' The fireman shook his head. 'By the time we got here, it was too late. We couldn't go inside. I suspect some kind of accelerant may have been used. The fire is ferocious. Deliberately lit, I'd say.'

Dupree stared into the flames and shuddered as the burning roof collapsed, conjuring up painful memories of the recent blaze that had destroyed his home and killed his son. Sensing his friend's distress, Lapointe turned to Dupree.

'I suppose we can tear up the arrest warrant?' he said. 'Our work's done here for now; what do you think?'

'Poetic justice?'

Lapointe shrugged. Then he reached into his pocket and pulled out his pipe.

68

Breakfast at La Closerie des Lilas, Paris: 8 March 2017

Mademoiselle Darrieux was waiting for Countess Kuragin at her usual table by the window. She had received an early morning phone call from her friend, inviting her to breakfast because she had something important to discuss. Sensing the seriousness of the occasion, Darrieux had decided to wear something conservative and subdued, which was somewhat out of character.

Darrieux watched the countess as the maître d' seated her at the table with his usual flair. To have such distinguished guests in his dining room for breakfast so early in the morning was a treat.

When Darrieux had a closer look at the countess, she knew instantly something was wrong. She recognised the all-too-familiar signs: the dark rings under the eyes hinted at sleepless nights, and the stern facial expression suggested stress and serious concern. Instead of wasting time with pleasantries, Darrieux decided to come straight to the point.

'You obviously didn't invite me here at this hour for a champagne breakfast, Katerina.'

'Of course not. What I'm about to tell you is in strictest confidence, although I expect it will soon become public.'

'You can count on my discretion.'

'I know I can. And I may need a favour ...'

'Anything.'

'It's about Jack.'

'Jack? But he's in Russia, making good progress with his investigation, I hear.'

'Yes, you've put him in touch with all the right people. That's not the problem.'

'Oh? There's a problem?'

'Yes, a very serious one,' said the countess. 'But before I tell you about that, there's something else you have to know first because it's all connected. Something sensational involving the two murders.'

'Really? There's been a development?'

'You can say that again. Lapointe and Dupree believe they have found the Black Widow and Le Fantôme, the woman who blackmailed you and played a part in the fire at Dupree's house and his son's tragic death.'

'But that's great! What a breakthrough, and so quickly.'

'Yes, but we may never know for sure—'

'Why?'

'Because they are both *dead*!'

'Are you serious?'

'They burned to death in a suspicious house fire yesterday with most, if not all, of the evidence going up in smoke. It's all very hush-hush at the moment because it's still under investigation. That's why there hasn't been anything in the press about this yet.'

'Incredible! But how's this connected to Jack in Russia?'

Close to tears and finding it difficult to speak, the countess looked at Darrieux. She reached into her handbag, pulled out a handkerchief and dabbed her teary eyes.

'My goodness, Katerina, what's wrong?'

'Jack's in intensive care in a hospital in Yekaterinburg,' whispered the countess. 'He almost died.'

Darrieux looked shocked. 'What happened?' she shrieked, making heads turn at the other tables.

'He's been stabbed. That's all I know.'

'*Stabbed?* What about that young woman he's travelling with?'

'Alina? She's missing. Let me tell you about her. You're in for a shock.'

The countess then told Darrieux about Quasimodo and the police investigation, the DNA analysis, and what that meant. She also told her about the difficult phone conversation with Jack regarding Alina the other day, and why she felt somehow responsible for what had happened to him.

'Are you suggesting that Alina tried to kill Jack?'

'Certainly looks that way.'

'And that she's the—'

'One who killed Aubert, and most likely Fabron as well,' said the countess.

'Seriously? A young woman like her?'

'The police certainly seem to think so. Apparently, the evidence is overwhelming.'

'This is bizarre,' said Darrieux, shaking her head.

'That's all I know at the moment. The Australian embassy has been notified, but you know how these things work. Consular assistance takes time, especially in Russia. Jack's on his own.'

'Have you been able to speak to him?'

'No. His phone's been dead ever since we found out about this. I don't know what happened to it, and besides I don't think he's in any condition to talk.'

'Jesus! Can't Dupree or Lapointe help?'

The countess shrugged. 'Not much they can do. At least not straight away. They are both frantically busy with this investigation.' The countess put her hand on Darrieux' arm. 'That's why I need your help.'

'All you have to do is ask, Katerina, you know that. I would go through fire for Jack. After all he's done for me.'

'I thought you would say that. Thank you, Adrienne.'

'So, what do you have in mind?'

'I'm going to Yekaterinburg to see what I can do—'

'You want me to come with you?' Darrieux cut in, becoming excited.

'Yes. You seem well connected in Russia, and I speak the language. And besides, I don't want to go by myself. Between us, I'm sure we can come up with something to help Jack.'

'Count me in! When do you want to leave?'

'Tomorrow morning. A ten-thirty flight. I have tickets. Is that a problem?'

'Absolutely not. Breakfast?'

'Yes please. I'm starving.'

69

Dorozhnaya Bol'nitsa, Yekaterinburg: 9 March 2017

As soon as they arrived in Yekaterinburg and had cleared customs at the airport, Countess Kuragin and Darrieux went straight to Dorozhnaya Bol'nitsa, the hospital where Jack was being treated. Before being allowed to visit him, they had to see the emergency doctor for a briefing.

The doctor, a young man in his thirties, told them that Jack had been incredibly lucky. The blade had missed major arteries and organs by millimetres and the catastrophic blood loss that could have killed him had been stemmed by a resident nurse at the hotel until the ambulance arrived. This had saved Jack's life. The damage caused to his chest had been surgically repaired, and all that was needed now was rest. Because the patient was otherwise healthy and strong, it was expected he would make a full recovery. The doctor warned them that Jack had been heavily sedated and would not be able to speak. However, it was likely that he would be conscious and able to hear them. In any event, the visit had to be short, because he already had a visitor in his room right now.

A visitor? thought the countess as she followed the nurse down a corridor smelling of cleaning fluids, the pungent odour making her feel nauseous.

'In there,' said the nurse. She pointed to a door and left. The countess looked at Darrieux for encouragement, took a deep breath, and then pushed the door open.

At first it was impossible to see anything in the dimly lit room as the countess stepped hesitantly inside. Then the outline of a bed came into view with a dark shape standing next to it like a sentinel guarding the patient lying in the bed, surrounded by blinking machines and with plastic tubes protruding from his mouth. A shiver of fear raced through the countess as her eyes became accustomed to the gloom.

Slowly she approached the bed, tears welling in her eyes and refusing to accept that the body lying motionless in front of her like a Frankensteinian corpse being kept alive by machines, was in fact Jack.

'Oh my God,' whispered the countess. Darrieux walked up to her from behind and gripped her hand. 'At least he's alive,' she whispered.

'He can hear you,' said a deep voice. The countess looked at the man in the black cloak standing next to the bed. 'I am Serapion, the abbot of the Novo-Tikhvinsky Convent. Mr Rogan came to see me a few days ago,' said the man.

'About Pavel Ustinov?' said Darrieux.

If the abbot was in any way surprised, he didn't show it. Instead he nodded and looked at Darrieux. 'He will get better soon, have no fear. We have been expecting him for a long time, and all of us at the monastery are praying for him.'

'*Expecting* him?' said the countess. 'How come?'

The abbot smiled. 'Because it has been foretold.'

'This is all about Kazanskaya Bogomater, isn't it?' said Darrieux, fascinated by the old man with the long white beard and pillbox hat who looked like some biblical saint straight out of a Rembrandt painting.

'Yes. We believe he's the one who will return the Protectress of Russia to where she belongs: right here in Yekaterinburg.'

'You say he can hear us?' said the countess, sounding concerned.

'Yes. I've been praying with him just before you walked in. That's why I know he's conscious and can hear us. I've been here several times since he was admitted. He's definitely getting better.'

'Praying?'

'Yes. He even had his eyes open,' said the abbot. 'The power of prayer is remarkable and will aid his recovery. Perhaps even more so than these machines here.'

'Thank you,' said the countess, recognising the kindness in the abbot's voice. 'It's good to know that our friend hasn't been alone. He is a strong believer in destiny.'

'I know, and so am I.'

'And you believe that destiny will guide him to Kazanskaya Bogomater?' said Darrieux, her curiosity aroused.

'Oh, yes; soon,' said the abbot. 'It has been foretold. But it is time for me to go. I can see Mr Rogan is among friends now. I am no longer needed.' With that, the abbot took a bow and headed for the door. Just before he opened it, he stopped and turned around. 'Angels watch over this man. Please take good care of him.'

'We will,' said the countess in Russian, deeply moved. 'We certainly will.'

The countess turned to Darrieux after a gruff nurse had ushered them out of the room a short time later. 'Do you think he heard us?' she asked.

'Yes, I think so. He even opened his eyes. You saw. He knows we're here, I'm sure of it. And I'm glad you told him about the Black Widow and the fire. At least now he knows. After all, she was the one who sent Alina ... The sooner he comes to terms with that, the better.'

'You don't think it was too much?'

'No. This is Jack, remember?'

The countess looked gratefully at Darrieux. 'I'm so glad you came along, Adrienne. This is much harder than I thought it would be.'

'I saw his eyes move when you mentioned Tristan and Anna, and told him they sent their love.'

'You did?'

'Yes.'

'We've got to get him out of here,' said the countess, 'and quickly.'

'I agree.'

'And I know exactly how we are going to do that.'

'*You do?*'

'Yes,' said the countess with a knowing smile.

'How?'

'Watch.'

The countess pulled her phone out of her handbag, and called Isis.

70

Time Machine Studios, London: 11 March 2017

Exhausted but elated after the long flight from Yekaterinburg on Isis's private jet, Countess Kuragin began to relax. Sipping a martini, she sat back in the comfortable lounge chair in Isis's penthouse above the Time Machine Studios, and looked pensively across the Thames and upriver towards the illuminated Tower Bridge. The familiar view had a calming effect after the turbulent few days full of tension and unexpected developments.

Jack had managed the flight without a hitch under the watchful eye of a nurse Isis had brought along from London. He was resting in the guest accommodation, which had been transformed into a state-of-the-art hospital room, with all the necessary equipment monitored by experienced carers around the clock.

'What a day!' said the countess. 'I still can't believe we pulled this off,' she said, shaking her head. 'And all thanks to you, Lola. It's truly amazing how you've arranged it all.'

Lola waved dismissively. 'It wasn't all that difficult,' she said. 'Once we told the local radio stations about Isis's visit and agreed to give a brief interview, it all fell into place. The old girl still has some pull. Even the usually prickly authorities were eager to help. In Russia, red tape is always the problem, but not this time. It all went from there.'

After the countess had contacted Isis, explained the situation and asked for her help, Isis and Lola had swung into action without hesitation. Calling in favours left over from Isis's iconic *Echoes from the Grave* World Tour in 2011, which still resonated strongly with fans in Russia who remembered Isis's spectacular concert at the Olympic Stadium in Moscow, Isis was welcomed in Yekaterinburg with open arms. While Lola and the countess arranged Jack's transfer from the hospital to *Pegasus*, Isis's private jet waiting at the airport, Isis was giving interviews and wowing lucky fans who had been allowed into the studio to see their idol.

Darrieux turned to Lola sitting next to her. 'Where is she?' she asked.

'Preparing to make her entrance, I imagine. It's a ritual before dinner,' said Lola, smiling. 'Especially when friends are present. She can't help herself. A consummate performer, even now in retirement. She misses the limelight terribly.'

She's not alone, thought the countess, who had witnessed these performances before. *Isis and Adrienne could be a double act.*

'An entrance? What do you mean?' asked Darrieux.

'You'll see in a moment. Here she comes now. There, top of the stairs; watch.'

Wearing riding boots, a full-length fur coat and a jaunty Karakul Kubanka Cossack hat she had worn during the interviews in Yekaterinburg, Isis looked like a film star straight out of *Dr Zhivago*.

Taking her time, she stopped at the top of the glass staircase and looked down into the spacious lounge area below. 'What do you think, guys?' she said, unbuttoning her coat. 'Perhaps a little over the top for someone my age?'

'Not at all,' said Darrieux. 'You look absolutely fabulous!'

'You really think so?'

'Very stylish. Fur coat looks great, and the Cossack hat suits you. The only thing missing is the beard,' said the countess, and lifted her glass in salute.

'I can't do much about that, now, can I? The fans loved it, that's the main thing, don't you think?'

'Quite so,' said Lola. She looked at the countess and rolled her eyes, trying hard not to laugh.

'Enough of that!' said Isis and turned around. 'We have a surprise dinner guest. Boris, bring him down.'

Moments later, Boris, Isis's bodyguard, appeared at the top of the stairs. He was carrying Jack in his powerful arms. Over the years, Boris and Jack had become quite close and formed a friendship, and

Boris, a former wrestling champion, was delighted to be able to carry his injured friend down to dinner.

Jack appeared in good spirits and was waving. *Incredible*, thought the countess, shaking her head. 'Isn't this a little premature?' she asked, as Isis and Boris came slowly down the stairs.

'Not really,' said Lola. 'The doctors actually suggested he should get up and exercise more. A little every day. And besides, keeping Jack in bed isn't easy, as you well know.'

'No, it isn't. I suppose he wasn't going to miss this: his friends, here, all in one place having dinner, especially as Adrienne and I are going back to Paris tomorrow.'

'No way! He could have walked down, you know,' continued Lola, lowering her voice, 'but Boris wouldn't let him.'

'This will do him good,' said Darrieux. 'He's a people person.'

'I could get used to this,' said Jack cheerfully as Boris lowered him into a comfortable chair.

'Don't,' said Boris, patting Jack on the back. 'We are going walking tomorrow morning, early. Doctor's orders.'

'What's for dinner?' asked Jack.

'Cottage pie; your favourite,' said Isis. 'What else?'

'Great! Real tucker at last! The food in the hospital was crap, I tell you.'

The countess winked at Darrieux. 'He's in good form,' she said.

'Looks that way.'

'This calls for a toast,' said Isis, her face aglow with excitement. She pointed to a large ice bucket full of champagne bottles and held up her empty glass. 'Boris, would you please do the honours? I'm dying of thirst.'

During dinner, Jack began to open up. It was the first opportunity for him to talk about his visit to Yekaterinburg, and the extraordinary encounter with the Seeker and the Guardians in the underground chamber below the church. He gave a detailed account of the meeting, but not once did he refer to Alina, or what had happened in the hotel room the night he almost died.

'This is amazing,' said Isis. 'So, what's your next move? You are not giving up now, surely?'

'*Giving up?* Are you kidding? In many ways, this is just the beginning. For the first time since we found that letter in the music box, I feel that I'm getting somewhere with this.' Jack pointed to his chest. 'But I have to let this heal first. After that—'

'Dupree called me this morning,' said the countess. 'I didn't have a chance to tell you earlier.'

'Oh? What about?'

'He had a message for you. He said it was a coming-home present.'

Jack looked at the countess. 'What kind of message?' he asked, curious.

'He said the third clue is about to pay off. Apparently, you would know what that meant.'

'Do you?' asked Isis.

'Yes, I think so.'

'How intriguing. Tell us about it, Jack. We would all like to know,' said Isis.

Feeling stronger and relaxed for the first time since the dreadful stabbing at the hotel, the storyteller in Jack didn't need much encouragement.

'According to Dupree, the investigation into the Amber Safe murder at the Ritz has generated three promising clues: a hair, a limp and a curious meeting in a casino in Paris.' Jack paused and looked dreamily across the Thames, reflecting myriad coloured lights pulsing through the vibrant city.

'The limp pointed the way to Emile Fabron, the safebreaker who was brutally killed on his boat after Dupree and I paid him a visit. Fabron left us a message before he died, a symbol painted in his own blood that pointed an accusing finger at the Black Widow, vindicating Dupree's hunch.'

Jack took a deep breath. 'And as you all know, the hair found under Aubert's fingernails exposed the killer ...'

401

He still finds it difficult to talk about this, thought the countess, watching Jack carefully. 'Malenkova, the Black Widow, and her assistant, Le Fantôme, are both dead,' said the countess, changing direction and coming to Jack's assistance. 'Killed in that recent house fire, effectively closing part of the case. So, what is this third clue all about?'

'The curious meeting at the casino?' said Jack and looked gratefully at the countess.

'Yes.'

'That's all about a Russian billionaire called Sokolov, living right here in the UK. A shady character with fingers in many underworld pies. The authorities here have tried to get their hands on him for years. Dupree's convinced that he's the one who bought the Rasputin Fabergé egg from Malenkova on the dark web. Dupree was following up a lead about this just before I left. It must have paid off.'

'And this could be significant?' asked the countess.

'Yes. If Dupree has made progress with the third clue, that would be of great help. To me.'

'How so?' asked Darrieux.

'Because it may lead me to the Fabergé egg stolen from the Amber Safe.'

'And that could be important?' said Darrieux. 'Apart from the money involved?'

'Yes. Because without it, we'll never unlock the mystery of Kazanskaya Bogomater and Mat' Rossiya,' said Jack. 'The Rasputin egg is the key here. My visit to the Yekaterinburg convent made that clear. Something's actually *inside* the egg.'

'How fascinating! So, that could be a welcome coming-home present?' said Darrieux.

'Looks that way. I can't wait to find out what Dupree has to say.'

'Maybe tomorrow, if you are a good boy,' said Isis, 'and let Boris take you back to bed now. Early night for recuperating patients under my roof, my friend. House rules.'

402

Jack held up his hands in mock surrender. 'The only thing I regret is having lost my notebook,' he said, looking quite dejected. 'It had a lot of information in it.'

'But you can manage without it?' said Isis.

'Yes. Thanks to what the abbot told me in the hospital, I can—'

'We met him when we arrived,' interjected the countess. 'He was right there. A fascinating man.'

'Oh yes, he's that, all right. He visited me several times and spoke to me. He sat with me for hours and told me stories. Even prayed for me. I was barely conscious, but I heard every word and can remember everything he said. Strange, don't you think?'

'Destiny?' ventured the countess, a sparkle in her eyes.

'You know me too well, Katerina. Yes, you could call it that. He showed me the way ...'

'To Kazanskaya Bogomater and Mat' Rossiya?' said Darrieux.

'Yes. He believes, you see.'

'Believes what?' asked Isis.

'That I am the one who will ...' Jack stopped in mid-sentence. 'I'm sorry, I feel suddenly quite tired.'

'*That's enough!*' said Isis. 'No more stories today, mate. Boris, take him back to bed – now.'

71

Finbar Castle, Scotland: 12 March 2017

'This guy has powerful friends,' said Sokolov, shaking his head. He looked out the library window to watch the early morning sea mist come rolling in from the east, and heard the huge waves crashing against the rocks below. It was a familiar, soothing sound he enjoyed because it helped him to relax and focus.

'True. Not many have a famous rock star friend with his own private jet they can call on to come to their rescue. I thought only Russian billionaires could pull off something like that. Especially in Russia,' said Aldar.

'So, he's in London, recuperating as a guest of this rock star? This could work for us, you know. We are lucky he survived.'

'What's on your mind?'

Sokolov turned around, walked over to his desk and picked up Jack's notebook. 'We've spent several days now, going through this stuff. I can't make sense of it. I'm sure the important bits are in Rogan's head and not in here,' said Sokolov.

'Could be.'

'Just listen to this: *"Is MR music by T as claimed by Y?"* According to Malenkova, this line is the key that can help us unlock the mystery surrounding Mat' Rossiya. But what does it *mean?*'

Aldar shrugged and lit a cigarette.

'Yet, I feel Rogan's getting close,' continued Sokolov. 'So much seems clear from what he has written down. Especially after Budapest, Prague and in particular, the convent visit in Yekaterinburg. He is very methodical and logical in how he follows this trail. Tenacious and quite ingenious in the way he does this. He uses contacts, common sense and intuition to put together the pieces of the puzzle. Clever, but without Malenkova to help us interpret this material, we are really on the back foot.'

'She was very good in making sense of snippets of information,' conceded Aldar. 'She could fill in the gaps, but she's gone. We are on our own.'

'We are. So, what are we going to do about it, my friend?' said Sokolov. 'We've been in tight spots before. This is no time to give up.'

'Certainly not, but whatever we do, we must do it *now* if we want to stay in this race,' said Aldar, 'or we lose the connection.'

'Agreed. And let's not forget that Chief Superintendent Lapointe is a good operator; you must admit that. The way he found Malenkova and Anielka so quickly is remarkable. He's a dangerous man who doesn't let go.'

'He is, and we mustn't underestimate him. But we are in the UK. Out of reach. Not his jurisdiction.'

'But there's Europol. Can be quite effective. We've seen that firsthand with the drugs, remember?' said Sokolov. 'Cost us a bloody fortune.'

'It has, but we know how to stay ahead of the game. We have contacts now, don't forget, in all the right places. Money talks.'

Sokolov put down Jack's notebook, walked back to the window and stared out at the crashing waves and rolling mist. 'If everything we need to know is in Rogan's head, then why don't we just ask him?'

'And you think he will just share that information with us? After all that's happened?'

'A little persuasion may be needed, but we know how to do that, don't we? We've done it many times, most effectively. Everyone has their weakness, their breaking point, and their price. The trick is to find out what it is, and then use it, mercilessly, until the subject cracks. And as we both know, most of them do.'

'True. And you think we could do this here?' asked Aldar.

'I have a few ideas … I believe I know at least one such weak spot that could open the door to Mr Rogan's memory castle and give us the information we need. Without too long a siege, I hope, and not too much collateral damage.'

'Despite betrayal and having had a knife stuck into his chest that almost killed him?'

'Oh yes, perhaps even because of it. Have no fear, certain things make a man blind. Even one as resourceful and resilient as our Mr Rogan. Trust me.'

'I know what you are thinking,' said Aldar, smiling. 'I hope you're right. And could that weak spot already be waiting for him right here, among these very walls?'

Sokolov began to laugh. 'You know it is. Waiting in my bed, actually, right now.'

'Good. But for this to work, we have to move quickly.'

'Agreed.'

'We have excellent contacts in London. Everything we need to pull this off is right there,' said Aldar.

'I know. Let's invite Mr Rogan for a chat and bring him up here as our guest. You can tell him the Scottish sea air will do him good. Help his recovery.'

'I'll get onto it straight away,' said Aldar and stubbed out his cigarette.

'You do that. In the meantime, I'll keep working on that weak spot to make sure it will sharpen Mr Rogan's memory when he gets here.'

72

Near the Tower Bridge, London: 14 March 2017

Aldar sat in a van parked in front of a building site near the Tower Bridge.

'As you can see, guys, he's a man who likes routine. Same walk twice a day,' he said and put down his binoculars. He had just watched Jack walk over the Tower Bridge. 'Except for one thing.' Aldar turned to the man sitting next to him. 'The big guy isn't with him today. Mr Rogan left his minder at home; perfect. We'll do it now, when he makes his way back to the studios.'

Aldar, a patient and cautious man, knew that preparation and meticulous planning were the key to success. He had carefully chosen the two men – both former Russian soldiers now working for the Russian Mafia – who would help him carry out the brazen abduction in the heart of busy London. With CCTV cameras covering almost every corner of the city and a well-trained police force on high alert – especially after the recent terrorist attacks that had put the whole of London on edge – such a project was not for the fainthearted.

Aldar lit a cigarette and sat back. 'I can tell you exactly what he will do next. Once he crosses the bridge, he will turn left and walk past the Tower along the Thames; watch. He will then make his way around the Tower moat, stop at the tube station to buy a paper, and then go down to St Katharine Docks and have a coffee at that place I showed you yesterday run by his Aussie mate. After that, he will walk around the Thistle Tower Hotel, take the stairs up onto the deck of the bridge, and then return to the Time Machine Studios the way he came—'

'And to do that, he has to walk straight past us here,' said the man sitting in the back.

'Correct. Isn't routine wonderful?' said Aldar. 'Without knowing it, Mr Rogan is handing us his freedom on a plate.'

Aldar opened the car window. 'So, let's go over it one more time,' he said. 'Are you absolutely sure there's no camera coverage here, Igor?'

'I am. Because of the building site here, they've taken the cameras down. I checked. This is a blind spot.'

'Perfect. And Mr Rogan will come along this street, just like yesterday. Only this time, he's not going back to the Time Machine Studios, but coming with us on a little trip north. Health reasons,' said Aldar, chuckling. 'Okay guys, let's get ready.'

Jack finished his coffee, picked up his paper, and stood up.

'Where's Boris?' asked the man behind the coffee machine.

'He let me go out by myself today. Thought I was ready. Good of him, don't you think?'

'Lucky you. Nice guy, but.'

'Gentle giant. It's not the same without him. Perhaps tomorrow. See you, mate.'

Jack waved and stepped outside. It was still quite early, but the traffic crossing the bridge was already heavy. It was overcast and had started to drizzle. Jack turned up his collar and tried to stay under cover wherever possible. He was cursing himself for having left his umbrella in his room.

'What's he doing?' asked Igor, watching Jack cross the street. 'Shit! I think he's taking a shortcut along the river because of the rain.'

'You're right,' said Aldar and slipped his gun into his pocket. 'No matter, we can't stop now. Stay right here, guys, and leave the rest to me.'

'Isn't that risky?' asked the man in the back seat.

'What isn't?' With that, Aldar opened the door, got out of the van and hurried after Jack, who had just turned into a side street. It was raining quite heavily by now and Jack didn't notice the man walking up to him from behind.

'In case you're wondering, Mr Rogan, this isn't my finger poking into your back, but a Beretta with a silencer,' said Aldar, calmly. 'So, I suggest you do exactly as I tell you, clear? You don't want another hole in your chest now, do you?'

Jack stopped in his tracks and glanced at the small man walking along beside him. The man was wearing a trench coat, and the slouch hat hiding most of his face reminded Jack of the hapless Inspector Clouseau.

'Keep walking,' said the man, 'and don't try anything stupid. A man in your condition has to be careful, right?'

He knows who I am and about my injury, thought Jack, evaluating the situation. The man's voice and confident demeanour radiated danger. Apart from a woman walking a dog and a couple getting into a car, the street was deserted. Attacking the man or making a run for it was out of the question.

'Where are we going?' asked Jack, trying to make conversation.

'Last time I was walking behind you, you were going to a convent in Yekaterinburg to meet the abbot,' said Aldar. 'This time, you're going to meet someone quite different, but just as exciting; promise.'

'I can't wait,' said Jack and smiled as he remembered Dupree's third clue. *Great coming-home present!* he thought.

Realising that any kind of resistance would be futile, Jack decided to play a little mind game instead and test the waters. 'Victor Sokolov, perhaps?' he mumbled.

If Aldar was in any way taken aback by Jack's question, he certainly didn't show it. 'How did you guess?' he said.

'Your accent gave it away: Russian.'

'Ah. I must keep that in mind. Please give me your new phone.'

'How did you know it was new?' asked Jack, genuinely surprised.

'Because I have your old one.'

'Things are getting more interesting by the second,' said Jack and handed Aldar his phone. 'If you have my old phone, perhaps you have my notebook as well?'

'Could be.'

'What's he like?'

'Sokolov?'

'Yes.'

'You'll find out soon enough. Now, turn around and go back the way you came.'

'All right.'

'Do you see that black van over there?' said Aldar as they crossed the street and turned the corner.

'Yes.'

'It would be nice to get out of the rain, don't you think?'

'Definitely.'

'Good. We'll now walk over to the van together and you will get into the back, understood?'

'Yes. Are you offering me a lift home? Is that it?' said Jack, cheerfully.

'Not quite,' said Aldar, actually enjoying the spirited banter. He was beginning to like Jack. 'We are going a little further afield.'

'Any hints?'

'Perhaps later. Now, *get in*!'

It took them less than an hour to get to Gatwick Airport. Half an hour later, they were in the air, flying north to Aberdeen in Sokolov's private jet.

73

Finbar Castle, Scotland: 14 March 2017

Jack couldn't take his eyes off the Imperial Fabergé Easter eggs displayed on the harpsichord by the window. He was about to ask Aldar for permission to have a closer look when Sokolov walked in. Casually dressed in a pair of cords and a heavy knitted Norwegian jumper, Sokolov looked relaxed and in control. He had intentionally left Jack waiting in the library for almost an hour after arriving on Sokolov's personal helicopter from Aberdeen. The raging storm had made landing almost impossible. Narrowly missing a wall, it took the pilot several hairy attempts before he could finally put the chopper down during a brief lull in the wind.

'All's well that ends well, isn't that so?' said Sokolov breezily. He walked over to a sideboard, put down his phone and poured himself a drink. 'For a moment there, we thought we almost lost you. Scary landing. Great pilot. Combat experience; Chechnya. He's used to dodging bullets, not Scottish winds, but he's getting used to it. Drink?'

'Yes please,' said Jack, watching Sokolov with interest. He reminded Jack of Alistair Macbeth, the charismatic founder of Blackburn Pharmaceuticals he had crossed swords with on the *Calypso*, the corporate flagship, in 2011. While Macbeth may have been in a wheelchair, the aura and polished manner were the same: urbane civility and charm, disguising an extremely dangerous man without moral compass, used to getting his own way.

'I saw you looking at those beauties over there,' said Sokolov, pointing to the Fabergé eggs. He handed Jack a large Scotch. 'Understandable. They are rather spectacular, don't you think?' he said. 'Would you like to have a closer look?'

'May I?' asked Jack, playing along. He recognised the contrived foreplay-dance of polite small talk, leading slowly to the subject of

411

real interest. It was the way to explore one's opponent and, if possible, find a weakness. Jack put down his glass and walked over to the harpsichord. 'So, that's where the Rasputin egg ended up,' he said. 'The dark web works in mysterious ways.'

'It has its purpose. Pity Malenkova can no longer enjoy the spoils,' said Sokolov, watching Jack carefully. 'Burned to death with her trusty assistant, Le Fantôme. What a terrible way to go, don't you think?'

'The last time I saw the Rasputin egg was in the Amber Safe in the Paris Ritz only a few weeks ago,' said Jack, ignoring the remark. 'Monsieur Aubert, the manager, was showing it to us. He, too, is dead now. Strange, how people associated with this masterpiece seem to die so violently.'

'You are right. And that, of course, includes the mad monk Rasputin and Empress Alexandra. Do you think the egg is cursed, Mr Rogan?'

'No, I don't think so. It's the people who come in contact with it who appear to be.'

'Interesting. So, why don't we make sure this doesn't include you ...'

'What do you mean?' said Jack, momentarily taken aback by the remark.

'Come on, Mr Rogan, a man of your experience knows exactly how these things work,' said Sokolov, sipping his Scotch. 'I haven't brought you here to drink my liquor or show you my art collection.'

'I didn't think so,' said Jack calmly and also took a sip. 'Excellent whisky.'

'Glad you like it. Shall we cut to the chase?'

'Always the best way.'

'Good. I knew we would understand each other. You have something I want, and in order to stay alive you will have to give it to me. Simple, isn't it?'

Jack nodded. 'Sounds like it.'

'Good.' Sokolov turned to Aldar. 'Would you please give Mr Rogan his notebook?'

Aldar walked over to the desk, opened the top drawer and took out Jack's notebook. Then he walked over to Jack and handed it to him.

'So, that's where it ended up,' said Jack, feigning surprise. 'I've lost my little book several times over the years, but somehow it always seems to find its way back to me. I remember once leaving it in a felucca sailing down the Nile. I was doing research for my first book, in Egypt. I thought it had gone for good that time, but a young deckhand tracked me down, brought it to our camp the next day, and returned it to me with great flourish.'

Gutsy guy, thought Sokolov, wondering where Jack was going with this. *He's just been brought to a remote castle against his will. He knows he may never leave here alive, yet here he is telling stories. Extraordinary!*

'And then there was this unforgettable occasion in the Kimberley in Western Australia,' continued Jack. 'I was writing *The Disappearance of Anna Popov*, my second book. Our Aboriginal guide took me to a remote cave to look at some ancient rock art, when the little book slipped out of my backpack and fell straight down into a deep gorge below. Fortunately, it didn't fall into the water, but landed on a sandbank full of crocodiles sunning themselves. Our guide had to retrieve the little book with a long stick while I distracted the curious reptiles by throwing pebbles at them from above—'

'You are obviously a lucky man, Mr Rogan,' interjected Sokolov. 'Perhaps this time, the little book may even save your life.'

'Oh? How so?'

'Because of what it contains. Or to put it more accurately, what it doesn't contain – because the missing parts are somewhere else.'

'How fascinating. Where, do you think?'

'In your head, Mr Rogan, and that's why you're here. I have to know what's in your head so that we can make sense of what's in the notebook—'

'Because it may lead you to Kazanskaya Bogomater and Mat' Rossiya?' interrupted Jack.

'Precisely.'

'And what makes you think that I know the way?'

'Come now, Mr Rogan, we both know you do! The meeting with the abbot in Yekaterinburg showed you the way, right?'

'What makes you so sure?'

Sokolov touched his nose. 'Instinct.'

'Ah. But instinct can be misleading.'

'It can. For that reason, I have to be sure. One way or the other.'

'I see. And how do you intend to accomplish that?'

'By finding the truth, of course. How else? And there are certain reliable ways to find it. Shall we begin?'

'Sure,' said Jack, calmly. 'But before we do, could I have a closer look? At the Rasputin egg?'

'By all means. Go ahead.'

Jack walked over to the harpsichord and touched the egg with the tips of his fingers. 'May I?' he asked.

Sokolov nodded. 'Open it. I'm sure you know how it works.'

'I've never seen the inside,' said Jack, enjoying the feel of the heavy egg in the palm of his hand.

'Then you are in for a big surprise; open it.'

'How?'

Sokolov walked over to Jack and pointed to a large diamond on top of the egg. 'Press here,' he said.

As soon as Jack pressed the diamond, the top half of the egg opened, revealing a diamond-encrusted gold cross with the Romanov double eagle on top. 'Fantastic,' he said, admiring the two oval miniature portraits on either side of the cross, one of Rasputin, the other of Alexandra.

'There's more,' said Sokolov. 'Lift up the cross, gently! It will take you into the little crypt below.'

Here it comes, thought Jack, striving to suppress his excitement as he carefully lifted up the cross and activated the hidden spring: *The moment of truth*.

Suddenly, the bottom half of the egg opened up all by itself. Jack stared at it, and gasped. He was looking at an exquisite miniature icon. *Kazanskaya Bogomater*, thought Jack, his head spinning. *A perfect replica.*

'Magnificent,' he whispered. 'This must be the most spectacular of all the Imperial Fabergé Easter eggs without a doubt.'

'I agree,' said Sokolov, obviously chuffed. 'And historically speaking, it's unique. Now, I have a few questions, if you don't mind.'

'Not at all,' said Jack. He carefully reassembled the egg and put it back on the harpsichord. 'Fire away.'

'You may not know this,' began Sokolov, 'but Malenkova and I have done quite a lot of business together in the past. Mainly dealing with artworks relating to Russian history; my passion. That's why she came to me with the Fabergé egg. She knew I would be interested and she was right. To cut a long story short, I purchased the Rasputin egg and here it is. Another drink?'

Jack nodded, and Sokolov filled up his glass.

'But that's not why we're here,' continued Sokolov. 'What brings us here is something much bigger and far more interesting. Something to do with a letter found hidden in a music box left to you by Madame Petrova, your great aunt,' said Sokolov, watching Jack carefully.

'You are well informed,' said Jack.

'Malenkova was very thorough and very enterprising. She came to me with a proposal, you see, regarding certain fascinating matters arising out of that letter: a mystery. No doubt the very same mystery that took you to St Petersburg, then to Budapest and Prague, and finally to the Novo-Tikhvinsky Convent in Yekaterinburg.'

'What kind of proposal?' asked Jack.

'Ah. Malenkova was convinced – obviously just as you are – that something big is involved here, something of great historical significance involving Empress Alexandra, Rasputin, and Russia. And it all has to do with Kazanskaya Bogomater and Mat' Rossiya.'

Sokolov paused and looked expectantly at Jack, waiting for a comment.

'What kind of proposal?' Jack asked again.

'Malenkova and I agreed that we would join forces and see where the trail would take us, and what may be discovered along the way.'

'What kind of trail?'

'You, of course, Mr Rogan,' said Sokolov, an infuriating smile spreading across his face. 'So far, we've been able to follow every one of your steps, all of your enquiries. We were right there, next to you, looking over your shoulder, literally.'

Jack nodded. Suddenly, it all made sense, and any doubts that may have lingered about Alina's involvement and intentions evaporated, leaving behind a painful sense of disappointment, emptiness and betrayal.

'Alina,' whispered Jack.

'Quite. Her real name's Anielka.' Jack tried not to show his surprise. 'She has been remarkably effective; clever girl. Until it all turned sour. Malenkova's death changed everything.'

'Is that why I'm here?'

'Yes. I suspect she didn't tell me everything she knew. Frieda was a cunning old witch, but that was to be expected. Part of the deal.'

'So, what do you want from me?'

'Isn't it obvious? To fill in the gaps, of course. You will help me find Kazanskaya Bogomater and Mat' Rossiya. Simple. I've been analysing the entries in your fascinating notebook here for a few days now, but I need you to help me make sense of it all. There's one particular line I find intriguing: *"Is MR music by T as claimed by Y?"* Malenkova thought this was the key to it all. She had a good nose for such things. No matter; I'm sure you will tell me what it means. You will tell me all I need to know,' said Sokolov, smiling. 'Isn't that right, Dmitri?'

Aldar nodded.

He obviously doesn't know too much, thought Jack, his mind racing. *That's good!* Yet he was telling Jack everything about his arrangements with Malenkova and his intentions. That could only mean one thing: once Jack told him what he wanted to know, he was finished. *I'll never get out of here alive!*

Jack had met men like Sokolov before. Ruthless, obsessively ambitious and cunning, but driven by fear of failure and always looking for approval. There was only one way to deal with someone like that. Jack had to keep calm and outfox him, but he realised time was running out. Then came the phone call that changed all that.

The phone Sokolov had casually put down on the sideboard rang. He walked over to it and answered the call. He spoke briefly in Russian and put the phone back on the sideboard, but didn't switch it off. That's when Jack decided to make his move.

'So, it was Alina ... I mean ... *Anielka*,' he said, pretending to have difficulty breathing. He pressed his hands against his chest as if in pain, and began to stagger towards the sideboard. '*Water*,' he mumbled and reached for a glass pitcher on the sideboard. As he knocked it over, the pitcher and the bottle of Scotch fell to the floor and shattered. Breathing heavily, Jack let himself fall against the sideboard for support. Bending over, he quickly grabbed Sokolov's phone, slipped it unnoticed into his pocket, and then collapsed onto the floor.

'What's wrong with him?' shouted Sokolov, looking alarmed.

'Long day. Excitement, stress, the flight. He just had a major operation,' said Aldar and bent down to feel Jack's pulse.

'I'll be fine,' said Jack weakly. 'Just have to lie down for a while.'

Sokolov turned to Aldar. 'Should we call a doctor?' he asked in Russian.

'No.' Aldar got up and walked to the door. He opened it, called in two bodyguards who stood outside, and then turned to Sokolov. 'He needs rest, that's all. Let's take him to his room and see how we go. Leave it until tomorrow; it's late.'

'*Der'mo!*' Sokolov swore and clenched his fist. 'I need a drink!'

As soon as the bodyguards had taken Jack to his room, thrown him on the bed and he found himself alone, he pulled Sokolov's phone out of his pocket and quickly sent a text message to the only number he could remember that counted. Then he turned off the phone, opened the window and threw the phone down into the boiling sea below.

417

74

Unable to fall asleep, Countess Kuragin turned restlessly in her bed. The disturbing news about Jack's sudden disappearance kept her awake. Isis had called her from her lawyer's office earlier and had told her what had happened. Jack had failed to return from his morning walk. Boris had retraced his steps and found nothing. Jack's phone had gone dead. Isis had immediately called Sir Charles Huntley, her lawyer, who first contacted the Metropolitan Police and then spoke to his contacts at MI5. The most logical explanation was that Jack had been abducted.

The countess heard her phone beep on the bedside table, signalling an incoming text message. She turned on the light, looked at the screen and paled. Then she called Dupree.

'Payback for the other day?' asked Dupree, sounding sleepy.

'No. Just received a text from Jack.'

'*What?*' said Dupree. 'Are you sure?'

'Yes.'

'What does it say?'

'Finbar Castle. Sokolov. Urgent! Jack.'

'Jesus! I'll call Lapointe.'

'I'll get dressed and come over.'

'You do that.'

The countess got out of bed, put on her dressing gown and then called Isis.

75

Dungeon at Finbar Castle: 15 March 2017, 4:00 am

Aldar burst into Jack's room followed by two of Sokolov's guards. It was four-thirty in the morning. Jack had been expecting something like this, but pretended to be asleep. Aldar switched on the lights. 'Search him and the room, now!' he bellowed.

The two guards walked over to the bed and pulled off the blankets. Jack opened his eyes. 'What's going on?' he said, squinting at the two angry faces staring down at him.

'Where is it?' asked Aldar.

'Where is *what?*' said Jack.

'No use pretending! I want the phone, *now!*'

'I don't know what you're talking about.'

'Search him!'

One of the guards pulled Jack to his feet and began to pat him down. 'Nothing,' he said, turning Jack's pockets inside out. The other guard took the bed apart and began to search the rest of the small room.

'It has to be here; keep looking!'

Aldar had turned the whole library upside down after the mess had been cleaned up, searching for the phone, and had spoken to all the staff involved. To think that one of them might have taken Sokolov's phone was absurd. Sokolov had had a lot to drink and could easily have misplaced it. It had happened before. Aldar had searched every possible location; nothing. That only left one logical explanation: *Jack.*

'Are you going to tell me what's going on?' said Jack, pressing his hands against his chest. 'I don't feel well.'

'You'll feel a lot worse if you don't tell me what you've done with it!' thundered Aldar.

'*What?*'

'Victor's phone. You took it.'

'This is crazy!'

'It's not here,' said one of the guards.

'Has to be,' said Aldar. Then his eyes fell on the window. *I wonder*, he thought. He walked over to the window, opened it and looked down. *That's what I would have done: make a call and dispose of the evidence quickly.* Victor would be furious!

'I can see we'll have to do this the hard way,' said Aldar. 'Take him to the dungeon.'

The 'dungeon' was a vaulted chamber hewn from virgin rock below the castle kitchen. Originally used for storage, Sokolov had turned it into his interrogation room. The dark, intimidating space without windows or electric light was perfectly suited for breaking even the most stubborn and determined spirit, and crushing any form of futile resistance. And when it came to doing that, Aldar was a master. Over the years, several 'subjects' had died in there. Their mutilated and often dismembered bodies were then disposed of at sea and disappeared without a trace.

In the middle of the chamber stood a high-backed metal chair with armrests, and leather straps to restrain the subject, like the electric chairs used in the US for executions, only more ornate. Displayed along one of the walls, a sinister collection of medieval torture instruments – including an Iron Maiden, Judas Cradle, a Pear of Anguish, The Scavenger's Daughter, and a finger press – were silent reminders of excruciating pain, broken bodies, fear, blood and slow, agonising death. It reminded Jack of the Museum of Old-Time Tortures in Zielona Góra, Poland, perhaps one of the darkest and most scary museums he had ever visited.

Aldar turned to one of the guards and pointed to a wooden stool in front of the torture chair facing the wall of exhibits. 'Take him over there,' he said.

'Very theatrical,' said Jack, and sat down. He realised that playing for time somehow would be his only chance to stay alive, and to do that he had to play along, however difficult that might turn out to be, and use his wits.

'You think so?' said Sokolov as he stepped through the low doorway and entered the dank, claustrophobic room smelling of dampness and decay. Illuminated by lanterns hanging from rusty hooks wedged into the moss-covered walls, the droplets of water clinging to the moss looked like eyes of evil demons, watching.

Jack glanced at Sokolov but didn't say anything. 'I can assure you, these items are not just for display,' continued Sokolov. 'Unfortunately, the time for pleasantries is over. You have blotted your copybook, Mr Rogan, and abused my hospitality. Very foolish of you. This has consequences; very unpleasant ones as you will soon see.'

Sokolov shook his head. 'I don't like ungrateful guests—'

'*Guests?* That's a bit rich,' interjected Jack, aware that any show of weakness would be exploited immediately. The only language a man like Sokolov understood was brazen defiance and lack of fear.

'I believe you have something that belongs to me,' continued Sokolov, ignoring the remark. 'I want it back – *now.*' Sokolov pointed to the Iron Maiden standing in the corner, its lethal-looking steel spikes casting frightening shadows against the moist wall behind it, like devil's claws, promising mutilation, unspeakable pain and slow death.

'We can do this the easy way, or the hard way. Your choice. But one thing I can promise you, the result will be the same. The only thing that will differ is the journey. One path could be easy, if you cooperate, that is. But should misguided obstinacy make you choose another, it will be paved with nails, if you get my drift. And my friend Dmitri here is a master of nails, and other nasty objects to tear flesh apart in very private, sensitive places, isn't that right?'

Aldar nodded.

'Here, let me show you one of my favourites.' Sokolov walked over to a wooden table next to the Iron Maiden. He picked up a rusty metal contraption the size and shape of a pear, and held it up. 'This is a medieval Pear of Anguish,' he said. 'A specialty of the Inquisition, especially when witches were involved. It works like this: As you can see, the "pear" is divided into four segments that expand and open up like the petals of a flower when you turn this screw here. The pear can be inserted, say, into the mouth to punish a blasphemer. When the pear expands in the mouth it can easily dislocate the jawbone and crush the teeth, causing not only excruciating pain, but also irreparable damage.' Sokolov turned the screw to illustrate the point. 'In the case of witches who were accused of consorting with the devil, the pear was inserted into a different orifice ... I will leave the place and the damage caused to your imagination.'

'If it is information you want, I am happy to provide it to you now,' said Jack casually. 'Bring me my notebook and we can begin, if you like.'

Sokolov shook his head. 'That can wait. Right now, I want my phone back.'

'I don't have it,' said Jack.

'*I don't believe you!* You staged a health event, pretended to be ill, stole my phone and then made a few quick calls, no doubt. Very clever. I want my phone back, and you will tell me who you called and what was said. Do we understand each other?'

'I have no idea what you're talking about.'

'The reply I expected.'

Jack thought he could detect a hint of grudging respect in Sokolov's voice. 'If you subject me to these wonderful instruments here and begin to tear me apart,' he said, 'you will never find Kazanskaya Bogomater, or Mat' Rossiya.' Jack pointed to his chest. 'You know I already have a serious injury. So, it wouldn't take much to—'

'Very good, Mr Rogan,' interjected Sokolov. 'I admire your tenacity and your spirit. To sit here in your position and actually make a threat takes balls, don't you think so, Dmitri?'

'It does, but it will do our friend here no good, as he's about to find out. He may even lose one or possibly both of his balls along the way,' said Aldar, laughing.

'But he's right,' said Sokolov. 'To give me what I want, I need him in good health. And in good health he shall remain for the time being. But that does not shield him from mental anguish, pain, or despair, does it, Dmitri?'

'Certainly not, and that's why our friend is sitting on a stool *facing* the torture chair and isn't strapped into it.'

'Exactly. Why? Because he will be a spectator, just like us. And because watching will be infinitely more agonising to bear than physical pain, he will answer all of our questions. What do you think?' said Sokolov.

'Absolutely.'

Jack felt a wave of uncertainty and fear wash over him. Sokolov's comments unnerved him. The duel of wits was suddenly moving in a direction he hadn't expected and didn't like.

'Well then, let's see if we're right, shall we?' Sokolov turned to one of the guards standing by the door. 'Bring her in!'

I wonder what they're up to? thought Jack. He was trying hard to stay calm, and kept watching the door as a feeling of dread made the hairs on the back of his neck tingle like a cube of ice melting slowly down his back.

Moments later, the door opened and Jack's heart missed a beat. Barefoot and wearing only a white nightshirt, Anielka stood in the doorway like an apparition. She stared at Jack with eyes wide open, shock and disbelief distorting her beautiful face. 'Is that really you?' she whispered, tears in her eyes. *'You are alive?'*

Jack shrugged. 'I'm afraid so. It wasn't my time. As you can see, following my breadcrumbs of destiny can be a dangerous business.' It was obvious that Anielka had no inkling that Jack was alive or had been brought to the castle.

'Stand over there,' barked Sokolov and pointed to the torture chair.

Obediently like a robot, Anielka walked over to the chair.

'Now take off your shirt.'

Slowly, Anielka slipped her shirt over her head, let it fall to the floor and kept looking at Jack with eyes so sad that he had to look away. Sokolov watched him and smiled. *Now that I know his weak spot, he will tell me everything I need to know,* thought Sokolov and turned to the guard standing beside him. 'Strap her in,' he said. 'We'll start with this little beauty here.' Sokolov held up the Pear of Anguish like a trophy, and smiled.

'Good choice,' said Aldar. 'I've never seen it fail, have you?'

76

Finbar Castle: 15 March 2017, sunrise

Following the rugged coastline and flying quite low, the two Chinook helicopters were approaching Finbar Castle. It was just before sunrise, and dense sea mist hovered above the waves crashing against the rocks below.

Operated by E-Squadron – arguably the most clandestine special operations unit in the UK – their mission, nicknamed Ruski, was to assist Police Scotland and the NCA in securing the castle. Because of its remote location – perched high on a barren clifftop – it was almost impossible to approach it unnoticed. Yet it was clear that the element of surprise was vital if the mission was to succeed.

Using surveillance and informers, both the NCA and MI5 had closely monitored Sokolov and his activities for quite some time. Linked to organised crime, especially money laundering on an industrial scale, and operations linked to the FSB – the KGB's main successor – involving assassinations and suspected terrorist activities, Sokolov was more than a person of interest. With slippery tentacles in many criminal pies reaching all the way to corrupt public servants in high places, nailing the shady Russian billionaire would be a major coup. When intelligence reached MI5 through Europol and the Paris Police about Jack's abduction, with a likely link to Sokolov, the NCA saw an unexpected opportunity. Realising that time was of the essence, it mobilised at once and decided to pounce.

The plan was for the elite taskforce to land just after sunrise, secure the castle and search the premises. If Jack was in fact held there, Police Scotland and the NCA would arrive later and take over. If not, the taskforce would leave, and the raid never happened.

After pretending not to care and engaging in a risky, high-stakes game of indifference, while at the same time trying to protect Anielka

425

from serious injury as she was being obscenely tortured, Jack was desperately playing for time. He realised that if his message got through and had triggered the desired response, every minute he gained counted. However, Jack finally capitulated just before the Pear of Anguish could cause serious damage, and when Aldar began to apply the finger press to turn up the heat, which would have crushed Anielka's fingers and crippled her hand. Time had run out.

'*Enough*!' said Jack. He held up his hand and then calmly proceeded to tell Sokolov that he had created the diversion to allow him to take the phone unnoticed. He also told him what he had done with it, and about the text message sent to Countess Kuragin.

Damn! thought Sokolov, clenching his fists in frustration, and turned to Aldar standing next to him. He knew he had been humiliatingly outmanoeuvred. *I would rip his guts out now if I didn't need him, and then feed him to the sharks. Later.* 'You were right. I should have listened to you earlier,' he said to Aldar. 'He played us like a violin and we danced to his tune. Where does this leave us?'

'Not in a good place,' said Aldar, shaking his head. 'With both of them here, and the information out there, we are exposed. We tripped up. They are a serious liability.'

Sokolov nodded. 'What do you suggest we should do?'

'*Outside*; not here,' said Aldar and opened the door.

Jack walked over to Anielka as soon as Sokolov and Aldar had left the chamber and they found themselves momentarily alone. He quickly removed the horrible device, covered in blood, untied Anielka and handed her the nightshirt. 'Put this on,' he said.

Shaking, Anielka slipped on the nightshirt without looking at Jack. 'I'm so sorry,' she whispered.

'Hush,' said Jack and began to stroke her hair.

Anielka burst into tears. 'What do you think will happen to us?'

'Don't know,' lied Jack. Judging by what he had just overheard, he was certain Sokolov would try to kill them before help arrived, and remove the evidence.

'Is it true that Frieda and Zuzanna are both dead?' asked Anielka.

'The Black Widow and Le Fantôme?' said Jack.

Anielka nodded.

'Yes.'

'I can't go back to prison. I'd rather die!' said Anielka.

'Why did you do it?'

Anielka pointed to her head. 'Demons, in here. Since I was a little girl. They entered the first time I was raped, and never left. The only way I can keep them under control is through my painting; nothing else works. What are we going to do?'

'We stay calm and keep our wits together,' said Jack, stroking Anielka's hair. That's when he saw the other torture instruments laid out in neat rows on the wooden table. Some looked like surgical instruments, sharp, with pointed, blade-like edges used for inflicting deep cuts, or for disembowelling recalcitrant subjects. Others were lethal-looking hook-like instruments for insertion into the ears to cause maximum pain and terror. Jack reached for one of the sharp instruments that looked like a knife with a long blade, and slipped it under his jumper.

'Give me one too,' said Anielka and held out her hand. 'At least if we go down, we go down fighting *together*.'

Jack nodded and handed her one of the rusty hooks.

Sokolov was talking to Aldar in the corridor, his voice raised, when one of the bodyguards came running down the stairs, agitated and breathless. 'Two choppers just landed outside. There are armed commandoes everywhere. They are breaking down the door right now!'

Aldar looked at Sokolov and nodded. What they had talked about moments earlier as a possibility, had just eventuated. He turned to the two guards standing in front of the heavy wooden door leading into the chamber.

'Finish them off and throw the bodies into the sea,' he shouted. 'You know where. The large window just up there on the landing, clear? It can't be seen from the front. And no guns! Understood?'

The guards nodded. 'Do it now, quickly!' said Aldar and then turned to Sokolov. 'Let's go upstairs, talk to our visitors and try to slow them down. All going well, there will be nothing left for them to find here. Come.'

The commandoes had broken down the heavy front doors and were securing the building by fanning out and moving methodically from room to room. Sokolov and Aldar hurried up the stairs, opened a concealed door, and walked into the large entry foyer teeming with armed men.

'Gentlemen,' Sokolov called out and held up his hand. 'There was no need for this. All you had to do is ring the bell! Who's in charge here?'

'I am. Who are you?' said one of the armed men, his face concealed behind a black balaclava.

'I own this place; who are you?'

'Stand over there and put your hands against the wall where I can see them,' said the man, ignoring the question.

Sokolov and Aldar did as they were told. 'I want to call my lawyer,' said Sokolov.

'Later. We have reason to believe that Jack Rogan is being held here. He was abducted in London yesterday. Is he here? It would save a lot of time if you could help me with that.'

'Never heard of him,' said Sokolov.

'Have it your way. Stay exactly where you are,' said the man and turned to one of the commandoes standing next to him. 'Make sure they aren't going anywhere,' he said, and then followed the others up the stairs.

Jack heard the key turn in the lock. 'Stand by the chair and attract their attention,' he hissed. He just managed to press himself against the wall next to the door, when the door opened and the two guards burst in. Both had knives in their hands, their intention obvious.

'You take *her*!' shouted one of the men and began to look around. 'Leave him to me!'

428

Realising what was about to happen, Anielka began to scream like a banshee. That's when Jack made his move. He raised his knife and slashed the man's throat from behind. The man dropped his knife in pain, and began to howl. Surprised, the other man spun around and was about to launch himself at Jack when Anielka ran forward and buried the rusty hook in his neck like a giant fishhook. Bleeding profusely, the man stopped in his tracks and, gasping for breath, fell to his knees. Jack picked up the knife from the floor and turned to face the other man who, holding his bleeding neck with both hands, was staggering towards the open door. Jack followed him outside, knife in hand. That's when he heard it: the unmistakable roar of rotor blades coming from above. *The cavalry has arrived*, he thought. *About bloody time!* He quickly took the key out of the door, stepped back into the chamber, and locked the door from the inside.

Anielka was kneeling beside the man lying on the floor. 'I think he's dead,' she said calmly and stood up. 'What do we do now?'

'We wait, said Jack. 'I think help has arrived.' He put his arms around Anielka and held her tight. 'Thank you,' he said.

'What for?'

'For saving my life.'

Lapointe sat in the back of a police car, nervously drumming his fingers against the armrest. The car, together with several others, was parked out of sight a few kilometres up the road from the castle. *They landed almost an hour ago*, he thought. *What if we got it wrong and he's not there?* Then the police radio crackled into life and the officer sitting in the front answered it. 'Understood,' he said and turned to the driver. 'Let's go!'

'They found Rogan?'

'Yes,' said the officer.

'Alive?'

'More or less.'

'What does that mean?'

'Let's go and find out.'

77

Finbar Castle: 15 March 2017, 8:30 am

Lapointe's unmarked police car crossed the narrow promontory leading to the castle and pulled up in front of the entrance, just as the strike force was preparing to leave. The Scottish police had already arrived and were taking over. The noise from the rotor blades was deafening, and Lapointe had to hold on to his hat and bend down low to make it safely to the entrance.

Jack saw Lapointe first as he walked into the busy foyer, took off his hat, and began to look around. Jack waved and walked over to him.

'What took you so long?' he said and held out his hand. Instead of shaking Jack's hand, Lapointe did something that would have surprised even those who knew him well: he embraced Jack and gave him a hug. It was a rare gesture of affection and relief by a serious, reserved man who always kept his emotions in check, and rarely gave even a hint of what he really felt inside.

A little surprised, but pleased, Jack patted Lapointe on the back. 'Just in time,' he said. 'Thanks. It couldn't have been easy to pull this off. Half an hour later—'

'That bad?'

'Only someone like you could possibly imagine what happened here this morning.'

'Tell me.'

'Before I do, have a look over there.' Jack pointed to a lounge by a large fireplace. Wrapped in a blanket, Anielka sat next to a female police officer who was handing her a glass of water.

'Is that ...? It can't be!' said Lapointe, astonished, *'Here?'* He took a couple of steps forward, then stopped and looked at Jack. 'How?'

'It's a long story.'

'Amazing. Dupree was right! He thought we would find her here.'

'There's more,' said Jack. 'I have another surprise for you.'

'I think I've had just about enough surprises for one day.'

'Perhaps, but I think you'll like this one.'

'What is it?'

'Upstairs in Sokolov's study, you'll find something that started it all.'

'Intriguing. What is it?'

'The Fabergé egg stolen from the Amber Safe.'

'Are you serious?'

'Absolutely,' said Jack, enjoying himself.

'Would you perhaps be interested in joining my squad? I know your French isn't all that good, but I'm sure if I put in a good word with the Prefect, he might agree. I could do with a man like you on my team.'

'I thought I already was,' retorted Jack, enjoying the banter. After the trauma of recent events, a little levity was a welcome relief.

'You are, informally. You know I have to arrest her for two murders right now. And that's just the start,' said Lapointe, turning serious.

Jack bit his lip. 'I know,' he said. 'But be gentle. She's been through a lot.'

Lapointe looked at Jack with sad eyes. 'She almost killed you.'

'I know, but still ...'

Lapointe shrugged. No matter how long he had been in the job, or what he had seen, human nature always had something up its sleeve to surprise. 'I have to do it right now, before the Scottish police charge her with who knows what.'

Jack nodded. He watched Lapointe walk over to Anielka and stand in front of her like an accusing harbinger of justice, talking quietly, as the police officer sitting next to Anielka looked on in amazement. That only seemed to heighten the gravity of the moment.

Slowly, Anielka put the glass of water on the table and stared at Lapointe with eyes wide open, as if she hadn't quite understood what he had just said. Even though he couldn't hear the words, the body language told Jack everything he needed to know. Lapointe was delivering the inevitable, crushing blow. The day of reckoning had arrived.

After a while, Anielka covered her face with her hands and just sat there, shaking all over. Jack resisted the urge to walk over to comfort her, as he felt an overwhelming sense of sadness. He realised that Anielka was now beyond his reach because the wheel of the inevitable had begun to turn, and there was nothing he could do to stop its relentless advance.

As Jack turned away because he couldn't bear to watch any longer, a chilling scream echoed through the crowded foyer. Anielka had jumped up, thrown off the blanket and was running towards the open door, barefoot, and only wearing her bloodied nightshirt. The surprised policewoman ran after her, followed by Lapointe.

Outside, it had begun to rain again. The helicopters had left and the morning mist was rising from the sea like a ghostly shroud. The edge of the steep cliff was close by, with only a low stone wall separating the courtyard from the abyss. Anielka ran over to the edge, climbed on top of the wall and looked down, her wet nightshirt flapping in the breeze like a white flag of surrender. The policewoman stopped, unsure what to do.

'Don't go any closer!' shouted Lapointe and walked over to her. 'We have to give her space.' Having witnessed similar situations before, Lapointe knew that the next few moments were critical and every word counted. He was about to say something when Jack grabbed his arm from behind. 'Let me; *please*,' he said.

'All right.'

'Please look at me, Anielka,' pleaded Jack, and took a step forward. Anielka turned around, her beautiful face distorted by confusion, wide-eyed fear and despair.

'I can't go back!' she said, feeling dizzy, and looked over the edge again. 'I feel so cold.'

'*Look at me!* This is not the answer,' said Jack and held out his hand. 'Come, give me your hand. I will help you banish the demons.'

'It's too late; can't you see? Perhaps in a different life I could have ... loved you.' Anielka closed her eyes. 'Forgive me, Jack,' she whispered, and let herself fall backwards.

Lapointe held his breath as Jack ran towards the edge, shouting '*Nooooo!*'

By the time he reached the little wall, Anielka had disappeared into the mist.

78

Kuragin chateau: 19 March 2017

Darrieux pulled up in her red Citroën and waved at the countess, waiting for her on the front steps. 'How is he?' she asked and handed the countess a big bunch of flowers.

'I've never seen him like this,' said the countess. 'He's in a dark place.'

'That bad? I know what it's like to feel down, but—'

'He's been interviewed for hours by the police and has to go back, of course, to give evidence later. Both in the UK and here in France. It's been traumatic to say the least.'

'Understandable.'

'I've tried my best to distract him and lift his spirits.' The countess shrugged. 'Not even Anna can get through to him. He isn't eating, either. Cook tried. And that's bad.'

'Then let's try something else,' said Darrieux, adjusting her dress. Since her 'coming out' she had put on some weight, which unfortunately made her already outrageously tight dresses even more eye-popping. The countess smiled and was hoping that this would cheer Jack up a little, because he noticed such things.

'What have you got in mind?'

'What's he doing now?'

'Working furiously; hasn't stopped. Going through his notes in the conservatory. He barely left the room since he got back from Scotland.'

'That's exactly what I thought he would do. He's trying to justify it all.'

The countess looked at Darrieux, surprised by the shrewd observation.

'Interesting. That's what I've been thinking as well,' she said.

'He won't rest until he's solved all this, you know. He can't stop now. He can't afford to fail, or—'

'It was all for nothing?'

'Exactly.'

'You're right. What will pull him out of this dark place is *action,*' said the countess.

'I've brought something that may help.'

'Oh? What?'

'Information.'

'Clever. Let's go and see him.'

Jack was sitting in his usual place by the window overlooking the garden. The first thing Darrieux noticed was that he hadn't shaved, his hair was dishevelled, and he was still wearing his pyjamas under an ill-fitting dressing gown.

'You look like I felt a couple of weeks ago,' said Darrieux.

'You mean like shit?' said Jack, struggling to stand up.

'Don't! No point in undoing the good work the Russian doctors have done to patch you up now, is there? How are the injuries?'

'Coming along. I haven't exactly been doing what I was supposed to since we last saw each other in London ...'

'I heard. Must have pissed Boris off big time. He was supposed to keep an eye on you.'

Jack looked at Darrieux and raised an eyebrow.

'I know what you're thinking,' said Darrieux. 'Neither have I, as you can see.'

'What on earth do you mean?' said Jack, pretending ignorance.

'You want me to spell it out? Look at me! Nothing fits! Too much champagne, too much of ... *everything!* And besides, bloody diets don't work, trust me! I could do with a drink.'

The countess burst out laughing, appreciating the clever performance. What she had tried to achieve since Jack came back two days ago, Darrieux had accomplished in a couple of minutes by making fun of herself.

'It's good to see you, Adrienne,' said Jack. 'Thanks for coming.'

'I don't come empty-handed.'

'You never do.'

Darrieux pointed to Jack's notebook on the table. 'Before I tell you what I have for you, why don't you tell us what you've found in Russia?'

By completely ignoring the recent events in Scotland, Darrieux was cleverly skirting the difficult questions, and was instead raising subjects Jack was obviously working on.

'But first, how about some champagne. Katerina?'

'At ten in the morning?' said the countess, going along with the light-hearted banter.

'Is it that late already?'

Feeling better, Jack put a photograph on the table.

'What's that?' asked Darrieux, taking a sip of champagne.

'I believe this is the picture that will lead us to Kazanskaya Bogomater,' said Jack quietly. 'And quite possibly to Mat' Rossiya, as well.'

Darrieux picked up the photograph and scrutinised it. It was a close-up of the inside of the Rasputin egg, taken by Lapointe in Sokolov's library. It clearly showed the intricate miniature icon in the tiny crypt beneath the golden cross.

'What am I looking at?' said Darrieux and handed the photo to the countess sitting next to her.

'You are looking at an image of the original Weeping Madonna of Kazan, the Kazanskaya Bogomater, presented by Rasputin to Empress Alexandra not long before she and her family were killed. It was supposed to protect her son, the tsarevich. Sadly, it didn't. This is most likely the only true copy in existence.'

'This was inside the Fabergé egg we found in the Amber Safe? The surprise?' said the countess.

'Yes.'

'And this is important?' said Darrieux.

'Oh yes, it is,' said Jack, becoming animated.

'Why?' asked the countess.

'Because I believe it will show us the way to the original icon, waiting somewhere out there to return home.'

'Because it has been foretold?' asked the countess.

'You've been speaking to the abbot at the hospital,' said Jack, smiling for the first time in days.

'We have. Like you, he's a strong believer in destiny. He thinks you are the chosen one—'

'To return the icon to Yekaterinburg where it belongs,' interjected Darrieux.

'Ah, destiny,' said Jack, looking out of the window. 'Destiny can be very cruel and relentless. Just think about that letter we found in Madame Petrova's music box not that long ago. That's what started all this, and look where we ended up. Just pause for a moment and consider what happened: we opened the lid of destiny and let it all out. So much tragedy, so much pain, so much death. Part of me is wishing we had never set eyes on that letter, but it's too late now.'

Jack covered his face with his hands and turned away.

Slowly, the countess stood up. She walked over to Jack, put her arms around him and held him tight. The comforting embrace acted as a trigger, releasing all the pent-up emotions and pain Jack had carefully kept hidden, afraid of the ghosts that had haunted his restless sleep since Anielka's death. Unable to hold back the tears any longer, Jack began to cry.

The countess, too, became emotional as she recalled that fateful telephone conversation with Jack about Anielka. *Perhaps I shouldn't have told him*, she thought, stroking Jack's hair.

'I should have done more,' whispered Jack.

'Hush. There was nothing more you could have done.'

'I can't help how I feel.' Jack pointed to his chest. 'Even after all this. Pathetic, isn't it?'

'Not at all,' said Darrieux. 'It's human.'

Jack looked at her with teary eyes. 'You're right. And we must never lose that, whatever the cost, or we lose everything.' Jack pulled a crumpled handkerchief out of his pocket and blew his nose. 'Now, where's that glass of champagne you promised?'

Darrieux handed Jack a glass of champagne. 'Are you going to tell us how that photograph will lead you to Kazanskaya Bogomater, or do we have to drink the whole bottle first?'

Feeling calmer, Jack sat back in his wicker chair, picked up his little notebook and opened it. 'While I was in some kind of coma at this hospital in Yekaterinburg, the abbot spoke to me. It was really weird. I could hear every word and can remember everything he told me.' Jack turned to face the countess. 'A bit like what happened to Tristan all those years ago when I first met him.'

The countess nodded.

'The abbot stayed with me for hours and told me stories,' continued Jack. 'In fact, I wrote everything down later.' Jack pointed to a page. 'It's all in here.'

'What did he talk about?' asked the countess.

'I already told you about the Seeker and the Guardians, remember? A very resourceful lot, as you will see in a moment. They are all scholars who have dedicated their lives to finding the precious icon and return it to Russia.'

'You told us in London.'

'They are all part of a brotherhood – the Brotherhood of the Weeping Madonna of Kazan. The Brotherhood has been searching for the icon since it was stolen by the Germans from the Tikhvin Assumption Monastery just outside St Petersburg in 1941. The abbot told me about the huge amount of information the Brotherhood has accumulated since then, and how they managed to trace the icon after it had been taken to Germany.'

'Fascinating,' said the countess.

'And it was all due to Pavel Ustinov, the Golem of Treblinka, I told you about.'

'How come?' asked Darrieux.

'He returned to Yekaterinburg after the war and became a member of the Brotherhood. He tracked down the German commander who was in charge during the occupation of Tikhvin in 1941. The Germans occupied the monastery for about a month, and it was during that time it was looted, the icon removed, and taken back to Germany. The commander was taken prisoner in Berlin by the Russians at the end of the war and was held in a camp in Siberia. He died there in 1953. Ustinov went to see him. That's when he found out about SS Major Axel Wolfbauer.'

'Who was that?'

'Someone close to Hitler. He was the one who stole the icon and took it back to Germany.'

'How interesting,' said Darrieux. 'Tell us more.'

'Before I tell you about the major, it's your turn. You said you didn't come empty-handed.'

'I didn't.'

'So, what have you got for me?'

'Last time we spoke about that letter in the music box, you asked me a question, remember?'

'Yes, I wanted to know if you had any idea why that letter had been hidden there, and didn't end up with all the others in the Amber Safe with the Fabergé egg.'

'Exactly.'

'And there was another, more important question, right?'

'Yes. Why were the precious Fabergé egg and those letters left behind in the Amber Safe in the first place? Abandoned, you could say, for all these years?'

'That's a good question,' said the countess.

'This has been bugging me for some time now,' said Jack. 'It's a loose end, and I don't like loose ends.'

'There's a good explanation for this,' said Darrieux. 'Quite a tragic one, actually, and it has to do with your grandmother, Countess Bezukhova.'

'Oh? In what way?'

'It's all about how, and where, she died ...'

'She died just before the end of the war; we know that,' said Jack.

'That's correct, but there's more to it. A lot more.'

'What do you mean, there is more?'

'There is. She'd been a widow for many years. Count Bezukhov died in 1935. He was much older. It wasn't a happy marriage, which was by no means unusual in those days. Many marriages were arranged.'

'We discussed all that. We know the reason she left the chateau – it wasn't far from here – and moved into the Ritz in Paris in 1942 with her two daughters,' said the countess.

'Madame Petrova, and my mother,' said Jack.

'Yes.'

'The Germans commandeered the chateau and used it as headquarters for the Abwehr, the German intelligence office, as it was close to Paris. They told the countess it would be better if she were to move out, and offered to accommodate her and her two daughters in the Ritz. A generous offer at the time, wouldn't you say?' said Jack. 'And one that Countess Bezukhova would have found tempting.'

'Exactly. And that offer was made by a dashing, high-ranking SS officer ...'

'What are you getting at?'

'Well, Countess Bezukhova was a cultured, attractive woman in her forties with two beautiful daughters. All spoke fluent German.'

'What are you suggesting, and why haven't you told me this before?'

'Because I made a promise.'

'What kind of promise?'

'I promised Madame Petrova to keep this out of her biography. She told me all this in strictest confidence. I even had to turn off the tape recorder.'

'Why?'

'You'll see why in a moment. I thought long and hard about this, because I don't break a promise lightly. As a biographer, there is a certain amount of trust that must not be broken, but considering what has happened here recently, well ...'

'Go on,' prompted Jack, leaning forward.

'While she lived in the Ritz, Countess Bezukhova and that officer formed a relationship—'

'Are you serious?' interrupted Jack.

'Yes, and is it really all that surprising? Look at what happened to your mother and Madame Petrova. These were extraordinary circumstances, and extraordinary times. We must look at all this in its proper context.'

'Sure. So, she had a fling with this officer while she was staying at the Ritz; is that it?'

'That's certainly part of it, but there's more, and it explains why the Fabergé egg was left in the Amber Safe.'

'Go on.'

'Countess Bezukhova didn't die of a heart attack at her chateau as we were led to believe.'

'No? Where then?'

'It happened just before the Germans evacuated Paris and pulled out of the Ritz in 1944.'

'What happened?'

'The day before Countess Bezukhova was due to return to her chateau, the SS officer and the countess went for a drive through Paris. They visited some of the iconic sites they had enjoyed together. A farewell trip, if you like. That's when it happened. On the Champs-Élysées, just near the Arc de Triomphe—'

'What happened?' demanded Jack impatiently.

'The French Resistance was very active by then. There were assassinations, bomb attacks—'

'What happened?' repeated Jack, raising his voice.

'There was a bomb attack. The major's car was blown up and he, the driver and the countess were all killed,' said Darrieux quietly.

'*Jesus!* That would explain—'

'Why no-one came to collect the contents of the safe,' said Darrieux, sounding relieved. 'No-one but the countess knew about it. Madame Petrova certainly didn't, and she lived at the Ritz with her mother. Why the music box letter didn't suffer the same fate is a matter of speculation, but I think it was because it arrived much later, sometime in 1943, well after the countess had moved into the Ritz

441

and deposited the Fabergé egg and the letters in the Amber Safe. She must have returned to the chateau from time to time, and hid the letter in the music box after it was delivered by the Feldpost. Obviously, she didn't want the Germans to see it. A letter from Treblinka? Something like that.'

'That's a bit of a bombshell,' said Jack. 'Forgive the pun. It explains a lot, but doesn't change anything.'

'I suppose not, but I thought you should know. It's part of your family history.'

'Thanks, Adrienne, I certainly appreciate this and it shall remain strictly among ourselves, agreed?'

Both Darrieux and the countess nodded.

'So, what about this Major Wolfbauer?' said the countess, changing direction, 'the abbot told you about?'

'Right,' said Jack. 'The abbot stayed with me for hours and spoke a lot about Ustinov. He must have been quite a guy, because he went back to Germany a year later and managed to find out what happened to Wolfbauer.'

'Incredible. How?'

'Through the Church; the Brotherhood had excellent connections throughout Europe, and Ustinov used these connections in his hunt for Wolfbauer. The major survived the war, managed to evade capture and found his way to Rome. As we know, after the war the Vatican helped many high-ranking Nazis to leave Europe. Apparently, Wolfbauer was one of them. He was given a new identity and went to New York, where he became an antiques dealer specialising in religious artefacts. And wait, now comes the best: he took the icon with him and used it to set up his business.'

'Do you know what happened to it?' asked Darrieux.

'That's when things become a little murky, I'm afraid. Of course, Wolfbauer recognised the true significance and value of the icon. He had several copies made and approached well-heeled collectors. You can see where this is heading, right? And that's our problem, because until now, no-one really knew what the original actually looked like.

And detail is important here, and authenticity is everything. You cannot venerate a fake, can you?'

Jack paused to collect his thoughts and took a sip of champagne.

'Once again, through their network of connections, the Brotherhood managed to make enquiries about this in New York. Wolfbauer was even approached by the Archbishop of Chicago, who offered to buy the icon, but by now it was too late because Wolfbauer had sold it and all the copies, as well. Several excellent copies were by now in circulation, and it was impossible to ascertain which one was the original and what had happened to it.'

'How disappointing,' said Darrieux, and poured herself another glass of champagne.

'Until now, that is.'

'What do you mean?' said the countess.

Jack held up the photo of the miniature icon inside the Rasputin egg.

'We have every reason to believe that this here is a true image of the original icon, perhaps the only one in existence. Therefore, for the first time, we *know* what the original actually looks like, and a lot of that has to do with its frame here, and the riza.' Jack pointed to the elaborate frame of the icon that could be seen clearly in the image.

'And this could help?'

'Yes.'

'How?'

'The Brotherhood has been looking for the icon for almost eighty years now, and has been able to identify and trace several possible contenders. Best of all, they know what they all look like. They have collected pictures from newspapers, magazine articles, exhibitions and auction catalogues, but unfortunately, all of them are slightly different, especially as far as the gems in the riza are concerned. I have already sent the abbot a copy of this photo and spoke to him early this morning.'

'You have been busy,' said the countess, shaking her head.

'Apparently, there are three serious candidates, and we know where they all are. However, one in particular stands out and is at the top of the list.'

'Do you know where it is?'

'Yes, I do.'

'Where?'

'Fatima, in Portugal.'

'Seriously?'

'The abbot was quite certain. I am planning to go there tomorrow to make enquiries.'

The countess was taken aback. 'So much for being a feeble patient in recovery,' she mumbled.

Jack picked up his glass and looked first at Darrieux, then the countess. 'Would you perhaps like to come along? I may need a little pampering along the way. A man in my condition ...'

Darrieux turned to the countess. 'The incorrigible rascal is back, don't you think?'

The countess rolled her eyes. 'Certainly looks that way,' she said. 'A little more champagne?'

79

Fatima, Portugal: 20 March 2017

'Not long now,' said Jack, and turned to the countess sitting next to him on the plane. 'Did you know that Fatima is named after a Moorish princess?'

'I had no idea.'

'She was kidnapped by Goncalo Hermigues, a Portuguese knight,' said Darrieux, 'and fell in love with him. She converted to Christianity, so the story goes, in order to be allowed to marry her abductor.'

'You see, that's why I asked Adrienne to come along,' said Jack. 'She knows useful stuff. No wonder I feel so safe sitting here between the two of you.'

'How do you feel?' said the countess.

'A bit like a pilgrim. After all that's happened lately ...'

During the flight, Jack had opened up a little and told Darrieux and the countess about what had happened in Scotland, and that he had to go back soon to give evidence. The countess reached for Jack's hand and just held it. It was a gesture of silent understanding and support by a true friend who really cared about him.

'Did you know that pilgrims have been coming here since early last century?' said Darrieux.

'Why exactly?' asked the countess.

'Well, it all began with three local shepherd children.'

'How so?'

'One day, while they were guarding the family's flock of sheep, they saw an apparition.'

'What kind of apparition?' asked Jack.

'A lady dressed all in white appeared on a rock nearby, shining with a blinding light as bright as the sun. This happened in May 1917, but it wasn't the first apparition.'

'It wasn't?'

'No. The year before, an angel had appeared twice to the children and prepared the way for what was to come. The children claimed to have seen the Marian apparition, as it is known, on six occasions. They even announced that the last appearance would be on thirteen October 1917.'

'And this was taken seriously?' asked Jack.

'Apparently so,' said Darrieux. 'Just listen to this: On the day in question, seventy-thousand faithful gathered at the site, and waited patiently for the Virgin Mary to appear—'

'You've obviously researched this,' interjected Jack.

'Perhaps just a little,' conceded Darrieux, smiling. 'It's always good to know where you're heading.'

'That's what I do,' said Jack, nodding appreciatively.

'Some observers reported that the sun behaved strangely, and this became known as the "Miracle of the Sun".'

'Come on ...' said the countess, sounding sceptical.

'Faith works in strange ways,' said Darrieux. 'We all see what we want to see and believe in what we need. It all went from there. First, a small chapel was built on the site in 1918 to commemorate the occasion. Since then, the chapel has been enclosed within a grand basilica and sanctuary. Today, between six and eight million pilgrims come here to pray every year.'

'Look! Down there, you can see it,' said Jack, and pointed out the window. 'The building with the large steeple.' The plane had begun its descent and was lining up for landing.

'I can see it. Magnificent!' said the countess.

'Two of the children who saw the apparitions died soon thereafter. Victims of the dreadful Spanish flu pandemic in 1920. The third, Lucinda dos Santos, became a nun and lived a long life. She died in 2005,' continued Darrieux. 'But it didn't end there. Miracles have a long reach. In 2000, the two children who died so young were beatified by Pope John Paul II, and later canonised in 2017, one hundred years after the first apparition.'

'All right, guys, let's buckle up. We are about to land,' said Jack. 'We can visit the basilica later today after my meeting with the trustee.'

'I hope your prayers will be answered here,' said the countess quietly, and let go of Jack's hand.

Jack took a deep breath. 'So do I,' he said and pressed his hand against his chest where the knife wound had begun to hurt again.

'We'll just make it,' said Jack and looked again at his watch. He opened the door of the taxi and got out. 'It always seems to take longer than you think.'

'Is this where we're staying?' said the countess and looked at the imposing building.

'Yes. Not bad, is it? Obviously there's money in pilgrims. This is the Domus Pacis Hotel. I'm meeting the trustee in there. He's part of the International Secretariat that runs all this. Big business, as you can see. You go and check in and have a look around. I'll see you after the meeting.'

'Welcome to Fatima, Mr Rogan,' said Luiz da Silva, a tall man of aristocratic bearing in his sixties, with an extravagant moustache that reminded Jack of Salvador Dali. 'I must say, I was intrigued by a phone call from Moscow I received about you this morning.'

'Oh? Who from, may I ask?'

'Patriarch Nicodemus of Moscow. You have friends in high places, Mr Rogan. It isn't often that the Primate of the Russian Orthodox Church calls one of us.'

Jack smiled without saying anything. He was hoping this would disguise his surprise. He had never met, nor even heard of the Patriarch.

'He knew we had arranged to meet today, and asked me to help you in any way I could, because you are the chosen one?' said da Silva and raised an eyebrow.

'I understand this meeting was arranged by Abbot Serapion of the Novo-Tikhvinsky Convent in Yekaterinburg,' said Jack, sidestepping the implied question.

'It was, and he indicated you were making enquiries about the Weeping Madonna of Kazan.'

'That's correct.'

'As I understand it, you are a journalist and a famous author, Mr Rogan. Is this part of some research for another book, perhaps?'

'It's more complicated than that. Look at me as a pilgrim following the breadcrumbs of destiny.'

Da Silva smiled. He seemed to like the answer. 'In that case, you've definitely come to the right place.'

'I am trying to piece together what happened to the icon after it was removed by the Germans from Tikhvin in 1941.'

'Stolen, you mean? You are helping the Brotherhood?'

'In a way, yes.'

'The Brotherhood of the Weeping Madonna of Kazan has been searching for the icon for decades. Unfortunately without success, it would seem.'

'That's correct.'

'So, why come here?'

'As you are no doubt aware, there are many contenders—'

'Claiming to be the original?' interjected da Silva.

'Yes. And that has been the problem, so far.'

'*So far?* What do you mean by that?'

'We believe that the original is in fact here, in Fatima.'

'But the Blue Army has always maintained that it had acquired the original back in 1970. The icon was extensively tested and examined at the time, and the experts agreed. So, what's new?'

'This,' said Jack. He reached into his pocket, pulled out the photograph taken by Lapointe of the miniature icon inside the Rasputin egg, and placed it on the table in front of da Silva.

'What is this?'

'Arguably, the only reliable image of the original icon in existence today.'

'Are you serious? What makes you so sure?'

'It was painted in 1918 by Fabergé in St Petersburg, and presented to the tsar as part of a secret Imperial Easter egg he commissioned for his wife, the Empress Alexandra.'

'How extraordinary,' said da Silva, surprised. 'How did you come by this?'

'It's a long story.'

'I would love to hear it. We have time.'

'And in return, will you show me the Weeping Madonna of Kazan purchased by the Blue Army in 1970?'

Da Silva looked pensively at Jack. 'I would if I could,' he said.

'What do you mean?'

'The icon isn't here.'

'*What?* It is not here in Fatima?'

'No.'

'Do you know where it is?'

'Yes, I do.'

'What happened to it?'

'I will tell you.'

By the time Jack walked into the foyer of the Domus Pacis Hotel looking for Darrieux and the countess, it was already dark.

'Three hours; quite a meeting,' said the countess. 'I hope it was worth it.'

'In more ways than I could possibly have imagined.'

'Are you going to tell us?'

'Of course. Let's have dinner. I'm starving!'

'You have heard of the Blue Army?' asked Jack, after the delicious entree of *pata negra*, paper-thin slices of cured ham, had been served.

'The Blue Army of Our Lady of Fatima, also known as the World Apostolate of Fatima,' said Darrieux, 'is an international, Christian association—'

'Founded in 1946 by Father Colgan in the US,' the countess chimed in.

'You are well informed.'

'We did our homework while we were waiting for you. We visited the magnificent basilica. It was a revelation,' said the countess.

'Good. This will help you understand what I'm about to tell you because most of it has to do with the Blue Army.'

'We can't wait,' said the countess, enjoying the excellent Portuguese wine Jack had ordered.

'Remember yesterday I told you that Wolfbauer had several high-quality copies made of the original icon, and offered them for sale to well-heeled collectors in the US?'

'Yes, you did tell us,' said the countess.

'Well, now I can tell you what appears to have happened to the original.'

'You can?' said Darrieux, surprised.

'I found out this afternoon. I also discovered that SS Major Wolfbauer changed his name to Adolphus – which means noble wolf – while he was staying at the Vatican after the war. All part of a new identity, and a new life waiting for him in America. His antiques business in New York was called Noble Wolf Antiques. Ironic, don't you think—'

'Is it here?' interjected the countess, sounding a little impatient. 'The original icon, I mean.'

'Before I answer that, I have to tell you a story; an extraordinary one as you will see. It begins with the World Trade Fair in New York in 1964 to '65, and you won't believe where it ends.'

The countess shrugged and looked at Darrieux. 'Here we go,' she said. 'He's in great form again.'

'Adolphus was a shrewd operator who recognised the power of publicity. He knew that the original icon of Our Lady of Kazan had great significance and was worth a lot of money, but to realise its value, he had to find the right buyer. And in order to flush out that buyer, the icon needed publicity and exposure.'

Jack paused and took a sip of wine.

'Can you think of a better way to gain exposure than to exhibit the icon at an international trade fair? Surely not. And that is exactly what Noble Wolf Antiques did,' continued Jack. 'With much fanfare, the icon was exhibited in the Russian Pavilion in 1964, and that was how the Blue Army of Our Lady of Fatima became aware of it. In fact, on thirteen September 1965, the Blue Army spent an entire night in the pavilion in veneration of the icon—'

'Seriously? Why was the Blue Army so interested in it?' interjected the countess.

'Because of what it meant to Christianity in Russia. It was one of the most holy and most revered icons in the entire country, and therefore inextricably linked to the Russian Orthodox Church. With the rise of the Bolsheviks in 1917, the Church suffered greatly. Monasteries were closed and destroyed, the clergy persecuted and Christianity suppressed. The Blue Army believed that Russia would once again embrace Christianity, and when that happened, the icon had to be returned to Russia so it could take its rightful place within the Russian Orthodox Church and be worshipped by the faithful.'

'How fascinating,' said Darrieux.

'It sure is. After the trade fair, the Blue Army entered into negotiations with Adolphus to purchase the icon and a year later, they bought it. The icon was brought here to Fatima and enshrined in the Byzantine Chapel.'

Jack paused, to let the anticipation grow.

'And is it still here?' asked the countess quietly.

Jack took his time before answering. 'No,' he said.

'Do you know where it is?'

'Yes, I do.'

'Are you going to tell us?'

'When Pope Pius XIII fell seriously ill last year and was close to death, the Blue Army presented the icon to him. It was hoped that it would save his life and restore his health, and it seems to have done just that,' said Jack smiling. 'Because controversy still surrounded the icon and as several copies were in circulation all purported to be the original, it was thought that if the icon *did* manage to save the pontiff, this would serve as further proof that it was indeed the real McCoy, worthy of veneration.'

'And you and Professor Delacroix played a significant part in the pope's recovery last year; isn't that so? It wasn't just the work of the icon,' said the countess. 'Medical research had something to do with it, right? Somehow, it's all coming together. Amazing!'

'What do you mean, Jack played a part in the pope's recovery?' asked Darrieux.

'Jack and Professor Delacroix, the Nobel laureate he was going to celebrate New Year's Eve with in Sydney before all this blew up, were instrumental in saving the pontiff's life last year. The discovery of a drug Delacroix was working on did the job; isn't that so, Jack?'

'It is. There's no doubt about it, it saved the pope's life.'

Darrieux looked dumbfounded. 'You do get around, Jack,' was all she managed to say.

'All part of the breadcrumbs ...'

The countess shook her head. 'You and your infuriating bread-crumbs. Where's the icon now?'

'In the pope's study in Rome, waiting to be returned to Russia when the time is right.'

'Seriously?' said Darrieux.

'Yes.'

'And you found all this out this afternoon?'

'I did. Luiz da Silva told me. He's one of the trustees here. He should know, don't you think?'

'So, what's your next move?'

'Going to Rome to talk to his Holiness, what else? I'll call Cardinal Borromeo in the morning. I'm sure he'll be able to arrange it.'

'Who's Cardinal Borromeo?' said Darrieux.

'He's the Dean of the College of Cardinals.'

'*You know him?*'

'Oh yes. I met him last year. In the Vatican kitchens of all places, while Lorenza – the Top Chef Europe winner – and I were cooking a life-saving dinner for the pontiff,' said Jack, smiling.

'You are pulling my leg!'

'Far from it,' said Jack, who was enjoying himself. 'That's exactly what happened. Our cooking saved the pope's life. An Ottoman dish called Hunkar Begendi. You should try it sometime. It's delicious and has medicinal qualities.'

Darrieux turned to the countess. 'Is this guy for real?' she asked. 'I think this Portuguese wine must be stronger than I thought.'

'I know it sounds far-fetched and strange, but it's all true. It happened just as he said. And Lorenza is engaged to Tristan. They are planning to marry later this year.'

Darrieux shook her head. 'It must be this place. I need another drink!'

80

Papal Apartments, Rome: 23 March 2017

Jack got out of the taxi and looked in awe at Bernini's familiar four-row colonnade extending an open-armed welcome to the faithful flocking to the Vatican. As he went through security, he remembered his visit the year before on a similar, sunny day. On that occasion, he had come to Rome to do some urgent research in the Vatican archives. He had been following the trail of an ancient manuscript that held the key to a medical breakthrough, which ultimately saved the pope's life.

Jack knew the way. He crossed St Peter's Square and went to a side entrance he had used before. The Swiss Guard looked at him with undisguised suspicion when he asked to see Cardinal Borromeo and showed him an email he had received from the cardinal the day before. People didn't just walk in off the street asking to see the Dean of the College of Cardinals. Jack was asked to wait.

The guard's demeanour changed when an elderly monsignor working in the diplomatic service of the Holy See came down the stairs and greeted Jack like an old friend. 'It's wonderful to see you again, Mr Rogan,' said the little man. 'Cardinal Borromeo is waiting for you upstairs. Please follow me.'

Cardinal Borromeo, an imposing man in his late seventies, radiated authority. As the Dean of the College of Cardinals he was a man of great influence and power, used to being obeyed.

'You never cease to surprise, Mr Rogan,' said the cardinal, extending his hand. 'It's been almost a year since we first met, right here in my office.'

'It's just as I remember it,' said Jack and pointed to the paintings crowding the walls of the palatial room overlooking the dome of St Peters. 'Not many offices have a Caravaggio and a Titian hanging on the walls, and a timeless view like that.'

'I am only a temporary occupant,' said the cardinal, smiling. 'Last time you were searching for an ancient medical text in our archives here—'

'Yes, Osman da Baggio's *al-Qanun*.'

'Quite. And look where that took us.'

'Destiny, Eminence.'

'Professor Delacroix' discovery, and Lorenza da Baggio's cooking – ably assisted by yourself, as I remember it – saved his Holiness's life.'

Jack waved his hand dismissively. 'We are but instruments of fate.'

'Indeed we are, and I was wondering if your visit here today is perhaps of a similar nature?'

'It may well be, Eminence. But before we talk about that, allow me to thank you for seeing me so promptly, and for arranging an audience.'

'For you, his Holiness's door is always, open, Mr Rogan, you know that. His Holiness was delighted to hear from you and is looking forward to meeting you this morning. He has just finished saying mass in the Sistine Chapel.'

'I am honoured.'

'I'm not sure if you fully realise what impact his Holiness's sudden recovery last year has had, not only on Church matters here in the Vatican, but on world peace.'

'As I remember it, he did manage to travel to the US and address Congress, and then opened constructive channels of negotiation for peace in the Middle East, especially in Syria. It's all looking very promising,' said Jack.

'A very sensitive subject, but yes, progress has been made. Are you suggesting that the reason for your visit here today may further assist his Holiness in that regard? From what you have told me so far, I gained the impression that this may be the case.'

Jack nodded. 'The subject in question concerns something that is very dear to the Russian Orthodox Church ...'

'How intriguing. Is that why you would like to see the icon?'

'Yes. It is here, isn't it?' asked Jack, a shadow of worry flashing across his face. It only lasted an instant, but Borromeo had noticed it.

'It is. I sense this means a great deal to you,' Mr Rogan. 'May I ask why?'

The cardinal, a consummate diplomat and Church politician, was steering the conversation back to the subject that was of real interest to him. He wanted to find out why Jack had asked to see the icon presented to the pope by the Blue Army the year before. And he wanted to know that preferably before Jack would meet the pope, so that he could take control of the meeting.

Jack felt the urgency in the cardinal's question. 'It's a very long story. Before I bore Your Eminence, and his Holiness for that matter, with it, it would be helpful if I could see the icon—'

'Why?' interjected the cardinal, frowning. He wasn't used to having his questions deflected or being sidelined.

'Because that story is only relevant if the icon is in fact the original Kazanskaya Bogomater, removed by the Germans from the Tikhvin Assumption Monastery in 1941. As I understand it, a lot of controversy still surrounds the authenticity of the icon, despite the fact the Blue Army is convinced it is in fact the original. Several excellent copies are currently in circulation, claiming to be the real thing.'

The cardinal looked at Jack, impressed. 'That is correct, and yes, that has been a problem for us here, as well. Are you suggesting you are in a position to establish whether it is in fact the original, Mr Rogan?'

'Yes, I believe I can.'

'What, just by looking at it?'

'That's part of it, but there's more. A lot more.'

'You are full of surprises, Mr Rogan,' said the cardinal, smiling. 'And I suppose you are going to tell us all about this when you see it?'

'Yes, I will.'

'In that case, let's go and do that.' The cardinal looked at his watch. 'His Holiness should be back in his study by now. He will see us there, because that's where the icon is.'

Pope Pius XIII, a sprightly man in his eighties, stood next to his desk by the open window. Jack was surprised how well he looked. Since the pope's recovery the year before, Jack had only seen him on TV. Jack walked slowly towards him, stopped, and bowed his head.

'Come closer, my friend,' said the pope.

Jack took a few more steps towards the pope and stopped again, unsure what to do next. The pope walked up to him and placed his right hand on Jack's shoulder. 'Last time it was Hunkar Begendi. I wonder what brings you here this time,' he said. 'Another sumptuous dish, perhaps?' The pope was referring to the life-saving dish Lorenza had prepared for him the year before based on a medicinal recipe discovered by Jack in Osman da Baggio's famous *al-Qanun*. 'Welcome.'

'Thank you, Holiness, and thank you for this opportunity. I know how precious your time is.'

'For you, I always have time. You know that. I am indebted to you in more ways than I can express.'

'Very kind of you to say so. What brings me here, Holiness, is not a culinary event, but ... *that*.' Jack pointed to the icon on the wall behind the pope's desk.

'Ah. Kazanskaya Bogomater, the famous Russian icon. It was presented to me by the Blue Army of Our Lady of Fatima last year, in the hope that it would help my recovery.'

'And it seems to have done just that, Holiness,' said Jack, unable to take his eyes off the icon.

'I'm sure it helped. It was in my bedroom and I saw it every day during that difficult time. But what is your interest in it, Mr Rogan?'

'It's a long story, Holiness—'

'Which Mr Rogan will gladly share with us once he has established something that has troubled us as well,' said Borromeo, coming to Jack's assistance.

The pope looked at the cardinal, surprised. 'And what might that be?'

'The icon's authenticity,' said Jack.

'Ah. You know about that?' said the pope. 'Yes, it's true. The icon's authenticity has been under a cloud of uncertainty for years, I'm afraid. With so many conflicting claims, it is impossible to be sure. Even the experts ...' The pope shrugged and pointed to the icon. 'And that's also the reason it is still here,' he said.

'I don't understand,' said Jack.

'The icon was given to his Holiness last year, not only so that the Virgin Mary could watch over his recovery,' said Borromeo, 'but because he was entrusted with a mission.'

'What kind of mission?'

'His Holiness was asked to return the icon to Russia and present it to the Russian Orthodox Church when he believed the time was right. Politically speaking that is, if you know what I mean. When religious freedom had once again returned to Russia. That was the reason the Blue Army purchased the icon in the first place. It was always meant to be returned to Russia.'

'That's correct,' said the pope. 'While much-improved conditions in Russia would now certainly allow that, I am reluctant to return an icon with my blessing that may not be the authentic original. I'm sure you can understand that and see my dilemma. Venerating a fake, well ...'

'Clearly, Your Holiness.'

'But Mr Rogan may be able to help us in that regard,' said Borromeo.

'How?'

'I believe I may have found a way that could establish the icon's authenticity beyond doubt,' said Jack.

'What? Here, right now?' asked the pope, surprised.

'Yes, Holiness.'

'Amazing. Could you please explain?'

Jack reached into his pocket and pulled out the photograph of the miniature icon inside the Rasputin egg, and explained what it was.

He also mentioned the abbot, the Brotherhood and the Seeker, and what they stood for.

'May I?' he asked and pointed to the icon.

'Please, go ahead,' said the pope.

Jack walked over to the icon and held up the photo. 'See? Exactly the same,' he said. 'Right down to the finest detail, including the heavy-gauge silver-gilt and repousse oklad here.' Jack pointed to the icon. 'This is a head-to-shoulders version of the icon of the Theotokos of the Hodegretia.'

'What makes you say that?' asked Borromeo.

'Well, it shows the Infant Christ sitting on Mary's arm, His right hand raised in a gesture of blessing, and holding a book in His left hand. A classic composition. But most important of all, if you look carefully, you will notice that the Virgin Mary appears to be weeping—'

'But surely that's not enough?' interjected Borromeo.

'Of course not,' said Jack. 'This is just the beginning. While I was in hospital in Yekaterinburg only a short time ago, recovering from a knife attack, the abbot of the Novo-Tikhvinsky Convent in Yekaterinburg, where the icon had been kept until the convent was closed by the Bolsheviks in 1920, came and spoke to me while I was in a coma. Strangely, I can remember every word he said. It was all about this icon and a special feature to do with its spectacular frame and riza, here, dating back to Byzantine times.' Jack pointed to the heavy, jewel-encrusted frame.

'What kind of feature?' asked the pope, coming closer.

'It concerns something no-one apart from the abbot and the Brotherhood I told you about seems to know.'

'What exactly?' asked Borromeo.

'According to legend, the original icon presented by Rasputin to Empress Alexandra had something extraordinary concealed in a se-cret compartment at the back of its frame. Apparently, this was by no means uncommon. Several special holy icons had such compart-ments.'

'What are we talking about here?' said Borromeo, sounding a little impatient.

'As you can see, this is a particularly heavy frame. Very solid, and quite thick. Much thicker than the painted wooden board.'

'Yes, I can see that,' said the pope. 'But what about that compartment? What was its purpose, and what could it contain?'

'A holy relic.'

'Are you serious?' said Borromeo. 'What kind of relic; do you know?'

'Yes, I do. A small splinter of wood taken from the crucifix ...'

The pope looked at Jack, stunned. 'Are we talking about the holy cross on which Our Saviour died?'

'Yes.' Jack took a deep breath, but decided not to mention what else he was hoping to find hidden in the secret compartment. If he had interpreted Madame Petrova's music box letter correctly, then another, worldlier treasure would be waiting for them inside.

Jack realised that the moment of truth had arrived. He looked at the pope and they locked eyes. 'Why don't we find out?' he said quietly.

The pope nodded. 'Let's do that,' he said.

'If this is indeed the original Kazanskaya Bogomater, then it should have such a secret compartment at the back, and I know how it can be opened.'

'You do?' said Borromeo. 'How?'

'We should take the icon off the wall, first. May I?'

'Go ahead,' said the pope.

Carefully, Jack lifted the heavy icon off the wall and rested it on top of the desk in an upright position.

'As you can see, there is nothing at the back to suggest there is some kind of hidden compartment in here. Everything is cleverly concealed, yet the entire back should open up if—'

'If what?' interjected Borromeo, bending forward for a better look.

'We press this gem here.' Jack pointed to a small ruby in the centre of the elaborate crown on Mary's head. 'I think it should be his Holiness who ...' said Jack, turning the frame towards the pope.

Aware of the gravity of the moment, the pope nodded and came closer. As he extended his arm and his frail fingers almost touched the head of the Virgin Mary, the bells of St Peter's began to toll. Smiling, the pope pressed the ruby. Because the bells were still tolling, Jack couldn't hear the click activating the spring that opened the back of the icon.

But then he saw it. The entire back had opened like the cover of a book, revealing the secrets hidden within. Jack placed the icon face down on the desk, and stared at Empress Alexandra's gift to her country that had so tragically forsaken her.

'I think now we know, Holiness,' he whispered once the bells had fallen silent, his voice quivering with emotion. 'This is no fake. Kazanskaya Bogomater can now safely give up her secrets, and begin her journey home.'

81

Patsy's Italian Restaurant, New York: 28 March 2017

Jack always enjoyed the few quiet minutes of contemplation just before take-off. The anticipation, and looking forward to the destination and things to come never failed to excite him, and never more so than on this occasion. Jack was heading for a meeting he knew would set a chain of events in motion that would not only have far-reaching consequences, but also make history. What had begun with a long-forgotten letter discovered by accident in a music box, was about to reach its climax in a way he could not have imagined in his wildest dreams just a few short weeks ago.

Jack let himself sink into the comfortable seat in the pointy end of the aircraft and was about to close his eyes, when the hostess walked up to him.

'May I offer you a drink before take-off, Mr Rogan?' she said, giving Jack her best smile. She always made sure that she knew the names of all the passengers in her care on the popular Paris-to-New York run, which was her special domain.

'Why not?' said Jack.

'A glass of champagne, perhaps, or something else?'

'How about a Scotch? I've just been to Scotland ...'

'A holiday?'

Jack shook his head. 'I wish ...'

The hostess noticed the sadness in Jack's eyes and was too tactful and polite to ask any more questions. 'Leave it to me,' she said. 'I have something special for you.'

'Great. No ice please. Just a little water on the side.'

'Of course.'

The hostess placed a glass on the armrest and showed Jack the bottle.

'A Talisker Storm single malt, twenty-five years old. Wow! A Hebridean drop from the Isle of Skye. You are spoiling me.'

'You know your whisky,' said the hostess and opened the bottle. 'Say when.'

'What if I say nothing?'

'I'll leave the bottle.'

'Don't tempt me. That's enough, thank you. I can certainly do with this,' said Jack and lifted his glass.

'Enjoy,' said the hostess and withdrew.

Jack took a sip, closed his eyes and savoured the smoky flavour of the splendid whisky. As he began to relax, he let himself drift back to the pope's study and the extraordinary surprise discovery that had been waiting inside the icon. *Did it all really happen?* he asked himself as the plane took off. *Or have my breadcrumbs of destiny been playing tricks on me again?*

Jack waited until the plane had reached its cruising altitude. Then he reached for his notebook and iPad in the seat pocket, opened his notebook and began to type on the iPad. The hostess returned several times and refilled Jack's glass. She even threw a blanket over him and put his notebook and iPad away after he had fallen asleep, and served him breakfast just before landing.

By the time Jack arrived in New York he had almost finished a whole bottle of Scotch, but felt surprisingly refreshed because he had typed up everything he'd written in his notebook. Writing had always had a cathartic effect on him. Somehow, the clarity of the written word focused his recollection, dispelled the ghosts of uncertainty and speculation, and showed him the way. Jack was ready to face the next challenge of his extraordinary journey: how to present Kazanskaya Bogomater and her secrets to the world in a way that did justice to those who had long ago passed into history, and could no longer speak and be heard.

Jack arrived at Patsy's Italian Restaurant between Broadway and Eighth Avenue a little early. Run by the Scognamillo family since 1944, the iconic restaurant was Jack's favourite in New York, and he never missed an opportunity to have a meal, or two, in the familiar establishment. He even had his preferred table near the hundreds of photos of famous patrons lining the walls. Frank Sinatra had been one of the regulars, and so had Burt Lancaster, Gene Kelly and Al Pacino, together with countless other glitterati who felt at home in the cosy, informal atmosphere radiating wellbeing, congeniality and the promise of excellent food.

However, on this evening there was another reason Jack had chosen Patsy's: it was close to Carnegie Hall, where Benjamin Krakowski, the celebrated composer, violin virtuoso and conductor, was giving a concert that evening. He was performing Tchaikovsky's Violin Concerto in D Major as a special tribute to Isaac Stern, the legendary violinist who had saved Carnegie Hall from demolition in the 1960s.

Catching up with Krakowski was never easy because he was always touring and had recording contracts all over the world. To get him to change his plans and pin him down to a dinner after the concert had only been possible because of a close friendship, shared adventures, and a unique bond that went back many years.

And then, of course, there was Jack's phone call from Rome after his meeting with the pope. Once Jack had briefly explained why he wanted to urgently meet with his friend he hadn't seen for quite some time, Krakowski was unable to resist the invitation once Jack had given him a few cryptic clues. Enough to tantalise, but without giving too much away.

The other guest Jack had invited to dinner was Celia Crawford, a leading journalist working for the *New York Times*, whom he knew well and had also formed a close friendship with. She and Krakowski knew each other through a sensational case involving a forgotten Monet, and a forgery that had almost ended in disaster for Isis, who had purchased the painting for 35 million pounds in 2014.

Celia had been working on a story in Chicago when Jack had called her from Rome and she had flown back to New York specially to attend the dinner. Once again, a cryptic phone call from Jack had made all the difference. Jack's stories and escapades were legendary, and Celia knew they had to be taken seriously as some of her best leads, sensational articles and breaking news had originated from them.

Celia was the first to arrive. Looking a little flustered, but still gorgeous, she followed the waiter to Jack's table.

'Straight from the airport?' asked Jack and kissed Celia on the cheek.

'What do you think? I just made it. This better be worth it, Jack, is all I can say. I abandoned a senator and his girlfriend, who were involved in a scandal and had finally agreed to an interview. I left them standing in a hotel lobby without an explanation, hopped into a taxi to the airport, and answered your siren call. My editor will kill me. I need a drink!'

'Have I ever disappointed you?' said Jack with a cheeky grin, as the waiter served Celia a vodka martini Jack had ordered for his guest.

'No. That's why I'm here. Cheers!'

It was the applause rippling through the crowded restaurant that told Jack that Krakowski must have arrived. As a high-profile celebrity, Krakowski was well known in New York and attracted attention wherever he went. It was by no means unusual for people to break into spontaneous applause and cheer when he made an entrance, and come over to his table to ask for an autograph. Always gracious and polite, Krakowski usually obliged with a smile. Like most people in the spotlight, he enjoyed his fame and didn't mind being the centre of attention.

'Just like good old times,' said Krakowski and embraced Celia. 'Lovely to see you both.' Krakowski looked at Jack. 'No more forgeries and eccentric art collectors, I hope,' he said and sat down. 'I disappointed an ambassador and broke an actress's heart by cancelling our post-concert arrangements just to be with you guys,' said Krakowski.

'It's tough being famous,' said Jack, rolling his eyes.

'To tell you the truth, I was delighted to be able to get away. The ambassador is a pompous bore with a nagging dragon of a wife, and the actress is well past her prime ...'

'I've done you a favour, then?' said Jack.

'Let's not be too hasty. First, show me what you've got and we'll see.'

'You're on. Shall we order dinner?'

'Absolutely,' said Celia. 'I haven't eaten all day.'

'May I suggest Patsy's Delicious Fried Shrimps as a starter?' said Jack, unfolding his serviette. 'Never disappoints.'

Celia turned to Krakowski. 'When it comes to food, we can always rely on Jack, don't you think?'

'Agreed. It's all the other stuff he promised us that worries me.'

'Me too, but let's eat first, shall we?'

'How would you like to make history?' said Jack and pushed his empty plate aside.

'Here we go,' said Krakowski and smiled good-naturedly at Jack.

'I'm serious,' said Jack and wiped his mouth with the serviette after he finished his bowl of Linguini San Giovanni, a house speciality pasta consisting of capers, onions, dried plum tomatoes and grilled portobello mushrooms. 'This was bloody good.'

'History? In what way?' said Celia and reached for her notebook.

'You can put that away,' said Jack. 'There's no need to write things down.'

'Oh? How come?'

'Because I've written it all down for you. On the way over in the plane. I'll email it to you later. So, all you have to do now is listen, because what I'm about to tell you will sound stranger than fiction.'

Jack reached for his glass and took a sip of wine.

'This story has it all. A murdered tsarina, a mad monk, a world-famous composer, a secretive brotherhood and a pope. And most important of all, a sacred thirteenth-century icon that holds all the secrets here, and all the answers. Interested?'

'Are you sure you're not talking about your next book here, full of fantasy and fiction?' said Celia, shaking her head.

'Shame on you, doubter!' Jack reached into his pocket, pulled out a copy of the music box letter, and put it in the middle of the table.

'What's that?' asked Krakowski.

'The beginning,' said Jack, reaching into his pocket again like a magician and holding up the photograph of the painted miniature icon from inside the Rasputin egg.

'And that?' said Celia.

'That's the key that finally opened the door.'

'What kind of door?' asked Krakowski.

'The door to this,' replied Jack. He put the photograph next to the letter, reached into his briefcase under the table and pulled out a bundle of papers, which he carefully placed in front of his friend.

'And what's that?' asked Krakowski.

Jack pushed the bundle towards Krakowski. 'Have a look and tell me what *you* think it is.'

Krakowski put on his reading glasses and picked up the bundle. Jack reached for his goblet, took a sip of wine and kept watching Krakowski. The expression on Krakowski's face changed from slight bemusement to surprise, then astonishment, and finally wonder, until his hands began to shake and he had to put the papers down because he had tears in his eyes and couldn't read any more. *'Where did you get this?'* he whispered, his voice barely audible.

'What is it, Benjamin?' said Celia, surprised by Krakowski's emotional reaction.

'Tell her, Benjamin.'

'Where did you get this?' Krakowski asked again.

Jack pulled another photograph out of his pocket and handed it to Krakowski. It was a photo of Kazanskaya Bogomater lying face down on the pope's desk. The back of the icon was open, with a bundle of papers lying next to it.

'What am I looking at?' said Krakowski.

'The back of a precious Russian icon that used to belong to Empress Alexandra. It was given to her by Rasputin to protect her son, the tsarevich.'

'*What?*' said Celia. 'Let me have a look!'

'For almost a hundred years, these papers were hidden inside a secret compartment at the back of the icon. It was only discovered a couple of days ago when I visited the pope in Rome. The icon was in his study.'

'This is unbelievable!' said Krakowski, recovering his composure.

'What are these papers?' asked Celia again.

'A handwritten musical score; a symphony,' said Jack.

'Seriously?'

'Yes.'

'Do we know who wrote it?'

'Yes. There's a dedication here at the beginning, and a signature.'

'A dedication?'

'Yes, to Tsar Alexander III, and it is signed Pyotr ... Ilych ... *Tchaikovsky,*' Jack said slowly.

'Let me have a look!'

Krakowski handed the bundle of papers to Celia.

'What are we talking about here? Is this authentic?' she said, sounding sceptical.

'These are copies, of course,' said Jack. 'The originals are with the pope in Rome. But it certainly looks authentic. A symphony by Tchaikovsky never seen before called *Mat' Rossiya* – Mother Russia. A name given to the work by Tchaikovsky himself right here at the front, see? What do you think, Benjamin?'

'Certainly looks like it. I'm familiar with all of Tchaikovsky's published works, and have seen many of his handwritten scores, but I've never seen this—'

'Come on, guys. Can this be for *real?*' asked Celia, becoming excited.

'More work would have to be done, of course, by experts, but it shouldn't be too difficult to get authentication,' said Krakowski.

'And that, Benjamin, is what I would like you to do. I'm entrusting Tchaikovsky's lost symphony into your care. Here, right now.'

'How did all this come about, Jack?' said Celia, shaking her head.

'It's a long story, but as I told you before, I've written it all down.'

'And you asked us to come here just to tell us all this? Extraordinary as it may be. Is that it? Where do Benjamin and I fit into all this?'

'There's more to all this, of course,' said Jack, enjoying himself. 'A lot more.'

'With you, there always is. What do you have in mind?'

'Making history. Once you've read the full story, all will become clear, Celia. But what I would like you to do right now, is to break the story and tell the world that a masterpiece by one of the greatest composers who's ever lived has just been discovered in circumstances that can only be described as epic.'

'Is that all? Do you realise what you are asking here? A story like this only comes along once in a lifetime. It could be the coup of the decade, if not the century! Are you sure you want *me* to do this?'

'Aha. Worth abandoning the senator and his girlfriend for this, you think?'

'You can be so infuriating!' said Celia, clenching her fists.

'And where do I fit into all this?' asked Krakowski quietly. 'Have you something in mind for me, as well?'

'Yes. A spectacular world premiere, with you as the conductor. Once the authenticity of the score has been established.'

'You've given this a lot of thought, haven't you?'

'I have. And I can think of no-one better qualified to perform the lost symphony than you, Benjamin, most likely in Russia, when the work is officially presented to the Russian people for whom it was originally intended. This will go down in history. Interested?'

82

Afternoon tea at the Kuragin chateau: 5 April 2017

Countess Kuragin and Darrieux were enjoying a glass of champagne in the music room, when Dupree walked in. 'You did say three o'clock?' he said and gave Darrieux a hug.

'That's right. Jack wanted us here at three,' said the countess and pointed to a delicious-looking orange teacake cook had prepared earlier that day. 'Have a slice of this.'

'I don't mind if I do. Where is he?'

'He's been skulking around all morning, waiting for something,' said the countess, lowering her voice.

'A changed man since our trip to Fatima,' said Darrieux.

Dupree put a slice of cake on his plate. 'An epiphany, perhaps?' he asked.

'I wouldn't go quite that far,' replied Darrieux.

'But he's almost back to his old self since his return from New York,' the countess cut in. 'With a spring in his step. He has spent hours on the phone every day. Another glass?'

Darrieux nodded and held up her empty glass. 'Getting over things, I suppose.'

'Takes time. He had a rough ride,' said Dupree, filling her glass and pouring one for himself. 'But outstanding results. That meeting with the pope in Rome ...' Dupree shook his head. 'Not many could have pulled that off, I tell you.'

Darrieux pointed to the music box on the mantelpiece. 'And to think that it all began with that.'

'One of Jack's breadcrumbs of destiny,' said the countess, smiling.

'Absolutely!' said Jack, who had overheard the remark as he walked into the room. 'But by no means the last one. Sorry to keep you waiting, guys, but this just came in.'

Jack put a bundle of papers on the coffee table. 'I need a drink.'

'What's that?' said the countess.

Jack walked over to the ice bucket and poured himself a glass of champagne. 'History.'

'Care to elaborate?' asked Darrieux.

'I can do better than that. I can *show* you.' Jack pointed to the coffee table. 'Take one. There's a copy for each of you. This is the article that will appear in the *New York Times* tomorrow, and set the music world on fire. It will tell the world about an extraordinary discovery in which all of you played a major part.'

The countess picked up a copy and read the headline: '*Fact stranger than fiction? Mat' Rossiya, Tchaikovsky's lost musical gift to his beloved Russia.*' The countess looked at Jack, then continued, '*The recent chance discovery of a letter written by Empress Alexandra the day before she and her family were murdered in Yekaterinburg ...*'

'Wow!' said Darrieux after she had read the article. 'Explosive stuff. The world media will go nuts as soon as this is published, and they'll come looking for you, my friend.'

'This is incredible, Jack,' said the countess and held up her copy. 'And you are comfortable with everything in here?'

'I am. All vetted and approved, even by the Vatican. Celia Crawford and her editors worked around the clock for almost a week to make this possible. Benjamin had the score examined by some of the most respected experts in the business. There's unanimous agreement and, as you can imagine, huge excitement in musical circles about this. The score is authentic. Can you imagine, a lost symphony by Tchaikovsky, never seen or heard before? This is the musical discovery of the century.'

'Unbelievable,' said Dupree. 'Congratulations, Jack!'

'You are all part of it,' said Jack and held up his glass. 'It wouldn't have happened without you!'

'What about the icon?' asked the countess, looking intently at Jack.

'Ah. That's another story altogether,' said Jack, enjoying himself. 'The Vatican has already been in contact with Patriarch Nicodemus of Moscow.'

'What about?' asked Darrieux.

'The return of Kazanskaya Bogomater to where it belongs: the Novo-Tikhvinsky Convent. An official handover is planned and, please keep this to yourselves for the moment, will most likely be attended by the pope himself, in Yekaterinburg. A historic visit.'

'When?' asked Darrieux.

'Soon, I believe. A visit to Russia by the pope would be really something, don't you think? Especially now, when Russia is on the nose because of those recent assassination attempts. He's the "peace pope", after all, and wants to be known as the great conciliator,' said Jack. 'That will be his legacy. I already spoke to Abbot Serapion and the Seeker about all this and gave them the good news. You can imagine the excitement—'

'They shouldn't be all that surprised,' interjected Darrieux, a sparkle in her eyes. 'After all, it was foretold; isn't that right, Jack? And aren't you the chosen one?'

Jack shrugged. 'Who knows? But I can tell you, this will be huge, that's for sure. The whole world will be watching.'

'What about the symphony?' asked Dupree.

'I discussed this with Cardinal Borromeo. Obviously, the work belongs to Russia, just like the icon, and should therefore be presented to the Russian people as it was originally intended by the composer.'

'How?' asked the countess.

'It has been suggested I should hand it over in St Petersburg where Tchaikovsky died and is buried—'

'*You?* That's fantastic, Jack!' said the countess.

'It is. And wait, it gets better. I already raised this with Benjamin. As you can imagine, he personally knows everyone who matters in the musical world today. Not only is he a celebrated composer and violinist, but a conductor as well. The present thinking is to arrange a premiere of the symphony in St Petersburg, to be performed by the Saint Petersburg Philharmonic Orchestra – the oldest symphony orchestra in Russia – with Benjamin as the conductor. He's been a guest conductor there before and would be an excellent choice. He has all the necessary contacts and is putting out feelers right now. After all, he's already seen the score, is familiar with it, and is working on it to get it ready.'

'And I suppose the original score could be formally presented at the beginning of the performance, is that it?' asked the countess. 'And handed over to the Russian people, as intended by Tchaikovsky?'

'Something like that. And do you know where?'

'Tell us,' said Darrieux.

'The Bolshoi Zal—'

'In the famous Great Hall of the St Petersburg Philharmonia,' the countess interrupted. 'An excellent choice!'

'It is. Tchaikovsky performed some of his best-known works there, and would most likely have presented *Mat' Rossiya* to the Tsar in that very venue had he lived long enough. Sadly, that wasn't to be.'

'No doubt about you, Jack ... You, and the pope, joining forces over—'

'Kazanskaya Bogomater, and *Mat' Rossiya*,' interjected Darrieux. 'A holy icon to be triumphantly returned to Russia by the pope, and a lost symphony by Tchaikovsky to be presented to the Russian people by you, Jack, the person who made it all possible. Not bad—'

'Publicity for my next book, you mean?' said Jack, grinning.

'Just as I thought,' said the countess and raised an eyebrow.

'To be expected from an incorrigible rascal, you mean?' teased Jack.

'You said it, not me. And what about the Fabergé egg?'

'That's evidence for the time being,' said Dupree, stepping in. 'Then it's up to the lawyers.'

'Does that worry you, Jack?' asked Darrieux.

Jack shrugged. 'Not really. What will be, will be,' he said. 'There are more important things at stake here at the moment.'

'I'm glad you see it that way,' said Dupree. 'I think this definitely calls for a toast.'

'I agree,' said Darrieux and held up her empty glass.

Dupree went around and filled up everyone's glass. 'To Kazanskaya Bogomater, and *Mat' Rossiya*,' he said. 'May the holy icon bring joy and peace to the faithful, and *Mat' Rossiya* dazzle the world with Tchaikovsky's genius.'

'To Kazanskaya Bogomater, and *Mat' Rossiya*,' echoed the others and raised their glasses.

'And one more thing,' said Jack. 'You are all invited!'

83

Alexander Nevsky Cathedral, Yekaterinburg: six weeks later

The first thing Jack noticed was the crowd. The streets leading to the sprawling Novo-Tikhvinsky Convent complex were lined with cheering people, many of them waving flags, and an electric atmosphere of excitement and anticipation hung in the air on that sunny morning. The pope's imminent arrival had put an entire city into a tailspin, and media from around the world had been flocking to Yekaterinburg for days in preparation for the historic event.

Countess Kuragin turned to Isis sitting next to her in the car. 'So, this is what it feels like to be a celebrity being greeted by adoring fans.'

'Something like that,' said Isis, and shrugged. She pointed to Jack sitting in the front seat. 'Only this time, *he's* the celebrity. Jack's become a household name here with all the press he's been getting lately. And have you seen some of those TV interviews? Amazing!'

'You must admit, it's quite a story.'

'Sure is. A storyteller's dream, and there's nobody better than our Jack when it comes to stories.'

'You are right about that.'

'I've never seen Jack in a suit,' said Darrieux, who had agonised for days over what to wear for the occasion. 'He looks great.'

'Okay, guys, no more wardrobe police stuff please,' said Jack and pointed out the window. 'There's the cathedral. Just look at that crowd. We're almost there.'

Isis had picked up Jack, the countess and Darrieux in her private jet in Paris on her way to Yekaterinburg the day before. Lola had arranged the flight and the accommodation, and local authorities had provided transport for them from their hotel to the cathedral for the official handover celebration of Kazanskaya Bogomater, scheduled to start at noon.

One by one, the cars of the arriving dignitaries pulled up in front of the steps leading to the entrance, and were met by a group of monks, who escorted the guests into the cathedral and seated them. Inside, the cathedral was so crowded it was difficult to move.

As Jack was about to take a seat next to Vasiliev, Kun and Rabbi Stein, who had arrived earlier, a monk tapped him on the shoulder. 'Please come with me,' he said.

Jack followed the monk to a cordoned-off area near the side altar he had visited before. The first thing he noticed were the stunning floral arrangements. There were so many, it was almost impossible to see the altar and the empty pedestal where the icon had once resided until 1920 when the convent was closed down by the Soviets.

Wearing spectacular, heavily embroidered vestments, Abbot Serapion was seated in the front row facing the altar, next to Patriarch Nicodemus, Patriarch of Moscow and all Rus, and Primate of the Russian Orthodox Church. When the abbot saw Jack coming towards him, his face lit up. 'Welcome,' he said and introduced him to the patriarch.

'This is a momentous day, Mr Rogan,' said the patriarch, and pointed to an empty seat next to him. 'Abbot Serapion has told me a lot about you. Thanks to you, Kazanskaya Bogomater is coming home, and for that we are forever in your debt.'

'We are all but instruments of fate, Holiness,' said Jack.

The patriarch smiled and patted Jack on the arm. 'We have been waiting for you for a long time.'

'It has been foretold,' said the abbot, nodding sagely. Then the chanting began, filling the crowded cathedral with uplifting, ancient harmonies as a group of monks holding candles entered the cathedral and walked slowly towards the altar.

'Not long now,' said the abbot. 'They must be on their way.'

The pope and his entourage had arrived the day before and were staying at the Novo-Tikhvinsky Convent. Because the weather was so beautiful, Cardinal Borromeo had suggested that the pope should walk the short distance from the convent to the cathedral and greet the faithful along the way. Always the consummate Church statesman, Borromeo realised that this would further enhance the papal visit and provide excellent photo opportunities for the waiting media. The suggestion was enthusiastically embraced by the Russian organisers, and arrangements were quickly made for a procession. The Guardians would carry the icon on a decorated stretcher on their shoulders in front of the pope for all to see, and enter the cathedral, followed by the pontiff and his entourage. This would create a spectacle none of those fortunate to witness it would ever forget.

The countess turned to Isis sitting next to her. 'I wonder what's going on outside?' she said, as the cheering and clapping became louder and more boisterous.

'We'll know soon enough,' said Isis. She looked over her shoulder towards the entry, just as the huge double doors opened slowly, and a shaft of bright sunlight crept along the stone floor towards the altar like a beacon of hope. Suddenly, the chanting stopped as the Guardians entered the cathedral followed by the pope, and the church bells began to toll.

As Kazanskaya Bogomater passed through the arched doorway, illuminated by the sun from behind, many sank to their knees in prayer. Then the Guardians began to recite the famous *Agni Parthene*, a mystical chant composed by Saint Nektarios, Archbishop of Aegina, their deep voices adding spine-tingling mystery to the solemn occasion:

'Most Holy Mother of God, save us.

O Virgin pure, immaculate, O Lady Theotokos ...'

The Guardians put down the decorated stretcher with the icon in front of the altar and stepped away. The pope genuflected and was shown to a seat between the abbot and the patriarch by one of the monks.

The patriarch waited until the Guardians had finished the *Agni Parthene*, and then formally welcomed the pope before addressing the faithful. Reaching back to Byzantine times, he told the story of Kazanskaya Bogomater from the very beginning, to a spellbound crowd hanging on his every word, and concluded by explaining how the icon had ended up in the Vatican, and why.

'And now, it is time for Kazanskaya Bogomater to once again take her rightful place right here, at home, where she belongs,' said the patriarch, and turned towards the pope.

Slowly, the pope stood up and walked over to the stretcher, elaborately decorated with flowers. Bending down, he carefully lifted up the icon and kissed it. Then he turned around and handed it to the patriarch standing behind him. By now, the monks had begun to chant again, and everyone expected the patriarch to carry the icon up to the altar and place it on its pedestal. Instead of doing so, he turned away from the altar and walked over to Jack.

'You kept your promise,' he said. 'It should be you who returns Kazanskaya Bogomater to where she belongs, not me.'

Deeply moved, Jack stood up. 'I am honoured, Holiness,' he said.

The countess turned to Darrieux sitting next to her. *'Can you believe this?'* she whispered as Jack was handed the icon by the patriarch. Jack turned around to face the faithful watching him in silence, held up the icon and bowed. Then he walked slowly up to the altar and carefully placed the icon on the pedestal.

For a long moment he just stood there, staring at Kazanskaya Bogomater, as he remembered Countess Bezukhova, the grandmother he had never met, and those vital clues left behind in the Amber Safe following her tragic death. Then his mind turned to Madame Petrova and her music box, with the hidden letter that had started it all. Taking his time, Jack waited until the chanting stopped, and then returned to his seat.

'See what can happen if you follow those breadcrumbs of destiny?' whispered Darrieux.

'Only if you are the chosen one,' replied the countess, tears in her eyes.

84

St Petersburg Philharmonia – Bolshoi Zal: three months later

'This is the big day, Jack. How do you feel?' said Countess Kuragin. 'Here, let me help you.' The countess walked over to Jack standing in front of the mirror and adjusted his bowtie. 'That's better. Dinner suit looks good on you. You should wear it more often.'

Jack glanced at the countess and raised an eyebrow. 'Really? It's just not me, and you know it.'

'You couldn't go to a premiere in the Bolshoi Zal without one.'

'I suppose not. And thanks for taking me shopping. Your Paris tailor was wonderful.'

'Patient, you mean?' said the countess, laughing. 'I heard all about it.'

'That too.'

For the sake of convenience, Jack had booked a grand suite with several bedrooms in the Four Seasons Hotel Lion Palace in St Petersburg for the occasion. This had allowed them all to stay together. With echoes of Imperial Russia, the opulent hotel was not only well located, but also offered every luxury and comfort imaginable.

'I wish I had a tailor like that,' said Darrieux as she walked into the room. 'What do you think, guys?'

Jack turned around and looked at Darrieux. 'Wow! You'll turn heads tonight, Adrienne, that's for sure.'

'Better than making them roll, right? Valentino never disappoints.'

A flash of sadness raced across Jack's face as he remembered the little black Valentino dress he had bought for Anielka and she had worn to the ballet only a few months earlier. He still found it difficult to come to terms with what had happened, and instinctively reached for his chest, which still hurt occasionally. It was a constant reminder of monstrous crimes, betrayal, and a great tragedy that had almost cost him his life.

Jack turned to the countess. 'I wonder what Isis will wear?' he said, lowering his voice. 'You look stunning, by the way.'

'Thanks, Jack. I suppose this is one of those once-in-a-lifetime occasions?'

'Is that why you've brought all that jewellery along?'

'Yep. If not here, now, then when?' These pearls and earrings belonged to my grandmother. Bought for her right here in St Petersburg a long time ago.'

'Ah, that's where you all are,' said Isis, as she swept into the room, followed by Lola. 'I've been looking for you. This place is huge. Must occupy the whole floor.'

'You look fabulous,' said the countess. 'Is that a Zac Posen?'

'You know your fashion,' said Isis, admiring herself in the mirror.

'You are in good company,' said Darrieux, a touch of envy in her voice. 'Michelle Obama, Naomi Campbell, Miley Cyrus have all worn Posen creations to special occasions.'

'She's been starving herself for weeks to fit into this,' said Lola.

'I'm paying you a small fortune to keep my secrets, not share them with the world,' said Isis. 'This has to stop!'

'Too late. Cat's out of the bag,' joked the countess. 'It obviously worked. Very slim.'

'Thanks, but you'll outshine us all with that jewellery. Fit for a tsarina, darling!'

Jack looked at his watch. 'Not long now; we better get ready.'

'Is it here?' asked Isis.

'Yes, in the safe just over there.'

'Could we see it?'

'Sure. I was just about to take it out. The security guys will be here in a minute. They'll take it to the cemetery. Safer that way. After that, it's no longer my problem. The governor arranged it all—'

'How exciting,' Darrieux cut in.

Jack walked over to the wall safe, opened it, and carefully took out a glass and steel case, which he placed on a small marble table by the window.

'Fascinating,' said Isis. 'I've never seen anything quite like it.'

'Not surprising. This is a state-of-the-art display case, especially designed to preserve precious manuscripts. It's a portable case within a case. One was manufactured just recently for Anne Frank's diaries, to limit natural deterioration as much as possible. That's why we have a case within a case. This allows us to protect the paper against humidity, temperature swings, air pollution and vibrations.'

'Amazing. How did you get it?'

'The Vatican museum arranged it. It has several of these.'

'It's good to have friends in high places,' said Darrieux. 'Don't you think so, Lola?'

'Jack has plenty of those.'

'Don't I know it!'

Isis looked at the score through the glass lid. 'Extraordinary. And to think that we are looking at the original, handwritten score of a timeless masterpiece. It's about as close as we can hope to get to a genius long gone. It gives me goose pimples,' said Isis, pretending to shudder.

'This is a national treasure that belongs to Russia,' said Jack. 'The symphony you will hear tonight will blow you away. Benjamin has been working on it for weeks with the St Petersburg Philharmonic orchestra. He cancelled all other engagements. It's been very challenging, especially the choral sections, like in Beethoven's ninth. Fortunately, Tchaikovsky's instructions were very specific. There's a Don Cossack choir, monks chanting Byzantine hymns, and guns and bells, like in the 1812 Overture. This symphony has it all. "A musical tour de force of the Russian soul", Benjamin called it. There's even a violin solo with a surprise,' said Jack and winked at the countess.

'So, what's the program?' asked Isis.

'First, we go to the Tikhvin Cemetery for the handover,' said Jack. 'Tchaikovsky is buried in what is known as the Necropolis of Art Masters. All the great Russian composers are buried there, side by side. It's an amazing place as you will see—'

'This was a special request by Jack,' interjected the countess.

481

'That's right. Rather than handing over the original score at the concert in the glare of all the hype, I thought it would be more appropriate, and a little more dignified and respectful, to do that in the cemetery where Tchaikovsky is buried. As his grave is right here in the centre of St Petersburg, this was quite easy to arrange.'

'Great idea,' said Isis.

'The Governor of St Petersburg thought so, too. He will meet us there. After that, we go straight to the concert for the premiere of *Mat' Rossiya*, Tchaikovsky's lost symphony. It should be an exciting evening.'

Jack pointed to an ice bucket in the corner with several bottles of champagne. 'But before we go, I think we have time for a quick drink,' he said.

'Excellent suggestion,' said Darrieux. 'I'm parched.'

'As we are all together, I would like to say something,' said Jack, looking thoughtful. 'This is a very special moment for me. It's the culmination of an extraordinary, very personal journey in which all of you have played an important part. It hasn't been easy, but I'm very fortunate to have friends like you who stood by me. As you know, I value friendship above all else. So, let's drink to friendship, the greatest treasure of them all. Cheers!'

The countess linked arms with Jack. 'That was very moving,' she said, as they were leaving the cemetery and returning to their waiting car. 'Placing the score on the grave for the governor to collect rather than handing it to him was a nice touch. There wasn't a dry eye anywhere.'

'I hope it worked and made sense. I was trying to return the score to Tchaikovsky so that *he* could present it to the governor. At least symbolically.'

'It worked,' said Isis. 'And those flowers – gorgeous. Thanks for allowing us all to participate in this. Placing flowers on the grave, I mean.'

'You are all part of this,' said Jack, and opened the car door for the countess. 'Enjoy this quiet moment, because I suspect what is about to happen now will be a little different.'

'I can't wait!' said Darrieux, adjusting her dress.

As Jack and his friends approached the impressive home of the St Petersburg Philharmonia in Mikhailovskaya Street, they saw the huge crowd almost completely blocking the street and the pavement. And then there were the vans with satellite dishes and TV crews from all the major international networks. The event had attracted huge worldwide attention and music lovers around the globe were glued to their TV screens, waiting with great anticipation for the premiere of Tchaikovsky's intriguing lost symphony, which had become an overnight sensation.

Built in 1839, the Bolshoi Zal, the Grand Hall – arguably the most famous music hall in Russia – had seen many exciting premieres of works by such musical giants as Borodin, Rimsky-Korsakov, Mussorgsky and, of course, Tchaikovsky. Some of the most celebrated musicians of the nineteenth century like Wagner, Liszt, Berlioz, Mahler and Schumann, had dazzled spellbound concertgoers with their performances. The Bolshoi Zal was therefore the perfect choice for the exciting premiere of a lost symphony by one of Russia's most loved composers.

'Look, even a red carpet,' said Darrieux as the limousine came to a halt and the car doors were opened. Someone in the crowd recognised Isis and began to shout. Even before Isis could get out of the car, excited fans were chanting 'Isis, Isis,' and furiously taking photos with their iPhones. Never one to disappoint fans or miss a photo opportunity, Isis waved and blew kisses.

Lola turned to Darrieux. 'Thank God she's been recognised,' she said, as they followed Isis into the building. 'Otherwise she'd be sulking for days.'

Inside the Great Hall, fifteen-hundred lucky concertgoers who had somehow managed to secure tickets to the musical event of the decade, were already seated and watching the arrival of the VIPs parading down the red carpet, with wide-eyed curiosity and unbridled interest.

'How about this, Jack? Did you expect something quite like this?' said the countess as she took her seat next to Jack in the front row. As she began to look around, she recognised several famous faces in the rows directly behind her. 'Do you think there will be speeches?'

'Possibly. I wasn't told much, and even Benjamin didn't know when I spoke to him yesterday. He's completely focused on the performance. So, let's sit back and enjoy the ride.'

'What an exciting life you lead, Jack. Who would have thought a few months ago when we had that memorable lunch with Adrienne in Paris and you showed her Madame Petrova's letter, that it would lead to this?'

'It's all about those breadcrumbs I keep telling you about,' said Jack, a teasing glint in his eyes.

Then the lights began to dim and slowly, the excited crowd fell silent as the Governor of St Petersburg walked on stage.

'Ladies and gentlemen, it gives me great pleasure to welcome you, and millions of viewers around the world, to a unique event the likes of which even this hallowed hall has never seen before,' he said. 'It is the premiere of a symphony by Pyotr Ilyich Tchaikovsky, one of our most loved composers, which had been lost for more than a hundred and twenty years, but has just been returned to us in extraordinary circumstances by Mr Jack Rogan, who is with us here this evening.'

The governor pointed to Jack in the front row, as a young girl dressed in national costume walked up to him and handed him a huge bouquet of flowers. Jack stood up, turned around and took a bow.

The governor held up his hand as spontaneous, thunderous applause erupted and rippled through the hall.

'Most of you would have read the remarkable story on the back of your program of the symphony's recent discovery, or have seen it on TV, but what you don't know is that less than an hour ago, Mr Rogan placed the original score, which is right here next to me, on

Tchaikovsky's grave.' The governor, an experienced speaker, paused and pointed to a lectern with the manuscript display case on top. 'With that moving, humble gesture, he returned *Mat' Rossiya* – a long-lost parting gift by a musical giant – to the Russian people.'

Once again, thunderous applause.

'But now, without further ado, I call upon Maestro Benjamin Krakowski and the St Petersburg Philharmonic orchestra to present to you *Mat' Rossiya*, Tchaikovsky's lost symphony.'

The governor raised his hand and pointed to the orchestra seated behind him as Krakowski walked on stage and took a bow.

'Before we begin, ladies and gentlemen, a few words,' said Krakowski, in fluent Russian. 'It isn't often that we are allowed to witness history in the making, but that is precisely what is happening here, tonight. The work you are about to hear is remarkable in a number of ways. I have no doubt that Tchaikovsky composed it over many years, because it has elements of several of his major works embedded in it in subtle ways. They are reminders of an illustrious musical career spanning a lifetime: *his* lifetime. For that reason alone, it is indeed a parting gift by a musical genius, to the country that shaped his soul and the people he loved.

'You will recognise many familiar, profoundly Russian character-istics in this symphony. Cheerful folk songs, solemn Byzantine chants, ballet music and dance, pious church bells and guns of war, all cleverly woven into Tchaikovsky's sublime music in effortless ways that will delight you, make you smile, and move you to tears. And finally, there is one more, personal matter I would like to share with you, if I may.'

Krakowski held up the violin he had brought with him on stage.

'It concerns this violin, *The Empress*, which many of you would be familiar with.'

Enthusiastic applause interrupted Krakowski, and he had to wait for a while before being able to continue.

'This violin, a Stradivarius, was given to my father by Count Esterhazy in 1905, because his violin had been stolen by gypsies the day before he was due to give a concert in Vienna. He was fourteen at the time and played Paganini, which the count loved. The reason I have decided to bring this violin with me tonight is because it, too, has had a remarkable journey not dissimilar to that of the lost symphony. It was stolen from my father in a German concentration camp and was lost for a long time, only to be rediscovered many years later in circumstances that can only be described as extraordinary. And what is even more remarkable, is the fact that Mr Rogan here played a major part in all that as well. Coincidence or fate, ladies and gentlemen? You be the judge.

'There is a delightful violin solo towards the end the symphony, which I will play for you on this violin because I know it will speak to you as only an instrument that has seen so much, can. Thank you.'

As more applause erupted around him, Krakowski walked slowly back to the orchestra seated behind him, and carefully placed the violin on an empty chair. Then he stepped onto the rostrum, and briefly glanced at the large music stand with the full score containing all the complex musical notations for all the instruments and voices he had worked on for weeks. Taking a deep breath, he lifted his baton as electrifying silence descended on the hall, throbbing with expectation.

Before giving the signal to begin, Krakowski made eye contact with the first violinist and gave him a brief nod. Moments later, Tchaikovsky's *Mat' Rossiya* opened with a moving, low bassoon melody in E minor, just as in his Symphony No. 6, before the violas made an appearance with a theme of the Allegro in B minor, leading into a breathtaking outburst from the orchestra, heralding a promise of exciting things to come.

Mat' Rossiya, a symphony in four movements, had finally appeared on the world stage and was taking its rightful place in musical history as one of the great Russian masterpieces of all time.

85

Peter and Paul Cathedral, St Petersburg: Easter 2018

Jack and Countess Kuragin arrived at the Peter and Paul Cathedral at eight am as arranged. At that time, the cathedral was still closed to the public, and the usually busy square in front was deserted. The Governor of St Petersburg and a small group of officials were waiting for them at the entrance, and the governor greeted Jack like an old friend. Jack had met him the year before at Tchaikovsky's grave for the handover of the *Mat' Rossiya* score before the historic premiere of the lost symphony.

'Thank you for arranging this for me,' said Jack and shook the governor's hand.

'It's the least I could do. We were all very touched by your request.'

'It's the end of a long journey,' said Jack and pointed to the small leather case under his arm.

'That it is. Please come inside. Everything is ready and we have a little surprise for you.'

After the police and the authorities had closed the case of Aubert's sensational murder in the Amber Safe and released the Fabergé egg because it was no longer required as evidence, the lawyers took over to determine ownership. Jack was represented by Countess Kuragin's legal team, who submitted Jack's claim based on his relationship with Countess Bezukhova, his grandmother, and Madame Petrova, his great aunt.

Due to the complexity of the claim, it was impossible to reach a negotiated resolution, and the matter went to court for determination. This resulted in several protracted hearings and complicated legal arguments, but in the end the case was decided on the basis that Jack was the only living relative with a valid claim, and ownership of the precious egg was awarded to him.

Many expected Jack to cash in on his good fortune and sell the rare, historic piece to the highest bidder, but he had other plans.

As soon as Jack entered the cathedral, he could hear familiar chanting and was wondering where he had heard it before. It was coming from the Chapel of St Catherine the Martyr on the right, where Tsar Nicholas and his family had been finally laid to rest in July 1998, eighty years after their murder.

'Please follow me,' said the governor and led the way to the chapel.

'What an amazing place,' said the countess as she walked past the silent rows of white sarcophagi of emperors and empresses long gone. Because the cathedral was empty, this only made the experience more personal and moving. As the chanting became louder, it reminded Jack of his visit to the Novo-Tikhvinsky Convent in Yekaterinburg and his encounter with the Seeker and the Guardians just before his almost fatal stabbing.

As soon as he turned the corner and could see into the chapel with the white marble sarcophagus marking the resting place of Russia's last tsar and his family, Jack stopped, surprised. Standing in a semicircle in the centre of the chapel, the six Guardians, each holding a lit candle, were waiting for Jack and took a bow as soon as he entered. The Seeker walked over to Jack and greeted him warmly. 'We meet again,' he said and also took a bow.

'I am honoured,' said Jack, choking with emotion. He had certainly not expected such a welcome. The governor had quietly made arrangements for the Guardians and the Seeker to attend the little ceremony Jack had asked for.

'You are closing the circle,' said the Seeker. 'The final piece is falling into place and we wanted to witness this, as you are the chosen one who has kept his promise.'

'Thank you. This means more to me than I can possibly express right now.'

Jack looked at the governor, who pointed to the white sarcophagus. 'Please, go ahead,' he said.

Slowly, Jack opened the leather case, carefully took out the Fabergé egg and handed the empty case to the countess. 'Here we go,' he whispered and walked across to the sarcophagus. The chanting became louder as the Guardians followed and formed a semicircle behind him, like a guard of honour.

Taking his time, Jack placed Fabergé's exquisite masterpiece, which had led him to Kazanskaya Bogomater and *Mat' Rossiya*, on top of the polished marble. Lost in thought, he stared at the beautiful, jewel-encrusted Easter gift presented by a loving husband to his heartbroken wife, as he remembered that fateful letter hidden in Madame Petrova's music box, the story of the Postmaster of Treblinka, and the ingenious Feldpost delivery of that letter which had started it all. After a while, Jack stepped away, turned around to face the Guardians and the governor, and held up his hand. The chanting stopped, all eyes on Jack, as silence descended on the chapel.

'This marks the end of a long, turbulent journey of a unique artefact: the last Imperial Russian Fabergé Easter egg,' Jack began softly. 'It was a token of love and affection commissioned by Tsar Nicholas II a hundred years ago and given to his wife, Empress Alexandra, as an Easter present in 1917.'

Jack pointed to the egg.

'Both are buried right here where I stand. Due to the political situation prevailing at the time, the precious egg was entrusted to Countess Bezukhova, my grandmother, for safekeeping, and she took it with her into exile in France. Sadly, she was killed during the war, and the Fabergé egg disappeared, like so much else during the madness, only to suddenly resurface in dramatic circumstances that can only be described as extraordinary.

'The courts have recently awarded legal ownership of it to me. That may be the case in the eyes of the law, but I don't believe it is possible, because in my eyes, there can only be one rightful owner, and that is, and always has been, Empress Alexandra. A lot of time may have passed, but the forces of destiny are not ruled by time alone. There are other, more powerful forces in play here: love, devotion, loyalty, friendship, and the true meaning of a promise, to name but a few.

'I have therefore decided to honour a promise made by my grandmother a long time ago and return the Fabergé egg to where it belongs. Right here.'

Jack touched the golden double eagle on top of the egg with his fingertips in a gesture of farewell, and then turned around and slowly walked back to the countess as the Guardians began to chant again.

'I'm proud of you, Jack,' whispered the countess.

'You don't think I'm a crazy romantic who's lost his marbles?'

'Far from it. You're an incorrigible rascal, who's never afraid to do what's right.'

* * *

The last of the legendary Russian Imperial Easter eggs was taken to the Fabergé Museum in St Petersburg, where it joined nine others already on display.

Instead of calling it Rasputin – the name given to it on the dark web – it was renamed Bezukhova, in honour of a friendship that had transcended the horrors of revolutions and war, and the relentless march of time.

* * *

A Parting Note From The Author:
Fact Stranger Than Fiction?

All my books are based on meticulous research and, whenever possible, I draw inspiration for my stories from well-documented historic events. To create a seamless storyline, I try to weave fact and fiction together, blurring the boundaries between the two so that the reader is never quite sure where one ends, and the other begins. This is, of course, quite deliberate as it creates the illusion of authenticity and reality in a work that is pure fiction.

A successful work of fiction is a balancing act: reality must rub shoulders with imagination in a way that is both entertaining and plausible. For that reason, I have decided to conclude the book with a brief reference to some well-documented historical material relating to a famous Russian icon: Our Lady of Kazan, also known as Mother of God of Kazan, or Kazanskaya Bogomater, which has served as inspiration for a major part of this book.

The origin of the icon is steeped in legend, shrouded in mystery, and surrounded by tradition. According to the Russian Orthodox Church, the original icon was brought to Russia from Constantinople in the thirteenth century and, after the establishment of the Khanate of Khazan in about 1438, it disappeared from the pages of history for over a century.

A chronicle written by Metropolitan Hermogenes in 1595 tells us how the icon was miraculously recovered through the intervention of the Virgin Mary, who appeared to a girl in a dream and showed her the place where the icon had been hidden to save it from the Tartars. After that, a number of important churches were built in honour of this revelation, and military commanders through the ages sought guidance and protection through the image of the Virgin Mary, who, it is believed, saved Russia from invasion and destruction on several occasions. A number of miracles were also attributed to the icon, which became one of the most revered and sacred in all of Russia.

491

But the story does not end there. In fact, it becomes even more fascinating. In 1904, the icon was stolen from the Convent of the Theotokos in Kazan, and its fate after that has been the subject of much speculation, and is closely linked to what has become generally known as the 'Fatima image'.

The 'Fatima image' is a sixteenth-century copy of the icon, stolen from St Petersburg in 1917. It reappeared in 1953 and was purchased by Frederick Mitchell-Hedges from the merchant Kazano Shevliagin. Once again, controversy surrounded the icon and the claim that it was the original Kazanskaya Bogomater was disputed. After extensive X-ray testing of the wood and the pigments, experts agreed that it was indeed an original sixteenth-century icon of extraordinary quality, but most likely a copy of the earlier, original Kazanskaya Bogomater brought to Russia from Constantinople.

By now the icon was world-famous, and was exhibited in the Russian Pavilion at the World Trade Fair in New York in 1964, where it was venerated in the pavilion by the Blue Army of Our Lady of Fatima – the World Apostolate of Fatima – during the night of 13 September 1965. The Blue Army eventually bought the icon from Mitchell-Hedges' adopted daughter, Anna Mitchell-Hedges, in 1970, and put it on display in the Byzantine Chapel in Fatima, Portugal.

In 1993, the icon was presented to Pope John Paul II so that he could determine how, and when, it should be returned to its native land. He took it back to Rome and kept it in his study in the Vatican, where it greeted him every morning and there it remained for the next eleven years.

During this time, the pope formed the view that the right time had arrived to return the icon to the Russian Orthodox Church. In August 2004, it was exhibited on the altar of St Peter's Basilica in Rome, and on 28 August, the Feast of the Dormition of the Mother of God in the Orthodox calendar, the precious icon was taken to Moscow by a Vatican delegation, and presented to the Patriarch of Moscow in the Cathedral of the Assumption in the Kremlin.

Today, the icon is enshrined in the Cathedral of the Exaltation of the Holy Cross, which stands on the site where the original icon of Our Lady of Kazan was found in 1579, after the Virgin Mary had revealed the hiding place to a girl in a dream.

Fact stranger than fiction? You be the judge.

Gabriel Farago
Leura, Blue Mountains, Australia
November 2020

MORE BOOKS BY THE AUTHOR

Jack Rogan Mysteries Series Starter Library
The Empress Holds the Key
The Disappearance of Anna Popov
The Hidden Genes of Professor K
Professor K: The Final Quest
The Curious Case of the Missing Head
Jack Rogan Mysteries Series Box Set Books 1-4

JACK ROGAN MYSTERIES STARTER LIBRARY

So, what exactly is a STARTER LIBRARY? I hear you ask. Well, it's a way to introduce myself and what I do, to new readers, and create interest in my writing. How? By providing little insights into my world, and the creative process involved in becoming an international thriller writer.

The Starter Library consists of four short books:
1. *Letters from The Attic* – a delightful collection of auto-biographical short stories;
2. *The Forgotten Painting* – a multi-award-winning Jack Rogan novella;
3. *The Kimberley Secret* – a much-anticipated prequel to the Jack Rogan Mysteries series;
4. *The Main Characters Profile* – provides some exciting background stories and insights into the main characters featured in the series.

The Starter Library is available right now, and can be downloaded for FREE by following this link: https://gabrielfarago.com.au/starter-library2/

Please share this with your friends and encourage them to download the Starter Library.

In 2013, I released my first adventure thriller –
The Empress Holds the Key.

THE EMPRESS HOLDS THE KEY

A disturbing, edge-of-your-seat historical mystery thriller

Jack Rogan Mysteries Book 1

Dark secrets. A holy relic. An ancient quest reignited.

Jack Rogan's discovery of a disturbing old photograph in the ashes of a rural Australian cottage draws the journalist into a dangerous hunt with the ultimate stakes.

The tangled web of clues – including hoards of Nazi gold, hidden Swiss bank accounts, and a long-forgotten mass grave – implicate wealthy banker Sir Eric Newman and lead to a trial with shocking revelations.

A holy relic mysteriously erased from the pages of history is suddenly up for grabs to those willing to sacrifice everything to find it. Rogan and his companions must follow historical leads through ancient Egypt to the Crusades and the Knights Templar to uncover a secret that could destroy the foundations of the Catholic Church and challenge the history of Christianity itself.

Will Rogan succeed in bringing the dark mystery into the light, or will the powers desperately working against him ensure the ancient truths remain buried forever?

The Empress Holds the Key is now available on Amazon

Encouraged by the reception of *The Empress Holds the Key*, I released my next thriller – *The Disappearance of Anna Popov* – in 2014.

THE DISAPPEARANCE OF ANNA POPOV

A dark, page-turning psychological thriller

Jack Rogan Mysteries Book 2

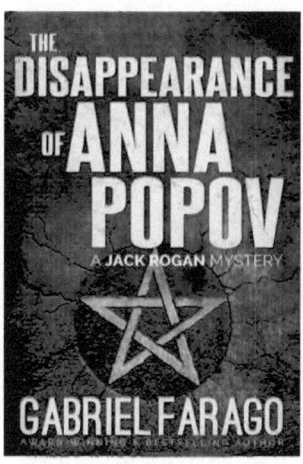

A mysterious disappearance. An outlaw biker gang. One dangerous investigation.

Journalist Jack Rogan cannot resist a good mystery. When he stumbles across a clue about the tragic disappearance of two girls from Alice Springs years earlier, he's determined to investigate.

Joining forces with his New York literary agent, a retired Aboriginal police officer, and Cassandra, an enigmatic psychic, Rogan enters the dangerous and dark world of an outlaw bikies gang ruled by an evil and enigmatic master.

Entangled in a web of violence, superstition and fear, Rogan and his friends follow the trail of the missing girls into the remote Dreamtime-wilderness of Outback Australia – where they must face even greater threats.

Cassandra hides a secret agenda and uses her occult powers to facilitate an epic showdown where the loser faces death and oblivion.

Will Rogan succeed in finding the truth, or will the forces of evil prevail, taking even more lives with them?

The Disappearance of Anna Popov is now available on Amazon

My next book, *The Hidden Genes of Professor K*, was released in 2016. Here's a short sample to pique your interest:

THE HIDDEN GENES OF PROFESSOR K

A dark, disturbing and nail-biting medical thriller

Jack Rogan Mysteries Book 3

"Outstanding Thriller" of 2017
Independent Author Network Book of the Year Awards

A medical breakthrough. A greedy pharmaceutical magnate. A brutal double-murder. One tangled web of lies.
World-renowned scientist Professor K is close to a ground-breaking discovery. He's also dying. With his last breath, he anoints Dr Alexandra Delacroix his successor and pleads with her to carry on his work.

But powerful forces will stop at nothing to possess the research, unwittingly plunging Delacroix into a treacherous world of unbridled ambition and greed.

Desperate and alone, she turns to celebrated author and journalist Jack Rogan.

Rogan must help Delacroix while also assisting famous rock star Isis in the seemingly unrelated investigation into the brutal murder of her parents.

With the support of Isis's resourceful PA, a former police officer, a tireless campaigner for the destitute and forgotten, and a gifted boy with psychic powers, Rogan exposes a complex web of fiercely guarded secrets and heinous crimes of the past that can ruin them all and change history.

Will the dreams of a visionary scientist with the power to change the future of medicine fall into the wrong hands, or will his genius benefit mankind and prevent untold misery and suffering for generations to come?

The Hidden Genes of Professor K **is now available on Amazon**

My next book, *Professor K: The Final Quest*, was released in October 2018. Here's a short sample to pique your interest.

PROFESSOR K: THE FINAL QUEST

An action-packed historical medical mystery

Jack Rogan Mysteries Book 4

Gold Medal Winner in the Fiction - Thriller - Medical genre!
2019 Readers' Favorite Annual Book Award Contest

A desperate plea from the Vatican. A kidnapped chef. An ambitious mob boss. One perilous game.

When Professor Alexandra Delacroix is called in to find a cure for the dying pope, she follows clues left by her mentor and friend, the late Professor K, which lead her on a breathtaking search through historical secrets, some of them deadly.

Her old friend Jack Rogan must step in to assist while also searching for kidnapped *Top Chef Europe* winner, Lorenza da Baggio.

He joins forces with his young friend and gifted psychic, Tristan, a dedicated mafia hunting prosecutor, a fearless young police officer, and an enigmatic Egyptian detective on a perilous hunt for a notorious IS terrorist.

Together, they stand off with the head of a powerful Mafia family in Florence and uncover a network of corruption and heinous crimes reaching to the very top.

Will Rogan and his friends succeed in finding Lorenza and curing the pope, or will the dark forces swirling around them prevail in their sinister plots?

Professor K: The Final Quest is now available on Amazon.

My next book, *The Curious Case of the Missing Head*, was released in November 2019. Here's a short sample to pique your interest.

THE CURIOUS CASE OF THE MISSING HEAD

A gripping medical thriller

Jack Rogan Mysteries Book 5

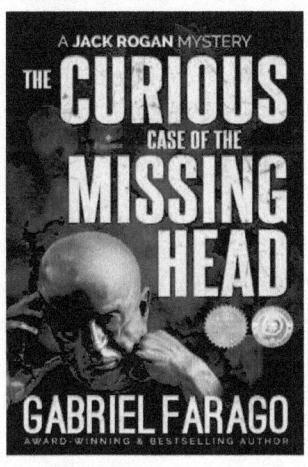

**Gold Medal Winner in the Fiction Thriller -
Conspiracy Thrillers Category!**
2020 Readers' Favorite Annual Book Award Contest

"Outstanding Thriller/Suspense" of 2020
Independent Author Network Book of the Year Awards

A headless body on a boat. An international conspiracy. Can he survive a controversial scientific discovery?
Esteemed Australian journalist Jack Rogan is on a mission to solve the disappearance of his mother in the 70s. But when a friend needs help rescuing a kidnapped world-renowned astrophysicist, he doesn't hesitate. Struggling with more questions than answers, his investiga-

tion leads them aboard a hellish hospital ship, where instead of finding the kidnap victim, he's confronted with a decapitated corpse.

As the search intensifies, Jack bumps up against diabolical cartels with hidden agendas. And when his research reveals dubious experiments, a criminal on death row, and a shocking revelation about his mother's fate, he must uncover how it's all linked.

Can Jack unravel the twisted connections and catch the scientist's killer, or will the next obituary published be his own?

The Curious Case of the Missing Head is the fifth standalone novel in the page-turning Jack Rogan Mysteries series. If you like meticulous theoretical science, exponentially increasing intensity, and astonishing surprises, then you'll love Gabriel Farago's hair-raising medical thriller.

The Curious Case of the Missing Head
is now available on Amazon.

JACK ROGAN MYSTERIES
BOX SET BOOKS 1-4

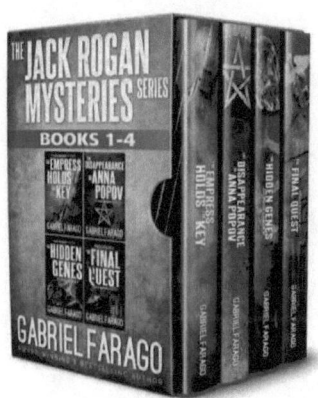

The Jack Rogan Mysteries Box Set is now available on Amazon

ABOUT THE AUTHOR

Gabriel Farago is the international, best-selling and multi-award-winning Australian author of the Jack Rogan Mysteries series for the thinking reader.

As a lawyer with a passion for history and archaeology, Gabriel Farago had to wait for many years before being able to pursue another passion – writing – in earnest. However, his love of books and storytelling started long before that.

'I remember as a young boy reading biographies and history books with a torch under the bed covers,' he recalls, 'and then writing stories about archaeologists and explorers the next day, instead of doing homework. While I regularly got into trouble for this, I believe we can only do well in our endeavours if we are passionate about the things we love. For me, writing has become a passion.'

Born in Budapest, Gabriel grew up in post-war Europe and, after fleeing Hungary with his parents during the Revolution in 1956, he went to school in Austria before arriving in Australia as a teenager. This allowed him to become multi-lingual and feel 'at home' in different countries and diverse cultures.

Shaped by a long legal career and experiences spanning several decades and continents, his is a mature voice that speaks in many tongues. Gabriel holds degrees in literature and law, speaks several languages and takes research and authenticity very seriously. Inquisitive by nature, he studied Egyptology and learned to read the hieroglyphs. He travels extensively and visits all of the locations mentioned in his books.

'I try to weave fact and fiction into a seamless storyline,' he explains. 'By blurring the boundaries between the two, the reader is never quite sure where one ends, and the other begins. This is of course quite deliberate as it creates the illusion of authenticity and reality in a work that is pure fiction. A successful work of fiction is a balancing act: reality must rub shoulders with imagination in a way that is both entertaining and plausible.'

Gabriel lives just outside Sydney, Australia, in the Blue Mountains, surrounded by a World Heritage National Park. 'The beauty and solitude of this unique environment,' he points out, 'gives me the inspiration and energy to weave my thoughts and ideas into stories that in turn, I sincerely hope, will entertain and inspire my readers.'

Gabriel Farago

AUTHOR'S NOTE

I hope you enjoyed reading this book as much as I enjoyed writing it. I'd be very grateful if you'd post a short review on Amazon. Your support really does make a difference.

CONNECT WITH THE AUTHOR

Website
https://gabrielfarago.com.au/

Amazon
http://www.amazon.com/Gabriel-Farago/e/B00GUVY2UW/

Goodreads
https://www.goodreads.com/author/show/7435911.Gabriel_Farago

Facebook
https://www.facebook.com/GabrielFaragoAuthor

BookBub
https://www.bookbub.com/profile/gabriel-farago

Signup for the author's New Releases mailing list and get a free copy of *The Forgotten Painting** Novella and find out where it all began …

https://gabrielfarago.com.au/free-download-forgotten-painting/

* I'm delighted to tell you that *The Forgotten Painting* has just received two major literary awards in the US. It was awarded the Gold Medal by Readers' Favorite in the Short Stories and Novellas category and was named the 'Outstanding Novella' of 2018 by the IAN Book of the Year Awards.

www.ingramcontent.com/pod-product-compliance
Lightning Source LLC
Chambersburg PA
CBHW020000120726
47903CB00004B/1065